UNDER

A

BLOOD MOON

CARRIGAN RICHARDS

♡ Carrigan Richards

Indie World
Publishing & Author Services

P.O. Box 819
Dewey, AZ 86327

DEDICATION

In memory of my grandfather, whose enthusiasm and
encouragement will stay with me forever.

ACKNOWLEDGMENTS

Huge thanks to all my readers. Without you, my dream wouldn't exist.

Music is such a huge part of my life, and I would love to thank all the musicians I listened to while I wrote this, but the list is way too long.

To Jennifer, the greatest best friend a girl could have. I hope you know just how much you are appreciated. To Chani for your editorial advice and for saving my documents. To Derrick, Angie, Rachel, and Laura. To Laura Gordon and her amazing job on the cover.

To my mom; my dad; Patrick, Morgan, and Alison. Your unwavering support never ceases to amaze me. I love you all. To my new family. I love your enthusiasm and support.

To Chris. Thank you for listening to me talk about my characters and their stories. You make me laugh every day; you challenge me and encourage me. My heart is yours.

PROLOGUE

The woman proudly smiled at the six frightened children assembled before her. They were so innocent now and unaware of just how powerful they would soon become.

"Can you believe they are already seven years old?" the woman asked her brother.

"No. They are lucky to be in such a peaceful time." He smiled. "Shall we get started?"

"Yes."

They had led the three boys and three girls into the conservatory, a large room with a globed glass ceiling. A purple velvet rug with a black pentacle design lay over the hardwood floor. Thousands of candles illuminated the room and the beautiful faces of the children. The woman gestured for each of them to stand on the black circle around the pentagram. As soon as all six of the children stepped onto the circle, it glowed.

"You are all special," her brother said. "We have brought you here to bind you together as a group. In ten years, you will come back to us, and you will accept your powers."

Savina made sure she spoke clearly. "To become part of this Circle, you must agree to this. You must invoke your powers." She glanced at Colden. "Now, before we begin, we need to gather blood from you all." She reached inside her robe and pulled out a small knife. A few of the children gasped, and Savina frowned. She instructed the frightened children to lift their arms. She dragged the blade across their skin and let the blood drip into a glass goblet that Colden held.

Then, her fingers lightly smoothed over the cut on their arms until the wounds vanished.

Savina pricked Colden's finger with the knife, let a few drops of blood into the goblet, and then healed it. She did the same with her finger. Savina took a sip of the warm blood and the metallic taste burst inside her mouth. The warmth of it filled her body and she felt connected to each of the children. Then, she passed the goblet to Colden.

"We belong together in this Circle. Just remember, you are sisters." She looked at the girls. "And you are brothers." She turned to the boys. "As you take a sip of the blood, let it fill you with warmth and comfort. This blood binds us together."

"Each of you is strong." Colden told them. "But your powers will not manifest until you are sixteen or seventeen. And in ten years, you will all meet here. May the Circle be open and remain unbroken. Do not speak a word to anyone about this. You must not break your promise."

After everyone drank from the goblet, Savina instructed them to hold hands. Then, she tilted her head and concentrated on the glass ceiling. She felt the power from each of the children emanating around the circle. Savina focused the powers of the children, and exhibited each one of their unique ability above in the glass ceiling. She watched as it slowly displayed a beautiful starry night with a full moon. Then, the bright reddish-orange hue of the sun shone through, dissolving the image of the moon. Its corona flickered on the sides. The sun faded as water splashed across the ceiling, like the ocean crashing onto the shore. A fierce hurricane wind took over and then the hypnotic flames of fire burst to life. Finally, an image of the Earth rotated in the glass until it vanished, and the empty night sky encompassed the ceiling.

Savina gasped.

Colden turned to her with a wary look.

She knew they were powerful but had had no inkling that they were the Elemental ones. *There is no reason to worry.* She mind-spoke to Colden. *Corbin is dead and no one will be looking for them.*

That we know. We must watch and protect them until they return here.

Savina nodded. It was dangerous living among the mortals, but she knew what would happen if the Elementals fell into the wrong hands.

CHAPTER ONE
BREATHING TRICKS

Ten Years Later

Ava Hannigan loved basking in the sun as she floated on top of the cool water. It relaxed her on the hot and humid day. She held her breath so she wouldn't sink and closed her eyes. The awful music Gillian just had to play was muffled since her ears were underwater. She leisurely moved from one end of the pool to the other. When she reached the deep end, she pulled upright and dipped her head under, cooling her face.

She heaved her body out of the water and walked past Gillian Madison and Melissa Rollins, her best friends, as they sun-bathed in pool chairs.

A rust-colored wooden fence attached to both sides of Melissa's house and enclosed them and the in-ground pool. Dogwoods, spaced out evenly for privacy, lined the fence. However, the nearest neighbor resided about a mile away across the vast field. Willow trees lazily danced in the wind in the backyard. Ava could hear a few cows moo in the distance, but couldn't see them.

"Can you please change the song, G?" Melissa groaned as she flipped onto her backside. Her tanned, long body glinted under the sun from the oil. She lifted the large square sunglasses from the top of her head and rested them on her straight, pointed nose, covering her green eyes. Her blond ponytail snaked its way down past her shoulders. Ava envied Melissa's tanned skin, for the tiniest bit of sun without protection made her burn—it was the Irish in her. Her skin could never tan.

"I like this song." Gillian continued to sing along off-key in her soft voice. She wore her red polka-dotted bikini since she lost five pounds, but she wanted to lose fifteen more so she could be Ava and Melissa's slender size. Ava thought the top was a little too snug, as if at any moment Gillian would pop out of it. Her black curls sprayed on the pool chair around her head. Her small pig-like nose, as Melissa used to call it, looked upward at the sky above her thick, full lips. A *Seventeen* magazine lay within reach beside her. Her blue eyes matched the pool water, and her olive skin darkened under the sun, without burning.

"Of course you would like that song because you like only what's popular."

"It's a catchy song."

"It's dumb," Melissa argued.

"No it isn't," Gillian said.

"Oh come on, her voice is nasally and she can't carry a tune to save her life. Or was that you trying to sing over her?"

Gillian sighed and picked up her magazine.

Ava rolled her eyes at their stupid bickering. It annoyed her so much that sometimes she wished she wasn't even there. She liked hanging out with her best friends, obviously, since they'd been friends since they were seven, but lately she had been enjoying time with Peter. They'd become good friends over the summer, but she found herself missing him a little since he left two weeks ago to visit his family in Boston.

Ava wanted to send him a text message, but didn't want to bother him. Instead, she applied another coat of sunblock to her skin.

"I can't believe our summer ends next week." Gillian

wrapped a black curl around her finger.

"Seriously. Two more years." Melissa grabbed a cigarette from her pack and lit it. "What a summer."

Ava shook her head. Melissa the stubborn chain-smoker. "I agree," she mumbled, though she was actually glad that school started on Monday because it gave her a chance to see Peter again.

"When does Peter come back, Ava?" Gillian asked as if she had just listened to her thoughts.

Ava shot a look at her, wondering why she would ask that in front of Melissa, since Melissa wasn't exactly privy to her and Peter hanging out.

"Peter? Peter McNabb?" Melissa inquired.

"Yes." Melissa would find out sooner or later.

She cocked an eyebrow and dumped ashes in an ashtray. "Are we talking about that scrawny kid with brown hair? The one who works at Foodland?"

"He's not scrawny."

"Compared to Lance and Thomas, he is."

"I think he's cute," Gillian said.

Melissa took a drag from her cigarette and exhaled. "Did you hang out with him over the summer?"

"Sometimes."

"Why were you hanging with *him*?"

"Well, you all were at some sort of sports camp or traveling. I had a lot of free time."

"True. What did you do?"

"We just watched baseball with Dad and saw some movies. He worked a lot. So it wasn't every night." It was the truth, but what Ava kept to herself was that they had hung out just about his every off day.

Melissa stubbed out her cigarette. "Boring. How am I the last to know these things?"

Gillian looked away from Melissa's narrowing green eyes.

"Does Thomas know?"

"Yeah. It's not like we're dating or anything. We're just friends."

"And Thomas is okay with that? How much does he actually know?"

"Exactly what I told you."

"So there's more?"

"Lay off, Melissa," Gillian said.

Ava sighed. "No there's not more. Please don't read into this like you do everything else."

"All right." She held up her arms. "He is kinda cute, though. Too bad you're attached."

Ava silently agreed.

"Give it time, though. Thomas will start to get annoyed. Especially the more you hang out with this guy."

"I'm sure we'll fall into the same routine as we always do when school starts." Unfortunately, Ava knew too well just how Thomas would react if he knew she started to prefer Peter's company to his.

"So did anything happen during the summer?"

"No. Why do you assume that?"

"You didn't notice anything...unusual?"

"Like what?"

Melissa pursed her lips. "Just something odd."

"No," she said slowly. "Why? Did you?"

Melissa and Gillian exchanged looks.

"What?" Ava asked.

Melissa shook her head. "Nothing."

"What are we doing tonight?" Gillian changed the subject.

"Probably the same thing we always do," Ava answered, still suspicious of them.

Melissa stood from her pool chair. "Do you two want anything to drink?"

"Water," Ava replied. What were they hiding from her?

"Diet Coke for me," Gillian requested and picked up her magazine.

Melissa walked through the sliding glass door to the one-story house, leaving it open.

"What's going on? And why did you have to mention Peter?" Ava asked Gillian.

"I'm sorry. I didn't think it was a secret."

"It's not. But you know how she blows things way out of proportion." Ava walked to the edge of the pool. "And you know Melissa will start putting ideas in Thomas's head."

"I'm sorry. Please don't be mad at me."

"I'm not mad, but Thomas overreacts."

"I know," she said and returned to her magazine.

Ava stared at the water glittering in the sun. She turned around to say something to Gillian, but as she did, arms grabbed Ava and pulled her into the pool.

Melissa always pulled these pranks, but when Ava looked, there was nothing but water. Ava felt arms and hands grasping her, but couldn't see anyone. She struggled to swim to the top but something still held her down. What was holding her down? She kicked and punched the invisible force. Her lungs burned. She needed to breathe.

She didn't know how much longer she could hold her breath. And then, she let go and inhaled.

She stiffened when air entered her nose instead of water. Was she dreaming? Of course. But the dream did not end. Ava continued sinking. Lungs aching for more air, she inhaled once more. She breathed in air again. Melissa appeared next to her in the water, clutched her arm, and pulled her toward the surface. Gillian helped Melissa drag her out of the water and onto the poolside.

"What did you do, Melissa?" Gillian shrieked.

"Ava?" Melissa screamed. "Ava, are you okay?"

Speechless, Ava studied Melissa.

"Ava!" She shook her. "I was totally joking around. I'm sorry."

"I-I'm fine."

Melissa let out a sigh of relief. "Why did you stop moving? Did you run out of air?"

"I. Just breathed. Underwater." As she said the words, they still made no sense.

"I knew it. That's so awesome," Melissa squealed. Her frightened face relaxed, and she smiled.

"You could've killed her, Mel," Gillian shouted.

"Whatever. Savina would have healed her."

"Yeah, she *heals*. Not bring people back from the dead."

Ava sat up. "Did you just make yourself," she paused. "Invisible?"

She nodded. "I knew your ability had developed. Ours have too." She acted as if she were a little kid telling her mom she could open her eyes underwater. "I've been waiting for this for ten years."

Ava looked to the water and watched it lap against the wall. She'd been dreading this day all summer ever since she got close to Peter. She'd turned sixteen almost a year ago, and had hoped it would never happen and that she would always be a normal girl. Her dad told her about it the day she came back from the Blackhart Manor. He sat her down and explained that she was an Enchanter with incredible powers that would develop around the age of sixteen. Of course, to her seven-year-old mind the thought was baffling yet curious. But over the years, she had read and heard stories about the wars and the Cimmerians who served Corbin Havok.

"Whatcha thinkin', Ava?" Melissa asked.

"Nothing. What can you do?" She looked up at Gillian.

A few small curls lifted with the wind around Gillian's baby face. Her dark eyebrows furrowed, and she bit her lip.

Melissa suddenly slapped her own face and then glared back at Gillian who meekly smiled.

"I can manipulate minds."

Ava's mouth hung open.

"You're not supposed to use it on us," Melissa reminded her.

"Come on. Ava had to see it for herself. I realized it one night when I asked my mom if Jeremy could stay over because the weather was so bad and I didn't want him going home in it. She and Dad were so relentless, and then I was able to change her mind. It was so bizarre, because for several minutes they kept saying no, but then I was being silly I guess thinking that if I stared at her long enough and made her think what I was thinking, she'd give in. And she did."

"Whoa." Ava knew Gillian's parents were strict and didn't allow her to do much of anything, let alone allow her boyfriend to stay over one night.

"What she doesn't know is that Jeremy was the one who created the violent winds that night." Gillian giggled. "But what's even more bizarre is that I've tried it again on my mom, but something is blocking me. It's like something's pushing at my mind when I try it against my mom."

"Wow," Ava said. She couldn't fathom the words they were speaking. They could actually do these things.

Melissa clapped her hands. "Maybe you should try it on some people at school. Now that I think of it, this year is going to be the best yet."

"What? You can't do that," Ava said.

"Why not? It's not like we're actually going to get to use our powers. There hasn't been a war in forever. Corbin's dead. Everyone knows that. Why not have some fun with our powers?"

"And do you remember what started those wars? Because Corbin used his powers on humans and killed them."

"Would you calm down?" Melissa grimaced. "We aren't going to kill anyone. Just have a little fun."

Gillian bit her lip. "Ava's right. It's not a good idea to use these on people."

"Oh come on. The only one who could really do anything to anyone is you. I might be able to scare people by appearing in front of them. And I don't think Ava could really hurt someone by breathing underwater."

"What about Lance?" Ava asked. "Has his power developed?"

Melissa pressed her lips in a tight line. "I think he has the same power as me. Which is really cool. What about Thomas?"

They looked at Ava expectantly, but she could only shrug. "So I guess this means we're still going back to Blackhart for the Initiation Ceremony."

"Well, yeah."

"Do you even think they're still there?"

Ava never mentioned that she'd visited the house several times after that night, but the man and woman weren't there and the house looked abandoned.

Melissa chuckled. "Of course they are."

But Ava didn't want to go back. She didn't want to be initiated into the coven. What was the use anyway? She took a deep breath. Ava still had two months not to worry about it.

"We should get ready for tonight." Melissa tossed her a towel.

Gillian placed a hand on Ava's shoulder. "Don't worry. Everything will be all right. Come on, let's go."

Ava had expressed her anxiety of this day to Gillian several times. But Gillian assured her each time. There hadn't been any evil Enchanters since Corbin, so there was no need to worry. But it wouldn't be easy being Peter's friend.

CHAPTER TWO
POWERFUL

Ava drove along the unlined country road to her house as the summer sun hung low in the pastel blue sky. She passed wide pastures on each side of the road with large bales of hay for the cows that hid under the lush green maples and oaks. Occasionally a house dotted the landscape along the way.

She turned down a gravel road and arrived shortly at the white quaint two-story home where she and her dad lived. After parking in the driveway, she turned off the engine. Shaded under southern oak trees, the cozy house was her mother's dream home. The steep roof with three dormer windows rested low to the ground shading the porch that ran the length of the house. The front door nestled between four windows with black shutters. A pale blue swing hung on the left side of the porch, while a table rested between two matching rocking chairs on the right side. Small columns were at the corners and entrance of the porch while rose bushes almost reached the railing.

Like Melissa's house, no neighbors lived around for miles. Across from the house were deep green woods with kudzu strangling onto the trees. Lifting her pool bag on her shoulder, she followed the small concrete path to the porch steps and then stepped inside.

"Hey Ava," her father said over the television.

"Hey." She closed the door.

He stretched out his gangly body in the blue recliner with his feet up. Freckles dotted his ashen legs and arms. His reddish-brown hair stuck out in several directions. It had slowly thinned over the years, but Ava chalked it up to stress he had endured since her mother's death. He still looked amazingly good for being forty, and his short bearded face hardly kept a wrinkle, a result of being an Enchanter. It was weird to think of her father as one.

"Did you not move all day?" She teased, noticing the same relaxed position she'd left him in earlier.

His green eyes smiled up at her. "I got up to eat."

"That's good. What did you have?"

"A hoagie." He patted his small protruding stomach. "Braves come on at seven." They had watched baseball together ever since she was little, but it meant something more after her mother died.

"I'm hanging out with Thomas and everyone tonight." She always hated turning him down.

Her dad muttered something under his breath as he pulled the lever on his chair, putting him in a sitting position. She knew he didn't exactly like Thomas and, since Peter had been coming around, he had formed a more appreciative relationship with Peter than he ever had with Thomas. He tilted up the soda can, took a final gulp, and then stood, towering over Ava.

"How was swimming with the girls?"

Oh, that. Well, Dad, apparently, I can breathe underwater. Ava refused to meet his eyes. "It was fine." She needed to tell him about her powers, but Ava didn't want to talk about it. Telling him would confirm it really happened. She didn't know why it freaked her out so much.

"Are you okay?" He scrutinized her face.

"Yeah. I'm fine." She was glad his ability to detect lying had faded. But she knew he would eventually figure out that her powers had developed since the parent's power disintegrated once their offspring developed theirs. But for now, she could hold off on telling him. "I'm gonna take a shower and change."

"Okay."

Ava walked up the stairs to her room and dropped her bag onto the floor next to her full-sized bed. She crossed to her bathroom to turn on the water in the sink. Plugging the drain, she waited until the basin filled, and then turned off the flowing water. Staring into her gray eyes in the mirror, she took a deep breath, and then submerged her face. She expected her instincts to force her to hold her breath, but she inhaled and exhaled as if she were not underwater. She lifted her head, water dripping onto the counter, and exhaled. She admitted it was cool, but she was still reluctant.

After taking a hot shower, Ava dried her straight, crimson hair that hung just below her shoulders and dressed in khakis and a gray t-shirt. She slid a gold ring that held a milky white opal stone in the center on her ring finger. It belonged to her grandmother, then her mother, and now her.

Her stomach groaned, reminding her that it was hungry. As she sank onto her bed, she picked up the postcard Peter had sent from Boston from her nightstand, next to the picture of her mom, dad, and her. A picture of Edgar Allan Poe's birthplace graced the front. Peter's short note to Ava on the back read:

Hey! I saw this and thought of you. Boston is seriously awesome, even if it's filled with Red Sox fans. Hope you're having fun. See you soon! Love, Peter

She sighed. She'd read it for the hundredth time. Each time she read it, her heart beat like an erratic drum. Ava placed it back on her nightstand and gripped the edge of the bed, hung her head, and closed her eyes.

What would Peter think if he knew? Ava didn't want this. She didn't want to be an Enchanter and take an oath binding her to a coven. *Two more months*. And then they'd return to Blackhart. She pictured that first night, eight months after her

14

mother died. She saw Savina, so otherworldly, sitting on a bench waiting for her. Ava remembered being scared, yet Savina and Colden somehow made her feel comfortable. The thought of drinking blood made Ava shudder.

There was a soft knock at her bedroom door, then the door slowly opened, and her dad appeared.

"Hey honey, Thomas is downstairs," he announced.

Ava sighed.

"Are you okay?"

"Yeah. I just hope he behaves tonight." She pushed herself off the bed.

"You don't have to go," her father said. "You *know* I don't like him. I can tell him to leave."

She smiled. "It's okay. I'm just thinking aloud." She kissed his cheek and walked out of her room.

Ava walked down the stairs, and her dread increased with each step. She used to enjoy being around Thomas and laughing at his dumb jokes or walking down the halls with him on her arm and secretly liking the jealous looks she got from the girls. But that was ages ago. She couldn't remember the last time she was happy to see him.

She crossed into the living room, but Thomas was too busy to notice because he was changing channels on the TV as if he owned the place. The smell of his musky cologne hit her like a wave slapping her in the face. The scent always made her sneeze. She hated the way his strawberry blond hair curled past his collar like it had the last four years. Thomas despised any sort of change and felt that his stupid hairstyle resulted in his godlike ability to throw a football and score points. And why on earth did he insist on wearing shirts that were so tight on him that his muscles threatened to rip apart the seams? Too bad his brain wasn't as big as his muscles.

He finally turned to her, his pale blue eyes roving up and down her body like he did every time they went out.

My eyes are up here, Thomas.

"Hey, Babe." He licked his lips before he pressed them to hers. Ava silently shuddered at his greeting but kissed him back. She hated it when he licked his lips. His kisses used to turn her inside out, but now they seemed lackluster.

Behind them, her father cleared his throat. Ava, thankful for the interruption, quickly pushed away from Thomas.

"Good evening, Sir." Thomas nodded, and handed the remote to her father.

"Hello, Thomas," her dad replied without an ounce of warmth.

"How are you?"

"I'm fine."

Even though Thomas was bigger than her dad, he always seemed so nervous around him. It made Ava laugh silently to herself.

"I'll see you later." She smiled and gave her father a quick hug. "I'll watch the game with you tomorrow. I love you."

"I love you, too. Have a good night," he called as they walked out into the humid night.

Once outside, they both climbed into Thomas's Jeep. After strapping in, he started the engine. With a jerk, the car backed onto the gravel road and then he slammed down on the gas, kicking gravel everywhere. The Jeep swerved slightly and then Thomas corrected it.

"Do you have to do that every time?" she asked. Her voice sounding annoyed. It was becoming a habit to talk like this to him. She tried to stop, but he just irritated her.

"It's fun."

She rolled her eyes and peered out the window. Why didn't she just drive her own car? Then she could listen to her own music and not be praying for her life.

"Why doesn't your dad like me?" Thomas asked.

"He likes you fine."

"You told him about the night before I left, didn't you?"

Ava exhaled noisily. She hated thinking of that night. They'd been making out, but Thomas didn't want to stop. They had a fight, and then Thomas went to football camp the next day, wild with anger. She wasn't ready for that next step in the relationship. After that night, she couldn't stop imagining how different her life would be if she were with Peter.

"Even though my dad and I are close, that doesn't mean I tell him every detail of my life."

"You know I'm sorry if I hurt you, Babe."

"Don't call me that. And yes, I know you're sorry. I got your letters and phone calls."

"But you hardly responded to the emails. And when I called, you couldn't talk long."

"Must we argue every time we're together? Is this how it's going to be from now on, until I give in?"

"Come on, Ava. Melissa and Lance have. So have Gillian and Jeremy. Every girl in that school would love a chance with me. Why not you?"

"Because I'm not ready," she snapped. "I've already told you this. If you're so desperate to get laid, why don't you just ask out every girl in the school, then?"

"Because they aren't like you, Ava. Don't you love me?"

"Yes, I love you," she said automatically and then looked at his profile. But did she really? He hadn't always been this aggressive. He used to be kind and caring. Maybe they were just growing apart. Or maybe she was just losing patience.

"I'm just confused. I mean, we've been together since seventh grade. How much more time do you need?"

Her temper flared. "I don't know. Okay? I'm sorry. But if you loved me, you'd understand and be patient about it and not hound me every five seconds."

"Whatever."

For the rest of the way to the small town, he turned up the radio, and she stared out the window, fidgeting with her opal ring. She briefly wondered what Peter was doing. Hanging out with him was easy. Like swimming. Calm and relaxing.

Thomas pulled into the usual spot at the high school hang out, an outside strip mall. There wasn't much to do in the small town, except loiter around the strip. Ava didn't like being there every night while Melissa, Lance, and Thomas mostly harassed other kids. But especially tonight. She really wanted to try her ability again. She had always loved the water, and for some reason, since learning this new trick, she felt alive.

Ava got out of the Jeep as fast as she could. The warm breeze made the humidity bearable, but it also helped that the sun wasn't beating down on her. Instead, bright florescent shop signs lit up the night. The moving clouds made the dull crescent moon barely visible.

She and Thomas walked silently toward Melissa, Gillian, Lance, and Jeremy, who all stood next to the brick building.

Melissa exuded coolness as she smoked a cigarette and stood in front of Lance. It wasn't the cigarette that made her cool, but the way she smoked it like she was slowly tasting and taking in every drag. Ava envied her nonchalant attitude and wished she could be more confident. Her blond hair was in loose waves and she wore heavy eye makeup as usual. "What's with you two?" She flicked ashes to the ground.

"Probably fighting again." Lance assumed. It annoyed Ava that they all joked about her and Thomas.

"Shut up," Thomas told him.

Lance shrugged and wound his muscular arms around Melissa's waist. Like Thomas, because of his chiseled abs and square jaw, many girls at school fantasized about him. His crew cut dark hair had a widow's peak. Though he had a friendly smile, his dark eyes made him mysterious. But it also could have been the fact that he kept to himself mostly and was around Melissa usually. He gave her a quick peck on the cheek and then turned to Thomas. "Come on, let's get something to eat."

"You want a vanilla milkshake?" Jeremy asked Gillian.

"Sure." She smiled sweetly and then kissed the tip of his long, narrow nose. He squeezed her shoulder before he followed Lance and Thomas down the sidewalk to the burger joint.

The girls walked to one of the empty wooden picnic tables and sat down.

Melissa stubbed out her cigarette in the flimsy aluminum

ashtray. "So, what happened on *Days of Our Lives*?"

Ava rolled her eyes. Melissa always compared Ava and Thomas's relationship to the soap opera. "He's still mad at me."

"Still?" Gillian checked her reflection in a compact mirror. She had to make sure everything was perfect. "That was like weeks ago."

Ava nodded. "Yep."

"You should just give it up already. Making him suffer, y'know?" Melissa rolled her green eyes as she lit a cigarette.

Ava crossed her arms in front of her.

"If she's not ready, she's not ready," Gillian said and then coughed. "And, can you wait five minutes before lighting another one of those things?" She reapplied red lipstick and pursed her lips together as if she were going to kiss the mirror.

Melissa batted her eyelashes, mocking Gillian. "We can't all be perfect and sweet like you."

"I didn't say I was perfect."

"Well, I know you're no longer a virgin."

Gillian blushed and looked away.

Melissa wrapped an arm around her. "It's nothing to be ashamed of, G. Though, you never did give us details—."

"Have you guys told your parents about your powers?" Ava cut her off, saving Gillian from having to talk about her private love life.

"I think my mom knows," Gillian said. "Especially since she's been blocking me."

"Yeah, I told my parents when it happened," Melissa said. "I was so excited. I thought they'd never develop."

"How would yours develop if you're adopted?" Gillian asked.

"Because when they adopted me, Savina linked our blood together," Melissa answered. "Have you told your dad, Ava?"

She shook her head.

"You're gonna have to eventually. Maybe you'll finally learn what kind of Enchanter your mom was."

Ava shifted uncomfortably. She hated talking about her mom. Luckily, for her, the guys came back with burgers, fries, drinks, and a salad for Melissa, who was vegetarian.

"Eww, there's little bits of Thomas on my salad." Melissa grimaced.

Ava watched her remove bacon bits from her salad, and then laughed.

"What are you talking about?" Thomas asked.

She picked up the bowl and pointed to the bacon. "See? Little bits of you."

Everyone laughed, but Thomas looked completely confused.

"How is it that you got this far in school? There's bacon on my salad. Bacon comes from a pig. Little bits of Thomas. Get it?" She turned to Lance who couldn't keep a straight face. "How many times does his head get hit in football practice?"

"I'm not a pig."

Ava bit back a laugh.

Thomas shook his head and engulfed a large bite of his double patty hamburger. Ketchup and mayonnaise stuck to his chin before he wiped it away. Ava never understood why he had to inhale his food like it was his last meal.

"Oh, Ava, I brought *On the Road* for you," Jeremy said. "I just finished it last night."

"Thanks. I'm looking forward to it."

"Did you know Hunter S. Thompson probably wouldn't have written *Fear and Loathing in Las Vegas* had it not been for this book?" Jeremy leaned forward, the way he always did when he was excited to talk about something he loved. His eager topaz eyes pierced through his rimless rectangular glasses.

"No, I didn't."

He shook his head like it was the most amazing fact. Ava grinned. She was close to Jeremy since she felt they were the outcasts in the group. No one else read as much as they did, and no one else surely talked about books for hours like they did. She would never forget when Jeremy fell severely ill with a lung disease when they were ten. Ava read to him every day while he was bedridden. Jeremy had always told her if it wasn't for that, he probably wouldn't love books as much as he did.

The girls at school never really drooled over Jeremy, but Ava assumed it was because he kept himself hidden behind a book. Like her, he didn't like a lot of attention. His sandy blond hair parted down the middle and fell on either side of his head, like an upside-down bowl. If Gillian wasn't playing with her own hair, she was sure to be playing with his. His frame was smaller than Lance and Thomas, but he still had muscles.

"Oh, look who's walking this way," Thomas announced after finishing his last bite of his second burger.

They all turned their heads to see Kristen Miller, an average-height girl with bushy brown hair and a plain face. She walked up the sidewalk with a chubby boy who held her hand. Ava exchanged exasperated looks with Gillian and Jeremy. They knew Thomas and Melissa were going to tease Kristen. She hated it when they did this. She didn't know why they needed to feel superior.

"Her hair looks like she teased the hell out of it. I should give her fashion advice," Melissa said.

"Hey, Kristen." Thomas flashed his famous sexy smile as Kristen walked by.

"Leave her alone," Ava warned under her breath.

Kristen's face immediately reddened. She and the guy stopped at their table. "Hi."

Melissa lit a cigarette. "Is that your boyfriend?"

"Yes." Her brown beady eyes lit in eagerness.

"Wow. That's incredible. It's like a match made in heaven."

Kristen smiled. "Thank you. We just started going out this summer."

Thomas sucked the last of his drink and then made that annoying slurping sound with his straw. Ava swiped the empty cup from him. "So, Brent is it?" he asked.

"Brett," he responded, his blue eyes glaring.

"Yeah. We're looking for another player for our team, y'know?"

"You are?"

"Yeah."

Ava kicked Thomas under the table, but he ignored it. She wished they would stop.

"Isn't it too late to join football?"

"No. Lance and I could totally get you in."

"What position? I tried out for the center."

"Oh yeah, we can talk to Coach about adding you." Lance joined in the conversation.

Thomas snickered. "Well, it won't be center. We need someone to wash our jock straps."

"I thought they needed a base for the cheerleader's pyramids." Lance laughed.

"Kristen could do that!"

Thomas, Melissa, and Lance laughed hysterically.

Kristen's face fell, and Ava knew she was about to cry while Brett just glared and urged her to start moving.

"Why do you have to be so mean?" Gillian said. "Like you three are so much better."

Melissa blew smoke in the air. "Oh come on, that was funny."

Ava shook her head. "No it wasn't. You should be ashamed of yourselves."

"Whatever. I'm sure they won't even give what we said a second thought," Thomas said.

"They'll be thinking of this constantly."

"Lighten up, will you?" Melissa asked.

"Come on, let's go throw the football," Thomas suggested as he stood from the table and walked away with the guys.

Melissa turned to Gillian. "You know what you should do?"

"You're going to make me apologize, aren't you?"

"No. Just, you know, use your ability."

Ava dropped her jaw. "She shouldn't do that."

"I agree, Melissa. It doesn't sound like a good idea."

"Why not? Why do you always have to follow the rules? Come on, it'll be fun."

Gillian pursed her lips together, contemplating.

"Don't do it, Gillian. Come on, let's get out of here."

"Will I get in trouble?" she asked, ignoring Ava.

Melissa flicked ashes in the ashtray. "From who? It won't hurt anything. Besides, you should see if it works on anyone besides your mom and me."

Gillian thought about it for a moment. "Okay." She stood and jogged to catch up to Brett and Kristen.

"Why do you always do that?" Ava asked.

"Do what?"

"You know what. You always make her do things, and she always listens to you. Why can't you just let her be?"

"It's not bad. She should live a little." She took a puff of the cigarette and exhaled.

"I don't think manipulating someone into doing what you want is living."

"For Gillian it is. She never does anything. It's like she's begging to come out of her shell."

"It could turn ugly."

"Stop being so paranoid."

Ava stared at her defiantly, and clenched her teeth. A lazy breeze blew, slightly cooling her, and she relaxed. She fiddled with the plastic lid on her empty water bottle and wondered what Peter was doing. Then chastised herself because she shouldn't be thinking about him so much when she had a boyfriend.

A few minutes later, Gillian rejoined them. She had a suspicious smile. "Well, they're no longer mad at us."

"What happened?" Ava asked.

"It was amazing. I was able to control both their minds at the same time. At first, they didn't want to talk to me, but then I told them they needed to hear what I had to say, and they stopped and turned around." Gillian sped through her words. "I just sent messages to their minds or something. I guess that's how it works."

Ava clumsily lost her grip on the bottle and it rolled across the table. She was shocked. Of course, she'd heard of Enchanters being able to do this, but it was uncanny to think her best friend could control a mind. "What were the messages?"

"Just that nothing happened between us and them. Afterward, they smiled at me as if it was the first time they saw me tonight. It was so weird."

"That's my girl." Melissa wrapped her arm around Gillian and pulled her into a hug.

Gillian smiled like a kid who had just earned an A on a test.

Ava eyed her speculatively. But she knew she didn't have to worry. Gillian was smart and conscientious. However, she wondered if Melissa would try to convince her to use her ability more than needed.

"Let's go swimming," Melissa suggested.

Though Ava was glad to finally leave and try her ability again, she didn't like the knowing look Melissa suddenly shot her.

As Thomas drove to the outer part of the city, the stars above blazed into view. Ava usually liked to poke her head out a little to feel the warm breeze through her hair. But tonight, she only stared out the window, twirling her ring around her finger.

"I'm sorry about earlier," Thomas said.

It was hard to tell if he meant it since he was handing apologies out quite often. But she didn't want to argue anymore. "It's fine."

"I'll understand if you want to wait. It's not right for me to force you."

He sounded so sincere it took Ava a second to respond. "Thanks." Little pieces of the Thomas she knew before that stupid night emerged, but it was becoming rare. And she still felt guilty for thinking about Peter so much.

Thomas pulled into the driveway of Melissa's brown split-level ranch house. Little round lights lined the sidewalk to the front door. Ava climbed out of the Jeep, and they went inside the house without knocking. Her parents had always treated all of them as if they were their own children.

Cailin Rollins greeted them with hugs and a warm smile. "Hey, Ava. If I had known y'all were comin', I would have baked you somethin'," she said through her thick Southern accent. Ava had to bend slightly to hug Melissa's petite mom. Her honey blond hair was cropped and Ava noticed crow's feet near her smiling brown eyes.

A lavender scent wafted by as Ava pulled away. "You don't always have to bake us something."

"Though anytime you wanna make some of those chocolate chip cookies, I won't mind," Thomas said.

Mrs. Rollins smiled and playfully patted his shoulder.

"We're going swimming." Melissa corralled everyone through the sliding glass doors to the pool.

"Okay, y'all be careful. Your Daddy and I are going to bed."

"Goodnight. Love you!" Melissa called then closed the door.

Thomas shed his shirt, revealing his smooth chest, and slipped off his flip-flops. He ran from a corner and cannonballed into the water, splashing Ava and Melissa. Lance followed. Jeremy and Gillian sat at the patio table. Ava and Melissa held hands and jumped in together.

When they surfaced, Melissa swam to Lance, and Thomas swam to Ava. Being in the water rinsed away Ava's worries.

"Hey, I have a great idea." Melissa looked at Ava. "Remember when we were kids and we'd hold our breaths under water to see how long we could hold them? I think we should have another competition."

Thomas rubbed his face. "Who holds the record?"

Lance held his head high and puffed out his chest. "That would be me."

"How many minutes?" Jeremy asked.

Lance exhaled. "Like two."

Melissa sat on the bottom step in the pool. "Okay, well I'll time everyone." She held up her hand. "Ready? Go!"

Ava grinned before she went under. After a couple of minutes, she watched the three guys struggle to keep going. Thomas went up first, then Lance, but Ava stayed under. The chatter above was stifled. She was relaxed beneath the water. It was comforting to her. Minutes ticked by.

"How long has she been under?" She heard Lance's muffled voice ask.

"Is she okay?" Jeremy asked.

Thomas grabbed her arms and pulled her up. She laughed along with Melissa and Gillian.

"What is so funny?" he demanded. "How could you hold your breath under there for so long? Did you cheat?"

Ava flashed a proud grin. "I can breathe underwater."

Jeremy moved to the edge of the pool. "What?" he gasped.

"You can what?" Thomas's jaw dropped.

"It's true," Melissa said. "And I can make myself invisible. So can Lance. Gillian can manipulate minds. Jeremy can create strong winds."

Thomas nodded. "You got a lighter and a candle?"

"Here." Gillian grabbed the citronella candle and the lighter from the table and handed it to him.

They all watched Thomas light the candle and then place his hand over the fire. His hand abruptly burst into flames.

Ava yelped and doused his hand with water from the pool.

He sighed. "Dammit, I'm trying to show you something." Again, his hand lit in a blaze.

Its warmth heated Ava's face. The orange glow fused into dark blue. She gasped as the flame moved to the palm of his hand in the form of a ball. He closed his hand and extinguished it.

"Yeah? Watch this." Jeremy challenged.

They waited and watched the trees around them rustle. The wind picked up strong, until it knocked a large branch to fall from a tree nearby. Then, the wind stopped.

Gillian squealed.

"Jeremy! Not so close to the house, okay?" Melissa said.

He chuckled. "Sorry."

It was all so amazing to Ava. But then her stomach tightened, and suddenly her hamburger and fries weren't sitting well. Thomas could manipulate Fire. Jeremy could control Air. Could she be a Water Enchanter? If that were the case, that would mean three of them were Elemental Enchanters. Exceedingly rare. And incredibly powerful.

"What's wrong, Babe?" Thomas moved in front of her as she leaned against the pool wall.

"You realize three of us might be Elemental?"

"So?"

"That's very rare."

He shrugged. "But oh so cool. Just think of what we can do now. Nothing can stop us. I'm gonna have so much fun with some of those people at school."

What were he and Melissa going to do exactly? Would they go so far as to hurt someone like Kristen? Would Thomas use his power against Peter if he found out how much Ava liked him? Her heart jumped.

"No." She pushed him away. "This is serious. These powers are not meant to use whenever you want. We're not supposed to use them on humans." She spoke to everyone.

Thomas cocked an eyebrow. "Whatever."

"Will you calm down?" Melissa said, and then narrowed her eyes. "Why are you really concerned about this?"

Ava knew that Melissa knew what she was thinking. "Because we're not supposed to. We could get in trouble."

"You sound like Gillian. Just trust us. We aren't going to do anything crazy." A wicked smile spread across her thin lips.

CHAPTER THREE
THE NEW KID

The first day of junior year started under a hazy sunny day. Ava would much rather be swimming than be stuck inside a drab building all day. However, she was actually a little excited as she pulled into the parking space near the four-story brick school building. She wondered if she would have any classes with Peter and hoped she'd at least get to see him.

She got out of her car. The morning took no time to become hot and sticky. The thick air made it difficult to breathe, but there was a cool breeze.

Thomas stood by the gray double doors, waiting for her.

"Morning, Babe." He licked his lips then gave her a quick peck on the lips. He placed his meaty arm around her shoulders and walked inside. Disheartened students walked to their lockers along the concrete walls under the boring fluorescent lights. No one wanted to be there, except maybe for the few who enjoyed school. Thomas walked Ava to her locker, kissed her, and then walked away.

Algebra two with Mrs. Duke started Ava's morning and luckily, Melissa was there to share the misery. Ava despised any type of math. The only ones in the group who were good at it were Jeremy and Lance.

Ava walked to the back of the classroom once she saw Melissa with her head down on the desk. She plopped her books onto the desk next to her, and jolted Melissa awake.

Ava chuckled and slid into the chair.

"Why do you have to do that?" She groaned.

Her appearance bemused Ava. She'd pulled her blond hair into a messy ponytail, and little hairs stood in several directions. Redness surrounded her green eyes, and she wasn't wearing makeup, not that Ava ever felt she needed to, but Melissa always wore it.

"What the hell happened to you?"

"Lance and I stayed up way too late," she murmured.

"Are you still drunk?"

Melissa smiled. "Probably. I can't tell."

"I can't believe your parents let you get so drunk, let alone drink."

"Technically, they aren't my parents, but I love them all the same."

Ava rolled her eyes. "You look like death warmed over."

"I feel it, too."

"Why are you even here?"

"What and miss this? Are you kidding?" she said. "You should've been there last night. We got G drunk." She snickered.

Ava knew it would happen sooner than later. It bothered her that Melissa could persuade Gillian into doing anything. She never understood why Gillian would do anything to please Melissa, like they'd stop being friends if she didn't.

"Ugh. I know what's going through your mind right now. And no, I did not force her to do it."

Ava met her eyes.

"Don't give me that look. I don't want to hear it either."

Ava shrugged and turned to the front where Mrs. Duke wrote on the dry erase board.

After a long and boring lecture, Ava sleepily found her way to chemistry—another boring subject of hers—until Peter strolled inside the classroom. Her heart leapt.

"Hey." Peter's vigorous smile was contagious, and it always reached his chestnut-colored eyes. His smile smoldered and revealed a genuine sexiness. It was intoxicating to her. His shaggy dark brown hair came above his collar, and his bangs almost reached his thick eyebrows.

"Hey, I'm so glad you're in this class." Ava stood and hugged him. She loved the way his arms perfectly fit around her and held her so tight, if only for a second. His lanky, muscular figure stood a couple of inches taller than her. He smelled wonderful. Fresh and clean, like water. Ava realized she missed him more than she thought which wasn't a good thing.

"Yeah, me too."

She returned to her seat and he took the desk next to hers in the back of the classroom.

He smiled widely. "I brought you something back."

"You did? What for?"

Peter shrugged. "I just felt like it. Plus, when I saw it, I immediately thought of you." He plopped his backpack on the top of the desk, unzipped it, and pulled out a small leather-bound book. He held it out to her, still smiling.

She looked at the cover. Edgar Allan Poe's poems. "Peter? Wow, thanks." His unprovoked generosity overwhelmed her as she flipped through the book. Her mom had always read Poe's stories to her as a child, and he was her favorite author.

"Yeah I thought that since you had a copy of his stories, you needed one of his poems."

"Thanks," she said. "So, how was Boston?"

"Ah, it was great. Got to see a baseball game and hung out. My dad had a good time. I have to confess though. I missed you."

Her heart skipped a beat. "Oh," she looked away. Inside she was smiling, but she couldn't put too much thought into it.

"How was the rest of your summer? Anything exciting happen?"

If only you knew. "Uh, no, nothing. Thanks for your

postcard. I liked it."

"Cool."

The bell rang, sending students to their seats.

Short, pudgy Mr. Horn didn't even greet the students as he walked through the room handing out the curriculum. The smell of Icy Hot drifted by Ava as Mr. Horn placed a packet on her desk. His wild white hair trembled in the strong currents of the air conditioner. When he returned to the front of the room, he droned on and on in a monotone voice explaining what the class would endure during the semester. His thick glasses magnified his hazel eyes and made him look over ninety.

Peter leaned closer to Ava. "So did anyone give you a hard time for hanging out with me this summer?" he whispered. She knew he was asking about Thomas.

"No."

"You know I'd still like to hang out. I hope that doesn't change."

"Of course not. I like hanging out with you."

He nodded and grinned.

Ava read her new Poe book and watched the clock slowly count down to lunch.

Once the bell rang, Peter walked with her to her locker. "Hey, you wanna eat with my friends today? They haven't met you."

She wanted to say yes. "I should probably eat with my friends. Might look a little odd if I sat with you. Thomas would get the wrong idea."

"But we're just friends."

"I'm sorry."

"So it's okay for him to flirt with every female in this school?" His eyes veered past her. "But you can't be friends with anyone else?"

Ava followed Peter's gaze and found Thomas talking to and touching some brunette on her arm. The girl was in awe of him, just like every other female in this place. Ava wouldn't be surprised if Thomas had started to have flings on the side since she had turned him down. She suppressed an irritated sigh and looked away from him.

"Why do you put up with that? I could never do that to my girlfriend."

"You get used to it."

"Uh huh. Is clenching your teeth a way of getting used to it?"

Ava let out a small laugh.

"I'll talk to you later. Call me," he said and then turned on his heel. He disappeared into the crowded hallway.

"Who was that?" Thomas asked as he came up from behind. He kissed her cheek and they followed a large group entering the lunchroom.

"Peter."

"Who?"

"Remember, I told you about him. We hung out during the summer."

"*That* was him?"

"Yeah."

"I thought he was some retarded kid you were helping out."

"Why would you think that?" She had to raise her voice as they came into the large cafeteria. With a high ceiling, the voices reverberated off the cement walls. Little rectangular windows at the top of the wall broke the monotony of the gray.

Thomas shrugged. "What did you do with him then?"

"I told you. Watched baseball with Dad."

"He's younger than us, isn't he? Like you're just being nice because he has no friends, right?"

"What? No, we're the same age. He's only a friend." She could see the muscles in his jaw clench. They walked to their usual table in the back, and Thomas dropped off his bag then went to the line to get their lunch.

"Did you hear? We're getting a new kid at school." Melissa sat at the lunch table next to Ava. She looked more awake now. Gillian took the seat across from her and didn't look the smallest bit hung-over.

"No. Who cares?" Ava shrugged and pulled Jack Kerouac's *On the Road* from her backpack.

"This girl in my English class told me he's really creepy. Like, when he looks at you all you can do is shudder and look away. But I think she's a wimp."

"You think everyone's a wimp," Ava said.

"Well, most of them are. Anyway, I'm curious to see the new kid. I wonder if he's in here." She looked up, searching the lunchroom for the mysterious new guy. "His name is Xavier Holstone."

Ava shook her head and opened the book, ignoring her constant babble about the new kid. She was almost done with the book, since that's how she spent her Sunday night after watching the game with her dad. That and daydreaming about Peter.

She read a couple of pages and then Jeremy sat down next to Gillian. "How do you like it?" he asked.

"It's good," Ava said. "I like his writing style. The story is so real."

"I know. It definitely——."

"What is all the commotion?" Thomas interrupted him as he sat down with his and Ava's trays of food. Lance joined them and squeezed in next to Melissa, who still searched for this new kid.

"What commotion?" Ava marked her place with a scrap of paper and shoved the book in her bag. She grabbed the packet of salad dressing, poured it over her salad, and began to eat.

"This new guy. I swear everyone's talking about him."

"Aww, Thomas, are you sad that he's stolen your spotlight?" Melissa teased.

"No."

Ava suppressed a laugh.

"Well, he could surpass you as the hottest guy here. Girls may not swoon over you anymore. They're already talking about how hot he is."

"Melissa, stop," he demanded.

She shrugged and bit off a piece of a carrot and crunched it loudly.

"I heard he already knows more than his classmates. I heard he was really smart." Gillian's tiny voice barely made it over the hundreds of echoed conversations in the room.

"We'll see. Ooh, I think that's him." Melissa was agape as she looked toward the doors. Ava followed her gaze.

It was as if her voice bounced off the walls, broadcasting his arrival, because all eyes were on the dark, mysterious young man. The conversations seemed to have hushed, and Ava imagined several girls' hearts skipping beats.

Xavier Holstone elegantly glided across the white tiled floor with a crooked smile as if he liked that everyone stared at his tanned skin and ash blond hair. His oval face was severe with high cheekbones and a perfectly straight nose. His muscular, but thin, build made a few girls blush, though his dark eyes saw no one as he made his way to an empty table in the back. Ava didn't really think he was attractive, but there was something dangerous about him.

Lance crumbled his milk carton and cocked an eyebrow. "Do I need to worry about your new fascination?"

"He *is* hot," she said.

"Wow. Thanks for boosting my self-esteem," he said with a playful smile.

Melissa winked at him.

"I don't see what the fuss is about. He's got no muscles. He's got nothing. I'm taller than him," Thomas said. "And a lot bigger."

Ava patted his hand. "Of course you are."

"Let's hope he's not as egotistical as you," Melissa said.

Jeremy pushed his glasses up to the top of his nose. "I don't think anyone could beat Thomas at that."

"Jeremy!" Gillian smacked his arm.

Melissa roared with laughter, which was contagious around the table but did not reach Thomas. Instead, he fumed as he picked up his tray and stormed off to the trash bin.

"Thomas, it was a joke." Jeremy called after him.

"Guess I'll go calm him down." Ava groaned as she stood. "See you guys later."

"Good luck." Melissa laughed.

"Thanks." She rolled her eyes as she carried her tray to the trash bin.

Glancing at Xavier, she noticed him reading, legs stretched out from him. He held a sense of mystery, and instead of being lustful, like every other female there, Ava felt more wary of him. As if he could sense her, his eyes peeked up from his book. She smiled, but instead of returning the friendliness as she expected, he glared. His steely gaze made her look away. Well, that was rude.

Shrugging it off, she walked toward the front of the cafeteria just as the bell rang. She found Thomas outside in the wide hallway. Ava caught up to him before he emerged through the double doors that led outside.

"Are you really upset?"

He turned around. "No. Mel gets annoying after a while."

"Yeah, she does."

"There's something about that kid that I don't like. I can't explain it," Thomas told her as he stared past her. She turned and saw Xavier coolly stride through the crowd. He seemed so out of place by how sophisticated he acted.

"Yeah, I got that, too." Ava looked up at Thomas. "When I returned my tray, I smiled at him, and he just glared at me."

He finally met her eyes. "Why were you checking him out?"

"I wasn't."

"Why were you smiling at him?"

"I was just being friendly."

"Friendly? You have a boyfriend."

Ava sighed. "Forget it." She followed the remaining crowd squeezing through the hallway to the classrooms.

The rest of the day went by like any other. English then psychology. She took notes and groaned when they announced homework. Once the bell rang, she, like all the other students, hurried out of the building to the parking lot. She was the only one in the group who didn't have any after-school activities so she would go home to work on homework for a couple of hours before her father arrived. Or read on the porch swing. She didn't mind though. She loved stretching out, inhaling the sweet roses, and feeling the breeze. And she did just that when she got home.

Except when she opened her book, Xavier's face popped up in her head. *What was with the glare?* She thought. And Thomas, of course, accusing her of liking the guy. If he got that bent out of shape because she had been friendly with someone, how would he act if he saw her talking to Peter every day?

She remembered Colden and Savina mentioned something about being bound and keeping the circle unbroken. But was she really bound to Thomas? And more important, was she potentially endangering Peter's life by being his friend?

CHAPTER FOUR
MISSING

A week later, Ava arrived at school under a black sky. Thunder had grumbled all morning. Flashes of lightning streaked across the sky. Just as the clouds released the rain, she made it through the double doors of the brick school and hustled through the disorganized crowd to her locker. Shoes squeaked all around her, and she couldn't help but notice the somber mood of the students. Rain usually made them quiet and moody, but then she noticed the low whispers of those who gathered around a part of the concrete wall opposite of the lockers.

Ava moved closer as some students walked away. Taped to the painted gray wall, a small yellow sheet of paper read, MISSING KRISTEN MILLER in large bold letters. Under her name, Kristen's small face, overshadowed by her thick hair, smiled shyly back at Ava. Last seen Monday August 27. Phone numbers were listed. She gawked at the poster. What had happened? She backed away in a daze and then slammed into someone.

"Sorry," she said automatically. Then she looked up and met the cold black eyes of Xavier Holstone. She shuddered and jumped back.

"You should pay more attention," he spat. His eyes narrowed. Then he walked away.

Ava exhaled, unaware she had been holding her breath. What was his problem? She meandered to her math class.

"Kristen Miller went missing," Ava told Melissa as she dumped her books onto the desk and slid into the seat.

"Yeah. They say she never came home from school last Monday. Get a new kid, and one goes missing." She opened her notebook to an empty page.

"Melissa, this is serious! Did they say who she was with when she was last seen?"

"No one saw her. She went to all her classes and vanished right after school. Her parents came to get her car today."

Ava's shoulders slumped. What an unsettling thing for her parents to have to do. "What about her boyfriend, Brett?"

"He's just as lost as her parents. He was the one posting the pictures up this morning. I think she's turned to drugs."

"Drugs?" Ava echoed. "In a week? She was fine that night, with the exception of you and Thomas making fun of her."

"We'll see."

"There's no way she's on drugs. She's too good. This is something else."

"Maybe she forgot where she lived and got a ride from a stranger."

"Melissa, stop."

"I think it's drugs. Care to make a wager?"

"You can be so insensitive."

Melissa shrugged. "Twenty bucks says she's doing drugs."

"Why do you think that?"

Concern flashed in her green eyes. "Because I'd rather it be drugs than something worse like being kidnapped. Or her lifeless body dumped somewhere. Now, are we placing a bet?"

Ava sighed. "Fine." She felt completely ashamed of herself.

Things like this were a rarity at their school. The police would find Kristen. Nothing bad had happened to her. But

Ava knew she was only trying to make herself feel better. She looked down at the empty page of the notebook on her desk and silently hoped Kristen was okay.

After class, they squeezed through the crowds to Melissa's locker and found Gillian sobbing.

"What's wrong?" Melissa asked.

Ava turned Gillian around to face them and she and Melissa blocked the onlookers with their bodies. Mascara ran down Gillian's smooth face in dark watery lines.

"It's my fault," she choked through her tears.

"What is?" Ava asked.

"Kristen. She ran away because we were so mean to her."

Melissa lifted an eyebrow. "I highly doubt that, G. Why would you think it's you? They don't even know if she ran away."

"Whatever. You told me to use my power on them that night. I tried to change their minds, but it didn't work."

"You didn't do this."

Her chin quivered, and fresh tears sprang from her eyes.

"Why'd you tell her to do that?" Ava asked Melissa.

Melissa gave an exasperated look. "Come on, G, let's get you cleaned up." She put an arm around Gillian and led her to the bathroom.

Ava knew it was a bad idea to use their powers. Not that she believed Gillian had anything to do with Kristen's disappearance. She took a deep breath and then went to chemistry. She took her seat next to Peter.

His lips curled into that smoldering smile that reached his eyes. "Good morning."

"Hey."

"Can you believe that about Kristen?"

"No."

"She sits in my English class. It's really weird seeing her seat empty every day. She never misses a single day of school."

"I can't believe that no one has a clue," she said. "There's a ton of people walking out of these doors to their cars after school. *Someone* must have seen her."

"I agree. Some people say she started talking to Xavier the day she went missing."

"Xavier? Why would Kristen ever talk to someone like him? Are they suspecting that he has anything to do with her disappearance?"

Peter shrugged. "You know how rumors start. People don't like the guy, so they're probably trying to make it unbearable for him."

"I hope they find her."

"Me, too."

The bell rang and students settled in their seats. Ava opened her book and notebook. But she thought about Xavier. What could he possibly want with Kristen Miller? Maybe she was overanalyzing. It was a rumor after all.

"Hey, do you wanna hang out Friday night?" Peter whispered.

Ava turned her head and gave an apologetic smile. "I can't. Football game."

"Oh, right. First one of the year. I might go." He turned back to his book.

She wanted to hang out with Peter, though. They hadn't hung out since he'd gotten back and she hated football games. But there was no way she could be with Peter instead of watching Thomas play.

Chemistry went by just as sluggish as it normally did, where every second seemed to drag. The bell rang, and everyone hurried for the door. Peter walked Ava to her locker, a new tradition, she guessed, but she liked it.

"Wanna sit with me today?" he asked in a hopeful tone.

"I'm sorry. I gotta sit with my friends today."

"You have to?"

"It's just, I have to see if Gillian's okay. That's all." She sifted through her locker.

"What's wrong?"

"She's just really sad about Kristen."

"Oh. Were they good friends?"

"Not exactly, but Gillian is just a very emotional girl. She cries when someone kills a roach." She closed her locker. It was the truth, but she couldn't exactly tell Peter the real reason.

Peter chuckled.

Ava bit her lip. "This whole Kristen thing has gotten to me for some reason."

"I can understand that. It's not every day someone from our school goes missing."

Something hard collided into Ava's back, making her lose balance and stagger forward. Her books slipped to the ground, but she found herself in Peter's arms instead of sprawled across the concrete floor.

"Hey," Peter called.

She looked up to see Xavier walking past Peter. "Hey, what gives?" She shouted at him, but he didn't turn around.

"Are you okay?" Peter asked as she steadied herself.

"Yeah. What the hell was that?"

Peter bent down to pick up her books and then handed them to her. "I don't know. He just *pushed* you."

"Thanks for catching me."

"You're welcome. I guess I'll talk to you later," Peter said.

Ava knew he saw Thomas nearing. "Okay, see ya."

Peter left as if on cue.

"Why is he always talking to you?" Thomas wrapped his arm around her and escorted her to the cafeteria.

"We're friends. We have chemistry together." She hoped he didn't read into that statement too much.

His jaw tightened.

"Don't be jealous."

Thomas shrugged. "It won't last long."

She narrowed her eyes. "What do you mean?"

"I just find it odd that he's talking to you. Knowing you're my girlfriend. Doesn't he realize that's automatically off-limits?"

"You can't tell me who I can and can't talk to."

Ava struggled against his tight grip on her, but he refused

to let go. Getting angrier, she pulled his thick arm away and released herself from him, with ease.

"Damn, have you been lifting weights or something?" He stopped, stunned, searching her eyes.

"No." But it was strange to be able to pull his arm away so easily. Maybe he just conceded.

How dare he tell her she couldn't talk to Peter? What was this? 1950? She could be friends with whomever she wanted. But Ava was fooling herself. Thomas could still seriously harm Peter.

CHAPTER FIVE
HOMECOMING

The day started with another thunderstorm. It had been pouring for almost two weeks straight. Ever since they found out Kristen Miller disappeared. It never rained this many days in a row, but it wasn't the only weird occurrence going on. Not only had Kristen vanished, Nicole Eckrich and Scott Tingle had also gone missing without a trace. The police of course were doing everything they could, but that still didn't quell the worries of parents and even students.

Ava pulled into her parking space and shut off the car engine. She hated the rain. The more it came down, the more she thought about her mom and the streaks of lightning that looked like brilliant white veins. The memory permanently seared her mind. The heavy rain soaking her as she cried for her mother...She shook her head but it didn't erase the images.

She jogged out of the cool rain and into the school. Her hair had probably ballooned into some big frizzy mess now even after she had straightened it this morning. Just as she opened the second set of doors, Thomas was there waiting. She hated how he always waited for her. She could walk to her locker on her own.

He smiled down at her, licked his lips, and then gave a quick kiss. "Good morning."

"Morning," she mumbled.

"Someone's grouchy."

She immediately felt defensive. "It's raining. And I hate mornings."

"True. I hope it stops. For both our sakes."

Ava looked up at him. Had Thomas actually remembered why she hated the rain? It impressed her. But she had to be sure. "What do you mean?"

"It sucks playing in this stuff, and I can imagine sitting in the bleachers watching must suck too. I'm tired of practicing in the mud. And if we don't win tomorrow..." He shook his head.

The impressiveness quickly vanished. Of course, he was more concerned with football than anything else. Ava wondered what her mom would say about her still being with Thomas.

"Ava! Thomas!" Gillian ran toward them.

"It's happened again," she cried. "Something's going on." Her body shook while tears leaked from her large blue eyes, and her chin quivered.

Thomas grimaced. "Damn, calm down."

"What's wrong?" Ava asked.

"Link Harris." Gillian caught her breath. "No one had seen him since Sunday. Jeremy said he missed basketball practice this whole week."

"What the hell is going on?" Thomas demanded.

"I don't know. There's more."

"What?" Ava and Thomas asked together.

"Kristen and Link are back. Unharmed."

Ava shifted. "What about Nicole?

"I haven't seen her. But apparently Kristen's parents claim they forgot she was with her grandmother."

Thomas lifted his eyebrows. "Yeah, okay."

"I'm not lying."

"How do you just *forget* your daughter is with her

grandmother?" Ava asked.

"I don't know. But you'll never recognize Kristen."

"Why?" Thomas asked. "Did she finally get that makeover Melissa's been wanting to give her?" He laughed.

Gillian glared at him. "You are such a jerk. She's completely different. And Link isn't nice anymore. He's so mean. You know Chasity Waddell? He totally just pushed her out of her wheelchair!"

Ava's mouth flew open.

Thomas laughed, probably from how uncharacteristic it was of Link Harris, but Ava knew better. "Wait, good 'ol boy Link? Like, the same Link that does all the soup kitchens and everything?"

"Yes!"

"Just on a whim, he shoves her out of her chair? Is he trying to be badass or something?" Thomas asked. "Link Harris? What's he trying to prove? He's so perfectly good."

"I don't know what's going on." Gillian covered her face and fell into Ava's shoulder.

Ava placed an arm around her. "I don't either."

The three of them walked to Ava's locker, where Melissa, Lance, and Jeremy lingered.

"You guys have to see this," Melissa said.

The loud voices in the hallway immediately hushed. Ava turned her head to see Kristen slowly saunter down the hallway confidently instead of her usual hunched-over walk. Everyone was aghast at the sight of the new Kristen, with a grin on her face that could get anything she wanted. The boys drooled, and everyone stared wide-eyed at the unbelievable transformation that had taken place. She no longer wore the grandmother cardigans. Today, she donned a black leather jacket, a short black skirt, and black patent heels. Her brown hair, no longer bushy, was sleeked into several twisted strands that bounced past her shoulders. With a hand on her hip, she headed straight for Ava and Thomas.

"Hey, Thomas," her now sultry voice greeted him, and she caressed his chin with her finger. She continued walking by as his eyes followed her backside. Ava elbowed him, but he only shrugged. Kristen continued to stroll until she stopped next to Xavier. They embraced as if they'd been together forever and kissed so passionately that Ava had to avert her eyes. Several gasps resonated off the walls, and then loud chatter resumed.

"Well, new kid is into drugs too," Melissa said. "Pay up, Ava."

"Shut up."

"And so is Link," Melissa added as he walked up next to Xavier and Kristen.

Link had dyed his blond hair jet black and now sported a five o'clock shadow. He looked as though he'd aged in the past few days. The three of them laughed and ignored all the stares and whispers. They carried on as if they had been friends for years. Ava couldn't take her eyes off the scene that unfolded before her.

The tardy bell rang, and students scrambled into their classrooms, including Melissa and Ava, who interrupted Mrs. Duke's monotone role calling. She gave them a stern look but continued. Once finished, she stood at the front of the room, slowly writing down numbers on the dry erase board and continuously sliding her glasses up her small nose.

Ava wasn't listening to anything Mrs. Duke said. Kristen and Link's new appearance circled in her head. How could Kristen's parents just forget something like that? Or was that just something Gillian said? Obviously, something wasn't right. Could someone have tampered with her parents' memory? Gillian? No. How could she even think her best friend was involved? Then again, Gillian did act a little too freaked out by it. Were they playing games with Xavier? He was the new kid, and no one liked him. Had Melissa and Gillian convinced Kristen and Link to hang out with Xavier? It seemed far-fetched, and it didn't explain their disappearing act. But the way Melissa acted lately she wouldn't put it past her.

Ava knew Melissa would be upset if she asked, but she

had to know for sure they weren't involved. Maybe she'd talk to Thomas first.

Class ended and Ava walked to chemistry and took her seat. The second she saw Peter, she smiled. No matter what, he always made her heart skip a beat.

"Good morning." Peter sat at his desk. "What's wrong?"

"Nothing." How did he even know something was wrong?

"Okay, liar," he teased.

"Even if I told you, you wouldn't believe a word I said," she told him.

"Try me."

She shook her head, knowing she could never tell him about their powers.

"Is everything okay?"

"Sure."

Class ended, and Peter accompanied her to her locker, where she switched out her books. She searched the hall for Thomas and waited.

"You know you can talk to me if you need to."

"I appreciate it," she said.

"I'll see you later."

"Okay."

Peter strolled down the hall, and she was immediately guilty for leaving it like that. The one time she'd gotten to see him today, she'd brushed him off. She was just too preoccupied.

Thomas walked up and kissed her cheek. "Hey, Babe."

"Do you think Melissa convinced Gillian to tamper with Kristen and Link's mind?"

"What? Why do you say that?"

She crossed her arms in front of her chest. "I know you and Melissa wanted to play games. Something is going on. I mean, don't you think it's odd?"

"What is wrong with you?" Thomas seized her arm and pulled her closer to him. His eyes burned into hers. "How can you even think we had anything to do with Kristen and Link's disappearing act?"

His stern tone and sudden hostility surprised her.

"I'm sorry, but how many people do you know who can control minds?"

He loosened his grip, and his eyes rolled in the back of his head. He lost his balance and leaned over. Ava caught him from collapsing to the floor, and with a gasp, wondered how she was easily able to hold him. She dropped him immediately, before anyone could notice.

"Thomas?" She slapped his face then glanced up to see Xavier, Kristen, and Link pass by, completely absorbed in their own worlds.

Thomas groaned and opened his eyes. "What happened?"

"You just fainted."

He sat up. "Seriously?"

"Yeah. Are you okay?"

"I'm fine." He got to his feet, and Ava positioned her body as if he were going to fall. "I'm not gonna do that again, okay?"

She dropped her hands and stood upright.

"Whatever you do, don't tell the others. I don't need Lance getting on my case."

"Did you get hurt in practice yesterday? Hit your head on something?"

"Ava? Come on. I don't get hurt."

She rolled her eyes. "Of course not. Do you think it's your blood sugar?"

"Stop worrying. I'll be fine."

"You just fainted. Don't you need to see the nurse?"

"Give it a rest," he snapped. "You're as bad as my mom."

"I'm just trying to help." Anytime his precious ego was wounded, he had to act like a jerk.

"I don't need your help. It's no big deal."

Ava threw up her arms and made her way to the lunchroom. She swung open the door and stormed to their usual table. Slamming down her book bag, she realized they had all looked up at her.

"What's wrong with you?" Melissa asked.

"Nothing," Ava said. "I just don't get this whole Kristen/Link thing."

"It was my fault," Gillian said.

Melissa sighed. "No it wasn't, okay? You didn't do anything."

"You know," Thomas blurted. "Ava thinks you convinced Gillian to mess with their minds."

Ava glared at him, and clenched her teeth.

Gillian's jaw dropped.

Melissa gave a disgusted look. "I can't believe you would even think that."

"It just crossed my mind for a second."

"Why would it?"

"You're the one who said you wanted to mess with people."

"Are you freaking kidding me, Ava?" Melissa snapped. "I was talking about stupid things, like pretending to be a ghost in the girl's bathroom or something. None of us knows what's going on. You've been acting so weird since our powers developed. What's with you?"

"What do you mean?"

"You're just freaking out over everything."

"And Gillian's not?"

Gillian huffed. "That's not fair."

Ava felt guilty. Did she really believe her friends had anything to do with all this craziness? Maybe she secretly wanted it all to be some prank because that lessened the fear. "I just wish I knew what was going on."

"We all do, okay?"

Ava nodded, and then looked up and met Xavier's cold eyes. He was staring at her with a dark grin on his face.

CHAPTER SIX
CONFRONTATION

A month passed and school was anything but normal. If the disappearance and sudden reappearance of Kristen and Link wasn't enough, three more students had disappeared and come back as if nothing happened. Scott Tingle, Liza Butler, and Nicole Eckrich had returned, dropped their friends, and joined Xavier. All of their parents dropped their cases and the police strangely concluded that everything was fine again. It didn't make any sense.

Ava constantly watched Xavier's demeanor, confused by how he controlled Kristen as if she were his property. They all acted as if they belonged together. And what was with their enormous personality change? They walked the halls of the school like kings and queens of a court but kept to themselves. Each one of them *hated* everyone else. They ignored them, pushed them, vandalized their cars, called them names—the list was endless, and somehow they never were caught. Xavier had started a gang, and it frightened several students, including Peter.

He slid into the chair next to Ava without a greeting. She looked up and saw his face twisted in bewilderment. He balled his hand into a fist and punched the desk.

"Peter? What's wrong?" She placed a hand on his shoulder. He was shaking.

"I can't believe this."

"What?"

"Seth is now Xavier's friend."

Ava was shocked. "What?"

"I thought he was sick, and that's why he'd missed the last three days. And then I saw him this morning. He completely ignored me, and told Amanda to leave him alone. Just this weekend they finally kissed."

She gripped his shaking hand, uncertain as how to calm him. "I'm so sorry."

"And then this morning, Andre Hill went to talk to Xavier because they wrote trash on his sister's car. Xavier laughed, and then they circled Andre. Then, he fell onto the floor. Just...collapsed. No one touched him to make him fall."

Ava thought of Thomas. "Maybe he just fainted."

Peter shook his head. "While he was out, Xavier stood back while Link, Scott, and Seth kicked him. And then left him there. If they can do that to him, what would they do to someone like me?"

"I-I don't know."

"And Andre remembers nothing. I was there, Ava. I stayed hidden in the bathroom stall. It happened so fast, I couldn't help him. After they left, I came out and woke him up."

Thomas hadn't remembered anything after he fainted either.

"I've had enough of this," she said. "I'm going to talk to Xavier today."

He met her eyes. "You can't."

"I want to know what's going on. You don't just come to school, not knowing a single person, and then kidnap students and suddenly they're your friends and then start bullying everyone who isn't in your gang or whatever. I want to know what he's up to."

"Please don't," he said.

"Why?"

"Because he could—you could be next."

"I won't let that happen."

"Ava—."

"He can't keep doing this and get away with it."

"He will *hurt* you," he said, and then blushed. "I couldn't take that."

"I'll talk to him after class. Would he attack me with all those kids there?"

"I'm coming with you. If something happens to you, I'd rather be there so that I can try to protect you."

"You shouldn't be there."

"Neither should you."

"You're so stubborn."

He raised his eyebrows. "*I'm* stubborn?"

When the incredibly dull lesson ended, the bell rang, Ava and Peter walked side-by-side out into the crowded hall. She knew he was scared, but he didn't let it show. Some students were already leaning against lockers, talking or kissing. Some were frantically trying to beat the late bell. Ava scanned the crowd for Xavier. Then, she saw him standing at the end of the hall against a wall of lockers, arm locked around Kristen, and laughing with his new friends, Seth included.

Peter cursed. Ava marched toward Xavier, her heart pounding, but she wasn't about to let him see her fear. She knew Thomas wouldn't see her standing by her locker and knew he'd be upset, but she had to know the truth.

As soon as Xavier saw Ava, his smile disappeared, and his eyes darkened. "What do you want?" His sallow face held so much darkness.

"What are you doing to these people?"

"What? I'm not allowed to have friends?" Xavier removed his arm from around Kristen and crossed it with his other in front of his chest. He straightened his stance, making him tower over Ava.

"You know what I mean," she said through clenched teeth.

"He didn't do anything, okay?" Kristen smiled. "We all just started talking, and well, he saved me. He saved all of us." She gazed up at him.

"What are you talking about?"

The late bell rang as the hallway cleared of the students, but Ava ignored it. She couldn't tear her gaze away from Xavier's eyes. The same frustrated look contorted his face as before.

"You should leave before this gets ugly," he said.

Ava glared at him. "I'm not afraid of you."

Xavier shortened the distance between them, and his thin lips stretched into a menacing grin. "That will change soon."

"Why did you beat up Andre? Why are you terrorizing these people?"

Peter tugged on her arm. "Come on, Ava. Let's go."

"I will find out."

"No doubt," Xavier said.

"I will put an end to this." She let Peter pull her away.

"I'd like to see you try."

Ava stopped and turned back, ready to accept his provocation, but Peter jerked her away. They walked down the empty hallway, turned a corner, and headed straight for the cafeteria. Ava relaxed.

"What is he doing with those kids?" she asked. "It's like he's completely brainwashed them. They are all so different now."

"Did you see Seth? He looked at me like we'd never been friends."

"I'm so sorry, Peter. Mel thinks they're doing drugs, but I don't agree. I'll find out."

He stopped her outside the cafeteria. "Please don't do anything. If we don't entice him, maybe he'll leave us alone. I mean, I can fight him, but I don't think I could take seven of them."

His eyes pleaded.

Ava loved how he cared about her. But he was right. If Xavier was meddling with something dangerous, she didn't want to make it worse. She cared about Peter, too, which was why she wanted to help Seth. "Okay."

"Come on."

"Um, you should enter first. I don't want Thomas thinking anything."

"Does he know we're just friends?"

"Yes. It's easier this way. I don't want him badgering me with questions, and I don't feel like dealing with his temper."

"Of course." He rolled his eyes, and then opened the door, leaving Ava outside.

She hated hiding, but she knew how Thomas would react by her showing up late to lunch with Peter. Ava waited a few seconds outside but then heard footsteps behind. She twisted her head and saw Xavier and his gang walking closer. She quickly placed her hand on the door handle. Just then, a blinding flash burst in her head, and then nothing.

CHAPTER SEVEN
ACCEPTANCE

Ava's face stung as it pressed against something cold and hard, and her head throbbed intensely. She felt a dull ache in her jaw, but had no recollection of anything.

"Ava, wake up." She heard Peter's voice. He sounded worried.

She felt his fingers carefully sweep her hair aside, which sent shivers down her spine. Then, her head stopped throbbing. The dull ache in her jaw vanished. Ava felt no pain. It was as if it disappeared at his touch.

"Ava?"

She opened her eyes slowly and realized she was lying face down on the white concrete floor at school in an empty hallway.

"Are you okay?" He helped her sit up. "What happened?" His worried expression changed to relief.

She touched the right side of her head and winced at its tenderness. "I don't know."

"Were you feeling lightheaded?"

"No. Not at all."

"You don't remember anything? I came into the lunchroom before you, but you never came in. And after a few minutes, you still weren't there. I just walked out here and found you sprawled on the ground." She felt him stiffen. "It was Xavier, wasn't it? Did he hurt you?"

"I-I don't know."

"I knew he would." He checked the back of her head. "You aren't bleeding. But you have a knot now. I'd still get that checked out. You must have been hit pretty hard if you can't remember—and since you totally blacked out. Do you hurt anywhere else?"

"No," she said. His touch stirred the butterflies in her stomach. "I don't feel any pain."

"I'm sure it'll start hurting soon. Come on, I'll take you to the nurse."

The bell shrilly sounded, echoing in the hallway, followed by loud voices over voices and the shuffling of students exiting the lunchroom. Just as Peter helped Ava to her feet, Thomas pushed him aside, and grasped her.

"What did you do to her?" Thomas demanded Peter while the rest of her friends circled around her.

Ava pressed her hand against his chest. "Thomas, don't."

"What? What is it, Babe?"

"What happened?" Melissa asked.

"I think Xavier knocked her out," Peter said.

"And I think we can handle it from here," Thomas replied.

Ava met Peter's eyes and silently apologized.

"Why would Xavier hit you?" Jeremy asked.

"I can't remember."

Thomas pulled her into an embrace. "I'll take care of him. He won't hurt you again."

He smoothed his hair and kissed her forehead. She loosened his grip slightly to tell Peter she'd talk to him later, but he had already walked away. The throbbing returned. Ava buried her head into Thomas's chest to ease the pain, but it only got worse.

"My head." She winced.

"Here." Gillian reached in her purse and then dumped

two pills in Ava's hand. "Take these."

"Do you remember anything at all?" Melissa asked.

"I sorta remember talking to Xavier. Trying to figure out what he was doing."

"You shouldn't have been talking to him," Gillian said. "Why can't you just leave it alone? It doesn't concern you. We don't need you to go disappearing on us and suddenly wind up in his court, okay?"

"Okay. But I saw him," Ava said. "That day you fainted." She looked up at Thomas. "He walked by at the same time. And then you couldn't remember anything. Could he...could he be like us?"

"Like us? How?" Melissa asked.

"Wait, you fainted?" Lance raised his eyebrows.

They all looked at Thomas.

"It might have happened. I don't remember."

Ava rolled her eyes and removed herself from his crushing grasp.

Jeremy pushed his glasses up. "I don't think he's like us. I think he's just some manipulative bully who persuaded Kristen and the rest to be his friends."

"I don't understand why he's doing this." Ava shook her head. "I'm going home."

"I'll take you." Thomas took her hand.

"No, it's okay. I'll just see you later."

He sighed. "Why won't you let me help you?"

"Not now. I'll call you later."

Lance grabbed his shoulder. "Come on, man, we've got practice."

Ava walked toward the door as the bell rang and out to her car. Who was Xavier Holstone? Was he like them? Did he have powers, too? Had the same thing happened to Thomas, Andre, and her?

Ava awoke to the sound of a car door closing. She raised her head to see the time. Five thirty. Sleep had erased her headache, for now at least. She yawned but then cried out.

The side of her jaw throbbed intensely. Her hands flew to her face and it felt puffy and tight.

"You've got to be kidding me," she muttered and went into the bathroom.

Ava flicked on the light and gasped. The ghastly bruise was a deep dark purple. There was no hiding this. What was that kid's problem? Did he get off on bullying people?

With a sigh, she slapped the light switch off and then met her father downstairs. "Hey."

He raised his eyebrows, and grimaced. "What happened to you?" he asked, his voice rough.

"I don't really know."

"Did someone hit you?"

"I don't remember. I woke up on the floor. And I had a bruise on my face and a knot on my head."

"Who did that to you? Did you go see the nurse? Go to the doctor?"

"No, I'm fine."

"Except that you can't remember anything. Come on."

"I'm fine. I remember everything except that. And my head doesn't hurt anymore."

He let out a conceding sigh and then sank into his recliner and removed his shoes.

"Dad, could an Enchanter make someone just pass out?"

He looked away and thought for a minute. "I can't say I ever knew one who could. Why?"

Ava sat on the couch facing his side. "This guy at school is terrorizing students. All these people went missing, and they returned like nothing happened, and they're all different. It's so weird. Including one of Peter's friends."

He looked up. "How different?"

"Like Kristen used to be so conservative and nice. Now, she picks on kids with her new gang, and she doesn't even dress the same. Seth used to be this laid-back, nice guy, but he just beat up some kid today."

Her father narrowed his eyes. "Did this kid start a cult or something?"

"I don't know. I confronted Xavier, but he acted all high and mighty. Then Peter and I walked to lunch, and the next thing I know I'm on the floor facedown with Peter waking me. He said he saw Xavier come into the lunchroom a few seconds after him."

"Didn't he see what happened?"

Ava shifted on the old blue couch. There was certain spot on it that already had a divot made after so many years. "He went inside before me."

Her father raised his eyebrows. "He just left you out there?"

"No, I told him to go ahead of me."

"Why?"

"Because I didn't want Thomas seeing us walk in together."

"Ava."

"Come on, Dad. Thomas gets jealous."

He shook his head, and she knew he was disappointed in her.

"Anyway, it doesn't matter. I'm an Enchanter, and I guess you should know my powers developed."

"Really?" His face lit, but she didn't see what all the fuss was about.

"Don't get too excited. I can breathe underwater."

"And?"

"And that's it."

His eyebrows furrowed. "Something's not right."

"What?"

"That can't be all you can do."

"What else is there? Other than the climate-control and strength."

"Well, all Enchanters have those. And soon you'll have incredible agility, stamina, speed, and your reflexes will be so quick." His eyes lit up like a kid in a theme park, and Ava couldn't help but smile.

"When does all this happen?" she asked.

"The more you practice." He looked away wistfully and

took his time answering. "Your mom was a Water Enchanter. She controlled it."

"Really?" Ava had never known what kind of powers her mother possessed. They hadn't talked a lot about her mom.

"She made it do whatever she wanted. She could generate it. Create rogue waves. She could absorb it so that if someone attacked her with say, a sword, it would just go right through her without damaging her."

"Wow." Just thinking about it made Ava excited. "So, I can do all those things too?"

"Every person is different. Only you will be able to figure that out. When do you see Savina and Colden?"

"Sunday. I'll be glad when it's over."

"When what's over?"

"You know. This whole Initiation thing. I just wanna be done with it so I can get back to…" She briefly thought Peter, but knew that probably wouldn't bode well for her father. "Normalcy. It's all Mel can talk about."

"This is our life, Ava." His stern voice told her she'd crossed a line. "It never ends."

"I know that." He'd rarely gotten angry with her, but when he did, she always felt guilty.

He shook his head in disappointment. "You should be proud of who and what you are."

"I never said I wasn't. I mean, I have been dreading all of it."

"Dreading?" he spat and narrowed his eyes. "Do you understand what you're saying?"

Ava was taken aback. "Dad—."

"Your mother never regretted who she was."

"I only meant I was dreading the change." She tried to ease the tension.

"Ava, I know it must be a scary thing to suddenly wake up with powers. But remember what your ancestors and your mother went through so you could live free." His tone was sharp.

"I'm sorry."

"Think about that the next time you dread it." His eyes moved to the TV, and he flipped it on, signaling the end of the conversation.

Ava swallowed the lump and released the pillow that she apparently had been gripping. She left, hoping he wouldn't notice her. When she reached her room, she closed the door and sat on her bed against the headboard with her knees to her chest.

Her dad had never spoken about her mom like that. Had he thought about her more because Ava was going to see Savina and Colden soon?

She picked up the picture of her and her parents from the nightstand. She had no idea who had taken it, but her dad was behind her mom and Ava, hugging them. Her mother's smile was pure happiness, and Ava wondered if any of her own ever looked so content. She loved the natural beauty and the absolute confidence her mother possessed. Though Ava shared her mother's almond-shaped gray eyes, she doubted they ever held such self-assurance. She had the same pale freckles across her cheeks and the copper hair, but Ava's was longer.

She wished she could remember more of her, and felt as time moved on, she'd forgotten too much. As she stared at the picture, guilt weighed even more on her. She hadn't meant to hurt her father's feelings, but she needed to take her heritage more seriously. She was an Enchanter. This was who she was. Nothing could change that.

CHAPTER EIGHT
BOYS

Ava tossed her pencil in the crease of her chemistry book. She didn't want to think about it. Nor did she want to think about her quasi-argument with her father last night. Or how she wound up unconscious in the hallway yesterday. She was sure the bruise on her jaw was extremely attractive. Had Xavier really hit her?

The crowd cheered, and a whistle blew. The announcer said something, but it was like listening to Charlie Brown's teacher. Very muffled.

"First down." Melissa nudged Ava.

"And I care?"

Like every Friday night at the football game, Ava didn't watch, but did her homework. What better time to do it? If it hadn't been for Thomas, she wouldn't even be there.

She always sat at the top of the concrete bleachers, away from the crowd so she could concentrate. Even in the sea of red-and-black Raiders fans, she managed to find a good spot. On the other side of the field, green-and-gold Spartans screamed and shook shakers.

Gillian cheered on the sidelines in her little uniform while Jeremy sat at the bottom near her, and of course, Thomas and Lance were playing.

Peter had sat with Ava every home game and actually helped with her homework, except tonight. She was glad Melissa hadn't antagonized Thomas about them sitting together, and Melissa actually seemed to like Peter's company.

"I don't see how you can concentrate on that here."

Ava shrugged. "I just drown out the noises."

Just as she looked out into the game, Ava saw number seven run back to the sidelines and after several teammates patted him, he pointed at her.

"I don't get why he always does that."

"Because. He just made an awesome play, and it was all for you," Melissa said in a dramatic voice. Her hands raked through her loose side ponytail.

"Whatever." Ava returned to her book.

"You know Thomas is going to be upset that you're not watching him."

"I don't care."

Melissa opened a package of candy and poured some into her hand. She ate one piece at a time. Something to keep her from smoking, Ava guessed. "What's the deal with you two? I mean, did it really spur from that night in the summer?"

"That night certainly didn't help." She pretended to read about atomic mass.

"Then what is it?"

Ava didn't want to say too much because Melissa wasn't exactly the best at keeping things to herself. "He's just different."

"We all are. Especially now. You two used to be so good together."

Ava looked up and saw, through the thick crowd of heads and shakers, Peter sitting with a couple of friends. Her heart leapt, and she wondered why he wasn't sitting with her.

"Would this have anything to do with Peter?"

Damn. Melissa caught her looking at him. "We're just friends."

Melissa popped a piece of candy in her mouth. "I mean, I

get why you like hanging around him. He's smart. He seems to hold a more interesting conversation than Thomas can."

"What are you getting at?"

"I just think it's a shame that he likes you so much, and you have a boyfriend."

"He likes me as a friend."

Melissa raised an eyebrow. "I doubt that. Do you know he's been sneaking glances at you all night?"

Ava shifted uncomfortably, but she secretly liked knowing that.

"It's like you two are star-crossed lovers."

"You're ridiculous," she said and faked a laugh.

"Well, maybe you're right. One of the girls he's with keeps glaring in your direction. She could be his girlfriend."

Ava looked up, and sure enough, the brunette girl was glowering right at her. Did Peter have a girlfriend? He would have told her. Was that why he wanted her to sit with his friends so much, so she could meet her? Her stomach turned. This was silly. He could have a girlfriend if he wanted to. Or maybe that was his friend Amanda who needed company after Seth became Xavier's friend. But that didn't explain the glares.

The loud cheering and the emptying bleachers signaled the end of the game. Ava closed her book and notebook and followed Melissa with the rest of the crowd down the side of the bleachers. They stopped at the bottom beside the concession stand.

"Hey." Gillian bounded up to them. "That was an awesome game, wasn't it?" Red and black ribbons tied her black curls into a ponytail with an exuberant bounce. Her blue eyes sparkled, and she held the black and red pompoms in her hands.

"Yeah it was so awesome. I wish we could do this every night," Melissa said sarcastically, and then walked closer to the locker rooms to wait on Lance.

Ava looked past Melissa and saw Peter and his friends following the crowd out of the stadium. He playfully tousled the brunette's hair, and she squealed. She hooked her arm with his. Ava felt a heavy weight in the pit of her stomach, and then looked away.

Gillian tugged on her arm. "I didn't know he had a girlfriend."

"So it would seem." She wanted to tell her the truth about Peter and needed to get it off her chest. "Gillian, if I tell you something, do you promise not to say anything to anyone?"

"I promise."

"Not even to Jeremy or Melissa?"

"Yeah. What is it?" Her eyes were eager for whatever juicy gossip Ava was about to tell her.

She took a deep breath, and hoped Gillian could keep the secret. "I really like Peter. And it gets worse the more I see him. I've tried ignoring how I feel, but there's just something about him. I want to break up with Thomas and be with Peter."

"Whoa." Her mouth was agape, and she brought her pom-pom filled hands to her mouth. "You can't," she whispered so softly. "You know that's forbidden."

She'd known about the unspoken rule regarding Enchanters mingling with humans. But if Corbin was dead and there wasn't a war, what was the harm?

"What am I supposed to do?" she asked. "I'm becoming more and more detached from Thomas, and he's aggressive and even more possessive."

"I've noticed that. Maybe you could just talk to him."

"I've talked and gotten nowhere."

"Don't do it."

Jeremy walked up behind Gillian and wrapped his arms around her. "You were great tonight." He kissed her cheek and hugged her tightly.

Ava looked away. The wind blew slightly, and she shivered. Goosebumps formed, but then she suddenly became warm as if the temperatures outside rose. And now she'd developed the climate-control ability, as she liked to call it. Enchanters could make themselves warm or cold to survive extreme weather. It was just one more reminder of how different she was.

"Are you two okay?" Jeremy asked.

"Fine," Ava said.

"We won, Babe," Lance said as he and Thomas came out of the locker room, clean and refreshed. He picked Melissa up and spun her around.

"That's 5 and 0," Thomas said. "We *finally* beat them." He took Ava's hand, and then they all walked up the hill to the parking lot of the school. "After three years of them beating us. Ah, that game was so awesome. I totally ragged them."

He launched into his review of the game while Ava ambled at his side, not paying attention.

Thomas squeezed her hand. "Earth to Ava, are you listening?"

"Yeah," she lied.

"Did you even watch the game?"

"Some of it."

He sighed and released her hand. "Dammit, Ava," he shouted. "Why can't you come and actually watch for once? I mean, what's the point of showing up if you're not even going to watch me?"

"Because you want me there. I had a lot of homework to do. Besides, I can't really tell what's going on or who has the ball and what all the flags mean."

"I've tried explaining it to you. It's not hard. It's not a sissy sport like baseball. This is a real sport."

As if she hadn't heard that a million times. "Yeah, yeah, yeah."

"Next Friday, for once, would you please just watch me? Is it really that hard? Or do you have to be so damn stubborn and uncaring?"

"It's not that I don't care. I'm sorry if I hurt your feelings. I just get bored."

"Great. So now I bore you?"

Ava groaned. "Stop acting like a baby."

"I'm a baby now?"

"Stop putting words in my mouth."

Lance shook his head. "And the fighting has begun. We'll see you at the bonfire." He and Melissa got into his car.

"We're gonna skip it tonight," Gillian said. "We'll see you later. I'll call you, Ava." She waved to them, and walked away with Jeremy.

Great. So now, Ava would have to endure Thomas's drunkenness while Melissa and Lance went to find a quiet spot in the woods. The night just kept getting better. She was a little miffed that Gillian had deserted her, knowing what Ava had just told her.

"Babe, ride with me," Thomas said.

"I wish you wouldn't call me that. You know I hate it."

He rolled his eyes. "Why?"

"You know why. It's patronizing. It makes me feel like I'm some toy."

"Whatever. Will you ride with me?"

"No. You'll get drunk, and then I'll have to find a way home."

"No I won't. But you could always drive us home."

"I hate driving your Jeep."

"I won't drink tonight. Promise. Please?"

He wouldn't give up. "Fine." She placed her books inside her car and then climbed inside his Jeep.

He turned the ignition, revved the engine, and drove out of the parking lot, following Lance and others in a caravan to the bonfire.

"I don't want to stay long," she told Thomas.

"You never do. By the way, thanks for telling everyone yesterday that I fainted. Good to know you can keep a secret."

"Oh, like you kept mine about me thinking Gillian manipulated Kristen."

"What are you talking about?"

"Do you have a crayon stuck in your brain?"

He wrinkled his eyebrows. "No. That was like a month ago."

"I still think something's going on with Xavier."

"Why are you so concerned with him? Who cares? If anything, he did Kristen and all them a favor."

"Favor? Why, because Kristen suddenly looks hot to you?"

Even in the dim blue dashboard lights, she could see the muscles in his jaw twitch. "What about Peter? You seem to have the hots for him."

"He has a girlfriend." She hoped that would make Thomas back down.

"Maybe he had something to do with your fainting."

She was aghast. "How could you even think that?"

"He's always around you. He was the only one out there with you yesterday. Maybe he and Xavier are working together. You never know."

"You can be such an ass."

Thomas parked the car at the end of the line in a field down from the bonfire and cut the engine.

Ava reached for her door, but he grabbed her arm and forced her to face him. "Don't call me that again." His blue eyes bored into hers.

She exhaled, defeated. "I'm so sick of this."

"Sick of what?"

"Fighting with you."

"Then don't." His eyes softened.

Then he cradled her face between his hands. He kissed her, gently at first, then harder.

She winced from the bruise. "Thomas," she groaned.

He leaned over, with his mouth still on hers, and pulled the seat lever, making it recline backward. His hands fervently tried to touch her, but she blocked him.

"Thomas, knock it off."

"Babe, come on, I'm ready."

"Well I'm not." She pushed him back.

He released a frustrated groan and then returned to his seat. "When are you ever going to be ready? We've been together forever. What's it gonna take?"

She pulled her seat back to the upright position. "Certainly not attacking me like that."

"I can't help it. I'm sorry. I really am." He brushed his fingers across her cheek. "I just love you so much. And I feel like I'm losing you."

She swallowed hard. He had a way of making her feel guilty.

He leaned over and kissed her cheek. "Let's go."

Ava nodded and then they got out of the car. She felt like crying, but with every fiber in her body, she held it in.

Together, they walked toward the large fire. As usual, music blared while people gathered around with beer or other alcoholic drinks, dancing, mingling, or just acting stupid. Like the time Chip Crenshaw fell into the fire because he was dancing to impress some girl. Lucky for him, he didn't burn.

Ava hated being here, and all she wanted to do was go home.

"You two get all that out of your system?" Melissa asked as Ava and Thomas joined her and Lance.

Ava clenched her teeth to keep down the lump that lurched inside her throat. She blinked away the tears.

"Shut up, Mel," Thomas snapped.

"I guess not," she said.

Lance patted Thomas's shoulder. "Come on, let's get a drink."

Ava grabbed Thomas's arm. "You said you wouldn't drink tonight."

"Whatever." He jerked his arm away and followed Lance.

"You okay?" Melissa asked.

"Fine." She knew she should've taken her own car.

Melissa lit a cigarette and exhaled the smoke as they watched Thomas telling his larger-than-life football story.

"It sure didn't take long for him to regale everyone with his precious football game," Melissa said. "He cracks me up with how animated he gets. You want anything to drink?"

"No, thanks."

Melissa walked away, and Ava continued to watch

Thomas, anger brimming. She stared at the fire and then tilted her head to the side. She couldn't be sure, but it looked as though the fire actually tried to reach out to Thomas. Yes, it seemed to follow his hand movements. Whether he moved up or down, the fire tagged along. She glanced around to see if anyone else noticed, but they all seemed too drunk or too enamored with him. Then, she saw Xavier.

He appeared to be staring right at Thomas's hands. She stiffened. Did he really see what she did? What was going through his mind? He didn't look shocked at all, but his gaze was so intense that it made her nervous.

"You're not getting any ideas, are you?"

Ava jerked around and met Peter's eyes. "What?"

"To mess with Xavier. It's not worth it."

"No, that's not what I was thinking."

"Good. Are you okay?" His brown eyes invited her to unload all her worries.

But she didn't.

"Sure."

"I'm sorry I didn't sit with you. Valerie and Amanda didn't want to sit alone since Seth, you know."

"It's okay. How are you all handling it?"

He sighed and shook his head. "I don't know."

"I'm sorry." Ava wished she could say something to make him feel better.

"Don't be. Seth made his decision."

But she wasn't sure Seth had a choice. She had to figure out what Xavier was doing. Something was going on.

"You get your homework done?" Peter asked after a few moments.

"I guess. I suck at chemistry."

"I know." He grinned. "Maybe I could tutor you."

"I don't think that would be a good idea."

"Why? Because of Thomas?"

Ava turned, and saw Peter's brunette friend watching them with her arms crossed. "I don't think your girlfriend would like it." At once, she wished she could take back those jealous words.

A crease formed between his eyebrows. "I don't have a girlfriend."

Ava was silently relieved. "Oh." She looked back where Xavier stood, but he was gone. She saw Thomas talking to a few cheerleaders away from the fire as if nothing had happened. Surely, he must have been aware.

"Would you like to meet my friends?" Peter asked.

"Don't take this the wrong way, but I don't think I'd be good company right now."

"Why don't we go for a drive?"

"What about your friends? How will they get home?"

"I took my own car. And Tony's with them now. Come on."

Alone time with Peter?

"Okay." She followed him to his car, hoping Thomas wouldn't see them together. But she decided that he was too drunk to notice. He would be upset, but she'd send him a message. The brunette girl would probably be even more upset that she was leaving with Peter. She suddenly felt wrong about taking a drive with him. If the girl wasn't his girlfriend, she obviously liked him, and Ava didn't want to step on any toes.

"Do you want to go to my house?" he asked.

"Sure," she said, and slid into passenger seat. What was she doing? She couldn't go to his house. Ava wanted to be there with him, but Gillian's words flashed in her mind like a blinking red light. *Forbidden. Forbidden. Forbidden.*

CHAPTER NINE
FORBIDDEN

Peter drove down the interstate a short distance and then exited. Ava ignored the rational part of her brain, and tried to push aside Gillian's annoying warning. They would just hang out like they did all those times during the summer. Besides, this way Thomas couldn't find her.

"What happened tonight?" he asked.

"Nothing." She twirled her opal ring around her finger.

"What's the nicest thing Thomas has ever done for you?"

The question took her off guard. "I don't know. He brought me flowers when he came back from camp."

"That's it?"

"What do you want me to say?"

Peter sighed. "I don't get why you're with him if he makes you so miserable."

"He's always been there." She paused. "When I was younger, I got sick with pneumonia, and he would talk to me on the phone every day. He's all I've ever known. But he's different now."

"Then why are you still with him? I mean, he doesn't seem to treat you well."

"He treats me fine"

"Is that why you looked like you were about to cry back there?"

She peered out the window, crossed her arms, feeling a little embarrassed. "Can we not talk about this?"

"I'm just worried about you."

"Peter, I appreciate your concern, but really, it's not necessary."

"Okay." He pulled into a driveway in front of a massive two-story house with a brick front and eight windows that faced the road. Peter and his dad lived in an old wealthy subdivision.

They walked up the short winding sidewalk to the front step. He opened the door to a quiet house, and she followed him through the narrow hall and into the living room.

Forbidden.

Soft yellow light poured from a lamp on an end table. Peter switched on the TV and flipped to a sports channel, while she took a seat in the deep brown plush couch.

"Are you hungry? Thirsty?" he asked.

"No, thanks."

He sat next to her, and her heart sprang to life.

After a few moments of silence and staring at the TV, he turned to her. "I didn't know you had pneumonia. How bad was it?"

She met his soft brown eyes. "I almost died."

His jaw dropped open. "Wow."

Ava fought the urge to hold his hand. This was bad. They would return to Savina and Colden's tomorrow night, but would she and Peter still have nights like this after the Initiation?

"What are you thinking about?" he asked.

"Just how everything is going to change."

"You mean after graduation?"

"Yeah," she lied.

"You can't worry about things that are out of your control."

"I know. It just sucks."

"Don't get down about it. This is our last year, so we need to make the best of it. Things will change, and friends will drift apart, but you'll gain some new ones. And those who really care will still be there. They won't abandon you."

His tone was bitter.

"Have you talked to Seth at all?" she asked.

He shook his head. "He still ignores me. He changed his number, and he's never at home. His parents don't even seem bothered by how different he is. I don't get it."

"I don't understand how someone can up and change like that, without warning."

"I've been wondering that myself for seven years."

Ava looked at Peter, unsure of what he meant.

"My mom left when I was ten," he said.

She gasped. "Peter, I'm so sorry." First, his mom had abandoned him, now his friend.

"Thanks. She just couldn't handle us I guess." He shrugged. "It happened one day after school. I came home, and she told us she was leaving. She said she wasn't cut out for this kind of life and left."

"That's awful. Has she ever tried contacting you?"

"No."

"Do you ever think about her? I mean, do you ever want to see her again?"

"I try *not* to think about her, honestly. And no, I don't want to see her." He spoke with resentment.

She reveled in the simple fact that they had something in common, something big, something no one she had ever known shared. They each had no mother.

"How come you never told me?" The words slipped out, but she knew the answer.

Another shrug. "It's just something I don't talk about."

"Yeah, I can understand." And she could.

"It's okay, though. I don't mind telling you about it. I'm very comfortable with you."

"Me too."

His hand brushed against hers, and slowly he intertwined

his fingers with hers. It felt so natural. The simple touch made her heart hammer against her ribcage.

Forbidden.

She dropped her gaze, and removed her hand.

The room was quiet, except for the people talking on TV. The wind outside forced the nearby branches to scratch the window. Her attention turned to the brewing storm. White veins descended from the dark clouds and illuminated the room. She flinched and looked away. No matter how many years had passed, she still hated lightning.

"You were there," he whispered. "Weren't you?"

She met his eyes. "Where?"

"With your mom?"

Her stomach tightened, as if someone had wrapped their hands around it and squeezed. It always felt like that when she thought of that day. "Yes."

"H how did she?" Peter shook his head. "No, sorry. That was rude."

"She was struck by lightning," she mumbled, and fidgeted with her ring.

Peter made a sound, but Ava wasn't quite sure what it was.

"I was outside playing—."

"You don't have to tell me. I don't want to upset you."

"It's okay." She drew in a shaky breath. "There was a storm coming. My mom came outside to get the sheets from the clothesline and told me to go inside. But I just took my time cleaning up my dolls." Tears blurred her vision. "If I had listened to her, I wouldn't have seen the lightning reflected in the glass doors."

"Ava."

She looked up and several tears fell. "The last memory I have of her…" Ava saw in her mind, the blood oozing from her mom's head and her singed body. "I kept screaming for her but she never woke up. How could such a thing have happened?"

Peter pulled her against him. "I—I wish I knew what to say."

"It feels weird knowing I've told someone else." She tilted her head up at him and searched his eyes. "Someone who understands me."

"I can't ever imagine how you must feel."

"Yes, you can. Your mom left."

"Yeah, but she had a choice. I do know how it feels not to have a mom. If she couldn't stand my dad so much, at least she could've made an effort for me. She could've given me advice or just been there for me. At least, we have each other."

"Yes. We do have that," she said, and their eyes locked.

Ava wanted to kiss him and knew she needed to leave before the desire became too much. She was getting in deeper. Why was she doing this to herself? It was only going to hurt even more. But she wanted this. This level of comfort and honesty. She couldn't remember the last time she and Thomas had such a sincere conversation. If ever. Peter was understanding and cared for her. Ava wanted to tell him that she wanted to be more than just friends.

Forbidden.

Her mouth went dry.

"I should go before Dad starts to worry." She stood from the couch, breaking the intense connection.

"Okay," Peter said. He picked up a dark blue jacket and handed it to her. "Here, take this. Looks like the bottom's about to fall out."

"Thanks." She smiled and put on the jacket. She inhaled. It smelled like him.

He opened the door for her and then followed her to his car. The wind blew, gaining strength, and the temperature outside warmed. Only in the South could it be warm one day and cold the next.

Peter got in the car after her and cranked it. "We should hang out more often. It's been a while."

"We hang out every Friday night."

He cocked an eyebrow. "I meant not at a football game. It's been like two months."

"I'm sorry. I've just been busy."

When they pulled up next to her car in the school parking lot, she dreaded leaving the moment and going back to reality. But she got out anyway.

Peter came around to her side. "I just want to make sure you're happy. I care about you, you know."

"I'll be fine. I had a good time."

"Me, too. I'm glad you came." He stepped closer, and her breath hitched.

Peter wrapped his arms around her tightly. It relaxed her, and for a moment, Ava wanted to draw him closer and run her hands through his hair. She was sure he could feel her pounding heartbeat.

She quickly pulled away. "Goodnight."

He grinned, showing the dimple in his cheek. "Goodnight."

Ava slid behind the wheel, and then he closed her door. She started the engine and drove away. The stupid warning from Gillian kept bothering her. But why was it forbidden? Other than keeping their kind a secret.

Her phone rang, startling her, and she answered, thinking it was Peter.

"Where are you?" Thomas asked, angrily.

His words slurred evidence that he was still drunk. She didn't even want to think how he got home.

"Home," she said. Like she was really going to tell him the truth.

"How'd you get back to your car?"

She didn't want to answer and knew she couldn't lie. "Peter."

"What's with this guy? You into him or something?"

"No. I'm just struggling with chemistry."

"Whatever."

Ava imagined his jaw clenching. "It's true. I'm failing."

"So you have to get some other guy to help you? Can't you ask Jeremy?"

"He was busy. What difference does it make? You got

drunk even though you promised you wouldn't."

"Yeah, because you pissed me off."

"I'm not doing this." She hung up. He was such a jerk.

Why did she have to be with him? Because of some stupid binding? How serious could Savina and Colden be, since they had been absent for ten years? Whatever happened to them always being there for Ava and the rest? Why should she go back tomorrow?

Ava turned up the radio to calm her anger. Guilt seeped into her thoughts as she remembered her father telling her that her mom never regretted what she was. Bet Mom never had feelings for a human, she thought.

Could it even be possible to be with Peter?

No matter though. Tomorrow she would end her relationship with Thomas. It was that simple. She had overanalyzed things once again, but the answer was right in front of her. Life would be good. At least, it would be better.

CHAPTER TEN
REUNION

On an extremely bitter, cold October night, it was time for the Initiation. Waiting for Thomas, Ava bit her lip and watched the fast moving clouds move across the darkening pink sky through her window. She didn't know why she was nervous, but she hadn't slept at all last night and couldn't sit still for one minute all day. Her dad tried to comfort her, but it didn't work.

She heard the doorbell and knew it was Thomas. Once they went to the Manor and came back, she would talk to him.

With a moan, she finally left her room and met him downstairs. "See ya later, Dad."

"Everything will be okay," he said.

Ava nodded and followed Thomas out the door.

"Took you long enough," he said.

"Don't start."

"Yeah, well, we'll just blame our lateness on you."

She opened the back door and squeezed in next to Gillian and Melissa. Thomas left the loud radio playing and the heat going for the others. Lance took the passenger seat, while Jeremy sat in the very back of the Jeep.

Melissa sighed. "Thomas, we're not late. It's not like we're going to the football game. By the way, what did Coach Jones do to you for being tardy Friday?" She laughed and lit a cigarette, inhaled, and exhaled the smoke.

Gillian coughed.

"He suspended him one game," Lance replied.

Melissa laughed. "Ouch. Bet that sucks."

"I was five minutes late," Thomas said. "Joey Davine is late all the time."

"Yeah, but Joey Davine isn't the star quarterback, now is he?" Lance said. "Coach couldn't care less about him. He's just some measly freshman."

Ava sighed and rolled her eyes. Thomas whined like an infant, while his precious Lance comforted him as always.

"Why *were* you late?" Melissa asked. "Were you finally getting it from Ava?"

"Shut up," she snapped. "Not tonight."

Melissa laughed uncontrollably. She rolled down the window further to release her cigarette butt. Her blond hair slapped over her face.

"Don't get upset," Gillian whispered so low that no one else could hear. "She's just in one of her moods."

Ava knew too well about her moods. She also could tell Melissa was excited, yet nervous. All of them were.

Melissa rolled up the window. "Well, you know it is about time. I mean, no wonder Thomas is grumpy, and you know, now that I think of it, you have been irritable." She glanced at Ava. "Just get it over with already."

Ava peered out of the window at the low moon that was the color of the sun, the beginning of a blood moon. It looked close enough to touch and seemed to swallow the sky. She was ready for this night to be over.

"Yeah, well, I'm not the one spending all my time with someone else," Thomas blurted.

He kept his eyes on the road, but Ava noticed his hands gripping the steering wheel so tightly he might break it off.

"And after tonight's meeting, you and I are going to fix

this."

"Fix what, Thomas?" Ava asked. Blood boiled within her pulsating veins.

"You and this guy."

Lance groaned. "Oh god—can you two wait until we're not around?"

"He's just some guy in my class," Ava said.

"Who?" Jeremy asked.

"Peter McNabb," Thomas said through clenched teeth.

Melissa let out a short, hard laugh. "You are threatened by him? Are you serious?"

"No. I've seen him sitting next to her at the games. And by her locker every day. Is that where you were last night?"

She swallowed. "Thomas, please. We've known each other for years now. Why should it bother you all of a sudden?"

"Because you've been spending so much time with him lately."

"Thomas, he's only really helping her with chemistry and math," Gillian said. "You know how terrible she is."

Ava met Gillian's eyes and mouthed the words "Thank you."

"We're not supposed to lure others into our group, Ava," Melissa said.

She rolled her eyes. Where was this coming from? "I'm not luring him."

"Okay, can everyone just settle down?" Jeremy asked. "Please?" He squeezed Ava's shoulder.

No one spoke for the remainder of the drive. Ava twirled her ring around her finger, thinking more of Peter, and just wishing she were somewhere else. The tight cramping in the pit of her stomach returned, as Thomas drove through the dark woods. She clamped her eyes shut, and Peter circled her mind. She propped her head up against her hand as she enjoyed the short daydream. She imagined his tall, slender, muscular body. His brown eyes. And then wished for his lips to touch hers.

"There it is," Gillian whispered, and Ava's eyes popped

open.

As they neared the great mansion, Ava gasped. She gawked out the window. The mansion was just as she remembered it the first time she came. How could that be? After all those years of visiting, it had clearly depicted abandonment. Now, it looked perfect—no caved-in roof, no kudzu, no broken gate, no overgrown vegetation.

Thomas put the car in park and turned off the engine. Ava stared straight ahead at the Victorian structure of gray stone. Sharp steeples projected from the mansard roofs. Several arched windows faced the front with diamond-shaped panes, like something out of a church. She didn't remember the two round turrets on each side of the heavy wooden door, but she did remember the raven statues.

"Now what?" Gillian asked, wrapping her black curls around her finger.

"We go in, genius." Melissa opened the car door and jumped out.

"What if they're not there?"

"Then we wouldn't have come tonight," Jeremy said. "It'll be okay."

Ava was glad she wasn't the only scared one. She slowly opened her door, and soon Thomas was by her side. He grabbed her hand and held it tightly.

"It'll be okay," he said, but she assumed he was reassuring himself.

They all walked together through the unbroken wrought-iron gate, between the garden with blooming purple orchids, orange lilies, and several other varieties of colors and flowers. Ava remembered the vivid colors. It was odd that such color could survive in October, and look so fresh. She couldn't really see them now, at dusk and shivered from the bitter cold, but then automatically, her body warmed. Thomas placed his arm around her waist, holding her tight against him as if she would vanish.

"Why is it so cold?" she mumbled. "It never is this time of year."

"I don't know, but I hope it's warmer inside," Thomas said and then knocked on the door.

Eerily silent woods surrounded the mansion. Another shiver reverberated throughout Ava's body. She didn't know what would happen to them. Her heart raced.

They waited only a few seconds before the massive wooden door opened. Behind it, stood Savina. Ten years had not aged the tall, slim woman. Her auburn hair was longer—below her waist, and straight. Small barrettes pulled it back from each side from her face. Her infectious smile reached her eyes. A ring of yellow surrounded the light green irises of her eyes.

"Hello, my children," she said with a Scottish accent. "I've missed you all so very much." She gave them tight hugs and kissed their cheeks. Ava breathed in the scent of oranges and remembered it from the first time she'd met Savina. "Please, make yourselves at home."

Ava hesitantly crossed the threshold, with Thomas helping her along, into the ornately designed home. She stared at the grand staircase that wound around to several stories and felt incredibly small under the intricate cathedral ceiling.

"I've prepared dinner for us all," Savina said. Her black robe-like dress drifted along the floor as she walked. The sleeves were long and wide. Ava couldn't stop looking at her.

She led the way into the dining room, and Ava's mind immediately flooded with the memory of that first night they all arrived. The paintings on the blood-red walls were dark and creepy. One was of the full moon behind bare trees and a woman floating in the air with a round, garnet pendant hanging from a chain around her neck. In another, a group of people dressed in black cloaks stood around a large fire bowing. It all reminded her of one of Edgar Allan Poe's stories. She loved those stories, but never wanted to live in them.

A steaming brown soup, warm bread, and several casseroles had been placed on the round black table. Pewter plates and glass goblets waited at each place setting. Ava remembered how good the food had tasted the last time, and her stomach growled.

"They're here," Colden stepped into the room and clapped his hands once. His long raven hair was pulled back in a ponytail, and his black eyes beamed. His tall slender body was cloaked in a long black robe that looked like a priest robe and he had pale ghostly skin. "It's so good to see you all. So healthy and so strong."

His smile gave Ava the creeps. She didn't know what it was about him, but she felt more comfortable around Savina. He was a Droll, a powerless Enchanter, which was very rare, but that wasn't the reason for her uneasiness.

When they all sat down, Savina smiled and motioned for them to begin. "I can't believe you all," she said. "It seems like yesterday when I saw you last. And what beautiful people you turned out to be."

"So what have you been up to all these years?" Ava didn't mean for her tone to sound so harsh.

"Looking out for all of you," Savina said.

"Among other things," Colden told her. "There is much to discuss, but we will get to that later."

"Why don't we get to it now? Where have you been all this time? You haven't been here in ten years."

Melissa nudged her. "Ava?"

"No, I want to know." She wasn't sure where all this was coming from. Or why she was suddenly so angry with them. Maybe it was just all those years of feeling abandoned and how she'd dreaded this day or that she had no choice in any of it.

"I know it may not seem like we were not here, but we were," Savina replied. "Only when you needed us the most. But we are here now. For good."

"Why?" Ava asked. "Because you need us?"

"Stop," Melissa said.

Savina held up her hand. "It's okay. Finish eating, and we will explain everything."

Embarrassed, Ava picked up the silver spoon and then

hesitated. She watched Thomas slurp his soup like it was his last meal on earth. Gillian daintily sipped hers, and Melissa looked at her as if she would hurt her if she didn't calm down.

"Please do not fear me," Savina whispered to her.

Why did she say that? Could she sense Ava's fear?

Ava drew a deep breath, and sipped the warm soup. It was rich and thick, and though she didn't want to admit it, it tasted heavenly.

Like the last meal with Savina and Colden, there wasn't much talking, but Ava couldn't ignore the stares from both of them. Once everyone finished, Savina motioned Ava and the rest into another large sitting room. Candles flickered all around. Savina moved to the black, marble fireplace, waved her hand across it, and a fire appeared.

Ava gasped. She had never seen an Enchanter use her power like that. An old painting of lively green rolling hills and tall mountains, presumably Scotland, where Savina and Colden were from, hung above the fireplace.

She sat on the L-shaped dark red couch and looked around at everyone's faces. They all looked content, comfortable, as if they belonged. As if they knew Savina and Colden would be here, but Ava felt sick, like a large weight had lodged in her stomach. She met Thomas's eyes and he took her hand.

Colden stood by the fireplace, and Savina sat in a Victorian chair that matched the couch.

"It has brought us such great joy to see you all," she began. "You are all so strong, mature, and so beautiful. Now it is time to understand the splendor of the Craft."

The knots would not stop forming in Ava's stomach. Thomas squeezed her hand, something he did when she gripped too hard, but she didn't let up.

"Each of you has a wonderful ability and we are here to solidify our Aureole," Colden said. "The Aureole is a circle that once we all stand on it, glows and connects us all. You have also come back to help us fulfill a mission."

Ava froze. A mission? She exchanged glances with the others and they looked just as confused.

Savina interlocked her hands. "Devon Maunsell has escaped the Cruciari."

Ava felt her jaw go slack. She didn't know who Devon Maunsell was, but for him to have escaped the famous Enchanter prison was enough for her to come unhinged.

CHAPTER ELEVEN
INITIATION

Ava took a deep breath and kept the stew from coming up. How could an Enchanter possibly escape the Cruciari? Water surrounded the fortress. A negation spell prevented the use of any powers. Enchanters were slowly tortured until death. Yet, somehow, one had escaped. What did this mean to them?

"How did he get out?" Her voice was shaky.

"We are still investigating that," Savina said.

Colden slowly paced in front of the fireplace, in deep thought. "We have been trying to find out if someone let him out or if the charm broke."

"So who is this guy?" Melissa asked. She didn't look as nervous as Ava felt.

Gillian chewed on her lip and curled and uncurled her hair around her finger while Jeremy held her other hand, seemingly calm.

Colden stopped pacing and then turned to them. "He is a Cimmerian, a Dark Enchanter. One of Corbin's biggest supporters."

A piercing silence fell on them. Corbin Havok. He was Colden's father and Savina's stepfather—the most evil

Enchanter in history. He had started wars with Enchanters and massacred mortal humans, or as they were known as Ephemerals. There hadn't been any wars since he died almost thirty years ago.

"When did he escape?" Ava asked.

"A few days ago," Colden said.

Jeremy shifted and leaned forward. "But his powers have been negated, and he's been tortured for years. What harm is he to us?"

Ava thought she saw a flicker of sympathy in Savina's eyes.

"He is a deranged man on the loose." Savina paused, as if gathering her thoughts. "We believe he has gained followers, but they leave no trace of their whereabouts."

"Followers for what?" Jeremy asked.

"Devon could be waging a war against us for revenge. While we search for him, we will need to prepare you all. We need to protect the Ephemerals and our kind."

"War?" Ava asked. Her throat tightened, and her heart stopped.

"Yes," Savina replied.

Thomas shook his leg, the way he did when he was nervous, which was rarely. "Where is this guy?"

Colden poked the fire, making small embers rise. "We do not know." There was a hint of irritation in his voice.

"Some of our Aureole are investigating and trying to track him down," Savina said. "The others are traveling here to train you all.

"Why would we need so many to train us?" Ava asked. "I thought only our coven leaders did that?"

Colden shook his head. "No. We cannot do this," he shouted at Savina. "They are too young, Savina." Ava detected concern in his voice.

She gave him a stern look, and Ava assumed she was speaking to his mind. What was she saying to him?

He took a deep breath and placed the poker back in its place. "Forgive me. We will explain more once we go into the conservatory." The scared look in his eyes worried Ava.

"Why is he seeking revenge?" Ava asked.

"For killing Corbin and forcing him and others into the Cruciari. He has also killed Ephemerals in his path but now he is making them into Enchanters for his army. He wants as many able bodies as he can get to fight us."

"Halflings in his army?" Ava asked. "That doesn't make sense." Devon must have been desperate for an army. Corbin had hated Ephemerals and there was no way he would make half-blooded Enchanters. He had only wanted pureblood for his military.

"He is willing to do anything to avenge Corbin," Colden said.

"I want you to know I can read minds, and you all will need to learn how to hide your thoughts," Savina said. "Along with healing, I can inflict mental pain. I must teach you how to use this craft well. Over the next few months, you will learn to master your power."

"But in the meantime, you must be aware of potential spies," Colden said. "And we are to execute those who are dangerous," Colden said.

"Why would anyone be spying on us?" Gillian asked.

"Comes with the territory of a possible war," Jeremy said. "He's seeking revenge against Savina and Colden, and we're a part of that. They probably want to know what we're up to or our every step."

This wasn't happening. It was all too much. They were going to die. Ava couldn't stop shaking, and she didn't even notice Thomas's arms around her.

"You all have come here tonight to pledge your dedication to your Aureole," Savina said. "This coven is founded upon commitment, trust, and love. You must not break it nor betray each other. Betrayal will lead to expulsion and loss of powers in most Aureoles," she explained as casually as if she were teaching history.

Ava gripped Thomas's hand once more. Her dad never mentioned any of that. She could not get over Benjamin escaping…impending war…potential spies…betraying the Aureole…Halflings. A bowling ball seemed to weigh inside her stomach and she felt dizzy. Several questions bubbled on her tongue, but she remained quiet. She felt as if her insides would pour out, but she held herself together.

Savina stood and walked to a cherry oak chest under a window and opened it. She pulled out six small, black velvet boxes and handed them out to Ava and the others.

Ava opened the box with shaky hands. Inside was a necklace similar to the ones her parents always wore. The pewter pendant that hung on a black leather rope was a pentacle, a star within a circle. An intricate Celtic design adorned the circle. Worked into the scrolls were five red garnet stones. A larger garnet was set in the center of the star. Each stone represented a person in the Aureole, the middle belonging to the wearer.

Ava pulled it out and, like the others, wrapped it around her neck, and clasped the ends together.

"This is my gift to you," Savina said. "Never be without it. These pendants are magical, and they give each of us an intuitive connection."

Ava remembered her dad talking about it when she was younger. It was like a mood necklace, and at the time, she thought it was the coolest thing. Now she wasn't sure she wanted the others to know how she felt at any given moment. But it was more than just moods. They'd be able to tell when any of them was in danger.

"I think mine's broken," Gillian said.

Savina smiled. "It will work once we call our powers." She moved her long hair from her chest and revealed the same necklace. Colden pulled his out from his cloak. "We will be able to feel you as well."

Melissa cleared her throat politely. "So will we be able to feel all emotions?"

"Yes. Especially, if it is intense." Savina eyed Melissa and Ava wondered if she was speaking to her mind. Ava knew what Melissa was thinking. This was going to be awkward.

"You must never remove the necklace, for your presence will not be felt, and I will assume the worst. If you feel someone in danger, you must protect them at all costs." Savina crossed the room with Colden and instructed them to follow. "Now, you must swear your oaths."

Ava still clutched onto Thomas's hand as they walked down the hallway that led to the large room with the massive glass ceiling. She shivered and then Thomas rubbed his hand on her arms to warm her. But the chills weren't just from the cold. She hated this. Savina could read her mind, and now they knew what she was feeling. She just wanted to be alone.

They reached the end of the corridor and entered a candlelit room. The same room that they stood in ten years ago appeared before them.

In the center of the room was a purple velvet rug with a large pentagram embroidered on it. Ava's stomach churned at the memory of drinking blood.

The simple beauty of this room once again awed her. She looked up into the domed ceiling at the stars and saw the orange-red moon low in the sky. She couldn't stop shaking.

Savina crossed to the center of the circle. "Swearing an oath is one of the most important events of your life. We were all born Enchanters and this is our destiny."

Ava tried listening, but only picked up every other word. Everything distracted her. The flickering candles. The way Colden and Savina stood calmly in front of them. The glass doors behind them, even though she couldn't see out of them, she wanted to get out of there.

"Everyone, get in a circle," Savina said.

Ava's pulse quickened and her palms sweated in Thomas's hand. She clenched her teeth to prevent them from chattering and followed the others to form a circle. She stood between Thomas and Jeremy. Colden moved next to Savina in the center.

He stood patiently, and clasped his hands in front of him. "Each of you is a part of nature. You are all Elemental Enchanters."

"There has never been a coven of Elementals," Savina said. "The Elements are the root of all existing matter. Each of you is exceptionally powerful, but together as a group, you can be omnipotent. With all these essentials combined, it could be severely dangerous. Which is why we must train you so you don't lose control."

Ava exchanged looks with Melissa.

Savina and Colden moved in the circle, and everyone held hands.

"Each of us will pledge one at a time," Savina said, and then spoke the oath. Melissa and Thomas followed, and then it was Ava's turn.

She took a deep breath, and swore her oath under the blood moon. "I bind myself to this Aureole. I solemnly swear that I will keep this coven under absolute secrecy, that I will use my power for the good, and that I will protect the members of my coven at all costs. I swear this upon my life, and should I break this most solemn oath, it would result in eternal unrest for my soul."

Lance gave his oath, then Gillian, Colden, and Jeremy.

"Our powers strengthen within this circle of perfect love and perfect trust," Savina said, and then moved in front of Gillian and touched her face. "Gillian, you are the Moon, the second most powerful entity. You calm us, help us regain our grounding, and help us in dire need. You keep balance inside the circle. The Moon affects moods, but more specifically, it affects our minds."

Ava wasn't sure what that meant. Did Gillian have the power to control their moods as well as their minds?

Savina placed her hands on Jeremy's face. "Jeremy, you are the Air. Cool and dry, you are associated with communication and intelligence. You are connected to the soul and the breath of life. You have the power to create gusts of wind so powerful that it could rip apart trees or boulders."

Ava had experienced a small example of Jeremy's power, but never knew just how immense it was.

Savina moved to Ava and lightly touched her face. Her

hands were warm and surprisingly comforting.

Ava, she spoke to her mind. Ava met her green eyes. *I promise you, everything will be fine. We are here now. Please do not be afraid—this is who you are.*

Something about Savina's tone reinforced her message to Ava that she had nothing to worry about.

"Ava, you are Water. Warm, intuitive, and cleansing. You deal with emotions such as love and joy but also pain and sorrow. High depths of emotion are associated with death. Be careful and do not let burdens weigh you down. Water is very strong as it is inside all of us. It will help cleanse ourselves and keep us hydrated. You have the ability to control water." Savina's hands fell and then she moved to Thomas.

Death? Why did she have to be associated with death? She quickly cleared her mind.

Savina looked up at Thomas, craning her neck. "Thomas, you are Fire," she began, touching his face as well. "Passionate, physical, and courageous. You can create fire. Be careful, it can get dangerous, but is very protective and warm."

"Melissa. You are the Earth. Beauty, nurturing, and caring. You are stable, but you have inevitable strong energy, just like the abundant power of an earthquake or volcano. You are here to guide and protect you all. A leader of all entities."

Ava met Melissa's eyes and Melissa had an almost giddy smile.

"And finally, Lance. You are our Sun. You are the most powerful as you guide our strength together. You bind us and open our eyes to see clearly. While the Moon is resting, you watch over us. The sun is like a magnet. It draws us to you, to soak you in. It is warm and bright. The sun also absorbs those around you."

"When you enter the circle, each of you must have absolute love and conviction," Colden said. "Now, each of you close your eyes and breathe softly. Think of your attribute of nature in a calming way."

Ava breathed deeply and thought of water. Off in the

distance, she heard waves…seagulls…smelled the salty air and felt the warmth of the sun. She was calm. The waves crashed harder and louder. She could see them growing in size. Warmth rushed over her, and then she opened her eyes. It was almost as if she had left her body and a stronger, more confident version of herself took over.

A vigorous force, like a wave, struck her, and she felt an immense amount of energy charging through her. A tingling sensation raced up and down her body, through her veins, pulsating inside of her.

Gillian's blue eyes widened, and she smiled. "Did you feel that?"

"Yes," Ava said. "I feel strong. There's so much energy."

"I felt very calm," Jeremy said. "And it was so quiet, but powerful."

Ava couldn't believe how different she felt. Seconds ago, she wanted to bolt through the glass doors, but now she believed as if nothing could harm her. As if she was unstoppable. "This is amazing. It's almost like I can do anything." Why had she been so scared before?

Savina smiled. "That's because you can, dear. Because you are in a coven together, the connection is unyielding."

"What can some of the other Enchanters do?" Jeremy asked.

"Some can morph into different people, move things with their minds, create the weather. You may face some who can make you see images of your past, or make you hallucinate."

Ava closed her eyes for a second. "Morph?"

"Yes. They are called shapeshifters. They can morph into anyone or anything."

Her pulse edged up. The invincible feeling quickly vanished. How could she know if anyone was really whom they appeared as and not some shapeshifter? "You mean they could just transform into anyone, and we'd never know it?"

"You can always tell if someone has morphed into someone else," Colden said. "A shifter can only use his own power, change his own appearance, and cannot inherit the

Enchanter's power."

Ava tried to keep her breathing level. "Okay."

Colden frowned. "Do not be afraid." His voice was smooth and quiet. "You will learn to be a stronger Enchanter."

She chewed her lip, the way she always did when she was nervous. "What if they morph into an Ephemeral?"

"You can still detect if they have power."

She nodded. She didn't know why Colden made her uncomfortable earlier, but now she felt fine around him.

"You must be careful because if you cannot control your power, it can get out of hand," Savina said. "You have to remember to focus. It is very important. You must practice focusing in case of an attack. I have to know you have control. It is a grave responsibility, but I know each of you is mature enough to handle this and care about each other because you are a family."

"There is a cabin in the woods, not far from here, near the Red Mountain," Colden said. "This is where you will practice without us. On nights that we will practice together, we will do it here. We have an enormous field beyond those doors. Savina placed a secrecy spell on your cabin. No one will be able to see it but us."

"But give your bodies a week to rest. Then you may start strengthening."

Savina moved from the circle. "Now, it is time to retire for the evening. May the circle be open and remain unbroken."

CHAPTER TWELVE
PARANOIA

Constant fear gripped Ava. They could go to war tomorrow or next week or tonight. Someone could attack them at any moment. There was no way to know for sure.

Thoughts of killing and death conjured gruesome images in Ava's mind. And spies. Someone could be following her or watching her every step. What if they found out where she lived? Or followed her at school? She shivered, and feared for, not only her life, but also others.

But she couldn't deny that energy roared within her, itching to break free. It was in her blood. The powers were an amazing gift, but part of her was afraid. Fear of the unknown. What were they supposed to do if someone attacked them? She didn't know how to kill. Was this what her parents did? It was all so much to take in, and she hadn't expected it.

"This is it?" Gillian complained.

Ava looked up just as Thomas pulled up to the front of a wooden cabin. They wanted to see it tonight, except Ava. She could have waited a few more days. Weeks. Months.

She took a deep breath and begrudgingly got out of the Jeep.

Thick woods bordered an open field that surrounded the

dark cabin. It looked like a one-story house made of logs with a stone chimney on the left side. Thomas took Ava's hand, and they walked up small wooden steps and entered.

It was dark until she found a switch and turned on the lights. A crystal chandelier hung above them in the foyer. There were hardwood floors throughout. An open kitchen with black speckled marble countertops and brand new appliances was to her right.

It was definitely more upscale than she had ever imagined. There was a sitting room to the left with two black suede loveseats facing each other and a matching couch between them in front of a stone fireplace. The bright shiny wooden walls reached the high ceiling with a hexagonal window near the ceiling.

"Wow," Lance said and pushed his way past them. "This place is awesome."

"Hey, what's down here?" Thomas pulled Ava down a hall next to the kitchen. They stopped at the first room and saw it was a plain room with a light-colored wooden bed.

"She gave us a house," Ava said. Why would she do that? Were they supposed to stay there every night?

"Mom said something about this. Every Aureole gets a house when they're practicing."

"Why? Wouldn't we just go home after practicing?"

Thomas raised an eyebrow and shook his hair. "Because. This is our own place. We can come here whenever we want. And stay as long as we like." He grinned wickedly and pressed her against the wall. Ava gripped the doorframe behind her. He leaned down, licked his lips, and kissed her softly, the way he used to. She had missed those kisses and could actually feel his affection for her now, which was the strangest thing. But then Peter flashed in her mind. She wanted to be with him, but it was impossible now.

Thomas pulled away with a yearning in his blue eyes.

She exhaled, unaware that she'd been holding her breath. "Let's see the rest of the cabin." Ava tried to move around him, but he grabbed her arm.

"I know I've become aggressive lately," he said. "And it clicked tonight with Savina. I'm Fire—passionate and can be aggressive. I'm afraid of what I can do. Afraid my anger will get the best of me, and I don't want to hurt you."

She felt an onslaught of tears but swallowed them. Ava was dejected at the thought of being stuck with Thomas forever and that she had to end it with Peter before it even began.

"What's wrong?" Thomas asked. "I can *feel* what you're feeling."

"What?" She looked down at her necklace. The garnet stones glowed red, and heat emanated from the pendant. This was going to take some getting used to.

"You're worried about something," he said. "And sad. That's the weirdest thing. What is it?"

Ava could not tell him about Peter. She had to make up something. Fast. What could she say? "I'm just scared. About all this." Which was true.

He drew her into a tight embrace, and she felt his breath on her head as he kissed her. "Don't be. You know I'll protect you." Ava could protect herself, but if that's what he wanted to think, that was fine. She'd rather him believe that than know what she was really thinking.

"Just think of what we are," he said. "We're the most powerful kind of Enchanters. No one's going to hurt us." He smiled as if he were a kid on Christmas.

Except for Devon.

"Of course." She faked a smile.

"Come on."

They found two more rooms, each with a similar bed. She hoped there were more rooms, but something told her they had to share. Ava wasn't going to stay here though.

When they made it back to the kitchen, she saw glowing candles through an entrance beyond the main room. She crossed to it and entered. Everyone else was in there checking it out.

Candles illuminated the room and, like Savina's

conservatory, there was a dark purple rug covering the floor with a pentagram printed on the center. Windows spanned the wall on the far end letting the silver light of the moon through. They had their own channeling room.

For the third time that night, chills scampered all over Ava. It was getting more and more real.

Melissa picked up a candle from the floor and watched the flame. "This is more than what I expected. I just figured we'd have our powers and have no reason to use them. But now?" A grin spread across her face, the candle casting shadows on her face, making it creepy. "Now we get to kill enemies."

Ava's stomach dropped. Her breathing hitched, and the room suddenly felt small. This was her destiny. She knew about the wars and knew there was a slight possibility she'd have to kill. But she never thought it would happen so quickly.

She thought of Peter again. What would he say if he knew this? She was going to be a killer, soon. Ava couldn't turn her back on Thomas or the others. She couldn't betray her Aureole, and they weren't very strong if it was broken. She wasn't ready for this. How were the others okay with it?

"Whoa." Gillian grabbed her necklace. "Ava, are you okay? I feel your worry."

"Me, too." Melissa pursed her lips. "I felt it earlier."

Ava cleared her throat. "Nothing."

"She's worried that we won't be able to fight off this Devon guy," Thomas said.

Melissa scrutinized her as if she knew exactly what made Ava afraid. She needed to get out of there. To clear her head so the others could stop feeling her. Then again, she guessed they'd always be able to feel her from now on. Unless she found a way to block them.

They finally left the cabin and Thomas dropped her off at home. He kissed her goodnight, and she walked inside.

Ava felt like at any minute she would fall apart. She sank onto the couch. Her head pounded from the tense night. So many thoughts, images, and words scrambled inside her mind, making her stomach ache.

Her father came into the room. "So? How'd it go?" His unworried tone didn't match the situation.

Ava looked up and her eyes filled with tears. "It's worse than we thought."

CHAPTER THIRTEEN
HOPELESS

The morning sun peeked inside Ava's room as she turned off the annoying alarm clock. Dreams of killing strangers and running for her life had interrupted her sleep. How long would she have to do this? But she knew the answer. She and her father had stayed up talking about everything she learned at the Blackhart Manor, but it had turned into an argument. He wasn't shocked about Devon Maunsell's revenge or that there could be spies who would attack at random, but he wasn't keen on the idea of Ava killing so soon.

"But several Enchanters started out young, too," he had reasoned. "You will be trained well."

"This is too much, Dad," she had yelled. "I'm not ready."

"You will be."

"It's insane."

"This is our life. You knew it would happen."

How could he be so cold about it? Why wasn't he comforting her? Would her mom have told her to deal with it?

Ava dressed for school, walked downstairs, and met her father in the kitchen. He was sipping coffee and reading the paper before work.

"Morning," he said.

"Morning." She fumed, but then regretted her attitude. She couldn't be mad at her father. It wasn't his fault. But was he even worried at all about Devon? And what would he think if he knew his daughter was slowly falling in love with an Ephemeral?

He smiled, but it only angered her. Her necklace began to glow.

He pointed to it. "What's wrong?"

Ava shifted her weight and hid it under her sweater. "Nothing."

"Ava, sit down."

"I'll stand."

Her father lay the paper down on the table, and then took a sip of the steaming coffee. He tilted his head up at her with a hard look in his eyes. "Do you really understand what's going on?"

"Yes." She wasn't dumb. "Devon escaped and is powerless. He's starting a war because his precious master was killed. He's killed Ephemerals and made some into Halflings for his army. Oh, and there could be Enchanters watching us constantly that could kill us. Did I leave anything out?"

He nodded once, and then rubbed his eyes with a sigh. He seemed hesitant. Or maybe he was trying to piece together his words.

Ava looked at the time on her phone. "Well, as lovely as this chat was, I have to go to school." She stepped out into the cool morning, and exhaled. Ava hated being so angry with her father. Did he and her mom really have to start killing the second they were initiated?

She arrived at school reluctant to see Thomas and hoped he wouldn't be waiting for her, but he was. He only served as a reminder that she was bound to him.

"Hey, Babe," he said and kissed her. His arm wound around her waist, but she pulled away.

"Stop calling me that," she shouted.

He raised his hands. "Whoa, what's with you? You've been angry all morning. Is it that time?"

She clenched her teeth. *Oh, right. Because the only time a woman's allowed to be angry is during her period.* "Leave me alone."

"Take some Midol," he said, and then left.

Ava released an aggravated groan, and then entered algebra.

Melissa cocked her eyebrow once Ava took her seat. "Little hot today aren't we?"

"I don't wanna talk about it."

"Of course not. Because it just wouldn't be you."

She sighed. "I just wasn't expecting us to do this so soon. And my dad seems to be fine and dandy about it."

"Are you sure that's why you're mad? Sure it has nothing to do with Peter?"

Melissa didn't know just how dead on she was. Or maybe she did.

"My father didn't seem the least bit worried."

"Maybe because there isn't anything to worry about."

"How can you say that?"

"I just can. By the way, Gillian and I need to talk to you."

"About what?"

"Later."

As if on cue, the bell rang. Ava sat through class staring at the board, but the numbers and letters were just blobs of blue ink. When class ended, she made her way to chemistry. She dropped her bag beside her desk, and propped her head up with her hand. A strange ache in her chest developed, knowing that seeing Peter would torture her.

"Are you gonna chew a hole in your lip?"

Ava woke from her reverie and met Peter's brown eyes. "What?"

"You were biting your lip. You do that when you're thinking hard about something."

"Oh." She turned back to her desk after a pang of sadness hit her stomach. Maybe if she acted aloof, he would stop talking to her, and then maybe it wouldn't be so hard.

"What's wrong?"

She faked a smile. "Nothing."

"Nice necklace," he said after a few seconds.

"Thanks." She hid it beneath her shirt.

"It's pretty. Is it garnet?"

"Yeah."

"Ah. I didn't know you were Wiccan."

"I'm not," she said sternly.

He raised his eyebrows and returned to his book. She felt bad for snapping at him, but she was on edge. Ava propped her head on her desk, trying to stay awake. She doodled on her notebook, and tried not to make eye contact with Peter, who kept eyeing her warily. She looked up at the clock and silently moaned—she still had 45 minutes left.

When the bell finally rang, Ava grabbed her books and meandered out into the hallway with Peter at her side.

"I don't think I can take much more of his class." He yawned. "How can he love this subject and sound so bored?"

Ava shrugged. "Beats me."

"At least some good comes out of it." He sheepishly grinned.

"Like what?" She stopped at her locker, turned the lock, and opened it.

"Seeing you every day."

Her heart stopped for a second, and then felt as if it would beat through her chest. She cleared her throat politely, and then closed her locker. "You should go."

He frowned. "Sorry. That was out of line, wasn't it?"

"Peter…"

"It's okay. I can take a hint. Guess I'll talk to you later." He walked away.

Ava wished she hadn't been so rude to Peter. He was sweet and caring. How could she continue to act like that with him? He'd been a good friend.

Thomas came up next to her, but she didn't say anything to him. He didn't push either. Once in the lunchroom, he went to get their food.

Ava glanced at Xavier's table filled with his smug friends. Xavier looked up and met her eyes. His eyebrows rose twice, obviously flirting with her. She looked away, disgusted. What was with him? One day he threatened her and then today he was trying to flirt with her? Maybe he really was on drugs. Creep.

She made her way to her table and sat next to Melissa.

"Have you been thinking about last night?" Gillian asked.

"What do you think?" She didn't mean for her tone to be so harsh but for some reason her anger returned.

Gillian sneered. "Why are you so snippy? You've been angry all morning."

"So what did you two want to talk about?" Ava asked.

Melissa shifted in her seat. "It's about Peter."

Ava stiffened. "What about him?"

"Mel and I think you should stop talking to him," Gillian said.

"Why?"

"Come on, Ava. It's obvious," Melissa said.

"Obvious? Because she told you?"

Gillian held up her hands. "I didn't tell her anything."

"Tell me what?" Melissa asked. "Is there something more to your friendship?"

"No, but this is ridiculous. I shouldn't have to stop talking to him."

"Please don't be upset," Gillian said. "It just doesn't make sense for you to be hanging out with him anymore. There's a lot of things going on, and he can't know anything. I mean, if he finds out about you, do you think he'd still want to be your friend?"

"Besides, you won't have time," Melissa added. "It could be dangerous. You are incredibly strong now and if he gets anywhere near us at the wrong time…"

"He could end up dead," Gillian finished.

Ava couldn't believe she said that.

Melissa exhaled noisily and gave Gillian a critical look. "We're just warning you." She turned back to Ava. "I don't want this Aureole to break. You're like my sister."

"What do you think I'm gonna do?"

Gillian wrapped a curl around her finger. "Nothing. It's just that." She paused. "You heard Savina. Don't betray the Aureole."

She was offended. "I'm not going to betray anyone, okay?"

The annoying pain in her stomach returned. Ava sat motionless, stunned, and hurt. End her friendship with Peter? It was bad enough that she could never be with him, but now she couldn't even *talk* to him? She felt sick.

Ava knew they were right but refused to admit it. She knew things would change. Knew it wasn't a good idea to continue getting close to Peter. But she couldn't just cut him out of her life.

The guys arrived with trays of food, but Ava had lost her appetite. She couldn't live with herself if something had happened to Peter. They were right. It was too dangerous.

When school ended, she didn't really feel like going home, to be there with her father alone, or to hang out with her friends. She just wanted the night to be done.

Maybe she could visit Peter at work. She used to during the summer when it was just the two of them. As she pulled up to the store and parked, she was reminded of the night they'd sat on the hood of his car watching the meteor shower. Then, she wasn't aware of how much she actually liked him.

Ava got out of her car and trudged inside. It looked a little busy but she hoped he wasn't. She wandered toward the produce but didn't see him.

"Are you stalking me?" Peter said from behind her.

She turned around. He smiled, showing his dimple. "No. I needed some mangos."

He lifted an eyebrow. "Come on. There are some in the back." He seized her hand and pulled her through the produce department and through the double doors. She always wondered was behind these doors.

But it was just boxes and shelves with fruit and silver

metal tables with cutting boards and knives.

"Hiding?" she asked.

"Yes. They might call me up front to ring up people. What are you up to?"

She shrugged. "Just thought I'd come and see you. And I wanted to apologize for earlier."

His eyebrows knitted together. "For what?"

"For being mean."

He rolled his eyes. "It was my fault. I shouldn't have said that."

"It's okay. I was just having a weird day."

"It's been weird for everyone lately."

"Seth is still ignoring you?"

He nodded. "I'm trying not to think about it, but it's like a light switch went off for him. Thirteen years of friendship just gone."

She didn't know if it was the sadness in his voice or the confusion in his eyes, but she wrapped her arms around him tightly. "I'm so sorry." She couldn't decide if that was the only thing she apologized for, or if it were that this was probably the last time they would hang out outside of school. She gripped him harder.

"Thank you," he whispered, hugging her back.

"I wish there was something I could say or do."

"You are."

The double doors flung open, slamming against the shelves. Ava jumped and pulled away. Peter's brunette friend stood with her hand on her hip and a fierce look in her brown eyes. She was short with long straight hair and bangs. Ava glanced down at her nametag. Valerie. For some reason, she felt guilty as if she'd been caught doing something wrong.

"What are you doing?" Valerie demanded. "We are swamped up there."

"I should go," Ava said, and then walked out. She would have introduced herself, but she was sure Valerie wouldn't have cared.

"What was she doing back here?" she heard Valerie yell.

"Stay away from her."

Did she know what Ava was? Why was she telling him that? Ava didn't want to hear anymore. Everyone seemed to know it was a bad idea for them to be together. Maybe she could talk to Savina or Colden.

Ava shook her head. What was she thinking? She had just taken an oath and couldn't undo it.

CHAPTER FOURTEEN
MEMORIES

The clock ticked achingly slow. It was as if it purposely taunted Ava, like it was some type of bully. She had given up on the chemistry lesson ages ago, and couldn't stop yawning. Sleep was not something she had been getting the last few weeks. Not since before the night she had returned to Blackhart Manor. How could anyone possibly sleep when someone could be spying on them?

None of them had even practiced or channeled yet, because of the lethargy. And fear. No one had really admitted it, but they could all feel what the other one felt.

Ava yawned again, bringing tears to her eyes, and then the bell finally rang. It was a sweet sound to her ears.

"Why are you always so tired?" Peter asked, grabbing his book.

She walked beside him out of the room. She hadn't told him they couldn't be friends; she just limited their talking, texting, hanging out. It wasn't easy because every fiber in her being wanted to be with him.

"Just a lot going on."

"You know I'm here for you," he said.

"Thanks." Would he still be there if he found out she was

an Enchanter?

"I'll see you later."

Thomas and Ava made their way to the lunchroom, got their lunches, and joined the group at their usual table.

"There has to be some cure to this no-sleep thing," Lance said, and then took a sip of milk.

"No kidding," Ava said.

"I keep thinking about Devon and those spies. They could be lurking around anywhere. Isn't there a way to tell if someone's an Enchanter or not?"

"I don't think so," Jeremy said.

Ava poked a carrot with her fork. "I still can't believe Devon would even use Halflings. Aren't they much weaker than Enchanters?"

Jeremy shrugged. "Maybe they're just pawns."

Thomas finished his water. "I'm sure Devon would want as many people as possible to distract us or something. Especially young people."

It made sense. Armies could use young people. They'd probably catch on quickly through training. What power could Ephemerals possess if they were changed?

Ava looked up and saw Xavier and his small army of minions. They still kept to themselves and tormented others. Just the other day Seth and Link shoved one of the football players into his locker and locked it. People were too afraid to tell any authority figure about it because they probably wouldn't do anything about it and Xavier's gang probably carried out threats. His minions all hung onto his every word and did anything and everything he said like he was some sort of leader.

Ava froze. She couldn't believe she didn't see it before. "Xavier," she blurted.

"What?" Thomas asked.

"He's an Enchanter. He made them all Enchanters."

Thomas laughed. "You're kidding me, right?"

"Yeah, that seems a little far-fetched," Melissa said.

"Think about it. Thomas and I have both passed out when

he was around. And we can't remember anything. And all his so-called friends are completely different."

Jeremy leaned forward. "She could be right."

"Please," Gillian scoffed. "You honestly think Devon would want Kristen Miller as part of his army?"

Ava exchanged looks with Jeremy. Since when was Gillian against Kristen? It sounded like something Melissa would say but not Gillian. "She's not the same anymore."

Thomas shook his head. "He's not an Enchanter. He's just some punk."

"Some punk who can mysteriously make you faint?"

"Maybe my blood sugar was down that day. I don't know. That was months ago."

"Why don't you believe me? I know I was fine before I got knocked out."

"You hit your head on the floor and that's what gave you a bruise."

"Then why would he bully and torture so many Ephemerals and get away with it?"

He rolled his eyes. "So anyone who bullies other kids automatically makes them an Enchanter? A Cimmerian no-less?"

"He made both of us pass out without touching us," she said through clenched teeth. He always had to disagree with Ava, no matter what it was about. She could tell him the sky was blue but he'd argue.

"Just drop it, Ava."

"Think about it. Every one of them at that table went missing for days, some of them for weeks, and they all returned and became friends with him."

Gillian groaned. "Stop arguing."

"Maybe we can ask Savina and Colden," Melissa said.

Thomas shook his head. "You'd be wasting your time."

"Maybe then they can tell me what I can do," Lance said. "If I'm the Sun, does that mean I can burn people? Blind them?"

Jeremy put his elbows on the table. "I'm sure you have

more than that," he said. "Think of the sun's rays. Or how pretty much all life on Earth is stimulated by the sunlight. It's extremely powerful and the atmosphere is there to filter some of that, but with you, I don't—."

"You can stop now," Gillian interrupted. "No one knows what you're talking about."

Ava looked at Gillian. Why was she so rude with Jeremy? She'd never been that way before.

"No, no, keep going," Lance said. "Is there a correlation with invisibility?"

Jeremy cleared his throat and thought for a minute. "No. But the sun absorbs electromagnetic radiation in the form of heat." He paused. "Maybe you absorb powers."

"That's it," Ava said. "Savina mentioned that. You've been using Mel's ability."

"But I can't do anything else. Like, I can't breathe underwater," he said, lowering his voice.

"Maybe because you've been around Mel a lot," Jeremy said.

"Maybe you can stop Devon if he gets to us," Ava told Lance.

Thomas sighed. "Ava, he's not even gonna find us."

Melissa popped a piece of gum into her mouth. "This is so amazing. We should start practicing tonight." She smiled.

"Definitely," Gillian said with a wicked grin. "I want to start manipulating minds."

Ava looked up at Jeremy. The wary look in his topaz eyes mirrored her feelings. What had happened to Gillian? First, she believed Ava was going to betray them, and she had been so supportive of her and Peter, or so Ava thought. And now Gillian couldn't wait to use her powers on Ephemerals. What was going on with them? They were all angry and edgy. Unless they were all freaked out about everything but wouldn't admit it.

When the day finally ended, all Ava wanted was to go home and relax. She dropped her bag at the foot of the stairs, and headed for the kitchen. She filled a glass with water, and took a sip. The house was quiet but her thoughts weren't. They were the same that had consumed her mind for the past few weeks. It was all so overwhelming. Had her parents accepted this life so easily? According to her dad, they had. And that her mom had never regretted it. But did he?

Her cell phone rang. She pulled it out of her pocket, saw Thomas's name flash, and then tossed it on the counter. Ava sighed, and raised the glass to take a sip but stopped. Like a magnet, the water shifted to the side that she held. She set it down, and then with her fingers, made it move from one side to the other. It followed her fingers every direction, just like the fire had done with Thomas at the bonfire.

She took a deep breath. Could her mom do the same? Dad mentioned her controlling it. And conjuring it. Ava didn't know the first thing about conjuring water. She wished her mom were there to tell her how. The ringing started again and she groaned in frustration but answered.

"Are you okay?" Thomas asked.

"Why do you keep calling?"

"Because I can tell you're sad. I got worried."

Blood burned her insides. Her teeth clenched and her slender fingers curled into a fist. "I'm fine." She didn't like having Thomas of all people know her every emotion. She was always so good at hiding them. Now, they were easily exposed. This would just reinforce Thomas's dominance.

"What's wrong?"

"I was just thinking about my mom," she said without thinking. It slipped out and she regretted it because now he was going to coddle her.

"Baby, don't be sad. I'm here. We can talk about it."

"No. I'll be there soon," she said, curtly.

When she pulled up to the cabin, the sky had darkened and there was a chill in the air. There was something eerie about the calmness outside.

Ava walked inside and Thomas immediately came up to her.

"Baby, I'm so sorry." He hugged her tightly and petted her hair as if she was a dog or something. "Come on." He pulled her down the hall into the first room and closed the door after them.

"Thomas?"

He crossed the room and took her hands in his. "What is it, Babe?"

"Why are we in here? Where is everyone?"

"You need comfort. Everyone else is in their room. Please don't be upset." He stroked her cheek. "Why are you thinking about your mom?"

"I don't want to talk about it."

"You never talk about her."

"Don't." She glared at him.

"Okay." He leaned down and pressed his lips to hers.

Why did he always think this would make her feel better?

He pressed harder and wrapped his arms around her. Heat emanated from his lips. She tried pushing him back, but he held her tighter.

"Thom—Thomas." She finally broke the kiss.

"What? What is it?" He asked breathless.

"Not so rough."

"Sorry." He kissed her and moved her backwards. She felt the edge of the bed pressing into the backs of her thighs. His hands moved slowly up her shirt but she stopped them.

She felt a surge of hatred toward him. Ava thought of Peter and immediately pushed Thomas away.

"Why are you so mad?" He held her at arm's length.

"What happened to being patient?"

"I can't help it. I've just got so much energy flowing through me." He crushed her to his chest and moved her hair aside. His lips grazed her neck. "I am patient. But you're so irresistible right now."

"You're irritating me."

He pulled back with a sigh. "Why? We used to make out all the time."

"This is getting so old."

"You're telling me? So does this mean you're ready?"

Ava sighed and pushed him away.

"Okay, okay. Let's stay here tonight." His tone softened. "Please? I won't go any further. I promise."

"I can't. I have homework." Ava felt somewhat guilty for lying, but she couldn't trust him.

He rolled his eyes. "You always have homework."

She needed to change the subject and then remembered earlier about the glass of water. "Do you wanna see what I did today?"

"I guess."

Ava opened the door and went into the kitchen to grab a glass.

"It's about time, you two," Melissa said, looking up from a magazine as she and the others sat on the couches. "What were you doing in there?" She laughed but stopped when Ava met her eyes. "Sorry. Couldn't resist."

Ava filled the glass with water and set it on the bar above the counter. "I noticed this earlier," she said and everyone gathered around. She moved her fingers up and down, and like before the water mimicked her motions.

Melissa's eyes widened. "That's cool."

"That's it?" Thomas said. "What are you going to do with that?"

Melissa slapped his arm. "She can control water. Just think of what she could do to a lake. Or a river. Or even the ocean."

Thomas looked skeptical. "Yeah, when she can do this with water, we'll talk." He held his palm facing up and a fireball abruptly appeared. He bounced it as if it were a baseball. Then, he threw it into the fireplace, startling Ava. The flames bulged and crackled for a moment.

"That's so cool," Lance said. "I wonder if I can do that."

Ava sighed and poured the water down the drain. He was such a jerk. She tuned out Lance and Thomas's admiration of his ability and walked outside. Her necklace warmed and glowed. The night had cooled and clouds moved across the dark sky. The door opened and she dreaded it would be Thomas, but she heard the click of a lighter and knew it was Melissa.

Melissa exhaled smoke. "Sorry."

"I can't believe I'm bound to *that*," she said, waving her arm toward the door.

"We're all bound to each other. Nothing will change that. But maybe one day you'll meet a hot Enchanter who actually cares about you."

Ava turned to her. "What, like have a fling on the side?"

Melissa laughed. "That would be interesting. No. Just because we're all bound together, doesn't mean you're destined to be with Thomas forever."

"What do you mean?"

"How much did your father tell you?"

"Apparently not enough. I'm kinda ignoring him."

Melissa raised her eyebrows. "Why?"

"We had a fight." Ava leaned against the wooden railing.

"Since when do you ever fight with your dad?"

Guilt rushed over Ava. She never fought with him. But she felt like he was holding something back from her. Like she wasn't completely in on the loop. "I just don't understand how he's completely okay with us possibly going to war or even killing."

"Because he had to do it in his life. There's nothing to worry about." Melissa stubbed out the cigarette and tossed it into the grass. She gave Ava a knowing look. "But I hardly think that's the real reason why you're fighting all this."

Ava looked away. "So I don't have to be with Thomas, but I can't be with…"

"It's forbidden. And too dangerous."

She silently cursed. She hated the word forbidden.

"I think once you and Thomas get through this hump, you two will be back to what you were."

"I don't want to be."

"That's because you like Peter. It'll pass though."

"You just don't get it, Mel. What if Lance were a human?"

116

"What do you think will happen? You fall in love with Peter and then what? You want Savina to turn him into one of us. Just like Devon is doing?"

"No."

"That's if you're still accepted in this Aureole. I know you don't want to betray us."

Melissa had a point but Ava wanted to ignore it. It was a dead-end situation.

The door to the cabin opened, and Thomas led everyone outside.

"You guys missed it," he said. "Lance mimicked me and can now create fire."

"Are you serious?" Melissa took Lance's hand. "I wanna see."

Just like Thomas, Lance made a fireball appear and bounced it in his hand. "I think I like this better than invisibility. Although, that has its advantages."

"You should try to do that with water," Thomas said to Ava. "But I doubt you could." The way he said it was so condescending. Like she was incompetent.

"I think I'll go home." She pushed her way through them, and walked to her car.

"Ava, what's wrong?" Thomas ran after her.

She opened her door and got in. "Nothing. I'll talk to you tomorrow." She tried closing her door but he held it firmly.

"Why are you so mad?"

Ava wished she could produce water and throw it in his face. "Let me go."

"If you're upset about your ability, I'm sure something will come of it."

"Great. Goodnight." She pulled on the door and closed it with success. Ava started the car, and felt Thomas's anger, but she didn't care. She was a bit miffed that she seemed to be the only one who lacked any real power. Even her dad said she was supposed to do more. What was she? The runt of the litter?

Once home, Ava took a hot shower, letting the water relax

her, and then changed into her pajamas. She turned out the lamp on her nightstand, and slipped under the covers. Her eyes searched the darkness. She wished she could see her mother. And that she could be with Peter. And for the tension between her and her dad to stop. That this Enchanter hadn't escaped. How was she supposed to sleep when there could be someone watching her?

The tears leaked out, streaming down her cheeks. With a heavy sigh, she rolled over on her side and saw that it was now after midnight.

She closed her eyes, and then saw a woman unpin laundry sheets from a clothing line. She squinted from the bright flashing light above. The wind lifted a sheet from the line and revealed the woman behind.

"Mom," she yelled. "Mom." Her heart sputtered, and she tried lifting her leg to walk but it was as if her feet were nailed into the ground. Ava knew that any second the lightning would strike. But she couldn't move. The woman never looked up from Ava's screams. Then, the flash struck the woman, and she collapsed.

"No, Mom!" she screamed. She struggled to move but to no avail. Then, something shook her.

"Ava, shh…" She heard a whisper.

Her eyes bolted open, and she saw her father. "Dad," she said breathless. Her heart jabbed into her ribs.

He leaned down and hugged her. "Shh…it's okay, sweetie. It was just a dream."

"Dad, she-she was right there…" She cried into his chest.

"Just a dream."

The amulet grew warm and Ava hoped no one would call.

"I'm sorry for waking you." She pulled away, and her breath slowed.

"It's okay," he said. "I had to make sure you were all right."

"Thanks. I'm okay now."

"Are you sure? Would you like to talk about it?"

"No. Go back to sleep."

He looked at her speculatively. "Something that helps me is to clear my mind before going to sleep. Just push all thoughts out."

"Okay."

He leaned over and kissed her forehead. "Goodnight."

"Goodnight, Dad."

He closed the door behind him.

Ava turned off the lamp and lay back down. She gripped the blanket, but couldn't stop shaking. She was afraid to close her eyes, for fear the dream would return. Taking a deep breath, she cleared her mind of any thoughts—just like her father suggested, and then closed her eyes.

CHAPTER FIFTEEN
FRIENDS

Ava pulled her sweater over her head, and then smoothed down her hair from the static electricity. She sluggishly walked into the bathroom, and braced for the light as she turned it on. She looked terrible. Her eyes were bloodshot and had black semicircles underneath. No different from any other day lately.

Her mom's face flashed in her mind. Why did Ava have such a nightmare? She hadn't dreamt of that day since she was a kid. The helplessness in the dream mirrored her real stance on things. She didn't feel any stronger, even though Savina said it would take a week or so for their strength to come back. Maybe she was a defective Enchanter. That was fine by her. Then maybe she wouldn't have to continue with this crazy lifestyle.

Tossing the dream and her incompetent thoughts aside, she reluctantly walked downstairs and didn't see her father. Maybe he'd gone into work early. Were they ever going to talk about things? Though, part of that was her fault since she had avoided him.

When she arrived at school, Thomas was leaning against the car next to hers. She'd seen all his missed calls from last night and figured he'd be eager to coddle her.

"Hey, Babe."

"I'm sure that person won't appreciate you touching his car."

He wrapped his arms around her and stroked her hair as if she were a pet.

"What happened last night?

"Nothing."

Thomas sighed. "Come on, Ava. Will you please talk to me? I was worried all night."

She felt her shoulders relax. Could she trust him again? "I just don't like talking about it."

"I know. But I'm here. Please? You never tell me anything."

"Because you can't keep anything to yourself."

"But we're all in this together. We shouldn't have any secrets. I just wanna be there for you, but you shut me out."

Ava looked up into his pale blue eyes, so sincere that she wanted to believe him. She took a deep breath. "I had a dream about my mom. I was trying to save her, but I couldn't move at all. I kept screaming her name, but she never heard me. And then..." She couldn't finish the sentence.

"That sucks. It was only a dream, though." He rubbed her arms.

"I know."

"Do you normally have dreams about her?"

"Not like that. I did when I was younger."

"Maybe it's just because you're thinking about her a lot."

Ava shrugged. "Do you ever wonder why you were chosen?"

He furrowed his eyebrows. "Chosen for what?"

"This life."

"We weren't. We were born into this. We were chosen for this particular Aureole. It feels natural. Like I was supposed to do this. Don't you?"

"I do, but a part of me keeps fighting with it, as if I'm not meant for this."

"You only think that because of your lack of powers. You'll get more. You're meant for this. Besides, if you weren't an Enchanter, I'd probably be with someone I didn't like." He smiled—a smile that could make any woman melt. Except Ava.

"*Do* you like me?"

Thomas grimaced. "Of course I do. I love you. Why would you think otherwise?"

"You've been so petulant. Ever since I turned you down."

"Petulant?"

She sighed at his ignorance. "Irritable. And you've been aggressive."

"Oh. Right. I'm sorry if I've been that way. It's just football and hormones. And this incredible energy flowing through me. Don't you feel it?"

"No. I don't."

"Maybe because you're afraid to give it your all. If you get all this emotional crap out of your system, you'll be able to focus. We need you and we can't have you unbalanced because of whatever's going on in your life."

Her heart sank, and the anger began to simmer inside her. Was he really more worried about the mission than her? She'd just opened her heart to him, and this was his suggestion? "You are an incredibly selfish jerk," she snapped, and pushed him away.

"What?"

"That's it. We're done." Ava clenched her teeth and took a step away from him, but he caught her arm.

"What's your problem? Dammit, Ava. I'm trying to help. Why do you get so pissed off?"

"I just opened up to you, and you want me to get this emotional crap out of my system? I'm sorry if my problems are impeding you."

"I didn't mean that." He held her in place. "I just meant, for you to feel all this energy, and for us to be prepared, you gotta clear your mind. You heard Colden and Savina. I know it's a hard time, but come on. I'm just trying to help."

"By making me feel like a burden?"

Thomas groaned. "You're not a burden."

"Yeah," she said icily and jerked her arm out of his grasp.

He tried holding her hand, once they entered the school, but she slapped it away. Ava saw Peter through the crowded hallway, and immediately looked away, hoping he wouldn't see her with Thomas. Ava reached her locker and opened it.

"Babe, don't be mad," Thomas said. "I suck at trying to explain myself. I'm sorry."

She grabbed the books she needed and slammed the door. "Whatever."

He sighed, and then leaned down. Ava tried backing away, but his lips were on hers. A rush of excitement enveloped her, and her insides twisted. She felt his love and was sure both their necklaces glowed.

"What was that?" she asked.

He leaned closer to her ear. "That's the fire burning inside me." It probably should have sent shivers down her spine, but it didn't.

When he pulled away, Ava was embarrassed seeing Melissa and Gillian walk up.

"Whoa." Melissa fanned them. "Someone put the fire out."

Gillian giggled. "You two are so cute."

"See ya later." Thomas smiled and left.

Ava sighed. Why did she have such an intense feeling when he kissed her? It had been a while since Thomas kissed her like that. Was it his powers? She strode to class with Melissa and took her seat still in a daze.

"What was that all about?" Melissa asked.

"Whoever made these necklaces was the dumbest person," Ava said.

She nodded. "Yeah, I agree. But I told you that you and Thomas would get back to where you were."

"Yeah. Sure. He told me to stop being so emotional because we needed to focus."

"Ah. So that's why you were angry earlier."

Curse this necklace.

After algebra, she went to chemistry, still thinking about Thomas's kiss. She opened her book to try to figure out derivatives. She had to or she wouldn't pass. Or maybe she just wanted to think about something else.

Peter slid into the desk next to her. "Hey."

"Hey." She felt her cheeks fill with blood. Why was she blushing around Peter? She never had before. Was it because she was thinking about Thomas and felt guilty, even though she should feel guilty thinking about Peter all the time.

"Will you be here tomorrow?" he asked, seemingly to be polite.

"I should be, why?"

"I wasn't sure if you would be absent or not for your birthday."

"Oh. I'll be here. Why?"

He hesitated. "I sorta got you something."

"You didn't have to do that." There was no way she could hide a present from Peter from Thomas. "Why don't you come over tonight?"

He paused. "Sure. I have work, but I'll swing by afterwards."

"Cool."

Peter wasn't his usual cheerful self. His eyes seemed sad. Or confused. Disappointed. Ava couldn't figure it out. He focused on the lecture, and at times, she would glance at him, but he didn't seem to notice. Was something bothering him?

He walked beside Ava to her locker but was quiet. The awkward silence annoyed her.

"Is something wrong?" she asked, and fished out her psychology book.

"No. I'll call you when I get off tonight," he said.

"Okay." She watched him walk down the hallway, and hoped he'd be all right. She wished she had more time to talk to him, but maybe they could later.

Thomas was right on time, and they made their way to the cafeteria. Ava looked at Xavier's table. They carried on like normal. If they really were Enchanters, why did they come to school every day? Unless they were scoping out more Ephemerals. No one believed her, but how could they explain someone like Kristen suddenly changing like that? Or Seth who completely avoided his friends. She shuddered, and sat across from Gillian.

"Oh, Ava, are you okay?" she asked, twirling a black curl around her finger.

"Yeah."

"Why were you sad last night?"

Melissa slammed her book on the table, and plopped down next to Ava. "Ugh, I swear I'm going to put a spell on Mrs. Norris."

"Why?" Ava asked. "What'd she do?"

"She gave me an F on my test. I studied for that thing." Melissa narrowed her green eyes. "She actually told me that maybe I should spend more time studying and less time being a teenager."

Gillian dropped her jaw. "She said that?"

"I thought you didn't believe in school work," Ava said.

"That's not the point," Melissa snapped.

"Mel, calm down," Lance said, and placed a tray with a salad in front of her.

"What's your deal?" Thomas asked.

"She wants to do something to Mrs. Norris," Ava replied.

Thomas laughed. "Like what? Turn invisible and scare her into having a heart attack?"

Melissa thought it over. "Actually, that's not a bad idea."

"What?" Ava asked. "You can't be serious."

Melissa shrugged. "She'd die of natural causes."

"What is with you? We're supposed to protect them."

"Yeah. I know why you want to." Ava hoped no one else knew what Melissa meant. "I'm so sick of you getting on my case like I'm a bad person."

"I'm not."

"I mean, do you really think I'm going to hurt anyone?"

"Mel, lay off," Thomas said. "She had a rough night last

night."

"I don't care."

What was with her today? Ava knew this attitude wasn't simply because of a test.

"You should care," Thomas told her. "She had a dream about her mom's death."

Ava's stomach dropped, and she threw Thomas a glare. "Why'd you say that?"

"They need to know."

"Your mom died years ago," Melissa said. "You should just get over it."

Ava shifted her glare to Melissa, and her necklace grew warm. "Go to hell."

"Babe, come on," Thomas said.

She snatched up her backpack, and hurried out of the lunchroom. She thrust open the bathroom door and it slammed into the concrete wall with a loud crack. Ava gripped the edges of the sink and took several deep breaths.

How could Melissa say such a thing? And Thomas lost her trust again. What was going on with them? Had their powers made them act so differently? Where was this perfect love and perfect trust?

She peered into the mirror, and the hole in the wall behind her drew her attention. What looked like the outline of the curved rectangular door handle had imprinted into the concrete wall.

Ava turned around and examined the damages. "Did I do this?" She brushed over the hole, and loose bits of concrete fell to the floor. "That's impossible."

The bell rang, startling her. She fled the room to avoid others from coming in there, and mingled with the dense crowd. She felt a hand pull her arm.

Thinking it was Melissa, she cursed, and then turned around. Ava felt her shoulders go limp with relief at the sight of Peter. "Hey."

He gave an uneasy grin, and pulled her outside into the small, empty courtyard. It was a space for seniors to enjoy their lunches, except it only held maybe ten picnic tables.

"I saw you rushing out of the lunchroom," he said. "What happened?"

"Oh. Melissa and Thomas upset me."

"I'm sorry. He upsets you a lot, you know that?"

"Just lately."

"What's going on? You seem distraught."

She twirled her ring around her finger. "It's just been a bad day."

The late bell rang, but they ignored it.

"I've been thinking about my mom a lot lately. Which is strange, because I usually only do that around the anniversary."

"I imagine since it's getting closer to your birthday and holidays thinking about her is stronger. At least, it's like that with me."

Ava nodded, but it was something else entirely that made her think about her mom. "I would give anything to talk to her again. I just miss her so much. There's not a day that goes by that I don't think about her. And I wonder if she would be proud of me. Or would she be disappointed in my choices?" She took a deep breath and pushed the tears back. "Melissa told me I should be over it."

"What? How dare she say that?"

"She's right. It's been ten years and I still get so upset."

"Ava, there's never a time limit on grief."

"I had a bad dream last night. And Thomas just told them all about it. I trusted him not to say anything. But he keeps saying they need to know."

"Why haven't you talked to them about it?"

Ava shrugged. "I just feel like they won't understand. And Melissa's comments clearly proved that. It's almost like I feel closer to you than them."

He took her hand in his. It was warm and comforting, and it jolted her heart awake.

"Ava, I have to ask something," he said.

She stiffened. "Okay."

"Have you only been talking to me because you've been having problems with him?"

"It does seem that way, doesn't it?"

"A bit."

"I'm so sorry," she said. "It's not like that at all. Everything about me now is just confusing. The only thing that makes sense anymore is you and me, but even that's getting difficult." Her lips trembled, but she let the words freely escape. "I'm changing, and there are…" She paused. How could she explain it to him? "Things I have to do now. Things that I'm unsure about and I don't know what to do. And I'm fearing…" She stopped. *Fearing for my life.*

Peter drew his brows together. His brown eyes were full of concern. "Ava, you're shaking. What kind of trouble are you in?"

Her eyes blurred. She didn't know how to answer that.

"Is there anything I can do?"

"No."

He wrapped his arms around her, holding her tightly. She rested her head on his shoulder, closed her eyes, and relaxed. Except that her heart pounded. Ava resisted the want, the need, the curiosity of having his lips on hers. So many urges she abstained forced tears to the forefront of her eyes. She took a deep breath.

"Ava." He paused. "Do you love Thomas?"

She drew back. "It's…complicated."

"Complicated," he echoed, shaking his head.

Ava wanted to brush her fingers through his thick hair and trace the smooth outline of his face. Feel the small dimple in his right cheek when he smiled. How was she supposed to end her friendship with him? This was ridiculous. She couldn't do that.

So what if her parents were Enchanters. Didn't she have a choice on how to live? Her friends had obviously not taken the oath seriously. Wouldn't she be safer from Devon if she carried on without using her powers? She couldn't tell her dad about her feelings. What about Colden? Would he help her? He had no power. Would he resent her for not wanting to be an Enchanter?

"Whoa, what's that?"

"What?"

Peter pointed to her necklace, and she froze. Ava looked down and silently cursed. She quickly moved the glowing pendant under her sweater. "It's nothing." A few seconds later, she felt her friends' worry. Would she ever get used to that?

He chuckled, bringing her up short. "That's neat. My cousin has a ring that does that. She presses a button, and it lights up."

She was relieved that he didn't think anything about the necklace.

"I should go," she said. "But we can talk tonight."

"I can call into work if you want."

"No. Your job is important."

"I think you're more important. It's a measly retail job, Ava. It's not like I'm going to stay there forever." He gave her a lopsided smile.

She would love to spend the entire evening with him, but she had to go to the cabin and channel with the others. "I just have to do something first. But I'll see you tonight."

"Yeah." He hugged her, and then she left the courtyard.

Ava wasn't going to class. She wanted to talk to Colden. Would he be there? Would he be upset that Ava came without invitation? Savina had mentioned that they were there for them.

CHAPTER SIXTEEN
DEVOTION

Driving on the same winding path as three weeks before, and just as nervous, she searched for the mansion. The road was lined with tall arched trees that blocked the sunlight. The lush green colors seemed odd in November. Ava braked at the entrance. A high stone wall surrounded the property with a black iron gate in the center held by two columns. Black raven statues perched atop each column. She let up on the brake and eased through the open gates.

To her amazement, the mansion was still intact. Her heart thrummed against her chest, and she couldn't seem to catch her breath. Her necklace warmed, and she grasped it.

Ava opened the car door. She hesitated a moment, and then got out. A breeze blew, removing some color off the trees. It was colder than it was when she left school. She closed the car, and made her way to the front door, never taking her eyes from it. Not knowing what to say, part of her wished Savina or Colden wouldn't be home. *Don't back out now.* She knocked on the door, and waited. Seconds later, it opened. Savina stood with a quizzical look on her pale face.

"Ava," she said. "What is bothering you?"

Ava's words seem to be stuck in her throat, but her

courage returned after a few seconds. "I'm sorry. I didn't know who else to talk to."

"Please, come inside." Savina moved aside to let her in.

Ava remained on the doorstep. "I would've come to you earlier, but you vanished." She raised her voice. "For ten years. I thought you were supposed to be there for us." She stared into Savina's green eyes.

"Please, Ava, come inside. We will talk." Her voice was firm, yet soft.

She crossed the threshold, and then followed Savina to the same room as the other night. She stopped in the doorway. Colden was talking to a man who stood by the fireplace with an arm propped on the mantle. Dressed in a black suit, the tall, slim man turned to her. His cropped brown hair looked almost black, as did his small goatee. He had slight laugh lines around his russet eyes, and he looked as if he were in his forties.

"Ava." The man beamed. "I am so grateful to meet you finally." He spoke eloquently in a Southern accent. "Savina has told me much about you. Are you not well?" His expression turned to concern. He reminded her of someone from the late 19th century. The only word that came to her mind was dashing.

"I..." Her words lodged in her throat.

"Ava, this is Aaron, my companion," Savina said.

He bowed his head, and she felt like she needed to curtsy, but didn't.

"Aaron, could you please give us time alone?"

"Of course. I shall return shortly." He shook Ava's hand, and then left.

"What has happened?" Colden asked, still standing by the fireplace.

Savina sat in her Victorian red chair. "She is worried."

Ava moved to the couch, and suddenly felt very awkward. How could she have behaved like that?

"I'm very sorry," she said. "I shouldn't have erupted like that."

Savina smiled warmly. "I understand." And the look in her eye proved that. "I suspect this hasn't been very easy for you."

"How'd you guess?" she asked, rudely, and regretted it. "Sorry." Ava could feel their gaze. She twirled her ring around her finger. Why had she come?

"You remind me so much of your mother," Colden said.

She looked up. "I do?"

"Yes. You are strong and independent, like her. She was a very determined woman, who could be a little hot tempered at times." He smiled, and Ava felt her cheeks warm.

"But she was very kind and loving and loyal," Savina said. "Your mother loved you so dearly. She did everything she could to protect you."

She cleared her throat politely. "Dad told me she was a Water Enchanter."

"She was. Just like you."

Ava shook her head. "I'm not like her. I'm not strong. All I can do is breathe underwater."

"It will come. You are strong, but you just have to find that strength within."

"I don't see it." She sighed. "All of this is too much. I don't belong."

"Why do you say that?" Colden asked.

"I'm the only one whose power is incredibly weak." She raised her voice. "And I don't want to kill."

Savina nodded. "You are not the only one with these concerns. I can tell you are fighting it, but you do belong here, with your Aureole."

"Why?"

"Your mother wanted you in this coven. Same one as her, different generation. I made a promise to your mother that you would be in my care if anything ever happened."

"You broke that promise."

Savina's green eyes cooled. "We have always been here, watching, and protecting you."

Colden held up his hand to her. "We never made our

presence known to you in all those years because we did not want to leave a trail for anyone."

"But Devon Maunsell knows about us, doesn't he? I mean, that's why there are Enchanters spying on us."

"He has spies because he wants revenge."

"What would happen if he found out what we are?"

Savina looked to Colden. They were obviously having a private conversation. After a few seconds, she turned back to Ava. "We suspect he could absorb all your powers for his own."

"But we are still investigating it," Colden quickly added. "If we capture the spies, we can get them to tell us where Devon is. If we kill them, they cannot go back to him."

Ava drew a ragged breath. "I don't want this."

"You swore an oath," Savina said.

"I know. I just didn't think all this would be happening so soon. I just want to live a normal life. I don't want to have to live in fear."

She gave her a tolerant look. "No one does, Ava."

"How many encounters have you had where you nearly died?" Colden asked.

She met his black eyes. "How could you know about them?"

"We know everything that's happened to you. Savina saved you when you had pneumonia. She healed Melissa's stomach virus, Jeremy's tuberculosis. When Gillian contracted a lung disease, Thomas's cancer, and Lance's severe fever, she saved them. If it had not been for her, none of you would be alive."

Ava's mind raced. They had been protecting her. How else would they have known of these incidences? "You...saved us?" she asked.

"I did, Ava. But you all healed each other as well. You stayed with each other throughout those dark times. You almost never left their bedsides and they reciprocated."

Ava nodded. "I remember."

"But we are not telling you this so you will think you owe

us. You do not by any means. We are telling you this to emphasize the strength of this Aureole. It is based on a bond that protects us. We are loyal and devoted to each other. You and your friends have been there for each other all of these years."

Guilt landed on Ava. "I guess I just never saw it that way."

"All of you are young and naïve. When you come back to practice, you will learn more of your loyalty and appreciate it more. We are a strong Aureole, but you must understand its meaning."

"I understand a lot more now," she said. Ava had experienced circumstances with the others that brought them closer together. She realized she had belonged to the Aureole all along, but why were her friends acting so hostile lately? Fear, probably. They just showed it differently than her. And how strange was it that they all almost died. "Do we know what caused us to become so ill?"

Savina pressed her lips together and exchanged a look with Colden. "There are theories."

"Like what? Were our powers too much for our bodies?" But then Ava thought of Corbin spreading illnesses. "Was it one of Corbin's men?"

"You should not be concerned."

"What do you mean? Who was it?"

"They are dead," she said with finality in her voice.

Ava wanted to know more, but it was obvious that Savina wasn't going to explain. Why wouldn't she tell her?

"How do you feel now?" Colden asked.

"Better. I just didn't think I could talk to my dad about it. He doesn't seem to understand a lot."

"He comprehends more than you think. Talk to him."

She would if it didn't turn into an argument lately. "I still don't feel like I'm ready to start...killing."

"I know," Savina said. "It is never an easy thing. I was like you. I never wanted to hurt a soul. But to stop those who could hurt the ones I love, I will."

That made sense. To keep her loved ones safe, including

134

herself, she would have to do this. Sacrifices would have to be made. She took a deep breath. "How exactly do we use our abilities? I mean, h-how do I kill someone?" She was still uneasy. Every time she said it, her stomach jumbled into knots.

"You are water. How can someone die by water?"

"Drowning?" Ava blurted.

"That's one way. When you want to drown someone, you imagine it. It will come to you naturally. You will find that you can do many things. You control Water, Ava."

Ava thought about moving the water in the glass. Could she really do that with larger bodies of water? "What about Melissa? She turns invisible."

"Melissa can produce poison—that's one of her several abilities."

"Produce poison?"

"Yes. It will take time for you all to learn everything that you can do."

"How exactly do we practice?"

"You will work with each other, using your abilities," Savina said.

"What if we get hurt?"

"You're able to sustain many injuries, but if anything is too severe, you can always come to me. Right now, I want all of you to learn to focus and your strengths. This Friday we will meet and train."

Ava let the information soak in. "Do you know of anyone actually spying on us?"

"No one that we have noticed yet."

"I-I think this boy at school is an Enchanter."

Colden furrowed his eyebrows.

Savina's face turned grim. "What makes you think this?"

"These kids went missing and came back to join his gang or whatever. They are completely different now. And I think he can make people faint."

"That's quite an accusation," Savina said. "If this boy was an Enchanter, and I'm assuming you believe he's made

Ephemerals into Enchanters, they would not be at school. They would be training to fight."

Ava felt her cheeks warm. Now she really felt like an idiot. Her friends were right all along. "Oh."

He clasped his hands in front of him. "You are not as worried as before. Have we helped?"

"Yes."

"I am glad."

Ava got to her feet, knowing she needed to leave. "Thank you."

"Anytime," he said.

Savina stood, and held Ava at arm's length. "Any time you need us for anything, we are here. As well as Aaron. Do not be afraid of the information we have given you. Learn from it."

She nodded, turned for the door, but stopped. "Is—is it okay to have friends outside the circle?"

"What sort of friends?" Colden asked.

"Ephemerals."

Ava sensed hesitation from Savina. "I don't think right now is such a good idea. If an Enchanter sees you with them, he or she could use them against you. We do not want to risk their lives."

"Of course."

"Come along, Dear. It is getting late, and your father must be worried." Savina lead her out of the room.

Ava stopped short. Aaron appeared just outside.

He tipped his head like a proper gentleman, and smiled warmly. "It was so nice to meet you, Ava."

"You, too."

Ava walked out into the dark night, and wondered what time it was. She slid behind the cold wheel of her car, and started the engine. Her body shivered from the cold, but then it warmed. She could get used to that.

There were several missed calls from Thomas, Melissa, and her dad. Being at Savina's seemed like it was ages since she had been at school. She called her dad and told him she'd been at the library. Ava wasn't sure why she lied, but because his powers had decreased, he couldn't tell.

She sent Thomas a text message telling him she was on her way to the cabin. Ava needed to talk to them. And Melissa, whom Ava felt her worry.

The talk with Savina and Colden certainly uplifted Ava's spirits. She was grateful to have an understanding and to have been chosen to be a part of a strong group. But she still didn't know what was up with Melissa.

CHAPTER SEVENTEEN
CLOSE CALL

When Ava pulled up to the cabin and got out of the car, Melissa ran to her. Her cheeks were tear-stained. Ava wasn't sure she was ready to face Melissa. It would take a while before she could forgive her, but for now she would practice as much as she could.

She stopped inches from Ava. "I'm so sorry," she cried. "I don't even know why I said it. It-it just came out."

"It really hurt. I don't know why you have to be so cruel."

"You have to know that I would never think that."

"I've tried understanding what could make you say such a thing."

"I don't know. Please, you have to believe me." Her eyes were so sincere. Melissa could be cruel, but nothing like this. Was it their powers that made them crazy or amplified feelings or thoughts?

"I talked to Savina and Colden just now."

"What? Did you tell them what I said?"

"No. I've just been scared of all this. But now I'm ready."

Melissa look surprised. "You are?"

"We need to talk. All of us."

"Okay. Do you forgive me? I have been feeling awful."

"I know. I feel you. Come on, let's go inside."

Melissa looped her arm with Ava as they walked to the porch. "By the way, what I think Thomas meant was, for you to feel like you are meant for this, you gotta give in. You're holding yourself back because you want other things." Melissa stopped her. "You gotta let go of Peter. And you have to block thoughts of your mom. These Enchanters can use it against you."

"I know."

"We're your friends. We care about you a lot. Let us in."

Ava nodded. "I will. But don't ever say anything like that again."

Her eyes watered and she nodded. "I know. I'm sorry."

They entered the cabin, and Thomas immediately rushed to her. He stroked her hair, and kissed her forehead. She pulled away and sat down on the hearth and he sat next to her. The heat from the fire was hot against her back, but she welcomed it. Lance, Gillian, Jeremy and Melissa sat across from them on the couch and loveseat.

"I talked to Savina and Colden today and I understand so much more now," she said. "I'm alive because of her. We all are. My mom wanted me in this Aureole and we need to protect the Ephemerals and us. I also asked about our abilities."

"What did they say?" Melissa asked.

"She said the more we practice, the more we'll be able to learn what we can do. She said you can produce poison."

Her mouth fell open. "What?"

"Yeah."

"What about the rest of us?" Thomas asked.

"She said that all we needed was to think of our element and what you can do with it. Since I'm Water, I can drown people. I just imagine that person drowning until they die."

Thomas raised his eyebrows. "Now *that's* cool."

"How exactly are we to practice?" Gillian asked.

"We just use our abilities on each other. If we get hurt badly enough, she can heal us."

Melissa eyes widened. "Let's go practice now."

Ava looked at the time. Seven-thirty. Peter was coming over tonight, and she didn't want to be late. She just somehow needed to explain that they couldn't hang out anymore. "I can't. I have a huge project—."

"Uh uh." Melissa shook her head. "I don't want to wait any longer."

"Something could happen."

"You worry too much," Gillian said. "We're just calling our powers."

Ava reluctantly followed them into the room. Once they crossed the threshold, the candles flickered alive.

"Okay, let's get started," Melissa said.

Standing around the glowing white circle, Ava closed her eyes, and thought of the ocean. The salty air she breathed was so real it felt as if she were at the beach. She could feel the heat warming her skin, the slight breeze through her hair, the soft sand beneath her, the sun lighting her way, and the moon calming her. Each Element giving her strength.

Then she focused solely on the waves, and they grew high above her, crashing powerfully against the shore. She opened her eyes and peered around the room at the others. All their necklaces glowed.

Ava tilted her head sideways, peering at Thomas. He grabbed her hand. A slight burning sensation filled her palm. It didn't hurt her though. They all held hands, completing the circle. Then tried focusing their energies again, starting with Melissa.

With her eyes closed, Ava saw each of them, in her mind, standing in a waist-high meadow. The skies were bright blue and just beyond the field, the ocean played. Melissa smiled as she handed them each a rose of a different color. Ava's was a light blue, like the ocean. She inhaled its floral aroma, and then realized that poison raced inside her. Her heart sped, and her air was slowly depleting. A few seconds later, it disappeared.

Lance walked beside each one of them, draining them of

their powers. A pulling sensation pricked her body as her powers dissipated. Then, they reappeared.

Gillian stared at Ava, and forced thoughts inside. Darkness loomed above her. It was so intense that she felt depressed. A large gust of wind billowed around her, like a tornado, and cut her skin. She watched the blood slowly creep from her arms. She looked to the ocean, and commanded the water to rush toward everyone. The water rose higher and higher until all of them were under, except her. Suddenly, a stinging, searing pain shot through her hand.

"Ow!" Ava cried, and jerked her hand from Thomas, breaking everyone's focus. She examined it. A burn in the shape of Thomas's hand covered hers. The pain throbbed with every heartbeat.

"What?" Thomas asked.

"My hand," she yelled. "You *burned* it."

Melissa gasped. She carefully lifted Ava's shaking arm and studied it. "Does it still hurt?"

"Yes!"

Gillian moved closer. "Thomas, what did you do?"

"I don't know. I'm so sorry." He held his hair back and his mouth was agape.

Ava looked up at Jeremy. "Did your hand burn?"

"Only for a little bit," he said. "But like everything else, it faded."

"Did you feel my drowning? I felt it all—your tornado-like winds, Melissa's poison, Gillian's thoughts, Lance taking my powers, but as soon as I felt them, it vanished, except yours, Thomas."

"I felt everything, too," Jeremy said.

"Yeah, same," Lance agreed.

"Maybe you weren't focusing hard enough," Gillian said.

"What?"

"Come on, don't fight." Melissa cradled Ava's arm, and steered her to the kitchen. "Let's get something to wrap this." She opened several cabinets, but they were all empty.

"Do we even have anything?" Ava asked.

"Doesn't look like it," she said, and searched the last cabinet.

"It's okay."

Thomas carefully lifted her arm. "How bad is it?"

"It feels like I pressed my hand onto a hot stove eye."

"I'm sorry. I didn't realize…"

"I'll just go to Savina's. Maybe she'll—."

"No," Thomas interrupted. "Please. She'll be upset. I didn't mean it. I'll take you home and bandage you up."

She was going to protest, but then the left side of her head pulsated. Ava squeezed her eyes shut, trying to block the pain that built. "I feel a migraine coming on."

"Whoa." Melissa steadied herself with the counter. "My head is killing me."

"Mine, too," Lance said.

"Who's doing this?" Gillian asked and plopped down on the couch with her head in her hands. Jeremy moved beside her.

When the pain subsided, Ava took a deep breath. "I don't think anyone is. I think we started too soon."

"It's been weeks though," Gillian said.

"That's enough for tonight," Melissa said. "We'll try again tomorrow."

Thomas took Ava's other hand. "Come on."

"No, Thomas. It's okay. I'll just—."

"I want to," he cut her off.

Much to her chagrin, Thomas followed her home. She didn't understand his insistence. She could take care of herself. Ava had to tell Peter not to come over, but driving with one hand, prevented her from calling.

When she pulled into her driveway, Thomas parked behind her, almost blinding her with his lights. Then, he rushed to her side.

"It's just a burn," she told him. "It's not like I'm bleeding all over the place."

"I'm sorry. I didn't do it on purpose. Don't be mad."

"I'm not." Not about that at least.

"What does this mean?"

Ava shrugged, and walked to the front door.

"Don't say anything to your dad. I don't need him hating me more."

She looked up at him. "You want me to lie to my dad?"

"Please, Ava. I don't want anyone to be angry."

Of course. Everything was always about him. She sighed, lowered her arm, and then pushed open the door. Thomas conveniently positioned himself to hide her hand. They entered the dimly lit living room. The TV was on, but her dad was fast asleep.

"Hey, Dad."

Her father jerked his eyes open. "Hey," he acknowledged them both. "Did you have a good day?"

"Sure. Thomas and I are going to watch a movie."

Her dad raised his eyebrows. "Okay."

Ava knew he could tell she was acting suspicious. She tried not to sound so rushed, but she had to do something soon. The pain ached too much. She and Thomas made their way to the stairs.

"Don't stay up past ten-thirty," her father called. Ava knew that was his secret code for Thomas to be gone by then.

"Okay," she called back, and then trudged upstairs.

Once in her room, she glanced at the clock on her nightstand. Eight forty-five. Peter would be off soon and on his way. Ava went to the medicine cabinet in her bathroom, and grabbed a tube of ointment. She had to think of a way to get Thomas out of there or call Peter.

"Shouldn't you run it under water first?" Thomas asked.

"I don't want anything stinging it," she said, and tried opening the tube one-handed. "Here, I'll do it."

"I got it."

Thomas sighed. "Give it to me." He snatched it from her hand.

"I'm not disabled, you know."

"What is with you? I said I was sorry." He took her hand,

squeezed some clear ointment out of a tube, and rubbed it over the imprint of his hand. "I can't believe I did this." He shook his head. Anger seeped into his rubbing. "How could I have done—?"

"Ow! Not so rough."

"Sorry. Do you have a bandage?"

Ava grabbed a wrap from the cabinet and put it in his hand. He needed to hurry up and leave. She shifted her weight and bit her lip.

"Will you stop fidgeting?"

She hadn't even realized she had been twirling her ring. "Sorry."

He unraveled the bandage and wrapped it around her hand. "What are you so worried about anyway?"

Ava forgot he could feel her worry. "Nothing."

He pinned the bandage from coming loose. "There. I hope it heals soon." He kissed her injured hand.

"Me, too." Of course, they could have avoided all this had they gone to Savina's.

"I don't understand what we did to get headaches like this. It feels like someone just hit me with a bat fifty times."

She handed him a bottle of headache medicine. "Here."

"I don't need it."

Ava rolled her eyes. "Of course not." She popped open the bottle, and swallowed two pills.

"I'd rather try something else." He leaned down, and kissed her softly.

She pulled back. "Thomas, you should go."

"What? I won't be so rough."

"Please."

"Let's just watch a movie. Come on."

"No. My head is killing me." *And I need to call Peter.*

He exhaled. "I'm not going to try anything."

"I don't feel good."

"I don't either, but let's just lie down."

"You can't fall asleep here." Why wouldn't he just leave? How was she going to talk to Peter with Thomas there?

"I won't."

"Fine." He was so stubborn. "I just have to get some water," she lied.

"Can you bring me some?"

"Sure."

Ava closed her bedroom door, and then walked downstairs to the dining room. Her father was on the other end still watching TV, or asleep. She pulled her phone from her pocket, called Peter, and he answered within seconds.

"Hey, I'm about to head over," he said. The sound of his soft, soothing voice brought her heart to a rapid beat. It was as if the throbbing pain from her head and hand moved to her heart. She needed to calm down so Thomas wouldn't ask questions.

"I have to cancel tonight."

"Oh. Is everything okay?"

"I'm just getting a migraine."

"Yikes. I hope you feel better."

"Thanks." Strangely enough, the pain had gone away. Maybe the medicine had kicked in.

"Hope I'll see you tomorrow," he said.

Her heart lurched. "Me too."

Ava hung up the phone, and almost on cue, the pain returned. How strange? Had she been so happy to hear his voice that any pain she felt was ignored? She thought that was a bit dramatic. Still though. That was a close call. And Ava couldn't afford to have anymore. She had to start ignoring Peter McNabb from now on.

CHAPTER EIGHTEEN
OUTCAST

Ava was probably the dumbest person. Why on earth had she gone to school with a migraine? On her birthday of all days. The bright fluorescent lights almost blinded her. Every sound made her cringe, and every movement she made stirred the uneasy feeling in her stomach. Her head would not stop pounding as she sat in algebra. She had decided to ignore all logic, and go to school. Apparently, she was so desperate to see Peter. But Ava missed him last night. Even if she had to break off their friendship, nothing could prevent her from seeing him at school.

Algebra was no picnic since Mrs. Duke spent forty-five minutes reprimanding a student. Melissa was absent, and she didn't see Thomas this morning. They had probably stayed home like smart people.

The bell shrilly rang, and she winced. How much more of this could she take?

Ava shuffled to chemistry, took her seat, and braced for the bell. She feared the nausea overtaking her, and held her head in her hands. And she wanted Peter to see her like this?

Then she felt a slight hand on her shoulder.

"Ava?"

She exhaled deeply with relief at the sound of Peter's voice.

"Are you okay?" he asked.

"Yeah."

"Are you sure? You look like you're going to be sick."

"I'm okay." She removed her hands, and met his dark brown eyes. Suddenly, the nausea disappeared, the throbbing in her head vanished, and the lights didn't seem as bright or the sounds as loud. How could all of it just fade away like that? What kind of sickness was this?

"What happened to your hand?" He asked, and then the bell rang, sending him to his seat.

She didn't flinch this time from the loud ring. "I…burned it."

"Ouch. How?"

"I took a hot pan out of the oven."

Peter cocked an eyebrow. "They invented pot holders for that reason you know?"

She rolled her eyes. "I wasn't thinking."

"Clearly."

Ava playfully hit his arm. "Don't be mean."

He chuckled. "You're starting to get some color back."

"That's good," she said, but wondered how she was about to hurl seconds before Peter came in and now she was fine.

"Happy birthday," he said, and placed a box on her desk.

"Peter, why did you get me a present?"

He shrugged. "I wanted to."

She opened the small box and pulled out a CD case. On the cover in Peter's handwriting was the title *Ava's Mix*. She looked at him, but he just grinned. "What's on it?"

"You'll like it, I promise."

Throughout class, she didn't pay attention to the lecture because she and Peter were flirting and passing notes. Like every day, he walked with her to her locker after class.

"Where's Thomas?" he asked.

She shrugged. "I don't think he came today."

"Shall *I* walk you to lunch, then?" He smiled, a little

smugly.

"Yes."

When they entered the cafeteria, Ava expected to see Gillian, Jeremy, and Lance, but the table was empty.

"Whoa, where is everyone?" Peter asked. "I don't think I've ever seen that table empty."

Had they all stayed home? Why hadn't any of them told her? "Could I sit with you today?" She didn't exactly want to sit with Valerie, but if it meant more time with Peter, she'd do it.

He smiled, showing his dimples. "Of course."

She followed him to the lunch line, but looking at the beef patty swimming in a brown sauce made her groan. Of course, there was always pizza and fries or a salad. But nothing appealed to her.

"You should probably eat something. You still look a little off. No offense," he quickly said.

"None taken."

"Let's just get some salad and fries."

"Okay." She liked the way he nonchalantly included her in this plan. After paying, he led her to his usual table. There sat one guy and two girls. Each of them stared at Ava with their mouths open. She sat next to Peter.

"This is Tony." Peter pointed to a boy with dark skin and black hair, who was to the left of Ava. He had a friendly smile, and she recognized him from the football games as the drum major. "Amanda." A girl with thick dirty blond hair and soft blue eyes that sat next to Tony. "And Valerie." She looked as if Ava was imposing on them. "Everyone, this is Ava."

She politely smiled, but felt awkward.

"Nice to meet you," Tony stumbled over his words.

"You too," she said.

"H-how are you?" he asked.

"I'm good, thanks." Why were they staring at her? Was she some sort of freak? Did she look that bad? Was it her bandaged hand? Could they sense that she was different?

Ava poked at her salad, still feeling their eyes on her. She'd never felt so self-conscious.

"What's wrong?" Peter whispered in her ear. "Are you starting to feel sick again?"

She shook her head. "No."

"What brings you to our table?" Valerie asked, and crossed her arms. "None of your friends are here."

"I invited her," Peter said with a hint of annoyance in his voice.

Valerie threw him a disapproving look. "Why?"

"Lay off, Val," Tony said. "You're welcome to sit with us anytime."

"Thanks," Ava said.

Valerie released a disgusted sigh, and glared at them.

"What's with the necklace?" Amanda asked.

Ava couldn't tell what was worse—Mel and Gillian tag teaming her over being friends with Peter, or Valerie and Amanda grilling her. She had never felt such animosity from others. Then again, the only one outside her circle she spoke to was Peter. She felt uncomfortable with them and realized she missed her friends.

"What about it?" Ava asked.

"Are you Wiccan or something?"

"No."

Valerie laughed. "She's in love with the devil."

"Valerie, stop." Peter snapped. "It's just a necklace."

Ava remained calm. "Why would you assume that I'm in love with the devil?"

"Because you're wearing his symbol. You and all your little friends."

"So did anyone watch the game last night?" Tony asked.

Ava balled her hands into fists. "It's not the devil's symbol, but what's it to you?"

Amanda leaned on the table. "Do you manipulate people like Xavier does?"

"Obviously," Valerie said. "She's got Peter wrapped around her little finger. Do you cast spells on anyone? I mean, that's what people are saying."

"What's the deal?" Peter asked.

"I don't care about your rumors," Ava said.

"Are you trying to get Peter to join your little group?" Amanda asked. "Like Xavier did with Seth."

"What? No."

"Whatever," Valerie said. "You're just like him."

What was with this girl? Ava glared. "How dare you say that?" Her necklace warmed. She needed to get out of there.

"Aww, did she hurt your feelings?" Amanda asked.

Tony nudged her. "Amanda."

"What is with you two?" Peter asked them.

Ava didn't care to know. She stood, grabbed her bag, and took a step.

"Ava, don't," Peter said.

"That's right, run away like you always do." Valerie mocked.

She had had enough. She stopped, turned, and got right in her face. "You *want* me to leave. You're afraid of me. Afraid of what I might do."

"Like you could really do anything."

"You don't know what I can do."

"I'm shaking," Valerie said, but Ava could see the fear in her eyes.

"Ava, wait." Peter called after her, but the bell sounded, and his voice was lost in the crowd.

The torturous lunch ended, and Ava was well on her way out the door. How could she have let Valerie get to her? She was stronger than that.

The second she left the lunchroom, her migraine returned. She couldn't possibly last the rest of the day with this pain and decided to go home.

Ava walked outside and trekked across the courtyard.

"Skipping today?" She heard Xavier's voice behind her.

She stopped abruptly. Her fingers curled into fists.

"What do you want?" she demanded.

He gave a cocky smile. "I thought we could talk."

"Yeah, you're the last person I'd ever want to talk to."

"I know my first impression was not friendly."

"What tipped you off?"

Xavier gave a small laugh. "I must apologize for that. I was only experimenting with something."

"I think you've done enough experimenting. What have you done to Seth and the others?"

He shrugged. "I just needed some friends. Speaking of, sounds like you could use some new ones. They don't seem very respectful of you. You would fit in perfectly with me and my group."

"Wow. Can I sign up now?"

"I love that fire in you." He smiled, but it only made her shudder. "I also love that necklace by the way. It's so...radiant." His black eyes taunted her. "Does your crush know what it means?"

Ava glared. Had he been spying on her and Peter? "What are you talking about?"

"I think you know exactly what I mean."

Did he know what kind of necklace she wore? Could it be true that he was an Enchanter? He had to be. And he had to know that she was.

"You don't scare me."

"Good. That's not my intent. I only want you as my friend."

"That won't happen."

"That's a shame. I think my next friend will be Peter McNabb. I suspect he is rather special. Something about him..." He shook his head.

Ava clenched her fists tight, and kept her breathing leveled. "Stay away from him."

"But he'll make a great addition"

"What is your deal? Why are you manipulating these people?"

He stroked his chin, and then smiled. "You'll find out soon."

Her hands suddenly felt wet, and she felt water around her

fists. She didn't want to look down at them for fear that Xavier would see. "Leave Peter alone."

Xavier chuckled, as if he was trying to be friendly. "I tell you what." He hooked his arm around her neck. "Why don't you become my new girlfriend, and I'll leave Peter alone."

Ava clenched her teeth, and pushed him away harshly. "Get away from me."

"Think about it. Until then." He saluted, and then walked away.

Ava was right all along. Xavier and his friends were Enchanters. And he was recruiting. How could she warn Peter? How could she protect him? Would she have to join him to keep Peter safe?

Once home, after taking medicine, she curled herself underneath the blankets, and fell asleep.

Ava leisurely opened her eyes, and saw that it was late afternoon. Nausea swirled in her stomach as she rose from her bed. She moved as though she were walking through cement. Her muscles ached. Her right hand throbbed in every crevice from Thomas's burn. She didn't understand why she still felt like this. Maybe she needed to see Savina.

The doorbell rang, and she hoped it wasn't Thomas.

She answered, and Peter stood on the other side. She was glad to see him, but still didn't know what to think about lunch.

"Hey," he said. "I tried calling, but you didn't answer."

"Sorry. I was taking a nap."

"Oh. You're looking better. How do you feel?"

She thought for a moment. Her head had stopped hurting and she wasn't nauseous. "Good."

Ava hesitated, but then stood aside and let him in. She closed the door, made her way to the kitchen, and Peter followed. She was going to grab a glass of water, but thought better of it, not wanting him to see what she could do, so she leaned against the counter.

"I'm so sorry about Valerie and Amanda."

"Did I do something wrong?" she asked.

"No. They just don't want me to be friends with you."

"Why?"

He wavered. "They think you're going to toy with me."

"Why would they think that?"

"Because you have a boyfriend." He looked away, acting as if he held something back.

"What else?"

"They think you and your friends are all in this thing with Xavier. And of course, people are spreading rumors about your necklaces. Valerie and Amanda think all of you are." He paused. "Strange."

Guessing by how Valerie and Amanda acted toward her, strange was probably nice compared to what they had actually said.

"They don't even know us," she said. "Why does she think I'm going to ask you to join my friends? What did she mean by that?"

Peter faltered once more. "Xavier's been watching us. At least, she thinks he is and that he'll take another one of us. Or whatever he's doing. I don't know. This whole thing has gotten all of us paranoid."

"You have to stay away from him."

"I plan on it."

Ava had to keep an eye on Xavier. "I'm not like him. And I would never hurt you. If she only knew what I went through to get to school today to see you—." She stopped. "Never mind."

"Wait. What happened?"

"Nothing."

"Ava." He urged.

She sighed. "I felt awful this morning. I was having a migraine, but I made myself come to school so I could." She paused. "So I could…" Ava didn't want to say the words.

"What? Tell me." His brown eyes encouraged her.

"Peter, please don't make me say it."

His face wrinkled. "Is it bad?"

"Depends on how you look at it."

"Tell me."

"So I could see you," she finally said, and buried her face in her hand. Why was she doing this to herself?

"Wow. That's interesting."

"Interesting? Oh, I shouldn't have told you." She groaned.

He pulled her arm away from her face, and closed the distance between them. His touch was like an electric shock. Her breathing accelerated.

"Don't be embarrassed," he said. "I'm relieved."

"Why?"

"To know you feel that way. Ava, I think about you all the time. The way you make me feel, it's like nothing I've ever experienced. I get so nervous before I see you, but when I do, it goes away because it feels right. And when we're together, it's like my insides are on fire." He blushed. "I don't know how to describe it, but you fill something inside me that's been empty for so long."

Her heart railed against her ribs so loudly. She couldn't believe this, and didn't know what to say.

"It's quite ridiculous actually, since you have a boyfriend. Which is why Valerie and Amanda don't like you. They don't want to see me get hurt."

"I think about you all the time, but I shouldn't," she blurted. She couldn't believe she had just admitted that.

"If you aren't happy with Thomas, break up with him."

"I can't."

"Why?"

Ava shook her head. "I can't say."

"Okay. So what are we doing?"

She tilted her head up slightly. He was so close, yet she did nothing to increase the distance. His intense gaze made her feel as though she would just turn into a pool of water. Whatever she wanted to say lodged in her throat.

"I want to be with you, Ava."

"What?" She wasn't sure she actually heard what he said.

"You heard me. And clearly you want the same thing."

"I have a boyfriend."

"Oh, come on. You don't love him."

"That doesn't matter."

"It *should* matter. Why won't you just break up with him?"

"It's complicated."

Peter let out an exasperated sigh and rolled his eyes. "Why is it complicated? If you don't love him, don't be with him."

"It's not that easy." Ava didn't want to argue with him.

"I don't get you." He raised his voice. "You're always saying bad things about Thomas, never anything good, and yet you are so attached to him…and your group for that matter. And it's like you're trying to break away but can't."

"They are my best friends. They would never hurt me."

"What about what Melissa said about your mom?"

"It was an accident. She didn't mean it."

"Do you hear yourself?"

"Peter, I don't want to argue."

"Sorry," he said calmly.

Ava knew she shouldn't have said anything. She was treading in dangerous waters now. She was only setting herself and Peter up for heartbreak. His friends were right. She was just toying with him.

"Are-are you *pregnant?*" he asked.

She let out a hard laugh. "No."

"I'm just trying to figure out why you started hanging out with me and admitted to liking me, but we can't be together. Is this a game?"

"No. You're a good friend. Is it wrong for us to be friends?"

"No, but you seem to like me more than that."

Ava looked away. "I shouldn't have said those things."

"But you did."

"We just can't be together. It's too dangerous."

"Why? Because of Thomas?"

"No."

"Then why would it be dangerous? We're in high school. Who cares if Thomas couldn't handle us being together?"

He wasn't making this easy. She couldn't say anything. Even if she could, she wouldn't know how to put it in words.

"Just let it go," she said.

"No."

She could feel the bulge in her throat forming, and knew her eyes would begin to tear up, but she pushed them away. "You need to move on, Peter. I'm so messed up right now. You don't want to get involved with me."

"Don't do that."

Her phone went off, and she was relieved for the interruption, but when she looked down at Thomas's name, she cursed. Her pendent warmed, and she immediately hid it beneath her sweater.

"What is it?"

She looked up. "You should go."

He arched his eyebrows. "What?"

The call went to voicemail, but then the phone rang again. And again.

She was angry knowing that Thomas could feel every strand of emotion she had for Peter, and the pain of knowing it could never happen. She wanted to stop restraining her feelings for him, but didn't have a choice. "I hate this," she shouted, and then tore the necklace from her chest.

"Did your necklace just automatically glow?"

"Don't say a word," she told him, and then answered.

"Ava, I'm on my way," Thomas said in a rushed voice. "I'll be there soon."

"No," she shouted. "Everything is fi—." She heard silence. He'd already hung up. Ava was exasperated.

"What's wrong?" Peter asked. "Are you okay?"

"You have to go." She grabbed his arm.

"Okay. Ow! Not so rough." He cried.

She dropped his hand instantly. "Did I hurt you?"

"Kinda." He gave her a wary look. "What the hell you been doing with that arm?"

"Sorry."

She heard the front door open, and then led Peter to the

living room. Her father entered.

"Hey," he said, and then furrowed his eyebrows. "Is everything okay?"

"Yeah," she said. "Peter was just leaving."

By the look in her father's eyes, she knew he could tell something was wrong "Okay. See you later."

"Yeah, you too," Peter said, and Ava pushed him outside.

A gust of wind welcomed them, a reminder of the colder nights, but she made herself warm.

"Peter, I'm really sorry, but you have to go."

A sudden realization flashed across his face. "He knows I'm here, doesn't he?"

"No."

"Why did he think something was wrong?"

How did he know that?"

"I could hear him shouting through the phone," he answered her silent question.

"I can't tell you."

"It's your necklace isn't it?"

Ava looked away. She had no answer.

"Is he going to hurt you?"

She knew any second Thomas would round the corner on the dark graveled road and find Peter there. She couldn't guarantee his safety and knew he had to leave.

"Peter, *please* go. I can't let him see you here."

"What are you hiding? If you're in any kind of trouble—."

"I care about you too much for you to be here right now."

"He can't hurt me."

"Listen to me." She put her hands on either side of his face. "Trust me. I need you to go."

He searched her eyes. "Fine," he muttered, defeat written all over his face. Then, he got in his car and backed out.

Ava felt her shoulders go limp with relief, once he was in the distance, but then her whole body froze the second Thomas pulled up. She knew he'd seen the taillights of Peter McNabb's car.

CHAPTER NINETEEN
TEMPERS

"What the hell is going on?" Thomas demanded as he stormed toward Ava. "What was Peter doing here? Where's your necklace?"

"Calm down. Everything is fine."

"Did he hurt you?" He pulled her close, forcing her head against his hard chest. "I swear, if he did anything…"

"No, he didn't," she said with clenched teeth, and releasing her head from his hands.

"I'm so glad you're okay." He pressed his lips to hers.

Ava pushed away from his hungry kiss. "Stop," she yelled.

"What is with you?" he asked.

"We're done, Thomas. I can't do this anymore."

He narrowed his eyes. "It's him, isn't it?" He shook her.

"Let go of me."

"What the hell were you two doing?"

"Nothing. He was helping me with chemistry. That's all."

"Don't lie to me. I felt you. You were in so much pain, and then I felt nothing."

"I told him about my mom." She'd just hit a new low.

"You what?"

"We were just talking, and he asked." She looked up into

his blue eyes, and hoped he bought that.

"Why would you tell him?" He shook her again. "What makes him so damn important?"

"Stop. You're hurting me." She struggled to break from his locked hands.

"Hey," her father yelled behind them. "What the hell is going on?"

Thomas released her. "I'm sorry, Sir. I was worried because she took off her necklace."

Ava glared at him. She knew he only said it to take the heat off him.

"You did what?" her father asked.

"Dad, I didn't mean to."

"Get inside."

"Okay," she said, and glanced at Thomas before making her way toward the door.

"And I don't ever want you to treat my daughter like that," he said with an authoritative voice that Ava had never heard before.

"I'm sorry, Sir. That was way out of hand."

"You're damn right it was."

Once Ava was inside, her dad came up behind her and slammed the door. She was humiliated, and couldn't believe Thomas had reacted like that. Especially, in front of her father.

She went to the kitchen, grabbed a glass from the cabinet, and filled it with water from the tap. The cold water soothed her parched throat.

Her father leaned against the doorframe, and crossed his arms. She knew he was going to yell at her for being irresponsible and foolish.

"How long has he been acting like this?"

"For a few months," she mumbled, refusing to meet his eyes.

"What happened to your hand?"

She self-consciously moved it aside. "Nothing."

"What did he do?"

"Burned it."

"Let me see it."

"It's fine."

"Ava," he demanded, and moved next to her.

She exhaled, and unraveled the bandage. He carefully took her hand, and examined it.

"I should strangle him," he muttered.

Ava wondered if he could make out the finger imprints from Thomas, but probably not since her whole hand was red. "He didn't do it on purpose."

He gave a dubious look. "He could help it. He wasn't focused enough. Have you talked to Savina about him?"

She shook her head. "No."

"You have to."

"And tell her what? That I'm bound to an overbearing jerk, and in love with an Ephemeral—." Oh no. No, no, no. The words had just slipped out. This was bad. She braced herself for the yelling, but when he didn't say anything, Ava looked up. His eyes were soft.

He rubbed his face, and sighed.

"Dad, I-I didn't mean that. Nothing will ever happen. I—."

"Ava," he cut her off. He seemed to struggle with his words.

"I'm sorry. I know it's wrong."

"I'm a Halfling."

The glass slipped from her grasp and shattered on the floor.

"What?"

"I was born a mortal."

He reached in the closet behind him, and retrieved a broom and dustpan. He swept the glass into a pile, but Ava didn't move.

How could he be an Ephemeral? That was impossible. It was well known that Halflings were inferior to those of pureblood. At least, that's how they were treated.

"Why didn't you ever tell me?" she asked.

"It never came up. And I was afraid."

"Didn't you ever trust me?"

He brushed the bits of glass into the dustpan and dropped it in the trashcan. "Of course I did."

"Does this make me a…?"

"No, you are all Enchanter. Those genes are very dominant, but I was made into an Enchanter before we had you."

She relaxed, but then felt guilty. "How is this possible? You said you had an ability."

"I did. It's fading now because yours is emerging."

"But how did you and mom end up together?"

"It wasn't easy," he admitted, looking away, lost in thought. "She struggled with it for quite a while. We had to convince her Aureole we were right for each other. She was stubborn and determined."

"How did you do that? Isn't it an unspoken rule that Enchanters aren't to fraternize with Ephemerals?"

"That was the hard part. Throughout the years, there have been several mixed couples, but they hide that. We went to Savina and Colden, and had to prove to the Aureole that we belonged together. They saw something in me and made me into an Enchanter."

"Wait, they made you an Enchanter? Isn't that what we're trying to prevent?"

"You're trying to prevent them from making an army. They only want fighters. It wasn't an easy thing to face your mom's coven, but they knew we loved each other. They felt it."

Her knees were weak and the room seemed to swirl. Ava pulled a chair out from the table, and then sank into it. She didn't know how to feel, but knew there was no way she could bring Peter into this. "So, they gave you powers?"

He nodded. "When I was accepted, it was like the first time you saw Savina and Colden."

She shuddered. "You had to drink blood, too?"

"Yes. It was as if I drank some of their abilities in a sense.

It took a couple of days to take effect, but when it did, I couldn't believe the change. They used me a lot when investigating enemies. It was a good way to tell what they were up to, if they blocked their minds from Savina. I could tell if they were lying, but I couldn't know the truth. Only if they lied."

"But now it's fading?"

"Yes. Unfortunately, I can feel it slipping from me." He sat down across from her.

"Do you wish it wasn't?"

"Absolutely. If there was a way I could protect you, I would. I've tried so much to protect you from them all these years. They almost took you…" He looked away.

"They? Wasn't Corbin dead before I was born?"

"We think it was one of his followers."

She knew it. They had tried to kill her and her entire coven. "I don't understand." She raised her voice. "Something doesn't add up. Corbin died, but you put all his supporters in prison. Yet, somehow, someone tried to kill us."

He frowned. "We missed some. Some went to Caprington to hide."

Caprington was Corbin's hideout, or home. Everyone knew that as a dark place, but Ava wondered if anyone had ever gone there after Corbin died and burned it. They could have missed thousands of Enchanters that went back.

"Why didn't Savina and Colden tell us?"

"They were trying to protect you. Luci always wanted you to be safe. And I thought I did my best."

"You did."

"I couldn't defend you from your sickness," he confessed with sadness in his eyes.

"But you couldn't stop them. You didn't know what they would do."

"No, but that doesn't change how I feel."

"Don't blame yourself, Dad." She was upset, but it wasn't her father's fault. "Why haven't you been concerned at all for me?"

"I am very much. But I also know how strong you are. You must understand just how powerful all of you together is. If this Devon guy finds out you are Elemental Enchanters…" He shook his head. "If he's anything like Corbin, he would stop at nothing to have you."

Chills tickled the back of her neck, and then she took a deep breath. "We really need to practice." Ava wondered if the others knew just how strong they were. She was curious to know what damage they could do together.

"Don't worry so much. I guarantee these spies he's using aren't anything to worry about, I promise you. I know you all can handle them. They're pawns."

"How do you know?"

"Devon Maunsell has been locked up and tormented for thirty years. He's not as strong as he used to be. And I don't think his supporters are powerful. They've been in hiding for so long."

"I think this kid at school, Xavier, knows what I am."

His eyes narrowed in a way that made her feel small. "Knows that you're an Enchanter or an Elemental?"

"Enchanter."

"How?"

"He made a comment about my necklace. And he was the one who hit me."

"What?" His eyes were angry.

"He had to have been. What if he is creating Halflings?"

"I wouldn't worry about him."

"Why?"

"If he really was creating Halflings, he wouldn't be at school."

"I think he's spying on us."

He shook his head. "You could just be paranoid. He hasn't done anything but be a bully. If he was a Cimmerian, he wouldn't just be bullying people. He'd be killing them."

She nodded, but wasn't so sure she agreed. "I'm sorry I got so angry with you about all this."

"You are so strong, so much like your mother. She had always accepted her responsibilities. Even from a young age. Why are you struggling?"

"I think you know," she murmured.

"Peter?"

"Yes." She didn't exactly want to talk to her dad about him, but some wishful thinking part of her wanted to know how being with him could be possible. "What did you think of all this when Mom told you?"

"I was actually pretty okay with it. Granted, it was hard to believe, until she showed me how she could control water. It was an amazing thing. She told me she would do anything to keep me safe, and that it was my decision if I wanted to be with her and be around all that."

Her mother was much braver than she was. "I don't think I could ever tell Peter what I am."

"It's not encouraged, as you know. But if you love Peter, you'll know what to do."

"The others don't see it as a good thing that I'm even friends with Peter."

"If Savina and Colden believe in it, they will give you permission."

"I don't think they would. If we have spies, Peter could be in danger. There's no way. I just can't." Her eyes brimmed with tears. And after Thomas's reaction, she definitely needed to detach herself from Peter. She needed to focus more on practicing and protecting the coven.

He reached across the table and squeezed her hand. "You need to tell Savina about Thomas. You cannot have him treating you like that. And she of all people would understand you."

"Okay."

"Will you talk to her?"

Ava didn't want to and felt it wasn't important. "Yes," she told him, and then stood to leave.

"One more thing."

"What?"

"Don't ever take off your necklace."

She was really hating his severe tone lately. "Yes, Sir."

CHAPTER TWENTY
SACRIFICE

After a sleepless night, Ava begrudgingly readied herself for school. She knew she'd have to face Thomas and briefly considered skipping school, but the thought of seeing Peter made her go. Her heart pounded as she felt Thomas's immense anger. She grabbed her pendant, and it grew warmer.

Ava arrived at school and her predictions were right when Thomas didn't meet her at her car. She knew he was upset, but also knew he'd come find her eventually. Or maybe he finally realized she was serious about breaking up.

Melissa was there, however, arms crossed in front of her, and angry. She wore a wide black band around her face, holding back her hair and yoga pants with a sweatshirt. Ava got out of her car, and Melissa immediately hugged her.

"Don't you ever do that to me," she said. "It was like you died. I couldn't feel you at all."

"I'm sorry."

"What happened?"

"Thomas freaked out as usual over nothing."

"You took your necklace off. I freaked out too. Tell me."

Ava just wanted to go to class, and knew she couldn't

avoid this conversation for too long, but she would try. "Why didn't we practice last night?"

"I still had somewhat of a migraine, but I talked to Savina and Colden yesterday. They said we weren't focusing hard enough. As for your hand, she said Thomas needed to try harder."

"Why didn't any of you tell me you weren't going to school yesterday?"

"None of us felt well. Why? Did you go?" Melissa narrowed her eyes.

Ava hated the way she looked at her, as if she was judging her. "I had a test," she mumbled.

"Was it called 'Peter'?"

"No."

"Oh come on, I know all about your homework and tests. Out with it."

"Fine. I went so I could see Peter. And you all weren't there so I had to sit with his friends, who hate me."

"I told you those people aren't worth our time."

"Peter was fine. Valerie and Amanda kept accusing me of being like Xavier. I don't understand their anger."

"We're different. We scare them."

"Maybe."

"How were you even able to talk to them? Didn't you feel awful?"

Ava took a breath. "About that. It was the weirdest thing. The second I saw Peter, the migraine vanished."

"Vanished?"

"Yes, and when we parted, it came back. When I collapsed after Xavier hit me, I woke and Peter was there. I felt no pain, but as soon as he left, I did."

"Really? Maybe you don't think about the pain when he's around."

"I don't know."

"What happened last night?"

Damn. She almost got away with it. "I don't want to tell you."

"You can trust me you know."

"Gillian said the same."

"She really didn't say anything to me about you and Peter. I just figured things out on my own. I see the way he looks at you."

"He came over last night to apologize for his friends. One thing led to another and I sorta told him I liked him. Of course, my necklace went off, and then Thomas came. He saw that Peter was leaving and got angry."

Melissa exhaled, and her green eyes held a stern look. "Ava," she took her hand. "You have to stop this. You can't let it get any deeper than it already is. What do you think will happen if Peter finds out what you are? Think he'll still be the same? Or do you think he'll agree with Valerie?"

"I know." She wanted to tell Melissa about her parents.

But didn't.

"I don't want us broken. And I don't want the elders getting angry because we can't keep our group together. Besides, maybe Xavier will leave Peter alone if you're not around him anymore."

"I got it."

Melissa hooked an arm around Ava's neck. "Come on. Let's get this day over with."

When they reached the courtyard, Melissa gave Ava an annoyed look and then rolled her eyes. It was teeming with shouting people, obvious that a fight was about to break out. Ava shook her head at the ignorance of boys and their need to brawl. She shuddered when she heard a loud smack and then the crowd oo'd in unison.

Melissa sighed. "Stupid boy—."

"Stay away from her!"

They both halted their steps. Thomas.

Fighting through the thick, boisterous crowd, Ava found him with his hand in a fist in the air aimed at someone she couldn't see. Her heart pounded as she pushed harder until she was in the open circle the crowd made. The other person on the ground was Peter.

"Thomas, stop," she screamed and pushed him. Ava glared at Thomas. His blue eyes were dark and full of rage. His hulking body towered over her, but she wasn't afraid.

"Move," he demanded in a grim voice.

"No." She glanced at Peter and when she saw his bloody lip, a lump formed in her throat. She wanted to console him but couldn't.

"What the hell are you doing?" Melissa yelled as she broke through the crowd.

"I'm about to pummel this kid," Thomas said.

"Yeah, you wish," Peter said.

Thomas's eyes shifted to behind Ava. He pushed her out of the way and Melissa caught her. Then, Thomas tackled Peter, and both of them threw punches.

"Stop," Ava screamed and then she and Melissa grabbed Thomas off Peter.

The bell sounded, and the crowd slowly dispersed, giving space to the circle they made.

Ava pressed her hands into Thomas's chest, but his eyes glared at Peter. Melissa was checking on Peter.

"Leave him alone," she said.

"Not until you stop seeing him," he demanded.

"You can't tell me what to do."

"No? You know what Gillian can do if you don't listen to me," he lowered his voice.

Ava's stomach dropped, and her breath lodged in her throat, but she continued the staring match with Thomas. There was no way she was going to allow Gillian to manipulate Peter's mind.

"Thomas, don't you dare," Melissa warned.

"Just leave her alone," Peter said.

"Peter, go," Ava insisted.

"Ava."

Thomas smiled. He pulled Ava against his hard chest and pressed his lips to hers. It was a kiss like before, passionate, making her knees weak. His intense love enveloped her, but there was something else. *Her* love for him. Where had that come from?

When it ended, she pushed him away, embarrassed. She turned around, but Peter was gone.

What was that? It had felt as if she were in a trance. Why did she have such a reaction to his kiss?

"What is wrong with you?" Melissa asked. "Did you really need to do that?"

Gillian came up behind Thomas, chewing gum. "What's going on?"

"Oh you just missed a schoolyard fight," Melissa said. "Because Thomas can't figure out how to calm down. What were you thinking?" she asked Thomas. "Fighting with an Ephemeral? Are you stupid?"

"He threw the first punch."

"I don't care. You could have killed him."

He shrugged. "Fine by me."

Ava balled her hands into a fist, and sent it across his face.

Gillian gasped. "Omigod, Ava. What's wrong with you?"

Thomas massaged his jaw, and then grinned, but it wasn't friendly. The muscle in his jaw twitched and he never said a word as he walked away.

Ava had to find Peter and make sure he was okay. She turned to walk away but Melissa grabbed her by the wrist.

"Where are you going?"

Ava released herself. "To see if he's okay," she said, and then jogged toward the parking lot.

A light mist trickled down onto her face, cooling it. Thomas made it clear that he would harm Peter further, and that Gillian would tamper with his mind if she kept seeing him. She couldn't believe it had gotten so out of hand that her friends threatened violence. There were others she needed to worry about, but never thought she'd have to protect him from her own friends.

She spotted him near his car, and then picked up her pace. "Peter," she called and he turned around.

When Ava neared, she winced at the sight of his swelling lip and bloodied nose. Anger, regret, and then sadness filled his eyes.

"Peter, I'm so sorry about that. Are you okay?"

"I'm fine," he snapped. He opened his car door and slung his backpack inside.

She moved closer, but he held up his hand.

"You know what I don't get?" he asked, and then gave a disgusted laugh. "How bad he treats you, and yet you're still so much in love with the guy."

She wanted to explain why she had such a response to Thomas's kiss, but she didn't know why. "Peter, we can't hang out anymore."

He gave a disappointed look. "Is this really what you want or did Thomas threaten you?"

"This is what I want." Her voice sounded strange, but she hoped he believed her. "What I said yesterday, I just meant I like you as a friend."

"You know I don't believe that."

"Believe what you want."

He shook his head, and then looked at her intensely. "You need to stay away from him, Ava."

"I can't."

"You could if you really wanted to. Ava, he's abusing you, and it's only going to get worse the longer you stay with him."

Her eyes blurred and she looked away from his heated gaze. "It's not what you think."

"You're so blind to it, because you're obviously still in love with him for some reason."

"Maybe you should just mind your own business," she snapped, though she immediately wished she could take back the harsh words.

"Fine. If this is really what you want, I'll leave you alone."

"Good." She walked away, and heard him drive off. She knew she had to let him keep believing she was still in love with Thomas. It gave her the out she needed to keep him safe. This was the right thing to do. To keep him out of danger, Ava had to make the sacrifice.

But Ava still couldn't understand why she had reacted as if she really was in love with Thomas when he kissed her. It was as if someone had made her feel that way.

Ava stiffened. Gillian. Had she used her power on her?

Later that night at the cabin, Ava entered still angry with Thomas and Gillian. She'd spent all afternoon trying to figure out what she was going to say to her so-called best friend of ten years. This was betrayal, and Ava was appalled and hurt.

They were all sitting in the main room around a blazing fire in the fireplace. Gillian was checking her reflection in her mirror and Jeremy was reading. Melissa and Lance were engaged in a conversation but stopped as Ava stood near the door.

Gillian looked up and smiled, but Ava wanted to wipe it from her face. How could she be so smug?

"Hey," she said. "Ready to practice?"

Ava clenched her teeth. "How dare you?"

She raised her eyebrows and looked from Melissa back to Ava. "I'm sorry?"

Jeremy lowered his book.

Ava folded her arms in front of her. "You used your power on me."

"What?" Melissa asked.

Gillian crossed her arms. "So what if I did?" She shrugged.

"What the hell did you do?" Melissa demanded.

"When Thomas kissed me this morning, she made me think I loved him," Ava said. "How could you do that? I can't believe you."

"It needed to be done," Gillian argued. "You aren't supposed to be flaunting around with some Ephemeral. Besides, you're supposed to be with Thomas."

"You what?" Jeremy asked. His mouth was agape and his topaz eyes widened in shock.

"G, we are *not* supposed to be doing that," Melissa said. "We're supposed to trust each other."

"Yeah, like that worked well." She grimaced. "She's been

sneaking around with Peter."

"I have not," Ava said.

Gillian let out a hard laugh. "What do you call last night? I can't believe you'd betray us like that."

"You used your power on me, and I'm the one who's disloyal?"

Jeremy rolled his eyes and sighed. "She's not betraying us, Gillian."

"Are you on her side now?"

"There are no sides." He raised his voice. "We're in this together. She hasn't done anything wrong. Do you want Thomas to keep hurting her?"

"He only hurts her because she spends so much time with Peter."

The door to the cabin opened and Ava moved out of Thomas's way. "What's going on?" He looked around.

"Gillian manipulated me," Ava said, without looking away from Gillian.

"Into liking Peter?" Thomas asked.

Ava twisted her head and met his eyes. "Into feeling like I did when you kissed me."

He furrowed his eyebrows and then looked past Ava at Gillian. "You did that?"

"I was helping you out," she said. "You should be happy."

Thomas shook his head. "You mean when I kissed her, I thought that was her wanting to kiss me back? But it was you making her?"

"Why are you getting mad at me? She lost our trust. She should be kicked out and her powers should be taken away."

"What's gotten into you?" Jeremy asked.

Ava shook her head. "We used to be friends. But now? You're nothing to me."

Ava turned and left. She knew it was a harsh thing to say, but she didn't care. If Gillian was going to use her power against her closest friend, Ava could say anything she wanted. And what was up with Thomas's reaction? He actually seemed hurt that Ava had kissed him back against her will.

CHAPTER TWENTY-ONE
MOVING ON

Ava watched the crescent moon through the trees. The night was cold, and she immediately warmed herself. She was ready to begin practicing fully for the mission. Ava was determined to never think about Peter, and to give in to her life as an Enchanter completely—something she should have done from the beginning. What would her mother have said if she saw her acting like this?

But she wasn't ready to forgive Thomas or Gillian for what they had done. She hadn't spoken to either of them since the incident a few days ago.

Melissa flicked her cigarette and stomped it out. "Okay, so maybe each of us should partner up. I'll be with Ava. Lance, you and Thomas, and Gillian and Jeremy. We'll switch it up."

"Sounds good to me," Thomas said, and he and Lance walked near the edge of the woods.

Melissa stood beside Ava. "You look like you could use a night out."

"I'm fine," Ava said.

"I'm sorry, but you had to know this could happen."

Ava sighed. "Did you know Xavier said he'd leave Peter alone if I became his girlfriend?"

174

"You didn't?"

"No. But ever since that stupid fight, he's left Peter alone."

"That's good, right?"

"Yes."

"I'm sorry that it hurts you, but it's for the best."

"I know."

"Come on, let's practice."

A sharp wind moved through the trees, bending them as if they were blades of grass. Dead pine straw and leaves lifted into the air. Ava lost her balance, but snatched Melissa's hand. They turned their head toward the woods as a cracking noise echoed. She gasped and brought her hand to her mouth.

Jeremy smirked, and pushed his glasses up his nose. "Something I've been working on."

"Wow." Lance raked his hands through his dark hair and still held his jaw open in astonishment. "Just think of what you could do to some of these spies. If they even exist."

"I hope you don't do that to me," Gillian shrieked.

Melissa rolled her eyes. "Your turn, G. And hurry up. I'm dying for a cigarette."

They waited for Gillian. Then Jeremy charged toward Melissa. Ava quickly moved out of the way. Melissa turned invisible, and then Gillian fell forward on her hands and knees onto the ground. Melissa reappeared behind her.

It was obvious Gillian had manipulated Jeremy to attack Melissa.

"Don't send Jeremy to do your dirty work," Ava said.

Gillian scowled. "Fine."

Melissa held a vacant stare, turned, and headed toward the cabin.

"Where are you going?" Ava asked.

Lance came up next to her. "What's she doing?"

"I don't know."

A few seconds later, Melissa returned with a knife in her hand, poised to cut across her wrist.

Ava gasped, and realized she was being controlled. "Gillian, stop."

Melissa poked the flesh enough to make it bleed. The knife made another incision.

"Gillian, stop it," Lance demanded, and rushed up to Melissa. He took the knife from her.

Ava visualized Gillian underwater. It was as if she stood over her in a pool of water. Gillian tried to break the surface, but Ava kept her down with her mind. Gillian grasped at her throat and choked until she fell once again to her knees. Her hold over Melissa broke and left Melissa completely disoriented. It was strange to Ava that she could do that to Gillian. Or anyone.

Melissa's eyebrows creased as she examined the knife in Lance's hand, and then her arm.

Gillian coughed. "What did you do to me? I couldn't breathe."

"Look what you did to her," Ava yelled.

"We're supposed to be practicing on each other. That was all I could think about doing."

"She didn't cut very deep." Melissa noted. "Or I should say she didn't make me cut myself very deep. That was the craziest thing. I was watching it, but I couldn't do anything about it."

"Are you okay?" Lance asked.

"I'm fine. Come on, let's practice." She turned toward Ava and slyly smiled.

"What?"

"Watch this," she whispered.

Ava waited until she saw dirt and rocks move and congregate around Gillian, forming a small wall.

"What are you doing?" Gillian screamed.

"I'm just practicing," Melissa smiled and shrugged. The wall lifted slightly, and then collapsed around her in a cloud of dust. "This is too much fun."

Ava had to admit how amazing it was to see them so powerful.

CHAPTER TWENTY-TWO
FRIENDLY CHAT

Ava tapped her pencil on her desk, and stared at the words on her chemistry test. It was all gibberish. The past month had been filled with practice and no studying. She lost her interest in school, and hardly even went anymore. But she liked to torture herself, just to see if Peter was safe. He never greeted her with a smile or asked how she was doing, or told her about his day so far. They never said a word to each other, but she was acutely aware of his presence. She wasn't sure what she was going to do during the winter break since she wouldn't see him.

"Ava, please keep the pencil still," Mr. Horn asked.

She stopped tapping, and then circled random answers on the final exam until she finished. When the bell rang, she turned in her test, and then left the room for the last time.

"Hey Babe." Thomas smiled. He still acted as if they were still together, but Ava did nothing to correct him. She didn't want to cause a rift in the group. They carried on as if nothing happened, and surprisingly he had begun acting like his old self.

"What do you want to eat?" he asked once they reached their table.

Ava sat down across from Gillian and Jeremy and next to Melissa. "Just some water and an apple."

"That's it?"

"Yeah, I'm not hungry."

"All right." He walked away.

"I totally bombed that chemistry exam," she said. "Who knows if I passed the class?"

Gillian opened a box of raisins and popped one in her mouth. "Why don't you get Jeremy to help you?"

Jeremy looked up from his *War and Peace* novel, and pushed his glasses up on the bridge of his nose. "What do you need help with?"

"All of it. It doesn't matter though. It's not like we're going to be in school forever. Besides, today's the last day."

"Until you have to retake the class." Gillian snorted.

"Don't you have the lab next semester?" Jeremy asked.

"Yeah. How's the book?" Ava asked.

"It's good. The characters are very enthralling and I like the dialogue in the story. I'm not that far into it, but I can't put it down."

"Well, don't read while we're at lunch." Gillian grabbed the book from him and placed it on the table.

"What's wrong with him reading?" Ava asked.

"It's rude."

Ava met Jeremy's eyes and silently apologized.

"Ugh, I'm so sick of this rain," Gillian said, and peered out the window.

"I know," Melissa said. "It's been raining so much lately."

"Can't you change it, Ava?"

"I'm not making it rain."

"No, make it snow or something," Gillian whined.

"Snow? Here?"

"Sure," Melissa said. "Freak weather happens all the time."

"I can't control the weather."

"Haven't you been practicing at all?" Gillian asked.

"Yes. Mostly to keep my focus."

"Same here," Jeremy said.

Gillian groaned. "That's nice. Come on, Ava."

"Why are you so eager?" Jeremy asked.

"I wanna see if she can do it."

"Yeah, me too," Melissa said.

Ava looked at them waiting for her to do something. When she didn't, they rolled their eyes and consumed themselves in a conversation. She leaned her head on her hand, barely listening. Could she actually change the rain to snow? She stared out the window, and focused on the pouring droplets until they moved slower, slower, until they were still. It became silent as small snowflakes stuck to the windows.

"Whoa, it's snowing," Gillian gaped. Her blue eyes widened as if she were a little kid.

Ava looked up. "It is? Wow. I guess freak weather does happen."

Melissa playfully punched her.

A buzz awakened the sleepy cafeteria as students watched the snowfall in amazement while it began sticking to the ground. It was as if they'd seen fireworks outside—but it was an amazing sight to see the snow, since it hardly snowed in the south.

Thomas set down the trays of food, and gawked at the window. "It's snowing."

Ava bit back a laugh.

"Imagine that," Melissa said.

"What's so funny?"

Ava shrugged.

"Are you doing this?"

"I don't know what you're talking about," she said, and then and glanced at Xavier's table. Of course, he was staring at her, like always. Did he know what she was doing? Suddenly, she let go and it began raining again.

The bell rang, sending students to the doors. Ava followed, and laughed to herself that they were still talking about the snow.

"You think that's impressive," Gillian said, and stopped in

front of the lockers.

"What are you gonna do?" Ava asked.

She smiled.

Melissa raised her eyebrows. "Are we supposed to see something?"

Ava leaned against the locker. Then, Jay McDonald, a blond guy in her math class, walked toward her.

He smiled. "Hi, Ava."

"Hi."

He leaned down, as if he was going to kiss her. She tried backing up, but couldn't.

"I really think you're hot," he whispered in her ear.

"Hey," Thomas said, and pulled him away from her. "What's your problem?"

Jay blinked a couple of times, looking confused, and then widened his eyes. "S-sorry." He walked away.

"Why did he just do that?" Thomas asked.

Kevin Burnley walked by, and then stopped, and turned. His eyes roved up and down Ava. "Wow, Ava." He closed the distance between them.

She sighed and shoved him. "Gillian, stop it."

Kevin smiled, and leaned closer. She pushed him, and Thomas grabbed him by the throat. Kevin's eyes grew large.

"Stop, Thomas," she yelled. "He doesn't know what he's doing."

He released him, and Kevin ran down the hall. Several people slowed down to watch, but then quickened their pace.

"Gillian, I can't believe you did that," Ava said.

"What? I thought you liked Ephemerals."

She sighed. "I gotta go." She walked down the hall, and saw Peter and his friends watching her. Her heart skipped a beat as she met his eyes. Did they see Gillian manipulating Kevin and Jay? Once she passed him, she relaxed.

Jeremy came up behind her. "I'm sorry about Gillian."

She shrugged. "It's not your fault."

"How are you doing this?"

"What?"

"You know what I'm talking about."

"I'm fine."

"Come on, I know this is all fake. You can't suddenly be back in love with Thomas as if nothing happened. I know you still have feelings for Peter."

She shook her head. "It's better off this way. He can't get hurt."

"No? He's hurting now. I can see it in his face. And you're not yourself. You seem so hollow and it's like you've become so passive."

That stung. Hadn't she tried to appear normal? But then again, Jeremy had always been so perceptive. "Even if I could be with him, there is no way I could hide what I am."

He slid his glasses up his nose. "Maybe you wouldn't have to."

"My mom didn't with my dad."

He arched his eyebrows. "What?"

She was unsure if she should say anything, but she could trust him. "My dad's a Halfling."

"Wow, that's incredible. How?"

She shifted, and lowered her voice. "Mom had to get acceptance from her coven. Savina saw how much she needed my dad, and my dad was willing to give up his life to become an Enchanter. But I'm not strong like my mom, and she didn't have a possessive boyfriend, either. And if Xavier is spying on us, he could hurt Peter."

The late bell echoed in the hallway.

"Fair enough. But I don't think he'd be scared if you told him the truth."

"If he knew, do you honestly think he would just accept it and move on? And if he did, there is no way that Thomas would ever accept him."

"You have my vote."

"Thanks."

"There has to be a way, Ava. You can't just be miserable forever."

"For his safety, I will. I just need to get over him. And

realize it will never happen."

Jeremy frowned. "Ava."

"Don't pity me. Come on, we're late." She pushed open the door, and took a step down, but stopped.

Xavier leaned against the wall at the bottom of the flight of stairs.

The door behind Ava and Jeremy closed with a click. Ava could go upstairs instead, but what if he made her faint or whatever he did?

He slowly climbed the stairs. "Shouldn't you be in class?" His black eyes taunted her, but then he looked to Jeremy.

Jeremy leaned forward, and tumbled down the stairs. His body was sprawled at the bottom in an unnatural position and he was unconscious.

She wanted to run to him, but knew she needed to keep an eye on Xavier. "What do you want?"

He shrugged, and brushed against her. "Friendly chat?"

She clenched her teeth. Then reached up, grabbed him by the throat, and slammed him against the concrete wall. Her hands tightened around his thick neck. "Leave us alone."

The door snapped opened and startled her. She softened at the sight of Peter. He looked at her as if she was a stranger. She reluctantly released Xavier and stepped back.

"What's going on?" Peter asked.

"Nothing you want to involve yourself with," she said.

Xavier rubbed his neck. "Just a misunderstanding is all. We'll talk later," he said, and casually walked through the door.

Jeremy moaned and Ava ran down to him.

"Come on, we gotta go," she said, and helped him to his feet. "Peter, go to class." She took a step, but Peter grabbed her arm. She tried to keep her breathing level.

"What the hell was that back there?" he asked. "You've got random guys trying to kiss you, and Thomas trying to attack them, and then you have Xavier by the throat."

"Just forget what you saw. I gotta go, but thanks for your help." She rushed through her words, and jogged down the stairs with Jeremy.

As soon as they left the stairwell, he halted. "My head," he said and doubled over, holding his head between his hands.

She knew all too well of the excruciating pain he experienced.

"I'm sorry. Come on." She put his arm around her neck, and her arm around his waist. "Can you walk?"

Jeremy nodded.

She helped him to her car, and then scrambled to the driver's side. "Do we need to go to Savina's?"

He shook his head.

She turned the engine, and backed out of the parking space. Her heart was pounding. Peter had possibly just saved them. Who knew what Xavier would have done? He could have made them both pass out and kidnapped all three of them.

"What happened?" he asked. "I don't remember anything."

"Xavier made you faint. You fell down the stairs. He didn't even touch you." There was no denying it. Xavier was an Enchanter. He had to be.

"What was Peter doing there?"

"I don't know. But he needs to stop following me."

"You ever stop to think that maybe it was a good thing he came?"

"Good thing? Xavier's had his eye on Peter, and I can't stop him. I've tried warning Peter as best I can."

"He won't take him."

Ava sighed. She knew he was just trying to make her feel better. "My dad didn't believe me when I told him about Xavier. But I know he's an Enchanter. He's spying on us."

"I believe you, but do you think he's working for Devon?"

"Yes! It's so obvious. Xavier is blatantly making Enchanters. He's helping Devon build his army."

"You're reaching. I believe he's an Enchanter, but I don't think he's making them."

"Then how do you explain Kristen and Link, all of their

personality changes?"

"Maybe they got a taste of popularity. You know how kids are. They get wrapped up in that stuff."

Ava sighed. She wasn't going to argue with him. She needed to gather proof. Maybe she should follow Xavier or Kristen around.

"What did you do to get rid of this pain?"

"I took some medicine. But then when I was—." Around Peter, she never felt pain. "When did it start hurting?"

"As soon as we got to the hallway. Why?"

"You didn't feel any pain when Peter was there?"

He furrowed his eyebrows. "I don't think so."

Did being around Peter relieve pain? It sounded so ridiculous, since he was an Ephemeral. Unless Xavier got to him early, and used him to spy on Ava. No, no. her imagination was running wild. But could it be true?

"We have to spy on Xavier, Jeremy."

He sighed. "I'd rather not until we know for sure."

"How much more proof do you need?" she yelled.

"Should we tell the others?"

"Maybe. Just in case things get out of hand. But we can't tell Savina or Colden."

Jeremy shook his head. "This isn't good. We shouldn't be keeping secrets from them."

"I don't want this anymore than you do. But Savina and Colden told us there would be spies. That's what we've been practicing for isn't it?"

"Are you doing this to protect us or strictly for Peter's sake?"

"Does it matter?"

He met her eyes. "No, I guess not."

"We'll watch him and follow him over the break."

He took a deep breath. "Okay."

Ava would find out exactly what Xavier Holstone was up to. She would do whatever it took to keep Peter safe.

CHAPTER TWENTY-THREE
TRAINING

Ava and her friends returned to Blackhart manor the next night. She passed through the gate, and admired the immense garden lit by the orange light of the torches lining the walkway.

Colden greeted them, and stood aside so they could enter. "We've much to do," he said, and then closed the door.

He led them through the conservatory. The purple velvet rug was gone, and only a few candles were lit. They crossed the bare hardwood floor to the outside.

He opened the wide door and Ava was amazed to see rolling hills that seemed to go on forever. She could only imagine how beautiful it must be in the daylight. The sliver of moon barely lit the charcoal sky, but torches lined the small area where Savina and Aaron stood, and around the edges of the mansion. Brown leaves embedded into the ground from the rains. A mix of empty maples and southern pine trees surrounded them on either side of the field.

Savina was waiting for them and did not greet them like she normally did. She stood assertively in her usual black robed dress. Her long hair swayed in the small breeze. "This is Aaron," she said. "To those who do not know. Now, what can you do with your powers?"

"I can create fire," Thomas replied.

"Show us."

He stepped forward and raised his palms, and emitted flames from his hands.

"What can you do with that?"

"Um." He attempted to hurl the fire but it extinguished.

"Too late," Savina told him. "You would be dead by now. Melissa, your turn."

"Wait." Jeremy held out his arm in front of her. "Do you hear that?"

Ava looked at him. "Hear what?"

"Stay focused, Jeremy," Savina warned.

"What does it sound like?" Lance asked.

"A woman is singing. It's beautiful."

Gillian fumed. "She said focus."

"I can't. It's too distracting."

Lance's face lit. "I hear it too. Do you hear it, Thomas?"

"Yeah. It's so beautiful," he said.

Ava looked up at him, and he was completely mesmerized with the mysterious sound. "What is it?"

"Am I missing something?" Melissa looked at Ava.

She shrugged. "I don't know." She looked at Savina, Colden, and Aaron who stood patiently as if they knew what the sound was.

"Look, do you see her?" Jeremy pointed a finger to the north of the woods, and a tall, elegant woman slowly, almost seductively emerged. Her slicked-back bobbed black hair crowned her round face, and her olive skin glowed against her orange chiffon dress. She crept closer and closer towards them.

The woman captivated all three of the guys, almost as if they were in a trance, but Ava watched her warily. Her full red lips held a sultry grin as she walked up to Jeremy and held his face between her slender hands. Black makeup shadowed her hazel eyes. It seemed as though there was no one else but that woman in Jeremy's eyes. Then, he collapsed.

Ava gasped, and glanced at Savina, Aaron, and Colden, who still stood, watching, not helping. Why weren't they doing anything? Was this a test?

"Jeremy," Gillian screamed, and started to run toward him, but she froze as if someone pressed stop on a movie.

"Gillian?" Melissa shook her but received no response. "What's wrong?"

Ava quickly envisioned the mysterious woman underwater before she did anything to Lance and Thomas. Soon, the woman fell to her knees gasping for air. Ava kept her focus until a blunt force knocked her to the ground. It was as if a train had hit her. But when she opened her eyes, her breath caught in her throat.

Snow covered the ground, the trees, everything. She groaned, and sat up. Where was she? Where were Thomas, Melissa, and everyone else? Her fingers dug into the snow.

"I'm sorry about that," someone said, with a gravelly voice.

Ava looked up and saw a man with short disheveled black hair with bangs that stood up on end. His crystal blue eyes locked onto hers, and his thick eyebrows pulled down toward the center of his smooth face, giving off a serious look. His nose was straight and narrow on his pale square face. He wore a necklace just like hers.

He held out his hand, but she didn't take it. Instead, she scrambled to her feet and backed up against a rock. They were inches from a cliff.

"Are you okay?" he asked. He was tall with broad shoulders and had a relaxed, but confident, stance. For some reason, he intimidated her.

"Who are you?" she asked. "Where are we?"

"I'm Gabriel. And we're in Russia."

Ava refused to let him out of her sight, but the beautiful landscape captivated her. They were surrounded by mountains so tall she couldn't see the tops of them. Below them was an aqua lake. "You teleported us?"

He cleared his throat. "I meant no harm. We're supposed

to be practicing with you all. I'm a part of the coven."

"Why did you do that?"

"You were drowning Natalia. I had to do something." He smirked.

"How did you know what I was doing?"

"You're Ava, right? The Water Enchanter."

She didn't like that he knew. What else did he know about her? "Take me back, now."

He held out his hand. "Okay. Let's go."

She looked at it, then his eyes. Something about him made her trust him. She took his hand, and a second later, she was back in the field.

"Ava," Thomas shouted and grabbed her.

"You shouldn't trust strangers so quickly," Gabriel told her.

"Who are you?" Thomas asked, and then shot a fireball right at him, but he disappeared and reappeared.

Thomas held Ava back behind him, protectively. Gabriel only smiled in a mocking manner. Then, he reached out, and grabbed something.

"You should really work on being stealthier," he said, and Melissa came into view, struggling against his grasp.

Ava tried to imagine him underwater, but someone grabbed her by the shoulders, breaking her concentration.

Just as Thomas turned around, a man, much shorter than him, overtook him and wrestled him to the ground.

"Let me go," Ava shouted and struggled against whoever held her.

Colden clapped his hands once. "Excellent."

"What's going on?" she demanded.

"This is the rest of our Aureole," Savina said, and the person holding Ava released her.

She turned around and saw a brunette man. He looked as if he were Aaron's younger brother or son with the same russet eyes. His twin fought with Thomas, but when she looked at Thomas, there was no one else around.

"I'm Eric," he said.

Thomas got to his feet. "There were two of you."

Eric laughed. "Gets them every time."

Ava backed away and joined Thomas. "What do you want?"

Eric cocked an eyebrow. "It's okay. I can duplicate myself."

"We are all friends here," Aaron said. "We wanted to see what you all could do after a couple of months practice. You'll need more."

Jeremy came out of his trance, as did Gillian. Lance held onto Melissa, just as Thomas did with Ava. She didn't know what to think. One minute she feared for her life, and the next she was supposed to act as if they were friends.

"In the meantime, I would like you to introduce you all," Savina said. "Natalia." She waved her hand to the woman who apparently could sing. Her hazel eyes looked impatient as she crossed her arms in front of her small chest. "Gabriel." The teleporter. "And Eric, Joss, Kira, and Maggie." She introduced them to a group of various aged and ethnic people. Kira and Maggie were Asian, and both had brown eyes. Kira had thick white hair that came to her lower back. Maggie's thick black hair parted off-center and covered her left eye. Her red lipstick stood out from her pale skin. She looked about Savina's age while Kira looked to be in her twenties.

The petite woman with light caramel skin and violet eyes came forward with a bright smile. "It's so nice to finally meet you all. I'm Joss," she said, cheerfully.

Ava wondered if she wore contacts. Her dark hair was pulled back from her small head in a ponytail. Eric stood next to her, and they held hands.

"Good to meet you all," Gabriel said.

Ava peered at him out of the corner of her eye. He was watching her, and then she quickly returned her eyes to Savina.

Thomas clutched her hand, and Ava thought it served as a reminder to Gabriel that he was still there.

"I brought them here to help you," Savina said. "We needed to show you all just how fast and focused you need to be. Ava reacted quickly to Jeremy, but you didn't realize anyone else was out there. When you attack, you need to listen for others. You need to protect each other. If one of you is incapacitated, do not run for them, you must keep your focus until all danger is gone."

"As for our beautiful Siren here, boys, you must ignore the sounds," Aaron said.

Jeremy shook his head. "I had never heard anything like it."

"What was so special about it?" Gillian demanded.

"It is a song that fills men's ears and all they see is her and all they hear is her song," Colden said. "It's an attack method. It allows Natalia to get close enough to touch so she can kill them. When she touches them, it is no longer a beautiful song, but can induce pain by a high-pitched sound so intense you fall unconscious or you die."

"But we never heard anything," Gillian said.

"It only works on men," Natalia said. "If I need to kill a woman, I use my high-pitched sound."

"And Gabriel can stop time for someone, as he did for Gillian, or teleport," Savina said.

"Whoa," Thomas said. "Is that what happened with you? One minute you were here, and the next you vanished.

"Yes," Ava replied.

"Aaron can diminish powers, or enhance them," Savina said. "As he did with you Thomas. Which is why you weren't able to do much with your fire. Kira induces poison with a single touch. Maggie can transform her body into a weapon."

Maggie gave a one-sided grin, and her arms and hands slowly transformed into metal Sai, a metal dagger with three prongs.

Ava shuddered.

"Eric has a duplication ability. And Joss can manipulate or create electricity."

"Now, Thomas could have thrown fire at Savina, but he

was nervous," Aaron said. "In order to ignore outside distractions, clear your mind and do not let anything interrupt your focus. When dealing with someone like Gabriel, you must be quick."

"Ava can drown people, but also can pull the water from within herself and create it."

"What? I can't create it."

"In order to practice this, it helps to be around water. But once you learn, you will be like Thomas. Now, Melissa…"

Ava tuned Savina out. She didn't know how to create water in the palm of her hand. "How do you do it?" she asked Thomas.

"It's simple," he said. "Just think of it."

She hated his arrogance, but was also jealous that he could do this so simply whereas she couldn't.

"I can help," Gabriel said.

"She can handle it herself," Thomas told him.

Though she despised his controlling attitude, she agreed with him. She wasn't sure she wanted Gabriel's help. Especially after he said not to trust strangers.

But she could feel him. He was incredibly calm.

"As we do with every practice," Aaron began. "Since there are so many of us, we pair off into twos. Whomever you are paired with, will be your permanent partner for now. We were hoping to have you all practice more with each other, but that failed."

Ava was embarrassed that they'd disappointed Aaron. He seemed like a person who was not afraid to punish. But instead of fighting, they really needed to focus.

Savina paired everyone, Ava with Gabriel; Jeremy and Maggie; Thomas and Natalia; Melissa and Eric; Lance with Kira; and Joss with Gillian.

Ava didn't dare show any frustration at being paired with Gabriel in front of Aaron. Soon the field rang with the sounds of combat training. Strong winds grew around Jeremy and Maggie. Fire exploded into mid-air from Thomas's hands. An invisible Melissa taunted her opponent. Natalia put

Thomas in a trance. Joss created electric arcs between her hands. Ava had never seen anything like all this. Some laughed as if they were truly having a good time. But Ava wasn't afraid, she was ready, at least she thought so.

A hard and brute force knocked her to the ground, leaving her breathless as she landed hard.

"I wish you'd stop doing that," she said, and got to her feet.

Gabriel raised an eyebrow. "I will once you fight me."

She pictured him in a pool of water, but nothing happened. He waited. She clenched her fists and thought of him drowning in the ocean. But he still made no movement. He only laughed.

She ran toward him and punched him the stomach. He fell to his knees, coughing, not laughing.

"Good hit," he said. "But you should never get so close to the enemy."

"Why?"

"Because they can do this." He snatched her and threw her hard against a tree. It happened so quickly, she didn't comprehend until she was flat on her face and broken branches and leaves fell around her as if it were snowing.

She was a little sore, but felt fine, amazingly.

"You must focus."

"I am."

"There are a lot of things going on with you. I can tell you're scared. Can you feel me?"

She waited only a second until she could. His head was clear of any thoughts, his heart beat rhythmically, and he breathed calmly.

Ava inhaled and exhaled. The ocean displayed in her mind with Gabriel in it. The waves grew, but they refused to crash. Instead, they fell all around him, but not on him.

"Focus," he urged.

"I am," she snapped.

"Don't get frustrated. Come on. Think of the water. How it feels. Smells. Sounds. Think of what you can do with it."

His voice was smooth, steady, and confident.

"I am. It's not working."

"Stop talking. Just listen to the water. You can do this."

She took another deep breath, and imagined how water felt. It was smooth, like silk. It smelled pure, clean, like rain, and could make the slightest of sounds or could be loud and thunderous.

She felt a tickle that ran down her arms, and when she looked, she gasped. Water dripped from her fingertips. She produced the water, and couldn't believe it. "I did it." Water rolled over each curve of her hand and each crevice. It was amazing. "Thank you."

"You're welcome. I knew you could. Now, you just need to learn to do it faster."

The water wrapped around her arms, building, and she shot it toward Gabriel, but he disappeared. He reappeared closer to her.

He had a beautiful smile, she thought, one that spread to his eyes. "Try again." His lean, but muscular, tall body exuded confidence through his patient manner. It seemed like time hadn't changed his face or body. He looked like he was in his early twenties, and perhaps he was. His blue eyes captivated hers with intensity.

Ava self-consciously cleared her throat. "Okay," she said, but he stared deep into her eyes. She dropped her gaze and felt slightly guilty for thinking how attractive he was.

Ava tried to discharge water, but narrowly missed him again.

His eyes held hers again. "Sweet dreams," he said.

Less than a second later, he stood behind her, with his hand lightly grasped around her neck. Breathing steadily, she froze. She hadn't even seen him move.

"If you were my enemy, you'd be dead right now," he whispered in her ear, causing her to quiver. She stared straight ahead and waited for him to release her. "But don't worry. I'm not going to kill you." He removed his hand and then stood in front of her.

What else could she do? Summoning water was hard, so she attempted to drown him again. The water was still, as she thought of cooling it. Ice crept over the water, hardening it.

Gabriel's teeth chattered and he seemed motionless. His eyes closed, and he fell to his knees. Then she released the hold over him.

He let out a breath. "Good. That's exactly what you need to do. If the drowning doesn't work, try other tactics."

Could her mother freeze water with her mind like that and actually kill someone? She wondered if she would eventually be able to transform her entire body into water. It all sounded so surreal. She wondered why they hadn't trained before with the other coven.

Gabriel stood. "Come on, let's work on being faster."

After training for several hours, Ava came home, and took a hot shower. Her body was sore, and the heat worked out the kinks. Training with Gabriel had helped her confidence. It gave her something to focus on and kept her mind off things. Nights were dreadful now since all she thought about was Peter. But she tried so hard to avoid it. She wondered what it would be like to have Gabriel's powers, and go anywhere she wanted, whenever. Like tonight, when he took her to Russia. She'd never been there, but it was beautiful, serene, and far away from here. If she had his power, she would be able to escape this and be free.

CHAPTER TWENTY-FIVE
THE FIRST KILL

Ava paced her room. She dressed in a simple black dress that came just above her knees for her stupid date with Thomas. She felt like kicking herself for agreeing to go out to dinner. He promised to be a better person. And that they could be who they once were. But she didn't want that. Ava had only agreed so that Thomas would stop begging. Besides, maybe it would throw the rest of them off from what she, Melissa, and Jeremy were up to later.

Tonight, they were going to spy on Xavier and his groupies. It hadn't exactly gone well when she and Jeremy brought up the idea to rest of the coven, but Melissa eventually agreed to the plan. The others were dismayed and so they decided to carry out the plan in secret.

Ava paused from her pacing and sank onto the edge of her bed. Was she actually ready to do this? Was it really a smart idea? She just needed to know who Xavier really was and what his game plan was.

Her phone vibrated next to her. Melissa texted asking if she was okay. She replied that she was, and then realized she needed to have a better grip on her feelings or the others would find out.

Ava walked downstairs and joined her dad in the kitchen. He was rinsing off the dishes and putting them in the dishwasher.

"Well, you sure look pretty," he said. "Where are you going?"

"Out with Thomas," she mumbled, and leaned against the doorframe.

He rolled his eyes. "Why?"

"I don't know. He wouldn't stop begging."

"Heard from Peter at all?"

"Dad, don't."

He shut off the water and closed the dishwasher. "You know you deserve better, Ava."

"It's just dinner."

The doorbell rang, and Ava took a deep breath. Time to put on a happy face. She smiled, but it felt all wrong, and then opened the door.

Thomas wore a baby blue button down and left it untucked from his jeans. Ava hated the style. It looked so sloppy.

He cocked an eyebrow. "Are you going to a funeral?"

"I'm not going if you're going to be a jerk."

"It was a joke, Ava. Chill out."

"Whatever." She walked out into the cold December night, and closed the door behind her. The sky was clear and the full moon cast its brightness over them. There was not a single sound. All was still, as if the night knew what the coming hours would bring. A strange excitement bubbled in Ava's stomach. "Can we hurry?"

Thomas stopped before reaching the driver's side door. "Why?"

"Because I don't want to be out all night."

They climbed into the Jeep and shut their doors.

"What's wrong with you? Why are you so nervous? You've been that way all day."

"Nothing. I'm fine."

"Melissa and Jeremy have, too. Is it related?"

"No."

"Don't lie to me. What are you guys doing?"

"Nothing."

"Why won't you ever tell me anything?"

"Because you'll just laugh."

He groaned. "Is this about that stupid Xavier crap?"

"No. It's nothing. So don't worry about it."

Even though he was angry, he let it go. Dinner was quiet and Ava couldn't wait until it was over. She didn't even know why she agreed to go in the first place. Did she really believe Thomas could be better?

Afterward, he drove them to the cabin, but he was sadly mistaken if he thought she was going into their room alone with him. Though, the closer they got to the cabin, the more Ava's dinner didn't sit well. All they were going to do was spy on Xavier. There was nothing to be afraid of.

They arrived and got out of the Jeep. Everyone was sitting outside, and Melissa met Ava by the car.

She lit a cigarette. "What is with you? Are you getting sick?" She kept her voice low and they walked away from the Jeep.

"No," Ava said.

"You're not getting cold feet are you? I thought you were ready?"

"Sorry. I've just never spied on anyone before."

"This was your idea."

"I know."

"What are you two whispering about?" Gillian asked. She chewed her gum so vigorously and constantly popped bubbles. Ava just wanted to rip it from her mouth the next time she blew a bubble.

"Nothing."

"You two are on edge. And so are you, Jeremy."

"They've been like that all day," Thomas said. "Ava won't tell me what's going on."

"Nothing," Jeremy mumbled.

"You're such a liar," Gillian snapped. "What are you up

to?"

"Why are you always biting our heads off?" Ava asked. "You're so different now."

Gillian shrugged, and wrapped a small ringlet of hair around her finger. "Deal with it."

"We're spying on Xavier tonight," Jeremy said.

Ava and Melissa exchanged looks. Why did he say that?

A chorus of shocked questions ensued from Gillian, Thomas, and Lance.

"Look," Ava shouted. "Xavier is planning something. I don't know what, but we have to find out."

Gillian groaned, and wrapped a small ringlet of hair around her finger. "Enough already."

"He's already attacked three of us," Ava said. "Why don't you believe me?"

"Because you are so paranoid that you've got psychotic notions in your brain," Gillian said.

"I thought we'd been through this already," Thomas said. "Xavier's not an Enchanter. We need to be looking for spies. Not some punk at school."

"Looking for spies? Thomas there hasn't been a single one. How else does Xavier know what we are?"

"Wait, he knows we're Enchanters?" Gillian stopped playing with her hair and glared at Ava. "Did you tell him?"

"Yeah, Gillian, I did. What do you think?"

Just stop, okay?" Thomas told her. "I don't know why you get so worked up over this. I'm sorry he knocked you out."

"Look, we've already got it planned out," Melissa said. "It's not that big of a deal. Besides, if you all think he's an Ephemeral, then there's no harm."

Gillian scoffed. "Except wasting our time with this when we should be preparing for when a spy does come. Are you just as deluded as Ava?"

"Just everyone stop," Jeremy yelled. "We'll be careful."

Gillian rolled her eyes. "This is so stupid."

"Nah, let them spy on this stupid Ephemeral," Thomas said. "They'll find out they were wrong."

Ava felt as if someone was watching them argue. She couldn't shake the feeling, but saw and heard nothing. She wondered if Xavier had found them, but he would have used his ability. She had to check this out. "I'll be back." She started for the woods.

"Where are you going?" Thomas asked, and followed her.

"Can you not feel that?"

"Feel what?"

"There's something out there. I can feel it watching us."

She stopped and listened. Dead silence.

Fire engulfed Thomas's hand, as if he lit a match, and he held it up so they could see.

"I don't feel it anymore. The light must have scared it."

"I didn't feel it." He shrugged.

She sighed and turned toward the cabin.

He doused the fire. "Are you sure you're okay?"

"I'm fine. Just wish you would believe me."

"Hey, hey," he said, and wrapped his muscular arms around her. "We're all a little scared. It's normal to feel a little paranoid. Everything's going to be okay. I promise."

"Please stop saying that."

"But it will be."

"You don't know that."

"Look." He lifted her chin with his thick hand. "Everything *will* be okay. I will not let anything happen to you or any of us." He leaned down and kissed her. She tried pulling away, but his hand gripped the back of her neck, forcing her to stay in place. His lips were warm as they slowly moved against hers. She wanted to be kissing Peter. "Come on."

With a hopeless sigh, she grudgingly took a step.

There was a snap behind her, as if someone had stepped on a twig. Thomas must have heard it as well because he froze with her. She met his eyes and heard it again. Her breath caught in her throat and she turned her head in its direction.

"Who's out there?" Thomas asked.

Like they would answer, she thought. Her eyes tried searching the darkness for any movement. Even the bright moon wasn't bright enough. Thomas lit a flame and she saw a silhouette of a person against a tree. She took a step forward, but Thomas caught her.

"Hello," she said.

The person moved forward slowly. They seemed to be having a difficult time and Ava saw a red liquid plastered to them.

"Ava," the stranger said.

She knew that voice. "Dad!" She rushed toward him and caught him as he collapsed. "What are you doing out here? What happened?"

"Ava, help me." He was bleeding from his stomach and she cradled his head in her lap.

Thomas moved to the other side.

"Dad," she wept. "What happened?"

"What's going on?" Melissa asked and she and the others came up behind them. "Mr. Hannigan?"

"We have to take him to Savina's," Ava said. Tears rushed down her cheeks. Her stomach clenched and everything around her spun. She clasped her father's hand. "Dad, can you walk?"

"Omigod." Gillian gasped.

"Lance, let's get Savina," Jeremy said. "We'll be right back Ava."

"Hurry," Melissa told them and knelt down beside Ava. "Mr. Hannigan, what happened?"

"Th-they got me."

"Who?" she asked.

"Get away from him," someone shouted somewhere from the woods.

Ava gripped her father tighter, and then looked up and saw Gabriel running towards them. Once he reached her, he grabbed her roughly by the shoulder and pulled her away.

"What are you doing?" she cried.

Melissa came up behind Gabriel, but he stopped her.

"I'm not here to hurt anyone," he said. "Thomas, kill him."

Ava fought against his iron grip. "What?" she screamed. "That's my father."

"Now, Thomas," Gabriel demanded.

"No!" She lunged forward but Gabriel's arms held her back.

With a flick of Thomas's hands, fire appeared. Ava's father looked at her with such fear in his eyes. The flames quickly latched onto him.

"Dad!"

Gabriel twisted her around to face him. "Listen to me," he demanded. The fire reflected in his blue eyes. "That isn't your dad. His name is Barkley Towers. He morphed into your father."

But the shrill screams that cried out into the night sounded just like her father's voice. Ava smelled a metallic scent mixed with a sulfurous smell so sharp and heavy it burned inside her lungs.

Ava struggled with him, but it was useless. The smell was enough to make her hurl, but she kept it down. She closed her eyes from the dizziness.

"Do you hear me?" Gabriel asked.

She nodded, and tried to look back at the body but he wouldn't let her.

"It isn't your dad," he kept repeating, but her father's cries reverberated inside her head.

Someone took her hand and pressed her head against his chest. She assumed it was Thomas, but everything was in a daze. Her body shook violently and all she saw was an orange glow.

"We killed the other one," someone said.

Ava looked up and saw Eric and Joss jogging toward them with Jeremy and Lance.

"Good," Gabriel said.

"What just happened?" Melissa asked.

"We felt someone around the area tonight," Eric said.

"We left the Manor to try and track them. Joss injured Barkley, who morphed into your dad, Ava. He knew where you all were so he thought that maybe you'd help him. Luckily, Gabriel got here just in time."

Ava finally calmed her breathing, and backed away from Thomas. The flames had burned out and all that was left was a scarred tree and a pile of ashes.

"So does that mean he's been spying on us for a while?" Melissa asked.

"Unfortunately," Joss replied. "I'm so sorry, Ava."

"I need to go home," she said. She wanted to see her father in the flesh, though she wasn't sure she'd ever be able to erase the image of him begging for her help and then burning alive.

Thomas took her hand. "I'll take you."

Ava sat with blood on her dress. Blood that she had to continue reminding herself belonged to Barkley Towers and not her father.

As soon as Thomas pulled into her driveway, she opened the door and got out. He met her on the other side.

"You can go home," she said.

He grabbed her arm. "I don't think we should split up now."

She jerked away from him. "I have to see my father."

"Ava, don't be angry with me."

"It was so easy for you to kill him, wasn't it?"

Thomas's eyebrows knitted together. "What are you talking about?"

"Without question, you just killed him."

"He wasn't your dad, though."

"You didn't know that," Ava screamed.

"I just thought-I mean, I'm pretty sure Gabriel wouldn't have told me that-."

"I have to go." She turned away from them and headed toward front door.

Feeling Thomas's eyes on her, she fumbled to get the keys out of her purse. Her hands shook as she turned the key and unlocked the door.

"Dad," she cried. "Dad!"

He came down the hallway, his face twisted confusion. "What's the matter, Ava?"

A sigh of relief left her lips, and she wrapped her arms around him.

CHAPTER TWENTY-SIX
RELIEF

It was hot. She pushed the covers aside, but it didn't help. Ava slowly opened her eyes and felt the warmth of the sun. Her clothes reeked of smoke and something else that she wanted to forget.

She groaned, and felt sick thinking about last night.

Seeing her father bleeding and in desperate need of help worried her enough. But hearing his pained cries as Thomas burned him alive would always haunt her.

Except, it wasn't her father. Some Enchanter had morphed into him. Ava was angry with Thomas for killing the man without question, but furious with herself for being so easily tricked. What were the spies trying to accomplish? It didn't matter at this point. She would be ready next time.

Ava wanted to get out of the clothes she was sweltering in, and take a shower. She got out of bed, started the water in the shower, and waited on the edge of the tub for the water to warm. They were killers now, but what was to stop Devon from sending more spies? Would they be killing incessantly? Why couldn't they just find Devon and kill him? Then end it all.

Once the steam rose from the hot water, she switched the shower on, and cleansed herself. The water immediately calmed and energized her. It was an incredible difference.

Ava stepped out of the shower and dried off. Once dressed in a wool jade sweater and jeans, she went downstairs.

"Good afternoon," her father said.

"Hey."

She was still in somewhat of a shock to see her father sitting next to her. The man last night looked and sounded just like him. How could she have ever known the truth if Gabriel hadn't shown up? Ava watched her father's eyes narrow as he read the paper. The way he stirred his coffee absent-mindedly and then brought it up to his lips to sip it slowly. Or the way he pursed his lips when he read something disagreeable.

"What is it?"

"He looked just like you, Dad. Your eyes. Your voice. Everything." Her eyes blurred from tears.

He lowered the paper. "He wasn't me."

"I know that now."

"How about we come up with a secret code?"

She couldn't help but laugh. "Really?"

"Why not?"

"Like what?"

"Dakota Seth."

It was her mother and father's middle names. She nodded. "Had anything like that ever happened to you?"

"No." He took her hand. "But you must prepare yourself for such things."

"How? How am I supposed to know it's not you?"

"Ask questions. But detailed questions that only you and that person know."

She buried her head in her hands. "This is ridiculous."

"Don't be like that. We will get through this, Ava."

"I'm just going to be wary of everyone now."

"It's not a bad idea."

The break had ended, but Ava didn't know if she was glad to be back at school. She hoped it would help keep her mind off Barkley Towers and the haunting image of her father supposedly dying. She hadn't gotten a good night's sleep in what felt like ages.

They'd gone back to Blackhart Manor after Barkley's death and trained some more with the Elders and the other Aureole. But it didn't do anything to stifle Ava's fear of spies. They could be anyone and anywhere. Gabriel had told her to remain calm and since she was able to feel Barkley's presence, that maybe she had the talent for being able to tell when Enchanters were near. It still didn't put her mind at ease, but maybe being at school would keep them safe.

Melissa, Jeremy, and Ava all agreed that spying on Xavier and his gang was probably one of the dumbest ideas. They realized the others were right about him. He might have manipulated and bullied people, but he never did anything like Barkley.

Ava took a seat in the chemistry lab at a table for two. She hoped she'd get a decent partner for the class. She looked toward the door and her heart raced as Peter strode inside the room. Their eyes met and he seemed to slow down as he neared. She opened her mouth to greet him, but he just walked past her without saying anything.

Ava bit her lip and turned her attention to the window. She was foolish to think he still wanted to talk to her. It was ridiculous that she even still thought about him.

But she did. Every day. And would fantasize about being with him.

She felt a presence and stiffened. It felt just like the night Barkley showed up. Ava turned her head toward the door, and Xavier Holstone took a seat next to her. She looked straight ahead. Why had she felt that odd sensation around Xavier?

"Good afternoon," he said. "You don't look so well. Are you okay?"

"Why are you sitting here?"

He cocked an eyebrow. "All of the other seats are taken."

"We are not going to be partners."

"Just give it a chance. I've decided to forgive you for almost choking me."

"You deserved it."

"Look, I'd like to put the past behind us and be friends. Besides, I think you and I have more in common than you think." He smiled.

"That'll never happen."

He shrugged smugly. "You never know."

This could not be happening. She had to change this. She was not going to spend an entire semester sitting next to him.

The bell rang, prompting the teacher to stand at the front of the class. He called roll and then mentioned that the person sitting next to them was their permanent partner for the semester. He didn't like to switch around things because it took up too much time.

Xavier leaned over. "Looks like we're stuck together."

The teacher handed out some random worksheets to do in class, of course with their partners.

"So, how was your winter break?" Xavier asked. "You look like you didn't sleep at all last night."

Why was he making small talk? Or even pretending that they were friends?

"Why don't you just do the assignment and shut up?"

"I'm really sorry for the miscommunication we seem to have had before."

"Miscommunication? Are you kidding me? You knocked me out."

"I apologized for that."

"Well it doesn't make it all better."

He leaned closer. "I thought you liked jerks."

"What?"

"That's why you're still with Thomas, isn't it?"

"I don't see how it's any of your business."

"Because I like you. I think you and I would be perfect

together."

"Don't make me sick."

He chuckled. "Think about it."

"Don't you have a girlfriend?"

"I like to keep my options open. As do you."

"What are you talking about?"

"I'm surprised Peter isn't sitting with you. Weren't you two secret lovers?"

"Leave me alone."

"Ah, it's a sore subject I take it. Well maybe I can help. He's looking a little lonely, too. Maybe my friends and I could cheer him up."

Ava clenched her teeth, but then took a breath. She had to play this cool. "I don't care."

Xavier scooted his chair closer and draped his arm across the back of her chair. "Must have been a bad breakup. Did he find out that you're a freak?"

Ava snapped her head in his direction. "What is your problem?"

He shrugged. "Your necklace tends to bring that out in people. Why *do* you wear it? I wonder."

Why did Xavier always talk about her necklace? It raised her suspicions again, but how could she possibly convince the others to spy on him?

When class ended, Xavier didn't say a word and left. Ava relaxed the second he was gone. She had to talk to the teacher about switching partners. She gathered her books together, stood up, and bumped into someone in the aisle. She looked up and met Peter's eyes.

"I'm sorry that I didn't sit with you," he said. "I didn't know Xavier was in this class."

It wasn't his fault, but she had to pretend that she didn't like Peter. "Whatever. Why don't you watch where you're going," she spat.

He furrowed his eyebrows and then left.

"So what?" Melissa said, after Ava explained what

happened in chemistry. They were hanging out at the cabin. "He'll stay out of harm's way now. What did the instructor say about switching partners?"

"He won't let me."

"Maybe you can get some information out of Xavier. You play the interrogator. See what he'll tell you."

"How do I even do that?"

"You might have to loosen up to him, and maybe start flirting with him," Melissa said slowly.

"Absolutely not."

"Oh come on, Ava. How else are we going to know for sure? Just take your time with it. It doesn't have to be tomorrow or anything."

"I don't know. Maybe we should just focus on training and school."

"Yeah, we should. But in the meantime, find out what he's up to."

"But he hasn't done anything except make new friends."

"That doesn't mean he's not on the prowl. He mentioned cheering up Peter."

"Why would you say that?" Ava asked. Melissa didn't even want Ava to be with Peter.

"Because I know you still think about him and you still care. You can still protect him from afar."

Ava hoped she was right. "Okay. Maybe I'll try in a few weeks."

"Good. I can't wait to hear what you've found out."

CHAPTER TWENTY-SEVEN
BURNED

Ava sat on the edge of the bed, wishing that she could just slide back under the covers and fall back asleep, but she'd already missed an entire week. She had several missed calls and texts from her friends and Thomas. Even Thomas had come by a couple of times during the week, but Ava didn't want to be around him. It didn't stop him from staying and watching TV with her dad though.

Once she dressed, Ava walked out into the cool March morning. It was overcast, but the storms were supposed to pass right over them. A heavy storm wind blew as she slid behind the wheel of her car. She took a deep breath, and then started the engine. Ava hated this time of year.

It had been ten years since that horrible day, but it never got easier.

The last couple of months were drab, and strangely calm. If Xavier really was an Enchanter working for Devon Maunsell, they sure were taking their time. Ava hadn't tried being nice to Xavier because he made it impossible, or maybe the thought of being nice to him repulsed her. The annoying banter with him went on daily about being his girlfriend or joining his group or trying to get Peter to join. It was nothing but empty threats. She did notice he had a tattoo on his arm of the numbers 042713. Everyone in his gang had the tattoo. It was strange. Xavier wrote it on everything, carving it into the lab table several times. She didn't know what it was.

There weren't any incidences with spies, but they still trained and practiced at Blackhart Manor, though Ava was beginning to think it was a waste of time. Even Xavier's gang seemed to have calmed down and the bullying and torments were losing their steam. Things were looking up.

And while she and Peter were still not talking to each other, they glanced at each other. He seemed to be fine, and she still thought about him daily. Especially since she and Thomas were sort of together and arguing as usual.

Ava walked into the chemistry lab room and sat at her usual table next to Xavier. Maybe today, she could suck it up and finally try to be nice to him and get some information out of him. Although, now it seemed like a lost cause since nothing had happened. Maybe he was just a lonely new kid. But it still didn't explain how Ava, Thomas, and Jeremy had mysteriously fainted.

"Welcome back," Xavier said. "Were you sick?"

"Sure," Ava mumbled.

"Glad you're back." He slid a postcard across the table to her.

"What's this?"

"An invitation. My friends and I are throwing an end of the year bash."

"Why are you inviting me?"

He sighed. "Must we dance around this obvious attraction every day? Besides, everyone will be there."

"I'm not everyone."

"Peter will be there. And so will your friends."

"You spoke to my friends?"

"Not yet. Everyone's invited."

She studied his face, trying to figure out what was up with him. "Why are you being nice? After being so cruel to everyone. It's like you've done a complete 360."

"I want to make it up to everyone. I know it was wrong of me to make them my friends and to bully the others."

"Then why did you do it?"

"I'm sure you can understand wanting to fit in. Besides, at my last school I wasn't anyone's favorite person. I was the outcast. So I came here wanting to start anew."

"So torturing people was your way of changing that?"

He smiled. "I learned my lesson. Which is why I've been a good boy this semester."

"How did you get all of them to be your friends? What happened? Why were they gone so long?"

"You ask so many questions."

"So do you."

"Fair enough. Let's just say I'm a very persuasive person."

"And they've forgiven you? I mean they are completely different people now."

"They didn't like who they were before. I look to find people who seem to be struggling."

"None of them were having issues."

"That you know of." He leaned closer. "And I know you have deep issues. So does Peter."

Her skin crawled at his closeness. "Is that why you're being so nice to me?"

"That and I like you. But I know you still have feelings for Peter."

"No I don't."

"Don't worry. Your secret's safe with me."

Ava couldn't believe how candid he was, if he was really telling the truth about everything. It still didn't make sense. And how could he tell she still liked Peter? Or that she had issues.

She flipped over the card and it read *End of the Year Party! It'll be explosive! 04/27/13*. Well, that explained the tattoo. How could someone be so excited over a party that they tattoo the date onto their skin?

When she got home, her phone rang. She pulled it out of her pocket and saw that it was Melissa.

"Hey," she answered.

"So what's the deal with Xavier's party?"

"I don't know. He's inviting everyone."

"Why is he suddenly being so nice? What's really going to happen at this party?"

"It does seem strange that they would have tattoos of the date."

"We need to find out more. He likes you, so he'll tell you anything."

Ava sighed. "Mel, his answers are vague and he gives me the creeps. We have one more month until school ends and I'm trying so hard not to make it even more miserable. I'm done. He's not a threat."

"Don't you think it's strange that everything just stopped? Xavier's bullying and the spying?"

"You don't know if anyone is watching us. But I've not felt anyone since Barkley." And Xavier in class, but she was getting used to him.

The doorbell rang, startling Ava. She opened the door, and inhaled a sharp breath. "I gotta go," she told Melissa and hung up the phone.

Staring back at her, with relief in his brown eyes, was Peter. She'd missed his eyes, his unkempt hair, and the dimples in his cheeks.

"Peter?"

"Hi," he sheepishly grinned.

She crossed her arms in front of her. "Why are you here?"

"I had to make sure you were okay. You weren't at school all last week. I was worried about you."

"Worried?"

"I thought Xavier had taken you. Given how chummy you two seem to be lately."

The thought hadn't crossed her mind that Peter would worry about her joining Xavier. She didn't even think Peter still cared or thought about her.

She closed the door behind her, and leaned against the porch railing. "No. He didn't take me. I didn't feel like being

213

at school last week."

"Oh. Crap. It was the anniversary, wasn't it?"

She nodded. "Yes. Is that really the reason you're here?"

The look in his eyes grew tense. "I also wanted to talk to your dad," he said with a serious tone.

"Why?"

"Ava, you've been skipping a lot of school lately and when you do come, you look like…well, you don't look so well. I'm worried about you."

"We haven't spoken in three months. Why should you suddenly start caring?"

"I never stopped."

"Well, you shouldn't. I'm fine." She hadn't expected him to be at her house ever again. But seeing him made all the emotions wash over her. Ignoring him and secretly glancing at him in school was easier than this.

"I don't believe you. I thought I could leave it alone, and I've tried for so long, but I can't stand seeing you like this. No matter what, you don't deserve this." He stepped closer, until he was right in front of her.

Her heart faltered. "What are you talking about?"

"Thomas. I think he's controlling you. Did he make you get back together with him?"

"No."

"Why do you stay with him, Ava? I see how you are around him, and I know you're miserable. I know it's hard to talk about, but please, you know I'm still here for you."

Be strong. "Thanks."

An awkward silence fell between them.

"I've missed you," he said.

She spoke without thinking. "I miss you too."

His gaze was deep, and she couldn't look away. She gripped the wooden railing for support, while he stood dangerously close. He slowly raised his hand, and softly touched her cheek. Her pulse edged up a degree, and her insides twisted. No one had ever made her feel this way. It had been so long, but her feelings for him were still very much there.

"I can't resist this temptation," he said, and leaned closer. "I want to be with you." His sweet breath made her jaw clench. She wanted to taste his lips, and feel his arms around her.

Her lips parted. She inhaled two short breaths and froze. No, no, no. She couldn't do this. "Peter."

He removed his hand, and stepped back.

She exhaled. Her heart throbbed against her chest. A surge of anger punched her, and her amulet warmed. She turned to stone. Thomas. Her phone rang, and she silenced it. Maybe she could make up an excuse by the time she got to the cabin. This wasn't going to be easy.

"What is it?" Peter asked.

"Why did you do that?" It was easier being angry with him because then it masked what she really felt.

"I didn't do anything."

"You almost kissed me. Why?"

"I wanted to."

"I have a boyfriend," she shouted and then pushed him.

"What am I supposed to do when I think about you all the time? This isn't some cute high school crush. At least, it doesn't feel that way to me."

"I'm sorry that I seemed to have led you on."

He stepped closer. "I know you still feel the same way about me as I do you."

"You're wrong."

"Why do you let him control you? You're better than that."

She shoved him again and he stumbled off the porch. "Get out of here."

"Has he threatened you? I've read cases about that. Girl can't leave boy because he threatens her—."

"Give it a rest," she snapped. "He's not abusing me."

"They warned me about you being blind to the fact."

Ava stood at the top of the stairs with her arms crossed. "They?"

He hesitated. "I spoke to someone. Anonymously. Look, it's okay that you're afraid. You just have to get away from him."

"Peter, you don't know what you're talking about, okay? I told you we can't be friends, so leave me alone."

"You've changed, you know that? You don't laugh anymore. You're always on edge, like you're expecting something to happen."

"Don't make me force you to leave," she said. She tightened her fists, constricting the blood. They throbbed from the pressure.

Peter glared at her. The staring match and silence made her impatient. She couldn't afford to be nice. She needed him to be safe from Thomas.

"Fine. But when Thomas puts you in the hospital, don't come crying to me."

That stung. "Just go."

With defeat in his eyes, he sighed, and then walked to his car. Ava stormed inside, slammed the door, and pressed her back against it. She took several breaths, trying to calm down. Her hands were shaking.

Ava couldn't believe what had just happened. She wished she could've let Peter kiss her, like any normal, sane girl would have. She'd missed him so much, and the ache of not being with him returned.

Hours later, Ava apprehensively arrived at the cabin. She'd done nothing wrong. They couldn't possibly have felt her, but she knew that was a lie. She hadn't exactly mastered hiding her feelings from the necklace.

Just as she entered, Thomas seized her arms, and slammed her against the wall. "I know you were with him."

"What are you talking about?"

His blue eyes glowered. "Don't lie to me."

"You're overreacting again. I was at home with Dad."

His hands squeezed harder and began to warm her skin. "I can feel you, Ava. Stop lying. I know he was there."

She inhaled. His hands, like hot irons, burned through her

sweater, and pressed into her skin. The stinging, scorching pain injected through her.

"Thomas," she cried. "Stop. It-it burns."

"Hey," she heard Melissa yell. Seconds later, she tried prying his hands from Ava. "Stop, Thomas," she demanded. "You're hurting her."

With a quick movement, he pushed Melissa away, forcing her to fall. "You will *never* see him again," he insisted.

The shock of the pain paralyzed her, and she could not focus enough to think of water. She blinked but all she saw was blinding flashes of white.

"Thomas!" Lance knocked him back, and crashed onto the floor.

Ava collapsed to her knees. The pain was so intense and it was hard to hear everything that was said. Melissa moved closer to her, and checked her arms.

"You've got to stay under control," Lance demanded.

"What am I supposed to do when she is with him?"

"Ava, is it true?" Lance asked, annoyed.

"He came over," she choked. Even though his hands were free of her arms, the burning throbbed. "He just wanted to know how I was doing. And then he left," she panted.

"See? Nothing happened. Jesus, Thomas, get a grip."

Melissa examined Ava's arms. "You burned her bad." The green sleeves of her sweater were tattered, revealing a dark red color where his hands had been. Blood oozed in small amounts.

Jeremy kneeled down. "Are you okay?"

"I think you need to get this taken care of," Melissa said.

"I-I'll go to Savina's."

"No," Thomas said, and got to his feet. "Oh god, Ava, I never meant to hurt you, I swear." A string of obscenities flew from his mouth in anger.

She looked at him, disgusted. Jeremy and Melissa helped her to her feet. "I'm going."

"No, please. How could I have done this?" He stepped closer to her, but Lance held him back. "Let me help."

"Stay away from me," she demanded.

"You're not going to follow her," Lance said. "You're staying here."

"She'll go to him."

"Right now, even as much as you are my brother, I'd rather she go to him. You cannot be like this with her. Ever. If she does not love you, you can't force her."

"But I love her."

"If you really did, you would never treat her like that."

Ava turned and Melissa helped her outside.

Melissa frowned. "This is bad. I'm sorry he did this to you."

She shook her head. "I'll be fine. Savina will heal me."

"I'll take you."

"No. I'll go alone."

"You're not going to Peter's are you?"

"I don't know." But all she wanted to do was see him. "I'm through pretending."

"You know I want you to be happy, but there's no way you can tell Peter any of this. You know as well as I do it isn't safe. And you know what will happen if you tell him."

"He doesn't know anything. I promise. I would not compromise us like that."

"Have you two been seeing each other this whole time?"

"No. Today was the first time we spoke in months. I don't know why he came to talk to me after so long. But I have to at least somehow explain it to him."

"It's too dangerous."

"Thomas is too dangerous," she cried. "I'm through with him. It's like he is just taking his power for granted and using it to the extreme."

"We'll figure something out."

"Please, Melissa. I just need to see Peter. Just long enough to tell him how I feel and then I'll leave him alone for good."

"What's wrong with leaving it alone?"

"I have to tell him something."

"What could you possibly say? If you feel so strongly

about him now, how do you think it's going to be when you leave him again? I don't want you to get hurt."

"Peter's never hurt me."

Melissa sighed, and opened Ava's car door. "I cannot believe I'm letting you do this. Just don't tell him a thing. And what will you tell Savina?"

"I'll figure it out."

"We'll keep Thomas here. Get that taken care of." She nodded to her aching arms.

"Thank you."

"If you say anything to him, you won't be thanking me."

CHAPTER TWENTY-EIGHT
RULED BY SECRECY

As Ava drove, she contemplated whether she should actually go to Peter's or not. But the thought of seeing him was like hearing the beep of an alarm clock in a dream—one that constantly sounded and didn't end. She wanted to give into her feelings, finally. She also wanted to test her theory—that if she was in pain, Peter could somehow take it away. She wouldn't know how to explain any of this to Savina anyway. Giving in

Pulling up to the curb outside Peter's house, she cut the engine, and waited for a moment. What could she possibly say to him? Would he even talk to her after today?

She opened the door and fumbled out of the car, trying to ignore the throbbing pain. As she carefully placed her jacket over her arms, the uneasy feeling of someone watching her returned, and then she froze. Had someone followed her or had they followed Peter? She looked around the quiet well-lit neighborhood.

A few porch lights were on a few houses down. There wasn't a single movement or sound. She put her hand on her car door handle. She needed to get out of there, but then a light behind her flicked on. The door opened and she turned around.

Mr. McNabb carried a bag of trash. "Ava? Is that you?"

"Hi," she said. "I know it's late."

"Are you okay?" She guessed that she must not have looked very well, given his reaction. He lifted the lid off the plastic trash bin at the curb and shoved the bag inside.

She nodded. "Is-is Peter—."

"Come on in, he's upstairs in his room." He invited her in with his hand and they walked up the sidewalk together. Just before she entered, she no longer felt the mysterious presence.

"Thank you." Ava forced a smile, and then walked passed him and up the stairs.

She appeared in the doorway of Peter's room. He wasn't there, but the shower sounded across the way. The nightstand lamp filled the spacious room with a soft yellow light. She crossed his room and peered out the window to see if she could see anything, hoping she hadn't led anyone to his house, but nothing stirred.

Easing herself on his unmade bed, she lay down and cuddled with one of his pillows in an attempt to ignore the agonizing burn. She closed her eyes.

"What are you doing here?" She jumped at his sharp tone, and sat up.

Peter hesitated in the doorway. His wet hair stuck out in different directions. She noticed how sexy he looked in just his gray jogging pants and tried not to stare at his smooth bare chest. Her heart thrummed against her ribcage.

She met his warm brown eyes and his jaw relaxed. "I came to talk about today. And the past few months."

"What's the point? I think you made it perfectly clear earlier that you feel nothing for me."

"I came to tell you the truth. This isn't some crush for me either."

He crossed his arms in front of his chest. "Why should I care now? Did you finally realize I was right about Thomas?"

"Peter, there's been so much going on with me and I can't

tell anyone about it. It hasn't been easy. So much has changed and I'm not the same person I once was." The words spewed from her lips as tears welled in her eyes. She didn't realize so much emotion had bottled up inside her. "I don't mean to play games with you. I just don't know what to do."

His eyes softened, and he sat down next to her. "I've noticed you changing, but I'm not talking about the front you've been putting up for me. You seem stronger and more aggressive actually. What's going on?"

"I can't tell you."

"You can tell me anything, Ava," he said.

She shook her head. "It's not that I don't want to, I just can't."

"Why?"

"I'm afraid of you…" Getting killed. "Look, if I tell you anything, they'll hurt you." She euphemized it for him.

"Who? Your friends?"

"No."

"Who?"

"I can't say."

"Okay."

She looked away and they sat in silence for a few minutes.

"I don't understand why we can't even be friends. I'm so frustrated by it all. It's been so hard for me these past few months without you. I know that sounds ridiculous."

"It doesn't. I've wanted to be with you," she whispered. "But we can never be together."

"Why? What is this hold that Thomas has over you? There has to be a way around this."

The conversation with her dad flashed in her mind. No, no, no, she argued with herself. Peter needed to stay out of this. "There isn't."

"Does your dad know how Thomas treats you?"

"Yes."

"And he's okay with this?"

"No. Dad doesn't like Thomas."

"He doesn't own you. I mean, if it comes down to it, we

can call the police on him. Or talk to his parents. Or—."

"No." She looked up into his worried eyes. "We're not together anymore, but it's complicated. I'm bound to them. There are things that we've done, and things we have to do, but I can't tell you what they are."

"What are you talking about? Bound to them? What does that even mean?"

"I can only tell you that there would be dangerous consequences if you and I were together. I can't promise your safety. I couldn't bear to see you get hurt."

"Is he forcing you to stay with him? Would he come after me again?"

She honestly didn't know if he would, but she wouldn't put it past him. "I wish I could tell you my situation," she said, and her eyes welled up again.

"What kind of danger are you in?"

Feeling him so close made her want to forget all her inhibitions and kiss him. She hadn't even felt the throbbing in her arms. Rebellious tears streaked down her face.

"Ava, what is it?" He swept her hair away from her face, which sent a shiver up her spine. She made herself stop crying before the necklace would glow.

"I knew this would be hard. This isn't fair to either of us, but I just had to come."

"I can't imagine what kind of situation you're in. I'll do whatever it takes to keep you safe from him. I just want to be with you. I can't explain it."

"I know. But please realize that Thomas isn't the one you have to worry about. I just needed to tell you how I feel."

"Would your friends seriously hurt me?"

They threatened before, but she wondered if Devon and his Cimmerians were still watching them. She couldn't take any chances. "Not my friends. There are others, Peter."

She'd said too much and needed to leave.

"Others?"

She didn't answer.

"So, you just came here to tell me your feelings and then

"Call it a forbidden love. Call it whatever you want, but yes. As much as I want this…You know, when you were going to kiss me today, it took everything I had to avoid it. Even after all this time, I still think about you."

"I promise you, if you left him, he would never hurt you again. I would see to it that he couldn't."

She reached up and touched his cheek. "You have to forget about me."

He shook his head. "No."

"I have to go now." She stood, but his hand caught her arm, pressing against the burns. "Ow!"

He immediately removed his hand and got to his feet. "What? What is it?"

"Nothing."

"Did he hurt you? Let me see."

"I guess I should take care of this." She removed her jacket.

Blood rushed to her cheeks as his eyes widened.

"What happened to you?"

"I got…burned."

"What?" He looked at her in disbelief, and then examined the loose strands of her sweater. "It's very red and swollen and drew blood. How did this happen?"

"It's nothing."

"He did this, didn't he?"

She remained silent.

"Come on," he told her, his voice unnerved. He led her to the enormous bathroom, complete with a garden tub and marble countertops with double sinks. The room could've been the size of a small bedroom. The green and blue striped shower curtain pulled against the edge, still wet from Peter's shower.

"Can you." He cleared his throat. "Remove your sweater?" His cheeks reddened.

She cautiously removed her sweater and looked away from his shocked eyes.

He gawked. "What the…It looks like hands. How did this happen?"

She swallowed and refused to meet his gaze.

"You're not going to tell me?"

"No."

He shook his head. "What is he? A pyro?"

She shifted. What could she say? "It doesn't hurt now."

"You're probably numb from the pain. You're lucky we have gauze in here."

Ava focused on his face as he grabbed a roll of gauze. His smooth features were wrinkled from worry and confusion. He unraveled it and wrapped it around each burn. She didn't wince once.

He grimaced. "Hopefully that'll heal soon. Does it hurt now after I messed with it?"

She shook her head, and smiled. "I had a distraction."

"Should I put a shirt on?"

"No."

She hesitantly raised her hand, and placed it over his heart. His heartbeat was sporadic. She liked that it did the same as hers. Then, she removed it, embarrassed. It was way past time to go.

"Do you have a shirt?"

"Yeah," he stammered. He turned out the light and they returned to his room. He pulled out a white tee from his dresser and handed it to her.

She pulled it over her head. "Thank you."

"You're welcome."

"For healing me too."

"I barely did anything. If it doesn't get better, you should go to the hospital."

"No. You healed me. I don't feel pain when I'm with you."

"I'm sure your arms are on fire now."

"They're not."

"Wait, you really feel *no* pain?"

"I've never quite figured it out. Remember that day I had a

migraine and I sat with your friends?"

"Yes."

"Once I saw you, it was gone. If I'm ever in pain, every time I'm near you, it vanishes."

His eyebrows furrowed. "How is that even possible?"

"I don't know. All I feel is an intense feeling."

"Wow. Are you just that happy to be around me?"

"It's not the happiness, I don't think. I think it's *you*. Or maybe I feel this way about you and it's stronger than any pain."

"I thought it was just me that felt this intense." He took her hand in his and stroked it. "I can't believe he did that to you. Why did he do it? Were you two fighting?"

She crossed the room to his window, and peered out into the dark night. "He knew you were at my house today."

"Is he spying on you now?"

Thomas wasn't spying but she couldn't say who was. They could be out there waiting for her to leave. Or waiting to hurt Peter. Maybe she could stay the night or somehow leave without being seen. How could she have gotten herself into this? Or Peter for that matter. She'd done so well over the past few months.

"What's wrong?" he asked. She saw his reflection in the window. He moved closer to peer outside. "Is someone out there?"

"No. I have to go now."

"Wait. Isn't there any way we could make this work? Ava, I would do anything for you."

"No." Hearing him say those words filled her heart.

"Well, if this is the last time we're going to speak, can't you stay longer at least?"

His eyes were begging her. She couldn't say no. "Okay. But just for a little bit."

"How would your friends find out about this? I mean, if we kept it a secret. There's no way they could know."

"They'd know," she said. "We can't talk to each other anymore. You can't come to my house. I'm sorry."

"I wish you could tell me something." He was so close to her.

"I know. But you have to trust me."

"Then trust me that I know we can find a way to get away from him."

He slowly raised his hand and softly touched her cheek. She tried calming her heartbeat, but it was impossible when she was with him. She silently prayed the necklace wouldn't give off any signs of her euphoria, but knew it would.

His fingertips edged along her neck, and drew her face closer to his. Looking up into his smoldering eyes, she surrendered.

Finally, his warm lips pressed against hers, sending a current throughout her body. She burned with an overwhelming passion that she had never felt before as his tongue found hers. She reached around his back and pulled him closer, losing herself in the kiss. She'd never felt more alive. She could feel his muscles tense as his arms wrapped around her, holding her so tight, as if she would run away.

They slowly pulled apart, breathless. Ava rested her head against his bare chest, listening to his erratic heartbeat. And then, just as she expected, Thomas's anger came like a wave. It was so strong.

"Your necklace is glowing. Why does it do that?"

"You can't ask questions." What was she doing? Was she actually considering being with him secretly?

"Okay." His lips brushed the top of her head.

"I don't deserve you," she whispered. "I'm not worth what you are."

"What are you talking about? Don't let Thomas make you believe that."

"I'm not perfect. Not by any means."

"No one is."

"I've committed a sin."

He shrugged. "Who hasn't?"

"You have to keep ignoring me at school, just like you've been doing."

"That's going to be easy," he said sarcastically. "How long is this to last?"

She sat on his bed, and hid her face with her hands. "I don't know."

The bed lowered next to her, and he pulled her close. She loved the feeling. "We'll get through this," he said. "I promise."

She wanted to believe him.

"How are your arms?"

"I guess they're okay. They haven't hurt since I've been here."

"That is the craziest thing I've ever heard."

Wait until you hear more of my life.

Peter intertwined his fingers with hers. "This is nice."

She angled her head upwards. He leaned in and kissed her longingly, moving his mouth rhythmically with hers, while his hand entangled in her hair and pulled her closer against him. She held him tightly, not wanting to let go.

"This is really going to be hard," he said.

"Yes, it is." She clutched her necklace. This was trouble, but she was willing to take the risk. She was risking it all. Including her life.

CHAPTER TWENTY-NINE
BLACK

A loud and constant tap resonated, dragging Ava from a deep sleep. When she opened her eyes, she realized it was the branches from a maple tree rapping against the window. The window groaned from the harsh winds.

Ava pushed the blankets aside, walked to the windows, and peered outside. Lightning flashed and she flinched. Then, she saw the silhouette of a man while the rains fell diagonally. The doorbell sounded.

She jumped and spun around. Who could it be at this hour? Thomas?

It rang once more. She hesitantly walked down the stairs, afraid of what was on the other side of the door.

Ava turned the knob, and touched her chest, trying to calm her frantically beating heart. The strong wind pushed the door open, and her hair brushed all around her face.

The hulking figure entered. His venomous eyes pierced hers.

"What are you doing here?" she demanded.

"You know why I'm here."

"Thomas, stop enjoying this so much." Melissa pushed her way past him, her blond hair wild from the wind, with a wicked grin on her face.

A silence hushed over them as the rest of them filed into the house.

"Seems as though you've betrayed us," Gillian said. "I knew it would happen."

"No I didn't."

Thomas grabbed her arms, reinforcing the burning, and forced her to look at him. "I warned you. I told you not to cheat on me." He dragged her through the door and out into the wintry wet night.

"Let go of me," she yelled. She hit him and pushed but he wasn't fazed. "Where are you taking me?"

"You'll see."

Thomas pulled her through the woods with the others following, laughing as if they were having a good time. She wondered if they were drunk.

"What are you doing?" The misty cold rain landed on her eyelashes and she tried to keep up with Thomas's rushed stride.

Her breath caught in her throat as he slowed near the fire-scarred tree from the other night.

Gillian pushed her hard against it. "We warned you to stay away from him."

"This is the end for you," Melissa said.

Savina emerged from nowhere, as far as Ava could tell. "I cannot believe that one of my children would do this."

"No," she screamed. She tried moving her hands, but they were somehow tied behind the tree. She didn't remember anyone tying them.

Thomas moved in front of her. "Think of what could have been," he whispered in her ear, and grabbed her arms. The stinging turned into searing as he gripped tighter.

"Ava," someone shouted.

Slowly, she came to, and opened her eyes. It was Peter.

"Are you okay?" he asked.

She drew ragged breaths, placed her hands on her sweaty forehead, and wiped her tears away. Her hands shook uncontrollably.

"Shh, it's okay," he whispered, and moved the hair out of her face. "What were you dreaming? You were screaming."

"I-I can't..." She panted.

"You can't what?"

Rain pounded against the window. Ava jumped out of bed and peered outside at the empty street blurred by water. Just a dream.

"Ava, what's wrong?" Peter placed a hand on her shoulder and turned her around.

"Nothing. Just had a bad dream."

"What was it about?"

She shook her head. Peter encircled his arms around her and pulled her close. She felt warm and safe. Protected. He held her, no questions asked, until she was calm.

When Ava woke the next morning, her eyes felt heavy, and her body begged for more rest. She'd fallen asleep in Peter's arms, and had stayed to protect him from potential spies stalking them. Somehow, she needed Savina to put a charm on his home.

"Good morning," Peter said and then tenderly kissed her forehead.

"Morning."

"I can't believe you're really here. I could get used to this." He smiled, his dimples showing. He leaned down and kissed her. Her heart thumped in delight.

She loved being in his arms and feeling his soft lips on her, but this wasn't supposed to happen. And after the dream last night, she knew she had made a mistake by coming here. But her mother hadn't died of betrayal from the coven. Nor was she cast out and stripped of her powers. They'd accepted her father. She could tell her friends about her parents. Maybe then, they'd understand. But what if someone morphed into Peter or worse, morphed into her and tricked him, luring him to his death?

"Are you already having second thoughts?"

Her necklace warmed. Her friends were worried about her and Thomas was angry. She sat up. "No," she lied. "Why would you ask that?"

"Because I know what the look on your face means. And I know you're a terrible liar."

"I was just thinking that I hope I didn't get you in trouble for staying." She had to get him off track.

"Dad won't mind. Besides, if he asks, I'll tell him you slept in the guest room." His hand brushed against hers and she got out of bed.

"We should get ready for school. Do you have a sweater I could borrow?"

He gave a lopsided grin. "Taking my clothes already I see." Peter walked to his closet, took a black sweater off its hanger, and handed it to her.

She pulled it over her head and raked a hand through her hair. "Thanks."

Peter walked up to her and their eyes locked. "Will you tell me what you're thinking? Please."

Ava felt her shoulders go slack. "I'm just scared."

He took her hands in his and brought them up to his chest. "We're in this together. Whatever happens, I'm here. I will protect you."

She nodded, even though it wasn't her life she worried about. It was his. "Let's skip today."

He raised an eyebrow. "I think you've missed enough days, slacker. Besides, you're going to have to face him sooner or later."

"I know. I just thought we could stay here for one day."

"He won't lay a hand on you. I promise."

"We can't talk. Or touch each other. We have to carry on like we have been."

"I know. But that doesn't mean I can't make sure you're safe."

She didn't know what it was, whether it was the intense look in his eyes, or the way he said it, but she pressed her lips to his and kissed him. She didn't hold anything back.

Ava felt his hands cradle her head and he kissed back with the same vigor, as if he knew the danger they were both in, but wouldn't let it stop them.

When it ended, she felt herself smile.

"Are you trying to seduce me?" he asked.

She playfully hit him. "Come on."

They drove to school separately, though Ava followed him the entire way. She didn't feel any strange presences at his house and hoped the day would go by problem-free. When she arrived at school, she saw Melissa waiting for her in the parking lot.

Ava opened her door and got out. "Okay before you get mad, just hear me out."

"Okay," Melissa said and folded her arms in front of her. Her green eyes were pale under the cloudy sky, like the color of jade.

"I was at Peter's last night."

"Yeah, I got that."

She sighed. "I went, but when I got there, I had that odd feeling. I was going to get back in my car and just go home, but then his dad came out. So then I went inside."

"What did you tell him?"

"Nothing about us. Just that we couldn't be together because of the danger. But then he said we could keep it a secret. He seems to think we can actually do this without getting caught. And he thinks all this is because of Thomas."

"Well let's keep it that way. Were you there this morning?"

"Yes. I was there all night."

Melissa raised her eyebrows. "Did you...?"

"No! I only stayed to keep him safe."

She shook her head. "I felt it, Ava. There was so much emotion from you, but you could have possibly let Devon's men get to Peter. Do you realize that?"

"Yes. I have to get Savina to put a charm on his house. In the meantime, I'll just divide my time between home and Peter's."

"No, Ava. You can't possibly even think about actually

being with him. How are you going to carry on a relationship when you have to lie to him constantly? I mean, what are you going to tell him when someone tries to kill him?"

"I can protect him."

"No. You're not doing this, Ava."

"My mom did with my dad. He's a Halfling."

Her eyes widened. "Are you serious? How?"

"My mom had to get approval from her coven and Savina and Colden."

"Hold on. Are you suggesting we bring Peter into the coven and make him an Enchanter?"

Ava looked away. "No. I wouldn't want that for him." It was true, but she didn't want to think about it. "My dad loved my mom so much he gave up everything to be with her and became an Enchanter."

"And do you think Peter would do the same?"

"I don't know."

"Then why did you go last night? Why bring him into this, Ava?"

Her eyes blurred from oncoming tears, but she quickly dispelled them. "I love him."

A look of pity displayed on Melissa's face. "What are we going to do?"

"I don't know."

Melissa hugged her. "We'll figure something out."

The rest of the day was surprisingly calm. She never saw Thomas, and she and Peter managed to act like nothing happened in chemistry. But inside, Ava was happy. She didn't know how long they could do this.

CHAPTER THIRTY
TAKEN

Ava waited for her favorite part of the day when Peter entered the chemistry lab. Student after student walked in disappointing her further. She watched as each student walked inside, and saw that the clock was winding down. The bell rang, and Peter still hadn't come inside.

It had been almost two weeks since they kissed, and every time she had texted him, he told her he was still sick with a stomach virus and nothing more. Keeping their relationship a secret was easier than she imagined, but they hadn't seen each other, or talked. She'd felt Thomas's anger, confusion, and guilt throughout the days. Who knew he could feel so many things at once? He had apologized over and over, but Ava was determined they were done.

During class, Ava stared at Peter's empty seat with an ache in her stomach and chest that had been there since the first day of his no-show. Peter had never missed this many days. She wanted to go check on him at home, but she didn't want to lead anyone to his house.

So she waited.

Another week passed, and still no show. And same with the next. Something wasn't right. Peter responded to her texts, but what was really going on? Was he really sick, or was he avoiding her? It was strange seeing his seat empty every day. Something Peter had said when Kristen Miller went missing popped in her mind. *'It's really weird seeing her seat empty every day. She never misses a single day of school.'*

She stiffened, and then her pulse quickened. Xavier's attendance the last month had been rather spotty. And he wasn't in class today, but she'd seen him earlier. She remembered hearing about a couple of students who were absent as well, but no one reported it. Her pendant warmed, and as the teacher lectured, she scooped up her books and fled the room. Her body shook and she couldn't calm her breathing. Ava pushed open a bathroom door and the books dropped to the floor.

He's been kidnapped.

She leaned against the wall for support and felt sick to her stomach. How could she not have seen this sooner? Where was he? Was he going to come back as Xavier's friend? But maybe he really was sick and her mind was being overactive. Perhaps Xavier was prepping for his end of the year party tonight.

She jumped when her phone vibrated, and then she pulled it out of her pocket. It was a message from Melissa. Then, a toilet flushed, and Kristen Miller emerged from one of the stalls.

Her hair was sleek and straight, and her brown eyes looked tired. She wore too much eye makeup now.

"You're looking a little pale," she said, and turned on the faucet. "Guess you came to the right place."

Ava glared at her. "What happened to you? You used to be nice."

Kristen shut off the water and grabbed a paper towel. "Was I not being nice? I'm sorry. Are you sick because Peter isn't here? I bet you really miss him. He really is a nice guy."

She clenched her teeth and lunged at Kristen, pressing her against the wall. "Where is he?" she yelled.

"Hey," she cried. "What's wrong with you?"

"What did you do with him?" She slammed her against the wall.

"You really should let me go."

"Not until you tell me where he is."

"Water and electricity don't mix well." Kristen grinned.

"If you shock me, we both go."

She tilted her head to the side, and pursed her lips. "Didn't your mother die of lightning? Wouldn't want her daughter dying of the same thing."

Ava loosened her grip on Kristen.

"I wouldn't threaten me anymore either. Or Peter may not come back. Have a good day," she said with a friendly smile, and then walked out.

It was true. She was right all along. What could she do? How could she find him? Maybe she could enlist Jeremy and Melissa to help follow them so they could save Peter.

The bell rang, and Ava rushed out, pushing through the crowd to the lunchroom. Her heart raced as she ran to their table. No one was there yet, but she sat, trying not to explode.

Melissa walked up with a worried expression, and sat. "What is it? I texted you."

"I'll explain when everyone gets here." And a few seconds later, the rest arrived.

"What's with you?" Gillian asked.

"Xavier's taken Peter."

Thomas groaned. "Not this again."

"Listen to me. Kristen admitted it to me. We have to follow them today."

"You are so paranoid," Gillian said, and pulled out her compact mirror.

"What did Kristen say?" Lance asked.

"She has an electrical power. Or lightning. And said if I bothered her again, Peter wouldn't come back. She asked if I missed him. Why would she ask that?"

Gillian rolled her eyes, and reapplied her glittery lipstick. "Probably because she knows you have some bizarre obsession with him."

"We have to save him."

"Save him?" Thomas shook his head. "If Xavier did take him, he's not going to kill him. We don't have to do anything."

"Thomas, I never went to Savina's to tell her you burned me. Or that you beat up Peter. I'm just asking for your help."

"Why should I?"

"This is what we're supposed to do. To protect the Ephemerals."

"There's no proof Xavier even took him."

"Forget it. I should've known I could never count on you."

"I'll come with you," Jeremy said.

Gillian wrinkled her face. "What?"

"Yeah, I'm going too," Melissa said.

Lance reached across the table and took Melissa's hand. "Whoa, hold on. We need to make sure they're Enchanters."

"Why would Kristen mention electricity? She knows I'm a Water Enchanter."

"How?" Melissa asked.

"I don't know."

Thomas turned around. "They don't even look like Enchanters. They just look like normal high school kids."

"So do we," Ava said. "Okay, so here's the plan. When the bell rings, we follow them. If they split up, I'll follow Xavier. Melissa, you follow Seth. Maybe he'll break and tell you something. He was Peter's friend. Jeremy, follow Link. Are you coming, Lance?"

"Yeah."

Thomas shook his head. "You guys are stupid. You think you're some hero or something. You didn't care this much when the others were absent."

"Actually, I did."

"And what do you plan on doing if you find Peter? You think you'll be able to hide all this from Savina and Colden? You know he would never become one of us."

"Why do you have to be so mean?"

"I don't know. Maybe because my girlfriend decided to cheat on me with some guy that for the life of me I can't figure out what's so damn special about him. That what you feel for this guy isn't even a tenth of what you feel for me."

"If you really loved me, you wouldn't have hurt me like you did."

"And I apologized for that. I hope you're right about this Xavier guy. Because if you go after innocent people, Savina and Colden won't be happy."

"Thomas, enough," Melissa said.

"I can't believe all of you are siding with her," Gillian said.

"And I can't believe you aren't being supportive." Melissa glared at her.

When lunch was over, Ava walked behind Jeremy, Melissa, and Lance. They waited outside the cafeteria in a circle, pretending to socialize. As Xavier and his group passed, they kept a trail on them but then they split up. Ava followed Xavier and Kristen until they stopped in front of a classroom. She stayed just around the corner, and hoped she wouldn't lose sight of them. Students walked by in both directions and Xavier had his tongue down Kristen's throat. Ava silently groaned. How much of a goodbye could they possibly need before class? They stayed like that until the late bell rang. Then Xavier pulled away, and Ava hid behind the corner again.

"Are you ready?" She heard him ask.

"Of course," Kristen said. "Are you?"

He laughed. "Baby, I have been patiently waiting for this for months."

"Sorry I'm late," she heard Link say. "One of them was following me."

"Did you get rid of them?" Xavier asked.

"He's in the trunk of my car."

Ava silently cursed. How had Link gotten Jeremy in his car? What happened? Her necklace hadn't even given a warning.

A phone rang, and Xavier let out an exasperated groan. "What now?"

A few seconds of silence.

"Well, try harder. Look, it's the only way to break this girl…If we get him, she'll follow, then the rest…I don't care…Just don't kill him…Because when he finally does break, he'll be useful, you idiot…Don't argue…We'll be there soon."

"Still can't break him?" Kristen asked.

"No. Come on, let's get this over with."

"My pleasure."

There was a loud crack outside, like something exploded, and all of the lights went out. Ava crouched to the floor. Muffled excited voices came from the students in the classrooms nearby. They were probably expressing their enthusiasm over the power being out. Had Kristen done that? What was going on?

Then another explosion erupted from down the hall, like a volcano. Ava saw a flash of orange and then was flung through the air and landed hard on concrete floor. She heard glass shattering. Debris and dust collapsed on her. She coughed from the thick smoke that filled the hallway. The fire alarms sounded and sprinklers went off. Screaming kids rushed out of the rooms and sprinklers went off.

She felt arms grab her just as something else detonated, shaking the building. She could barely hear anything and couldn't see. Her eyes and throat burned from the smoke.

"This was easier than I thought." Xavier. He was talking to her and carrying her.

"What are you doing?" Her voice sounded weak. She felt a liquid running down her face.

"Getting you out of here."

Ava couldn't move or struggle against him. She heard muffled screams and cries. What was going on? And then darkness came over her.

CHAPTER THIRTY-ONE
ESCAPE

Ava slowly peeled her eyelids back, but all she could see was black. Her teeth chattered, and her face pressed against something hard and cold. Her body was sore and there was still a loud ringing in her ears. She slowly sat up, ignoring the pain in her back and head, and then her hand brushed up against something.

Someone groaned.

"Hello?" Where was she? What had happened? Why couldn't she see?

"Ava?"

"Jeremy?"

"I can't see anything."

"Neither can I. Where are we?"

"I have no idea. Last thing I remember was following Link."

The conversation Ava overheard between Xavier, Kristen, and Link slowly came back. "The trunk."

"What?"

"Link put you in the trunk of his car."

"How?"

"I don't know. I overheard him talking to Xavier and

Kristen. And then there was so much chaos. Kids were screaming. Something exploded and there was debris and the fire alarms were going off."

Someone moaned and stirred.

"Lance?" Jeremy asked. "Melissa?"

"It's me," Lance said. "Where are we?"

"I'm awake, too," Melissa groaned.

"We don't know," Ava said. She touched her face and felt a sticky substance, and then licked her lips. She tasted something metallic and salty. Blood. "What happened?"

"I remember bombs going off," Lance said.

"Bombs?" Ava asked. That would explain the ringing in her ears. "Why would Xavier bomb the school?"

"This was his party," Jeremy said. "Think about it. They tattooed this date and even on that invitation it said explosive."

"He's been planning this all along," Ava said.

"What happened when you followed him?" Melissa asked. Ava could hear the pain in her voice.

"He and Kristen were talking. And then Link came up and they were asking each other if they were ready. Then Xavier got a phone call. Talked about not being able to break someone and that they needed to keep him alive."

"Do you think they were talking about Peter?" Jeremy asked.

Ava eyes filled with tears. It made sense. "Probably," she said, her voice cracking. "We've got to get out of here and find him." She slowly got to her feet and steadied herself from the dizziness.

She blindly walked forward with her hands out in front of her until she felt something. It was cold and smooth and there was a gritty substance along the surface of the wall. Dirt probably. She moved slowly and traced along the wall with her hands, feeling for a door.

Her foot caught something and she fell on top. The object was pliable and the more she touched it, she realized it was a body and quickly moved away.

"What are you doing?" Jeremy asked. "Did you find a door?"

"No. I tripped on a body."

"Omigod," Melissa moaned.

"Wait," Lance said and then a light came on.

Ava blinked and when her eyes came into focus, she saw that it was a fire. The last thing Lance had absorbed was fire.

"Oh thank you," Melissa said. There was a large gash across her forehead and her blond hair was matted and dirty.

Lance looked like he was in better condition and he stood. He walked over to the body near Ava and as soon as the light touched it, she stiffened.

It was Peter. He was still in the same clothes from the day after they had kissed.

"Peter," she shouted. Her breathing accelerated and she reached for him. Jeremy and Melissa came over and held Ava.

Lance kneeled beside Peter and pressed his unlit hand to Peter's neck. "He's alive. But his heart rate is slow."

"Omigod, Peter." Ava didn't care that she was crying. She took his hand in hers, and brushed his hair from his eyes. His bottom lip was split open and his left eye was swollen shut. His leg rested in an abnormal position.

Melissa rested a hand on Ava's shoulder. "He'll be okay."

"Savina has to heal him," Ava said, and then met Melissa's eyes. "We have to get out of here. Do you think you can break open these stones?"

She nodded. "I might need some help."

"Okay," Lance said.

"Wait." Ava held out her hand. "We should see if there are others in here that are hurt."

Lance nodded and then with his flamed hands, walked to the other side of the room. Ava gasped once she saw two still bodies and then she returned her attention to Peter. She didn't want to know if they were dead.

"They're alive," Lance said. "But we have to get out of here now."

"How did we even get in here if there's no door?" Jeremy

asked.

"I don't know," Melissa said. "Come on, Lance."

He extinguished the light, and Ava clutched onto Peter's hand, hoping they could break through the stones.

The room began to shake, and then she felt a wind tunneling around them. Ava reluctantly released Peter's hand to help the others. Water dripped from her hands and she concentrated hard. It built and when she felt strong enough, she threw the water in front of her.

Finally, the wall gave and earth collapsed inside. Moonlight flooded into the gray-walled room. Once the dirt settled, Ava saw that they were deep underground in some room.

"They buried us?" Melissa said.

"There has to be a way in and out of this place," Jeremy said.

Lance climbed over the heap of earth and helped Melissa out. Ava and Jeremy grabbed Peter's limp body and handed him to Lance. Then, they helped the others out.

Ava clambered on the moist dirt and rocks, and pulled herself higher. Her head broke through the opening, and she looked around. There were surrounded by woods in a deep fog and there was a small house with a few lights on resting on the hill. Lance helped pull her out of the mysterious room, then Jeremy.

"Where are we?" Ava asked.

"I don't know, but there's some cars up there," Lance said. "We can take one and get out of here."

Ava looked up at him. "Without attacking? This is our chance to kill him."

"Be quiet," he whispered loudly. "We can't go up there and start a war right now. Not with these injured people."

"Lance is right," Melissa said. "We need to be healed first. We're in no shape to fight. I promise we'll come back."

Ava wanted Xavier dead for what he had done to Peter and all those kids. For what he had done to her coven. But they were right. Now wasn't the time. "Okay. But do you know how to steal a car?"

Lance grinned. "Yeah."

"How do you know?"

"Thomas taught me."

She shook her head. "Of course."

"I'm going for the silver SUV." He pointed to the one furthest away from the house. "Ava, put it in neutral and steer and I'll push. Just until we get to the road. Melissa and Jeremy take the other two bodies with you through the woods and we'll meet up. We'll take Peter with us."

"Why are we splitting up?" Ava asked.

"Because Mel is weak right now, and I need you to help me while Jeremy helps Mel. Besides, the less movement, the better."

Jeremy and Melissa hoisted a body over each of their shoulders and walked through the woods as quietly as they could. Lance carried Peter, and Ava followed him in a crouched run toward the SUV.

Her heart was racing and she hoped the car was unlocked so they wouldn't have to break a window. Lance slowed behind a tree and Ava watched the house. She saw shadows of people moving around inside beside the windows. Luckily, there were curtains covering them. When they moved away, Lance and Ava continued.

They finally reached the SUV, and Ava suppressed a sigh of relief once the door opened. Lance lay Peter down in the backseat and motioned for Ava to get in the driver's seat. She got in and carefully closed the door. The car still had a new car smell to it. How in the world could one of them afford a Cadillac?

Her body shook as she waited for Lance to come out from underneath the car. How did Thomas even know all this? Had they stolen cars before?

Ava shook her head. None of that mattered now. They had to hurry in order to save Peter and the others. A light came on in the back, flooding a vast majority of the woods. She froze. And then she saw shadows of a couple of people walking toward the storm cellar where they had been kept.

Lance popped up and she jumped, and then pointed toward the woods. Once he saw, he moved to the front of the car and pushed. It slowly rolled backwards on the grass. She turned the wheel and then Lance moved to the back and she turned it once more. He pushed until they were a ways down the long drive. She braked and then opened the door for him. Ava climbed to the passenger seat and Lance got in, put a key in the ignition, and started it.

"Where did you get the key?"

He jerked the car in motion. "Someone apparently locks themselves out of their car often," he said. "Found it under the car."

She couldn't believe their luck. With this being a new car, she was sure the alarm would have gone off. "They're going to know we escaped."

"I know."

"They're going to come after us," she shouted. "We should have attacked them."

"Ava, calm down. We'll go to Savina's and be safe. Then, we'll go after them."

"What if they aren't there when we come back?"

"I don't know, okay? Right now, we need to get to the Manor."

He slowed the car once he saw Melissa and Jeremy. Ava moved to the back with Peter and Melissa and Jeremy put the two unconscious people in the very back and then climbed in. Then, they left.

Ava cradled Peter's head in her lap. She couldn't believe she'd endangered Peter's life. It had gone too far. Warm tears rolled down her face. "This is all my fault."

"Don't blame yourself," Jeremy said.

She looked up at him. His face was covered in black soot and had several cuts and gashes. The blood had dried.

"If I had stayed away from him, Xavier wouldn't have used him for bait," she said. "What if they made him into an Enchanter?"

"I don't think he is," Jeremy said. "Didn't you say Xavier

and Kristen were talking about him before the bombs went off? Maybe he blocked them somehow."

Melissa twisted around to face them. "That makes sense. You don't feel pain around him. Maybe somehow he can protect himself or something."

"I don't know," Ava said. "He could've been talking about any of the ones we found tonight."

Peter groaned, and opened his eye. "Ava?"

"Peter," she cried, and leaned down and kissed his forehead. "How are you feeling?"

He looked around and wrinkled his face. He wheezed and held his stomach. "It hurts to breathe."

Lance turned on the interior light.

"What happened?" She carefully lifted his shirt and gasped. His skin was dark purple from bruising all around his ribs. "Oh no. What do we do?"

"We're almost there," Lance said.

"What's going on?" Peter asked, struggling with each word. "What happened to you?"

She realized she must have looked bad, after surviving an explosion, and who knows what in that underground room.

"Xavier. We're getting you help, Peter."

"It hurts."

Ava hated seeing him in so much pain. "I know. I'm sorry."

Lance drove through the entrance to the Manor, but it wasn't fast enough for Ava. The car came to a stop and he put it in park.

"I'm sorry, Peter, but we're going to have to move you now."

He nodded, but she knew he was bracing himself.

Jeremy got out first and slowly pulled him out. He cried out but they kept on. Jeremy lifted him and then the door to the manor opened.

"Good gracious," Savina said. "What has happened?"

Ava was relieved that she was there because Peter would be healed, yet afraid that she'd gone against the rules. She hesitantly walked closer. "We found some injured Ephemerals. Xavier kidnapped them and us. They need help. I'm so sorry. I didn't know where else to go."

Savina held up her hand. "Bring them inside."

Ava followed Jeremy inside to the parlor. He eased Peter down on the red couch. Then, Melissa, Lance, and Savina came in with the still unconscious bodies.

Savina knelt beside Peter. "What is your name, dear?"

"Peter."

"I am Savina," she said calmly. "You are safe here. I will heal you, but it may hurt."

He furrowed his eyebrows, and held a look of fear in his brown eyes. Then, he looked to Ava as if asking what was going on.

Savina brought her hands over Peter's chest, then to his ribcage, hovering in the air. Then, a loud crack sounded, and Peter cried out.

Ava took a step forward, but Jeremy held her back.

Savina moved her hands over his legs, and there was another crack. Peter cursed, and Ava winced. Savina shifted to his face, and slowly, the swelling around his eye faded and his eyelid opened. His lip was sewn back together, and he took a deep breath.

He slowly sat up, still with a wary look in his eyes. "How did you…What just hap—."

"You will need some rest," Savina said. "But you will be fine."

"Thank you," he stammered.

She stood. "You are welcome. Where are Gillian and Thomas?"

"They're at the cabin," Melissa said. "I sent Gillian a message. They're okay."

Savina made her way to the other bodies. "Lance, could you and Jeremy please take them upstairs to a room? They will need extensive healing."

"Are they going to be okay?" Ava asked as Lance and Jeremy carried the two people out of the room.

"Yes." Savina walked up to Melissa and healed the gash in her head. "Better?"

Melissa nodded. "Yes. Thank you."

"Always," she said, and then looked to Peter. "May I ask what happened to you?"

"This kid at school kidnapped me, and kept me in this dark room," Peter said. "They kept beating me up. Saying they could never get through to me. I don't know what they were talking about. I don't know how long I was there."

"A month," Ava whispered. So that's who Xavier and Kristen were talking about. She felt sick knowing Peter had spent an entire month in a dark cellar beaten daily. How could she have done this? She led them to him that night they kissed.

"How many were there?" Savina asked.

"Two. They would come at different times."

"Do you remember what they looked like?"

He thought for a minute. "The woman had blond hair and was kinda overweight. The guy was thin with glasses. It was so dark and that's all I remember. She kept ordering the guy around and he seemed fine with it. And even when he was beating me, there was something odd about it. Like he didn't know what he was doing."

"I am very sorry this has happened," Savina said. "I promise that you are safe now."

"Thanks," he said, but still held a wary look.

"Melissa, would you and Peter please excuse us? Perhaps he would enjoy the library."

"Sure."

Peter stood and Ava met his eyes and then he walked out. She couldn't imagine what he was thinking.

Savina raised her hand to Ava's forehead and Ava could feel her skin pulling together to seal the wound.

"Are you hurt anywhere else?" she asked.

Ava shook her head. "No."

"Does Peter have a power? I cannot read his mind."

She gasped. "Did they make him into an Enchanter?"

"No. I can tell he is not. I believe he may be a Paramortal with a sort of protection."

"A what?"

"It means extraordinary human." She paused. "Ava, please sit," she said.

Ava moved to the couch and sat next to Savina. She knew this wasn't going to be good.

"Does this boy know anything about us?"

She shook her head. "No, but we must keep him safe."

"He will be. Do not worry. You care for him very much. I can tell."

"Yes, I do. He is my friend." There was no way she was going to tell Savina he was much more to her than that.

Savina nodded. "I was in love with an Ephemeral once. Long ago."

Ava looked up in her green eyes. She hadn't expected that. "You were?"

"Yes. His name was George. We were very much in love and I knew he would ask me to marry him."

"What happened?"

Her lips pressed tightly together and her eyes softened. "This happened around the same time that Corbin and his sister returned to Caprington. She had murdered her husband after finding out he was an Enchanter hunter. When Corbin returned, he was angrier. He became volatile and hated Ephemerals. That was when Corbin spread a plague around the village. He refused to allow me to help them, but even if I could, there were too many that were dying."

"Why was Corbin so set on killing the Ephemerals?"

"Revenge. But if he had not made a spectacle, none of them would have died."

"What happened to George?" Ava asked, but deep down she knew what happened to him.

"George contracted the illness, and I was able to save him. I tried to make him leave town before things got worse. But he refused."

Ava knew where this was going.

"Rumors of me being an Enchanter circulated and I was taken as a prisoner. They sentenced me to death, all because Corbin spread the illness, and blamed it on me. George came to me that night and told me he loved me and that it didn't matter what I was. Colden helped me escape, but that was when Corbin and his army obliterated the village. George was killed in the process."

Ava felt sick. She knew what Savina was trying to tell her about being with Peter. That it was too dangerous and she could get him killed. She knew this all along. Why wasn't she strong enough to fight her feelings?

"Sometimes your feelings are trying to tell you something, Ava. I was naïve. I didn't think Corbin would ever have done that. I told you not to get involved, for this reason exactly. I will keep him protected and heal his mind of these traumatic events."

Her heart dropped. "What do you mean?"

"His mind will be erased of all this."

Ava cleared her throat. "How will you do that?"

"Same way I healed his physical injuries."

"When will you do this?" Her pulse quickened.

"After tonight."

Ava twirled her ring. "What if he protects his mind?"

"I have an elixir that will relax his mind so I can get through."

"How much are you going to erase?" Her voice cracked.

Savina gave her a knowing look. "It's safer that he only know you as a classmate."

Ava bit back tears. Everything they had ever shared would be as if it never happened. He would only know her as some girl in his chemistry class. She didn't want that to happen. But what choice did she have?

CHAPTER THIRTY-TWO
HOLDING ON AND LETTING GO

Ava tried holding back her thoughts and feelings. But the fact of the matter was she was devastated. Savina was going to erase Peter's memory of Ava.

The only thing she wanted to do was leave the Manor and take Peter home. Just so she could have a few last moments with him.

Ava was grateful when Lance and Jeremy entered the room because it gave her something else to focus on. She'd been doing a somewhat good job of putting aside her thoughts, but any second she would explode.

"Thank you for taking them to their rooms," Savina told them. "Now, who is this boy at school?"

"Xavier Holstone," Ava said.

"He seemed to have been trying to brainwash Peter into joining."

Brainwashed. That's what happened to Kristen and the others.

"What others?" Savina asked, having read Ava's mind.

"A whole group of them went missing and came back being Xavier's friends. And they bombed our school. He kept threatening me to join his group."

"Did he ever mention Devon?"

"No, but I'm sure he's working for him."

"The woman Peter described as his attacker, sounds like Trudy McVaine. We must kill her tonight."

"Who is she?" Jeremy asked.

"I'll discuss it with you later. Do you remember how to get back to their hideout?"

"Yes," Lance said.

"What about Xavier?" Ava asked.

"Not until we know who he is for sure."

"He kidnapped all of us," she shouted.

"He may have been turned into an Enchanter like the rest of them. Completely compelled. We will not kill the innocent."

"Xavier is not innocent. He's helping Devon build his army."

"Yeah, I think I'm with Ava on this one," Jeremy said.

"I will meet you all at the cabin to discuss Trudy," Savina said with finality.

"Where is everyone else?" Lance asked.

"Colden has taken the other Aureole to find Devon."

"They found him?" Ava asked.

"Colden received information. Now, I will be at the cabin in thirty minutes. Be safe."

Why was Savina being so vague? Was there more that she wasn't telling?

"And Ava?"

Ava halted. "Yes."

"Give this to Peter." She handed her a tiny vial of a clear-yellow liquid. "I will come to him tomorrow after Trudy is dead."

She nodded begrudgingly made her way out of the room. She wasn't sure what she was even going to say to him, but she just wanted to be near him.

Melissa and Peter came out of the library and Ava's stomach clenched. She felt cold and ashamed for what was going to happen to him. She couldn't meet his eyes, and they all walked outside in silence.

The rain poured hard, soaking them. They climbed into the SUV and Lance started the engine. Ava sat in between Peter and Jeremy.

"Just drive to the cabin and I'll take Peter home," Ava said, and then turned to Peter. "How are you?"

"What did she-how did she do that?"

"Savina's..." How could she word this? "Special."

"How did you find me? Did you guys fight Xavier or something?"

"No," Ava said. "Xavier took us."

"How?"

"He and his friends bombed the school and carried us out. I blacked out and woke up in the same room as you."

"Bombs?" His mouth dropped and then he took Ava's hand. Her heart accelerated. "Are you okay?"

"I'm fine," Ava said, but her voice was empty of any feeling. She subtly removed her hand from Peter's grip.

"How did we escape?" he asked.

Well, we used our powers to break out of the underground cellar. "We found a door."

"I never found one. Then again, I pretty much stayed unconscious. What does he want? Why did he do this?"

"I don't know."

"Was anyone else hurt in the bombing?"

"We don't know," Melissa said.

"I should call my friends."

Ava felt even guiltier. What if his friends had been hurt? And he'd wake up the day after not knowing about the bombing? Or was Savina going to tamper with his mind in that regard?

"How did he kidnap you?" Melissa asked.

"I drove home from school, and when I got out, Xavier pulled up. He just smiled and then someone from behind put a cloth bag or something over my head. They kept telling me to stop blocking them, which I'm not sure what that meant. Then they'd get frustrated and start hitting me."

Ava bit her lip and blinked away her tears. She knew

Xavier would not live much longer after this. She would kill Trudy, but then Xavier would be next.

Lance pulled up at the cabin, and Ava was glad to see her car, but wondered how it got there. They got out of the car and while the others were walking toward the cabin, Ava and Peter went to her car.

"Thanks for your help," Peter told them.

Melissa, Jeremy, and Lance turned around.

"You're welcome," Melissa smiled. "We'll see you soon, Ava."

She nodded and then turned to see Peter within inches of her. Seeing him, alive and standing before her, relief overcame her. "I'm so glad you're okay. I was so worried about you."

"I thought about you the whole time." He wrapped his arms around her and she relaxed. "Ava, I don't care what it takes anymore. I don't want to be apart from you."

His words made her stomach twist tighter into knots. He wouldn't remember any of this tomorrow. Or every laugh they'd shared. Every intimate secret. Each look or touch. The few, but heart-stopping kisses. Every bit of it would be gone.

She pulled away. "Come on. I need to take you home."

"Okay."

The drive to his house was quiet, except for the downpour that pummeled her car, like marbles, in the humid night.

Ava knew he was exhausted and scared and his mind was muddled. She couldn't imagine what he'd gone through in that month. But if she had just stayed away from him from the beginning, none of this would have ever happened. It was too late now to worry about what ifs though.

When she pulled into his driveway to his house with a lone light on in the front, she put the car in park.

"Did my dad come looking for me?"

Ava shook her head. She realized someone had tampered with his mind. She turned to him. "I'm so sorry you got hurt," she said. "I tried so hard—."

He reached over, pulled her face to his, and kissed her. His lips were urgent and eager as they moved with hers. She wrapped her hand around his neck to make the kiss longer. She never wanted it to end, but time was running out. Ava wanted to relish this moment before she said goodbye.

"Thank you for saving me," he whispered.

"You shouldn't thank me."

"If it wasn't for you, who knows what would have happened. Ava, I can't be without you. I want us to be together."

Ava looked away, even though she could barely see his face from the soft glow of the blue interior lights, she felt his eyes on her. "This is bigger than you and me, Peter. I'm so tired of denying my feelings and pushing you away."

"Then don't."

"I have to." Ava glanced at the clock, and then reached in her pocket and pulled out the vial. "This is for you."

He took it. "What is it?"

She cleared her throat, and stared at the small lines of water streaming down her window. She wasn't sure how much longer she could hold back the tears. "It's to help you. I-I have to go."

"Please stay."

The sadness in his voice made her ache more. "I wish I could, but I can't. You need to rest and see your father."

"I don't want to let you go. The last time I did, I…"

"You're safe. I promise."

"Will you come back?"

She didn't answer.

"Why does it seem like you're holding back information? Are you avoiding me?"

"I can't do this, Peter." She spoke to the window. "You need to go."

"Why do I feel like this is a goodbye?"

Ava took a deep breath, and then met his eyes. They were full of confusion and sadness. Her eyes blurred. "I'll be back in the morning," she said, and then kissed him quickly before it completely consumed her.

"Promise?"

She swallowed the lump in her throat. "I promise." Even though he wouldn't remember, she still felt ashamed of lying to him.

"I'll be waiting," he said, and then got out of the car. He jogged to the front door and went inside.

Ava took a shaky breath and buried her face in her hands. She gave into the tears, but only for a moment. She wiped her eyes and readied for the next kill.

CHAPTER THIRTY-THREE
HYSTERIA

Ava pulled up to the cabin and saw, through the heavy rain, Melissa on the porch smoking a cigarette. She got out of the car and jogged toward Melissa.

"Is everything okay?" Melissa asked, and then inhaled the smoke. "Why were you so sad?"

Ava was trying so hard to keep it together. "Peter is having his memory erased of me."

Her jaw flew open. "What?"

"Savina said it would be better if he only knew me as a classmate."

"And you're going to let her do this?"

"I can't stop her."

"He can become one of us."

She shook her head. "No. It's forbidden. Isn't that what you've been telling me this whole time?"

"Forget what I said. Peter loves you no matter what. I mean, he didn't even freak out that Savina healed him."

"He's just confused right now. He doesn't know what to think."

Melissa narrowed her green eyes. "Did you even try to stop Savina or persuade her not to?"

"She told me to stay away from him, Mel. And I didn't. She told me about George, the Ephemeral she fell in love with, but Corbin killed him. Right in front of her."

"Corbin's dead—."

"And Devon isn't."

"Why are you giving up so easily? Where's the stubborn Ava I've known my entire life?"

"Didn't you see what happened to him? How can I stop Savina when I feel so guilty that I almost got him killed? I don't deserve him, Mel. He needs this."

Melissa shook her head. "Why don't you let him decide what's best? It's his choice. Savina's only taking the easy way out because she doesn't know what he is to you."

"She knows, Mel. She can feel it." Ava walked past Melissa toward the door. "Just let it be." She didn't want to think about it anymore. She walked inside the cabin and everyone looked up.

Thomas rushed up to her and crushed her against him. "I'm sorry I didn't believe you. I'm so glad you're okay."

Gillian hugged her once Thomas released her. "Thankfully we have these necklaces. We wanted to help you, but the bombs demolished half of the school. We helped the Ephemerals escape. But we were so worried about you."

"I'm fine."

But she wasn't. She was seconds from falling apart at the seams. She couldn't wait to be done with this night.

Moments later, Savina arrived. They were all tired, filthy, yet ready to execute Trudy. She only hoped by killing her, Xavier would fight back. Ava knew Xavier wasn't a Halfling. But what if Savina was right? What if he was only doing this because he was bound? She hoped Colden and the other Aureole would take care of Devon and all of it would end.

"Trudy McVaine is very powerful," Savina said. "She can turn invisible and make you see images from your past or anything she wants."

"How is that possible?" Jeremy asked.

"She reaches inside your mind and pulls painful memories

to the forefront. You see nothing else but those images. But she can also project new images."

Ava drew an unsteady breath. "How do we stop it?"

"You must keep your mind clear."

"So wait, why are we killing Trudy and not Xavier?" Thomas asked. "Wasn't he the one who kidnapped them?"

"She has been keeping Ephemerals as prisoners and changing them into Enchanters. Xavier and his group could all be Halflings under compulsion. Also, Trudy is using a man to help her. He is being coerced and we must not kill him. Gillian, you must overpower his mind."

"What if we go back and we're ambushed by the Halflings?" Ava asked. "Are we supposed to save them or kill them?"

"Only kill in self-defense. I would prefer you save them."

"Where will you be?" Melissa asked.

"I will be tending to the Ephemerals you all found tonight," Savina said. "You will be fine. There are only two. You only need to kill Trudy. You will come back to the Manor when you've finished your task. I will see you all soon," she said, and then left.

"Are we all ready?" Melissa asked.

"More than ever," Ava said.

Xavier might have kidnapped them, but Trudy had tortured the Ephemerals, including Peter. She had almost killed him, but tonight she would die. Ava was sure of it.

She followed her friends out the door, and waited a moment with them on the porch, watching and listening to the rain, mentally preparing. Energy and vengeance flowed through each of them.

"Does it have to be raining?" Gillian asked. "Can't we take the fancy new SUV?"

Lance laughed. "Great way to sneak up on Enchanters. Come on, it's not that far."

Ava smugly stepped off the porch and used her invisible umbrella, not getting wet.

"How are you doing that? Can't you do it to us? It's

messing up my hair."

She shrugged. "I don't know."

Melissa chuckled and then looped her arm with Ava. "If we hurry, we can save him."

Ava shook her head. "No. This is for the best. If he doesn't get involved, he can live a normal, happy life."

"I hardly think he'll have one without you."

"He won't even know we were friends."

"Stop gabbing," Gillian said. "Let's hurry up."

Ava and Melissa led the way through the forest behind the cabin to Trudy McVaine's hideout. Enemy Enchanters were so close to them, yet they couldn't see the cabin because of the protective charm.

A few miles later, they arrived back where Ava had started the evening. The lights outside of the house were turned out, but there was a soft blue hue in the front room. She assumed it was a TV.

She was grateful for the rain since it silenced their footsteps. They hunched down behind tall bushes in front of the house.

"Is this where you all were?" Thomas asked.

"No. We were stuck in an underground room."

She felt his hand on her shoulder, and then he squeezed. "I'm sorry I doubted you."

"Thanks."

"They're going to die tonight," he vowed.

She nodded.

Through the window, Ava could see a blond woman kissing a brunette man on the couch.

"I think I'm going to gag," Melissa said.

"Can we hurry up and get this over with?" Gillian asked. "I hate getting wet."

Ava didn't mind getting wet, but the constant pelting was annoying. "Melissa, you're going to have to turn invisible and sneak in. Then keep them distracted or something so we can get inside."

The man stopped kissing her and smiled. Then, he pulled

something out of his jeans pocket.

Melissa turned away. "Oh, they are not about to do what I think they are."

"No, he just pulled out a ring box," Lance said.

"He's definitely possessed. She's so ugly. He's gonna have to get a pulley or something to get that ring around her fat finger. Good to know the Enchanter world is balanced with uggos and pretties."

Ava rolled her eyes. "Go on."

Melissa turned invisible, but Ava could tell where she was since the rain bounced off her. They waited, and watched Trudy gloat as Milo slid the ring on her and they continued kissing. If Melissa didn't hurry, they were sure to go further.

Ava averted her eyes, but felt someone watching her. She turned toward the woods, but she saw no one. She shuddered. Was Xavier there?

Her pulse accelerated.

"What?" Thomas asked.

"I feel it again. Like someone's watching us."

He looked around. "I don't see anyone."

"We just have to be careful. Gillian, as soon as we're inside, you've got to control Milo."

"Got it."

"Lance, try to absorb her powers and I'll drown her." She met Thomas's eyes. "You'll need to burn her once she's dead."

He smiled. "I like this new you."

She pretended she didn't hear that.

Something crashed to the floor inside, and Ava gasped.

Trudy and Milo stopped kissing. "Who's there?" she shouted.

The front door opened as if by a ghost. It wasn't exactly what Ava had in mind, but they pounced on it. She rushed inside with the others behind her.

"What the hell do you think you're doing?" Trudy yelled, sitting up. Her yellow hair matted around her round face, and her deep blue eyes glared.

"I'm sorry, are we interrupting something?" an invisible Melissa said.

"Who are you?" Milo asked, putting his rail-thin body in front of Trudy. His brown hair split down the middle and came to his shoulders in small waves. He wheezed, and his eyes twitched from one person to the next. He had no idea any of them were Enchanters. And Ava assumed he had not known they had been held captive.

"You don't know us or this woman." Gillian peered into his eyes and it was amazing to see how quickly he fell into a trance.

Trudy smiled. "So you came back. Good luck trying to kill me." And like that, she disappeared.

Gillian inhaled a sharp breath, losing her power over Milo. "Where did she go?"

"Gillian," Ava screamed, and then ran outside the cabin. She heard Melissa and Gillian bickering, but tried to focus on finding an invisible woman.

Jeremy came up beside her.

"Can you hear her?" she asked.

"This way," he said and took off.

The trees shielded quite a bit of the rain, but it was still hard to see and hear. She stopped at one point and sensed something or someone, and then she moved as quietly as she could to capture it.

"Trudy!" Milo's voice muffled through the rain. It was apparent that Gillian's control didn't work very well.

A branch cracked to Ava's right, and she twisted her head in that direction. She could barely see the water bounce off an unseen object. She darted for her, tackling her invisible body to the ground. It was easy for her to hold Trudy down, even though she was almost twice Ava's size.

"I got her," she called out, and jerked Trudy to her feet.

"You know, you really are powerful. Havok will love your powers," Trudy said.

"Who?"

"He's weak right now, but once he has all your powers,

the world will be a better place."

Devon was now calling himself Havok. Could he be more obsessed with Corbin? And he was set on obtaining the Elemental powers. She hoped Devon was being killed this very moment.

"He will never get our powers. And I hardly think a world of war is a better place."

"Only for a short time. Until all those Ephemerals are dead. Speaking of, how is your precious Ephemeral?"

She gripped Trudy's arm, and imagined her underwater.

Trudy chuckled. "I know you all think you can kill me, but it won't happen."

"What makes you so sure?" Melissa asked as she and Gillian arrived with Milo in tow. Jeremy walked behind them.

Where were Lance and Thomas?

Trudy smiled. "Because I have my own army." Then a deafening crack echoed in the suddenly bright night. A tree branch broke and collapsed to the ground. Ava darted out of the way and lost her grip on Trudy. She landed on the ground inches from the smoking branch.

"Ava," Gillian screamed angrily.

Ava clutched onto Trudy's leg, which made Trudy fall with a thud. She got to her knees and forced Trudy on hers. She imagined her in the ocean. The waves angrily crashed over her, but she didn't gasp.

She smiled. "Is that all you've got?"

"What the hell is going on?" Milo asked. His eyes darted all around him and he struggled against Melissa.

"Gillian, control him," she yelled, and then her eyes rolled back and she collapsed.

"Melissa," Gillian shouted and ran to her.

Milo rushed toward Ava and Trudy, but then Jeremy grabbed him.

Something hard struck Ava on the head and then again. She tried to duck and realized it was hail the size of baseballs, but they weren't falling randomly from the sky. Instead, they were directed right at her. One hit the side of her face, her back, and her legs. It infuriated her.

"Do something," Gillian yelled, trying to shield herself from the hail.

Ava tried generating water, but nothing happened.

Focus!

She took a breath, but then saw a woman unpinning laundry. The sky was gray with a building wind. She looked around at her own backyard. Then her eyes fixated on the woman who was taking down sheets from a laundry line and advising her daughter to go inside the house. Once the daughter was out of sight, she could feel a smile spread across her face. Feeling the building wind through her hair, electricity surged within her. Lightning cracked above her, waiting for her to tell it where to hit. Seconds later, the long beautiful veins reached down and struck the redheaded woman. Then, the woman collapsed, dead.

Ava cried out and tried moving. It was as if she were stuck inside the memory. She was frozen. Her mother's dead, bloody face lodged in her vision. She shook her head as if to remove the images from her mind.

Trudy laughed heartily, and then Ava could see the present again. But something about the memory wasn't right. It felt as if she were the one that coerced the lightning to strike her mother.

"Your mother was so weak, it was sickening," Trudy said. "Too bad she died. Havok would have had one of the Elemental powers."

"Devon killed her?" Ava clenched her teeth. Water ran down her arms, and then lightning cracked inches from her, breaking her hold on Trudy.

Another strike landed near Jeremy and Milo and he jumped out of the way. A third strike hit another tree causing a fire next to Ava. Jeremy scrambled to his feet, created an intense wind that directed toward Trudy, like a freight train, but Milo moved to protect her. The callous wind ripped Milo's head from his body. Trudy quickly escaped and disappeared into the curtain of heavy rain as lightning continued to connect to the ground and trees.

It seemed as if the hail and lightning stopped immediately. Once the wind stopped, Milo's head dropped onto the ground at Ava's feet. His horror-struck eyes peered up at Ava and the rain rinsed the blood away.

She turned her head but the nausea was too quick for her. She hurled until her sides ached. A hammer pounded inside her head and her eyes refused to focus. Without looking back, she ran in Trudy's direction.

"Ava," Melissa called after her, and Ava guessed she had just awakened.

She charged through the thick forest, ignoring the briars and branches that snagged her clothes and the raindrops that pelted her skin stinging it. Her eyes blurred from the water. She wanted to kill Trudy, but how could she if she was outnumbered? And why couldn't she focus enough?

Her heart sped along with her legs as the tightness filled her lungs. They ached for more air. Tripping on roots, she shoved the branches out of her way. The rain and the wind made her tremble even more through the thick fog that hovered in the woods.

Once she reached a break in the woods, her legs wobbled, and she dropped to her knees. Tears leaked from her eyes as she rocked back and forth and held her stomach. Her body shook violently. An angry red glowed from her necklace. The images of her mother. The lightning strikes. Milo's severed head flashed in her mind.

She knew someone could place images in her head but didn't really think it would feel as if she were there again. Reliving it all over, only to realize her mother had been murdered.

"Ava?" She heard a trembling voice behind her.

Impossible. He couldn't be here. Everything ceased, including her breathing. She didn't hear the rain splashing into the soft ground, or felt it against her.

"Ava?" She felt strong hands on her shoulders.

She whirled around to see his face. "Peter?"

CHAPTER THIRTY-FOUR
GIVING IN

Rain bounced off Ava as her knees sunk deeper into the muddy ground while Peter stood over her with wide eyes, mouth opened, and rushed breathing. His face paled as he bent over and gripped his knees, to steady himself. His brown hair, like hers, was soaked.

"Wh-what's going on?" he shouted. "Is-is this your secret? Did you all just...*kill* him?" He glared.

"What are you doing here?" she yelled. "How did you get here?"

"I followed you."

"Why?"

"Why did you do that?"

She opened her mouth to answer, but then saw Melissa breaking through the forest. Her eyes widened as she made eye contact with Ava. She turned back and shouted to the others that Ava had left. There was no way her coven could see Peter here. And she didn't know if Trudy was hiding out somewhere waiting to attack. She had to get him out of there.

"Peter, we have to go," she screamed, and stood.

"I don't think—," his voice wavered.

"Come on." She grabbed his hand and pulled him along

through the forest.

"What's going on?"

"Just keep running."

Once they finally reached the cabin, she raced to her car.

Peter stopped and bent over, resting his hands on his knees.

"Let's go," she yelled.

"I-I can't believe..." he murmured, and then fell to his knees and collapsed onto the ground.

"Peter!" She lifted him under his arms and dragged him inside her car. Then, she hurried onto the driver's side, started the engine, and drove away.

Ava's mind raced as fast as her heartbeat. Savina was not going to be happy that Peter had followed Ava. She couldn't decide if she actually wished Savina had gotten to him before he saw what he did.

Even if Savina decided not to erase his memory, he would never want anything to do with Ava. But she wanted to try to salvage what she could by explaining everything to him. It was time he knew, especially after what he had witnessed. And maybe she could convince Savina to stop.

For now, she had to get him back to his house, and return to the Manor.

Peter groaned as he stirred awake. "What the hell happened?"

"You fainted." Her voice was a dry whisper. "Are you okay?"

"Yeah. Fine." His hand propped his head up.

The blue glow of the interior lights reflected on him. Water dripped from his hair and rolled down his face.

"What was *that* tonight?" he demanded.

"Guess you now know my secrets."

"*That's* what you've been hiding?" He shook his head. "I thought I was dreaming. But I wasn't, was I?"

"W-what did you see?"

"What do you think I saw?" he yelled. "The four of you terrorizing that poor girl and guy. And then...then...oh, Ava.

You *killed* him."

"Do you even know who they were?"

"Like it matters. Whatever they did couldn't possibly have warranted you killing them."

"They were the ones torturing you. How could you not want them dead?"

She could see out of the corner of her eye, his mouth agape. "What is wrong with you? You turn them into the police. What could ever make you want to kill someone?"

"Do you remember me telling you that I wasn't completely good? And you told me there wasn't anything that could make you leave me?" Rebellious tears rolled down her cheek and she quickly swiped them away.

He gave a disgusted laugh. "Seriously, Ava? I didn't think you were *killing* people," he shouted.

She flinched. "Well, you shouldn't have followed. I warned you."

"I'm not sorry I did that. At least now I know."

"But you don't know all of it."

"There's more? What could there possibly be?"

Ava took a deep breath, and pulled into his driveway. The sleet had finally stopped. "Peter—."

He opened the door, and got out. "Yeah I don't need an explanation. I can't believe you. Stay away from me," he said with such venom in his voice, and then slammed the door.

Ava fumbled to open her door and got out. "Peter, wait."

He turned around. "Stay away from me."

"Do you still have the elixir I gave you?"

"Why? Is it poison?"

"If you want to forget everything that's happened to you lately," she paused. "Including me. Drink it."

He stared at her for a moment, and then marched inside the house without looking back.

Ava thought she prepared for Peter's reaction, but the way the words twisted inside her ached more than she imagined. Her breathing refused to calm, but she had no time to grieve. She jerked the car in reverse and sped back to the cabin.

She got out of the car, and five angry Enchanters advanced on her. Her necklace warmed and glowed. There was anger, confusion, disappointment, and worry all bundled together.

Thomas took a step closer to Ava, and took her hands in his. "What happened back there?"

"I—."

"Where the hell did you go?" Gillian demanded, with a hand on her hip. Her black curly hair was now one big ball of frizz. Her eyes glared, and her face was crumpled. "Why didn't you kill her? Why'd you leave us?"

Jeremy held Gillian back. "Calm down."

"No," she shouted. "We were supposed to kill her."

Ava crossed her arms in front of her chest. "Well, what were you doing? You could've killed her too."

"We were all unable."

"Thomas, Lance, and I had passed out," Melissa said. "What happened?"

"Ava was just standing there like an idiot, and let Trudy go and made Jeremy kill Milo," Gillian said.

"I tried to drown her, but it didn't work."

"Why weren't you focused?"

"I was. Nothing I did harmed her."

"You were distracted, weren't you? It's Peter isn't it?"

Thomas stiffened. "What?"

"I know it's him," Gillian said. "He's the cause of her weakness. That's why she couldn't kill Trudy."

"G, get a grip," Melissa said.

"She made me see my mother die," Ava blurted. "I couldn't block her."

Melissa's jaw dropped. "She made you see that?"

"What's going on?" a voice demanded.

Ava turned around and froze. Savina and Aaron walked toward them.

"What happened?" Aaron asked again.

"Trudy didn't die," Melissa said. "We tried, but she was stronger than us."

"She made me see things," Ava said. "I couldn't move. I couldn't do anything. It was like I was someone else."

"She escaped." Gillian added. "And because of Ava's lack of focus, she made Jeremy kill Milo."

"Stop it," Jeremy told her.

"All of you, inside, right now," Aaron demanded.

Gillian tossed her hands up in the air, frustrated and stomped into the cabin. Ava hesitated, but Thomas tugged on her arm, and she went inside.

With a wave of Savina's hand, a fire appeared in the fireplace. Aaron stood next to her with his arms crossed in front of his broad chest and a stern look in his russet eyes.

"Tell us what happened," Savina asked.

Ava's chin quivered before she spoke. "We sneaked inside their house, and Trudy turned invisible instantly. Gillian lost her control over Milo and the rest of us went chasing after Trudy. I captured her, and tried to kill her, but then I saw my mom die again."

"And then there was the lightning and hail," Jeremy said. "It was as if it were directed right at us. Like she was controlling it or something. And Lance, Thomas, and Melissa blacked out."

"Trudy cannot cause lightning or hail," Savina said. "Someone else was there."

Controlled lightning, Ava thought. "Kristen."

"Who?" Melissa asked.

"Kristen Miller. It was her. Xavier made you three pass out, and Kristen was aiming lightning at us. I knew they'd be there."

"Why weren't you prepared for others to be there?" Aaron asked.

"We never saw them," Ava replied.

Savina moved closer. "What happened after Trudy put images in your head?"

"She ran, and Jeremy tried killing her, but Milo got in the way." Ava bowed her head. "I tried running after her, but—."

"Please," Gillian said. "You ran away like a scared little

girl."

"Enough," Savina insisted. "There is quite a lot of animosity. I hope you all have it sorted out soon."

"You all will need more practice, for sure," Aaron said. "I thought we taught you to be on the lookout for others."

"I'm sorry," Ava said. "It's my fault."

"You should not take full blame," Savina said. "We should have prepared you better. I realize it has been a while since they have made an appearance, but you should never let your guard down. I hope you all will learn from this."

"We have," Melissa said.

Aaron uncrossed his arms. "Get some rest. We will meet soon." He gently took Savina by the elbow and they started for the door.

"What about Devon?" Ava blurted. "Did you find him?"

Aaron turned back to them. "We will discuss that tomorrow."

That was a big fat no.

"Trudy kept mentioning Havok."

She could feel everyone's eyes on her now. "She told me he wanted the Elemental powers so that he could wipe out all the Ephemerals. That was his goal all along, wasn't it? To gain all our powers and become what Corbin never was."

Aaron and Savina looked at each other as if they were having a silent conversation and then Aaron turned to them.

"Do not leave this cabin," he demanded. "And if you must, go home, or to the Manor. Those are the only safe places. We will discuss this tomorrow." He opened the door and they left.

Ava felt as if the wind had been knocked out of her. Their refusal to talk about anything only confirmed her worst fears. Devon, or Havok, was after them. The fear among her group was strong as all their necklaces glowed.

"Omigod," Gillian said. "What are we supposed to do?"

"Why didn't we see this before?" Lance asked.

"Because we didn't take any of this serious enough," Melissa said.

Ava wanted to get out of there. She hadn't signed up for this. They weren't ready. She walked outside and took several deep breaths. Melissa and Lance followed.

She paced beside her car and clutched her pentacle. "I can't believe this."

Melissa put her hands on Ava's shoulders and stopped her. "Calm down. We'll figure this out."

"Why didn't they see this?" Ava asked. "Aren't they supposed to be our leaders or something?"

"I think now they realize there's more to this than revenge," Lance said.

"What did you do with Milo?" she asked.

"Thomas and I buried his body."

Melissa lit a cigarette. "Ava, what exactly did Peter see?"

"I don't know. But I know he saw Milo."

"What did he say? What did you do?"

"He was shocked, angry. I didn't really do anything. I took him home and he told me to stay away. I never meant for him to see this. To see me that way." She broke down, and Melissa pulled her into a hug. Her body shook from the aching pain that enveloped her.

"We have to tell Savina."

"Can we hold off on that? I need to talk to him."

Lance cocked an eyebrow. "Talk to him about what?"

"About me. I have to tell him."

His dark eyes widened. "Whoa, I don't think that's such a good idea."

"I have to." She looked away from him. "I want to."

Melissa exhaled smoke. "I can't believe how far out of hand this has gotten. You should tell him. He has a right to know."

"What?" Lance asked. "No she doesn't. What he saw is tragic. Gillian can erase that from his mind."

She shook her head. "I don't want anyone to mess with his mind."

"Ava, it's too dangerous. I can't be held accountable if something happens to him. You can't bring him around

Thomas."

"After what happened to him, he needs to know."

"Can't it wait? Until after we've finished off Xavier?"

"No."

"Why don't you talk to Savina first?"

"Because Savina is going to erase me from his memory tomorrow. She wants me to stay away from him. But I won't let that happen."

"Do you think he's going to stick around now? He thinks you're a killer, Ava."

"I'll explain it to him."

"We have to tell Savina," Melissa said. "And if you tell Peter, I'm behind you."

"Mel?"

"Oh come on, Lance. He already saw things, and they've already threatened his life. Her dad is a Halfling. It makes sense."

Lance looked from Melissa to Ava. "He is?"

"Yes."

"What are you going to say?" Melissa asked.

"I don't know. I really don't. I have to go home and then I'll go to Peter's first thing in the morning."

Ava drove home through the sleepy rain and thick fog. It was dark and there was only a few streetlamps on the desolate country road. She was tired, scared, and worried about Peter. Most of all, she was disappointed in herself for how things had gone.

She pulled her car into the driveway and slowed it to a stop. The light was on, and she got out and closed the car door. Her dad came outside and rushed toward her.

He drew her into his arms, and held her tightly. "I was so worried about you. The school bombing was all over the news. Why haven't you called? Where have you been?"

"Xavier kidnapped us. We found Peter and a couple other Ephemerals. Then, we escaped and had to go kill Trudy. But she ran away."

"What?" Her father looked down at her.

"Let's go inside."

He held her hand and they walked inside the house. It felt good to be home.

"Your face is all bruised. Do you need to go to Savina's?"

"No, she and Aaron told us to get some rest and they'd see us tomorrow," she said with a hint of aggravation.

"Tell me everything."

Ava was wet and dirty and her stomach growled. She couldn't even remember the last time she'd eaten. But it was three in the morning and the only thing she wanted to do was clean up and then sleep.

"Can I tell you after I take a shower and eat?"

He frowned. "I'm sorry. I'll fix you something to eat. Go get cleaned."

She trudged upstairs, went to the bathroom, and turned the shower on to hot. She stripped off her dingy clothes and glanced in the mirror. Red welts cluttered her face and body. Her hair was tangled into a clumpy mess. The more she thought about the evening, the more enraged she felt.

Ava stepped into the shower and immediately relaxed as the hot water trickled through her hair and down her back. She watched blood and dirt collect and then swirl down the drain.

After cleaning herself twice, Ava turned off the water and dried off, then dressed in a navy tank top and black shorts. Once the mirror defogged, she noticed the welts on her face were gone. She checked her body but they were still visible. That's weird, she thought.

Ava took a deep breath and smelled sausage and eggs and biscuits. It was good to be home. She walked downstairs, stopped in the doorway of the kitchen, and watched her dad. Like always when he cooked, he kept a towel on his shoulder. He stirred gravy and tasted it every so often, adding salt, or pepper. She had missed him and suddenly the want to have Devon dead overcame her.

Her father turned to pour the steaming gravy in a bowl and glanced up at her. "Feel better?"

She moved to the table and sat. "Somewhat. You didn't have to go through the trouble of making an entire meal."

"You need to eat."

He set the gravy bowl on the table and then grabbed water for her and a cup of coffee for him.

Ava picked up a sausage patty and placed it on her plate. Then a biscuit, eggs, grits, and then she poured gravy on her biscuit.

The only sounds were the occasional scrape of the fork on the plate and their chewing. She loved every bite and wished every day could start out like this. It wasn't just the food. It was being there with her dad, feeling safe, and normal.

"Have you eaten enough?" he asked.

She pushed her plate away. "Yeah. Too much."

"Good."

"I don't even know where to start. This day has been so long; it has felt like several." Ava launched into explaining everything that had happened, starting with school and the bombs, and ending with Trudy. She told him about the vision, but left out the part that it was from someone else's point of view, feeling it just wasn't right. Her father listened intently and hardly asked questions.

"I am sorry, Ava," he said. "Savina and Aaron are disappointed, but Aaron is right. You all should have practiced more."

"I know. I wasn't expecting to see her again. Not like that." She wiped a tear.

"You will get better at blocking those things from your mind."

"Maybe. So is Devon that obsessed with Corbin that he calls himself Havok? I mean, could there be someone else?"

"It seems unlikely. The Elders would know. Devon has been locked up thinking about this and has been tortured. He's crazy. Especially if he thinks he's going to absorb all of the Elemental powers." He reached across the table and took her hand. "He's not going to succeed."

Ava nodded, but still felt fear. She wanted to tell him

about Peter, but was afraid. "Dad, there's a couple of things I left out."

"Like what?"

"When I took Peter home, it was supposed to be for good. Savina is going to take his memories of me. But instead of drinking the mixture, he..." Just say it. "He followed me."

"He what?"

"And he saw us kill Milo."

Her father cursed. "Where is he now?"

"I took him home. Dad, I'm telling him everything today. I want him to be a part of this. But I'm scared that he hates me now after what he saw."

"I can't even imagine what's going through that kid's head right now. Just try explaining it the best you can. If he decides to walk away, you have to let him."

"What will happen to him? Xavier already kidnapped him once. What if Devon finds out he's a Paramortal?"

"Devon won't find out because he will die."

"What about Savina?"

"You have to talk to her."

"I wish I had your confidence."

"You do. You're just tired and feeling defeated right now." He touched her chin and raised her head to look at him. "Don't let those feelings take over. You are strong and very confident."

She reached over and wrapped her arms around her father.

He squeezed her and then kissed the top of her head. "I'm so proud of you and glad you're okay. I would give anything to put myself in your place."

"I can do this."

She had to. Xavier, Trudy, and Devon had to die.

CHAPTER THIRTY-FIVE
CONFESSIONS

The sun never rose. At least, it wasn't visible behind the thick, pewter clouds that multiplied. Ava half-expected to see Peter even walk outside and brave the world after what he saw last night. But she hoped with everything she had that he would read the text messages she sent, and come outside. It was too early to knock on the door and wake his father.

Deciding to stretch her legs, she exited the car and leaned against it. She shoved her hands into her hoodie pockets. She inhaled the cool, brisk April air but stayed warm. It came almost natural to her, to use her ability to stay warm.

She jumped when she heard a door shut, forcing the knocker to slam against its base. She almost dreaded looking up. Peter's cold eyes bored into her as he walked closer. Her heart dropped to the pit of her stomach as she got a closer look. His eyes were red and dark puffy bags clung underneath. The disgust emanating from his body was almost too much for her but she knew she deserved it.

"What do you want?" he demanded. His voice was tired and rough.

"I dropped off your car."

"Thanks. You can leave now." His tone was harsh.

"Peter, I'm really sorry."

"Sorry?" He seethed. "That's all you have to say?"

"You weren't supposed to see that."

"Yeah. I can't imagine why. And thanks for the thousands of nightmares I had last night and the many more I'm sure to have for the rest of my life."

She wanted to apologize again, but it wasn't enough. "You won't tell anyone will you?"

He glared. "It's good to know what you really care about. I don't think anyone would believe me even if I did. I don't know what to do now. I just—I don't get why you did it." Confusion leaked through his angry voice.

"You don't understand. It isn't what it seems. I didn't ask for this. Don't you see? This is who I am. I'm not on drugs. Thomas isn't abusing me. We aren't psycho serial killers or anything. I can't break free from this."

"Why?"

She exhaled. She was tired of placating him. "They'll kill me, Peter."

"Who? That innocent girl was going to kill you last night?"

"She could've. There's more to it than that. I don't want to break free from it."

"Oh, so you enjoy killing people?"

She raised her head and peered out into the bleak morning. No sound but the wind whistled in the cool, damp air. How could she possibly tell him?

"I'm waiting."

The wind picked up, sweeping her hair into her face. "We can't talk here."

"Okay. Where?"

"Let's go for a drive."

"Why? So you can take me to some secret place and kill me too?"

That stung. "I would *never* hurt you."

He scrutinized her eyes and relented. "Fine."

"Mind if I drive?"

"Go right ahead. You never know. I mean, after what you

all did to that guy last night. Why am I any different?" he mumbled, and got in.

Ava's attention maintained on the road, and she watched the rain splatter against the windshield, followed shortly by the wipers clearing the drops. The white dotted line ran past her so fast it looked like a solid line as they traveled down the interstate. She could feel Peter's eyes piercing at her from the side. How could she explain this? How would he understand? Was it possible for that? And why couldn't she just stay away from him like she was supposed to have?

"What you saw last night isn't what you think," she finally spoke. Her throat was incredibly dry.

"Oh no? I didn't see the four of you crowding around that girl while holding back the guy? I didn't see..." He shook his head. "I think I'm going to be sick again."

"I knew I should've kept being mean to you and ignoring you. I've seriously messed up and put you in danger."

"Are you blaming yourself for what Xavier did?"

"Yes. But all of this would have been fixed last night had you stayed home and drunk the elixir. Why did you follow me?"

"What would you have done? I mean, I was just healed by that woman, somehow. Just healed me without even touching me. And you were acting so weird, so I followed you."

"You shouldn't have done that."

"Yeah, I got that. So that's all I had to do. Drink that vial and I'd be done with all of this?"

Ava gripped the steering wheel, as if it helped keep her together. She wasn't sure how he would react if she told him the truth. But she already knew he was ashamed of her. She took a deep breath. "It was to relax your mind so that Savina could erase your memory of all of this. And me. She's supposed to do it today."

"What? How is that even possible? What the hell is going on?"

"I don't even know where to start."

"You can start from the beginning. I mean, you've been swearing this whole time that Thomas isn't abusing you, yet you show up with horrible burn marks on your arms. I was kidnapped. Some strange woman miraculously heals me. And then last night."

"What did you see?"

"I saw the whole thing, Ava."

She cringed.

"I couldn't hear anything that was being said because of the rain. And then the lightning was striking, and then I saw what looked like hail attacking you and Jeremy. Then there was this powerful wind like a." He paused. "Like a tornado and it...you know. I ran and hid but then I saw you running through the woods and crying."

Last night was already traumatic enough for Ava. She could only imagine how much worse it was for Peter. "I'm so sorry I did this."

"What's going on?"

"It was my fault Xavier took you. He was trying to get to me. I tried so hard to keep you safe."

"Stop being so cryptic. Just tell me," he said, losing the edge in his voice.

She pressed her lips together. "I'm an Enchanter," she finally confessed. "We're all Enchanters...Thomas, Melissa, Gillian, Lance, and Jeremy."

"That explains so much," he said sarcastically. "You like pretending you can actually cast spells on people. Do you all have wands and use broomsticks, too?"

She rolled her eyes and pressed further down on the gas pedal. "This is serious."

"Right. Like Rachel Higgins and Marie Adaire casting spells on people. It's ridiculous and they just want attention."

"Do you think I'm like them?"

"No. But what am I supposed to think when you say something like that?"

"I don't know. I was born an Enchanter, Peter. I actually have powers unlike Marie and Rachel."

"Like what? Force someone to fall in love with you?"

She ignored his bitter tone. "We are very strong, fast, and can change our internal temperature. We have strong stamina and are agile. All of these abilities surpass Ephemerals by far."

"Surpass what?"

"Humans. We call them Ephemerals."

"But you're a human."

"I hardly classify myself as human when I can breathe underwater."

She could see his jaw drop out of the corner of her eye.

"What?"

"Yeah."

He shook his head, as if trying to clear the nonsense. "What do you mean by internal temperature?"

"I can make myself warm when I'm cold or vice versa."

"How?"

She placed her hand against his warm arm and as quickly as the thought arrived, her hand cooled his skin.

"Whoa. How'd you do that?"

Ava returned her hand to the steering wheel and gripped it as her heart raced. "I think of it, and it happens." She wished so much she knew what he was thinking, but then thought better of it. She wanted to see his face—his reaction—but refused to look, for fear he might be afraid of her.

"That was amazing."

"What?" She had to peek. His eyes found hers and before she could get lost, she turned back to the wet, speeding road ahead.

"Oh come on, you must think that's cool."

She hesitated. "Well, yes. There are quite a lot of advantages. But Peter, you saw what we do last night. You noticed Jeremy didn't use a weapon, at least none that you could see. He used his ability with air."

"He did what?"

"He is an Air Enchanter. He can create wind gusts so powerful that they can, you know, decapitate someone. But even more than that."

"Why did you kill him?"

Her pulse quickened, and her amulet glowed. "I'm worried."

"About?"

"Your reaction."

"Your necklace is glowing. Why does it do that? Is it a tracking device or something?"

"Sorta. If any of us are in danger, we can find each other. We can sense one another through these necklaces. They can all feel me now."

"Feel you?"

"They know what I'm feeling right now. It's like an alarm to keep us safe if anything happens."

"Well, that explains some things. What exactly did Thomas feel from you?"

She swallowed. "I was sad, angry, and confused. He thought I was in danger when I removed my necklace that day and clearly overreacted."

"I'll say," he mumbled. "When I was about to kiss you..."

"He endured what I felt for you. Which is why he started a fight with you."

"Couldn't you have used your powers against him or something? To leave you alone?"

"I tried actually, but the pain was too much. Besides, I don't want use my powers against them for that. We are in the same Aureole."

"Same what?"

"It's a coven."

"Okay. But he obviously used his powers against you."

"The first time was because he wasn't focused enough. The second time, he just got out of control."

"Bastard," he muttered. "You're not indestructible?"

"No, but if anything happens Savina heals us."

"Why didn't you go to her that night he burned you?"

"I wanted to see you." She paused and noticed the subtle pink of the morning sun struggling for attention with the dark blue clouds. She couldn't tear her eyes from the beautiful colors. It was as if she were the sun trying to overcome the darkness. "When I'm with you, I feel no pain. I don't know why." Maybe he was a Paramortal, but she wasn't going to get into that right now.

"Is Savina like your leader?"

"Yeah."

"How many are in your coven?"

"Seven if you count Savina. But there are more Aureoles out there. We've only met one other."

"Back to the guy and girl. Why did you kill him?"

"Milo wasn't supposed to die. He was an Ephemeral."

"H-how many have you killed?"

"One Ephemeral and one Enchanter." So far. "This man had morphed into my father, tricking me, but we killed him."

"Wait. A man *morphed* into your father?"

"Yes. Some Enchanters have the power to transform into someone else changing their appearance completely. They can make themselves look like anyone they want. Like a shapeshifter."

"Whoa. How did you know it wasn't your dad?"

"I didn't. Gabriel, another Enchanter, told me. It wasn't easy watching him die."

"I don't imagine it was. What did he want?"

"He was a spy for Devon as well."

"Who is he?"

"It's kinda a long story."

"Well, looks like we both have all day."

She inhaled and then exhaled. "Savina was born in 1643 Scotland. Both her parents died, but before her mom died, she had met a man named Corbin Havok. They had a son, Colden. Corbin raised them but began to have a disdain for Colden because he didn't seem to have a power like most Enchanters."

"Why?"

Ava shrugged. "He's a Droll. An Enchanter born without powers. Anyway, his sister had killed her husband, who was secretly an Enchanter hunter, and then we think that's when

Corbin snapped. He hated Ephemerals. He wanted to kill them all. So he began spreading diseases among villages, so harsh that Savina couldn't save them all. He continued this for centuries, building armies along the way, and fought with Savina and Colden constantly."

"Damn. So they've been warring for over three-hundred years?"

"Yes, but about thirty years ago, Corbin showed up extremely weakened and Savina killed him. No one knows what happened to him, but everything was at peace until recently when Devon Maunsell escaped the Cruciari."

"What's that?"

"A prison for Enchanters that's completely surrounded by water. They negate your powers once you enter."

"How did he escape?"

"I don't know, but Savina and Colden seem to have a theory that they apparently don't think we're capable of hearing it."

Ava couldn't believe how honest she'd been with him, or how much she had told him. She was digging a hole for herself deep in the earth.

"Devon is creating an army to seek revenge against Savina and Colden for killing Corbin and imprisoning him and his counterparts. He wants all our powers for himself so he'll be the strongest Enchanter alive."

"What would happen if he were?"

"He'd carry out Corbin's vision of having an Ephemeral-free world."

"So where do I or Xavier or Seth fit in with all this?"

"He's using Ephemerals in his army. Meaning, he's changing them into Enchanters. That's what Trudy, the woman from last night, was trying to do to you. Milo, the man, was compelled. He had no idea what he was doing."

"So Seth is an Enchanter?" His voice rose.

"He's a Halfling. Part Ephemeral, part Enchanter. But he was coerced into it."

"And Xavier did that?"

"Savina seems to think Xavier is just doing as he's told as well. I don't believe it though."

"Do you think he did that with all of them in his group?"

"I know he did. Or someone compelled them."

He shook his head. "Why didn't they make me an Enchanter? Or Halfling?"

"I think you can protect yourself. Savina seems to think you're a Paramortal, an extraordinary human. She couldn't read your mind last night."

"She can do that?"

"Unfortunately. I overheard Xavier talking about someone who wouldn't budge. I think they were talking about you. How did you stop them from getting inside your head?"

"I don't know. I just wanted out of there. I refused to give them what they wanted. But if I could protect myself, I don't think I would have come out of that place with as many broken bones as I did."

"It might be a mental thing. I really don't know. It's all speculation."

He shook his head. "That's crazy to think. How old are you? Are you immortal?"

"Enchanters aren't immortal, we just have longevity. And I'm still seventeen. Once we grow into our adult bodies, the aging slows."

"How old were you when all this began?"

"Technically, when I was born. My mother was an Enchanter, who belonged to Savina's Aureole. But we all met Savina and Colden when we were seven."

"What happened when you met them? Did your parents just take you there one day?"

"For me, it was right after my mom died. I saw Savina sitting on a bench one day. It was uncanny how much she looked like my mom. She took my hand and led me to the Manor. I wasn't afraid of her, but when I got there, I got scared and didn't want to be there. She and Colden wiccaned us that night."

"What does that mean?"

"It just means to discover our powers."

"How does that happen?"

"She and Colden drew blood from each of us, we drank it, and then we saw these amazing illusions in the glass ceiling. I'll never forget it."

"What kind of illusions?"

"They represented our powers. There was the sun, moon, the earth, ocean, fire, and the wind. We are the Elemental Enchanters, the rarest of our kind and all in the same coven."

"So if Devon wants all your powers, does that mean you all are the strongest?"

"In theory. We're still young and very naïve."

"How are you okay with all of this? I mean, were you conditioned from day one that this would be your life?"

"Not me. I'm sure if my mom was alive, then yes. I struggled with it for so long because it meant I had to give you up."

"Are Enchanters and Ephemerals not allowed to be together?"

"It's difficult. I'm breaking my oath by telling you everything. But my dad recently told me he was a Halfling. My mother had to convince her Aureole that they belonged together. My dad loved her so much that he gave up his Ephemeral life to become an Enchanter."

"How does a human become one?"

She hesitated. "The Ephemeral drinks blood of the Enchanters, ingesting bits of their powers."

"So your dad has powers?"

"They're fading. They do that when your offspring develops their power. If you never have kids, you become strong like Savina and Aaron."

"What about Corbin? Why didn't his powers ever weaken when he had Colden?"

"Because Colden never developed his ability."

"Why doesn't he live his life as a human? I mean, what does he do?"

"He can do most of things that all Enchanters can, but

doesn't have a unique power. And he isn't very strong."

"How does he stand that? Everyone around him is powerful."

"He hated everything his father stood for so much, that he'll do anything to keep us and the Ephemerals safe."

Peter peered out the window, and Ava wondered what he was thinking. Instead, she just kept driving. Impatiently waiting for him to say something.

"What will happen to you now that you've told me all this?"

Her dream of Savina and her Aureole about to kill her came back to her and it made her shudder. "I don't know."

"It's something bad, huh?"

"I could incur a harsh punishment. I didn't talk to them before telling you all this. And I took you today, which Savina won't be happy about at all."

"Would they hurt you?"

"They could. I don't know what my penalty will be."

"But you haven't done anything wrong. Think about it. If you hadn't saved me, I would have known about Devon and you regardless."

He had a point. "But since we did save you, you weren't going to know anything. You would have been safe."

"And how long do you think it would take for Xavier to come after me again? Especially if Savina had erased my mind. I wouldn't know who he was or that he was bad."

"She said she would have kept you safe."

"What does that mean? Was she going to ship me off somewhere like I was in some sort of witness protection?"

"Possibly."

They were both quiet for a long while. The rain stopped as she pulled her car onto an exit ramp. She made a turn and drove on to a long, high bridge. The crystal blue ocean partially shimmered below them under the partly cloudy sky. Once she crossed, she drove through the long hotel strip, found a public part of the beach, and parked her car in the small lot. The beach was deserted, especially since there was a hurricane threat. She got out and Peter followed as the wind picked up, whipping her hair in her face.

"I can't believe we're at the beach," he said. "It seemed like a short drive. How fast were you going?"

Ava shrugged, tucked her hands in her hoodie pockets, and trudged through the white sand toward the water. "I don't know."

"You mentioned those illusions reflecting your powers. Which one was yours?"

She felt her lips twitch into a smile. "The ocean. I'm a Water Enchanter. I can conjure it, imagine people downing in it, and breathe underwater. Remember that day it snowed?"

"Yeah."

"I turned the rain into snow. I can't make it rain or anything, but I can turn water into ice or make it boil. At least, I think I can. I haven't really tried."

"Wow. What about the others?"

"Thomas is fire. He can create it."

"How did he burn you?" He gritted his teeth, pointing to her arms, which had already healed.

"Because he can't seem to control his anger, he grabbed me by the arms and squeezed. It felt like he had wrapped my arms in hot coils."

He shook his head. "I can't believe he did that to you. What can the others do?"

"Melissa is an Earth Enchanter," she said. "She can move dirt, rocks, and things like that. And can poison people. Lance is the Sun, and can absorb powers. Gillian is the Moon, and controls minds."

Peter stopped. "Did she mess with me?"

She turned and met his frightened eyes. "No."

"But she could?"

Ava nodded. "That day you and Thomas fought, he threatened he would get Gillian to mess with your mind. That's why I didn't correct you when you thought I was still in love with Thomas."

"But when he kissed you—."

"That was Gillian making me feel that way," she said and then stared out among the building waves. Red flags flapped hard in the wind cautioning anyone to go into the water. The constant thunder of the water colliding with itself calmed her. The salty air blew in gusts as seagulls and pelicans glided above in search of food. A large pelican landed on the water, and waded, like a duck in a pond. Its eyes watched the fish below, waiting to grab one.

"That day in the hallway," Peter said. "When all those guys walked up to you…"

"She did that, too. We're not supposed to harm or kill Ephemerals. But Gillian likes to play."

"This feels so surreal. Like a dream."

"I promise you, it's not."

"Well, at least I understand a bit more."

"You *must* keep this a secret. No one can know."

He reached inside her pocket, pulled her hand out, and intertwined his fingers with hers. His hand was cold, but she warmed it. "I promise. I won't tell anyone."

The pelican dipped its long beak into the water and pulled it back out, lifting it to the sky to swallow its meal. Ava crossed her legs and sat in the sand, and Peter followed.

"Okay, so you accidentally killed this Ephemeral guy when you meant to off the girl, right?"

"Yes."

"How—how were you going to, you know…?"

"Drown her."

"What happened? I mean, why didn't it work?"

"She put images in my head so I couldn't focus."

"Like what?"

She looked down and her eyes watered. "She made me see my mom die again."

"What?" he shrieked.

"I realize now she was murdered."

He cursed. "H-how do you know?"

"She gave me the killer's memory of that day. Not mine. She made me feel as if I were the one who made the lightning…" Ava shook her head.

He cursed again. "Was the killer there last night?"

"No. Kristen was there. She can produce lightning."

Peter took a deep breath. "Does this mean Seth has an ability, too?"

"Yes."

"Is there any way to save him? I know he's a good person."

"I think I finally convinced my coven that Xavier isn't a Halfling and that he and Trudy made the Ephemerals into Halflings. Since we didn't kill Trudy, she and Xavier have gone back to Devon. Colden led an Aureole to find him, but I haven't heard the outcome of that yet."

"Would it all be over if Devon were dead?"

"One could only hope." She turned her head back to the ocean. The dark clouds speedily passed over them, covering the sun completely. "How are you not freaked out?"

"I was last night. But now that I understand more." He shrugged. "I don't know. It doesn't matter to me what you are."

"Just what I do."

"No. It isn't like you're out there killing people for no reason. You are protecting humans and yourself. Besides, haven't you noticed? I'm so much in love with you that it's overpowering any other sense I might have."

Her heart skipped a beat. "Oh, Peter."

"This Devon guy won't win. He won't take you."

"I hope." She stood and moved closer to the edge of the water. "I wanted to explain everything to you to give you a choice instead of Savina taking it from you. I'm hoping this will give you a reason to leave."

But that wasn't true. She selfishly wanted him to stay.

"Leave?" Peter's voice came from behind her. "No. You said every time you're in pain and you see me, the pain is gone." He took her arm and turned her around until they were face to face. "So what if I can protect you against him? I'm prepared to take on whatever I need."

She searched his eyes. He seemed so confident. "I thought this would be harder. I never expected you to take my being an Enchanter so—so calmly. I feel like you're letting me off the hook too easily and I'm waiting for the other shoe to drop."

"You worry too much."

"I don't want to be the reason if you die."

"You won't be."

"You saw us kill someone. Don't you see what we are? We're hunters."

"You kill bad Enchanters."

"You are so stubborn."

"Yeah. Think we've established that we both are. But I'm not backing down."

"I just want you to be safe. That's all. I can't bring you in this."

"It's a little late, don't you think? Besides, you think I'm just going to let you take me back home and that be it? Just go about my life when I know you are in danger. Your mom had to convince her Aureole that she and your dad belonged together. You can do the same."

Her lips pressed tightly together and her eyes narrowed at him. "No."

"You know I'm not going to leave you unprotected."

"No," she insisted, but she felt her chin quiver.

"Why are you fighting this so much? This is the only way."

"Because I love you, Peter," she said. "And I can't stand the idea of you getting hurt." She sighed as tears fell down her cheek.

Peter reached out, brushed them away, and his brown eyes held hers. He placed his cool hands on either side of her face. "When we kissed, it was like…like an explosion. It was so powerful and I just knew it was right. I love you so much that I will fight and die for you. We're in this together."

Another tear fell.

"It won't work," she said. "I would have to convince Thomas and Gillian. They don't exactly like the idea of you, at all."

He shrugged. "Savina and Colden would have the final word right? You said they knew your parents loved each other. They can sense it with us, too. We just need to get their approval."

"Savina told me to stay away from you. And I didn't." She removed his hands from her face, and turned back toward the waves. They grew, but were inviting to her.

"She won't hurt you," he said. "Or me. Can't we talk about this somewhere else? I think we should go. It looks like a bad storm is coming."

"It's okay."

Ava wanted to show him what she could do. If he wasn't afraid, he really needed to see. She slipped off her shoes, and then eased her feet into the cold water.

"What are you doing? Ava, don't go in there."

Using her mind, the water quickly turned warm, as if turning a knob to hot, just like the day at the waterfall. She twisted around and held out her hand for him.

"Did you mean every word you just said?" she asked.

"Of course I did." He moved closer. "I'll do whatever it takes to be with you."

"Do you trust me?"

"Yes, I do, but come on. Seriously, it's getting worse out here."

"Do you trust me?"

"Yes."

"I need to show you something."

The wind whipped through her hair. The water crashed against sand, and as it retreated to the ocean, her feet sank in the wet sand.

"That water has got to be freezing."

"Take off your shoes, and take my hand."

"What are we doing?"

"You'll see. Walk slowly into the water."

He stepped into the freezing water, and caught her hand, never taking his eyes off her. His hair was messy from the wind. She focused her energy to pass into him.

"Wow, it's warm. Are you doing that?"

She could feel herself smile. "Yes."

"It's amazing." His voice shook. "But shouldn't we get out before we drown from the waves?"

"No."

A wave rolled toward them, and grew. Ava forced it to grow higher, making a rogue wave. She held it up for a moment, and then let it collapse around them. She felt Peter tremble.

"You want to be a part of this? Then you have to see what I'm capable of doing. Come." Ava slowly moved deeper into the water. She wanted to share all of this with him, even though it was stupid and reckless.

"Ava," he wavered.

"Trust me."

He nodded, tightly held her hand, and then moved with her deeper until the water was waist high. She felt him relax.

"It's like the water moves with you. It's so calm around you, but so violent everywhere else."

She pulled him closer, until their faces were just inches apart. The water began swirling, faster and faster until it rose above them, like walls. The water spun around them like a whirlpool, barely sprinkling on them. It was like their private bubble.

"This is so unreal," he said, watching the water.

"What are you thinking?"

"Wondering how you're doing this."

She tilted her head upwards, and closed her eyes. Their lips touched, igniting the thunderous explosion of her heart, sending the blood throughout her body like lava from a volcano. He held her closer and his lips matched the urgency of hers.

CHAPTER THIRTY-SIX
THE POINT OF NO RETURN

The drive home was rather quiet. The sun had set and the only light that guided her was the bright silver moon that peeked through the many broken clouds. Peter slept in the passenger seat. Sleep tugged at her body and she realized she hadn't really slept since two days prior.

Ava knew the others were angry. She didn't have to have a necklace to know that. Her cell phone showed several missed calls and messages from Melissa. She didn't even want to think about what Savina and Colden would do to her. She would take Peter home first, and then talk to her friends, though she wasn't sure what to say to make them understand.

The kiss, the ocean, creating the rogue wave had left Ava on some sort of high. Every bit of it was exhilarating. She couldn't deny that Peter strengthened her, and that she deeply loved him. It was unbelievable how easily he accepted her supernatural world. Maybe he was like her father in that he was willing to give up his human life for her. The gesture awed her, but it still left her feeling guilty.

"If you keep chewing on your lip, you'll make it bleed," Peter said, stirring from his sleep.

She sighed. "Sorry."

"Why are you still so tense?"

"I'm trying to figure out what to say to them."

"Tell them the truth. We'll make them understand."

"You're not coming with me."

He let out a frustrated groan. "Yes, I am. It will be better if I'm there."

"You can't come. What if Thomas attacks you? Or Gillian tries to manipulate you into hurting yourself? You know she made Melissa almost slash her wrists open."

"Stop fighting me," he said. She could sense irritation in his voice. "Don't you think Gillian or Thomas would have at least tried something on me by now?"

"That doesn't mean they won't tonight."

"If you take me home, I'm only going to follow you again."

Ava shook her head.

How was she even going to do this? Could Peter still become an Enchanter if two members of the Aureole disagreed? And what about Savina? Would she even listen to Ava? She had failed the mission. Broken her oath and her coven. Prevented her from erasing Peter's memory.

She felt Peter's hand take hers. "We can do this, Ava."

"If there's any sign of danger, will you promise to run?"

"Not without you."

"You're impossible."

He squeezed her hand. "It will be fine."

How could he be so sure?

"Stop doubting me, please," he said.

"Are you reading my thoughts?"

"No, but I can read your face like a book. I know what you're thinking when I say certain things because you bite your lip or you furrow your eyebrows."

He knew her well.

Moments of silence passed. She didn't know what Peter was thinking, but she stayed nervous as if her insides would give way at any moment from the stress. She wanted to do this, but was afraid.

Ava drove into the woods, down the narrow path, through the trees. She tried keeping her breathing normal, but once her necklace glowed, she knew her friends perceived her emotions.

She edged closer to the cabin, shifted the car in park, and killed the engine.

"Are you sure you want to do this?" she asked.

He leaned over and softly brushed his lips against hers. "Yes. I'm sure."

With a nod, she got out, and they walked hand-in-hand to the door. She took a deep breath and slowly turned the knob and opened it.

"Ava, where have you been?" Gillian stood from the couch with Jeremy. "Savina was looking for you." Her glower quickly faded into surprise once she saw Peter. "What the hell is he doing here?"

Melissa and Lance moved closer as Peter came fully into view beside Ava. She clutched his hand so tight. Her heart pounded so fast she thought it would knock a hole in her chest.

"I need to talk to all of you."

"What happened?" Thomas's voice came from down the hall. He abruptly stopped. Anger flashed in his eyes, and his fists clenched.

Ava tightened her grip on Peter's hand and stiffened. "Thomas, please listen."

"You brought him here?"

She held out her hand as if to stop him from getting any closer. "Just please listen."

But it was no use. Thomas bolted toward her. She braced herself, ready to block him. As she anticipated Thomas's impact, Peter's body struck her, forcing her to fall over. She landed on the hardwood floor, turned her head sharply, and saw Peter slam into Thomas, knocking them both to the ground.

They struggled with each other until Lance seized Thomas and held him back. Melissa hustled to guard Ava and Peter.

"Let me go," Thomas yelled. "I want to break him."

"Calm down." Melissa said.

Gillian folded her arms across her chest. "Are you siding with her now?"

"G, now is not the time."

"You're damn right this isn't," she snapped. "This isn't the time to be bringing your new boyfriend into our home while he tries to attack us."

"Are you okay?" Peter asked Ava, and helped her to her feet.

"Yes." She nodded, and looked at him. How could he have knocked Thomas over like that? Could being a Paramortal have extra strength, too?

"You will not hurt her anymore," he demanded, glaring at Thomas.

Thomas laughed hard. "What are you gonna do?"

"I'm stronger than you think."

Ava glanced sideways at Peter. What was he doing? Was he an idiot? "Stop arguing."

Thomas rolled his eyes. "Yeah. I'm sure some measly Ephemeral can defeat me." Then, his cold blue eyes sliced to Ava. "Is this what you want? To betray our coven for him?"

"I don't want to betray us."

"Well you just did," Gillian said. "You brought an outsider and told him everything."

"He won't hurt us."

"You're joking right? You just saw what he tried to do."

Melissa moved in between Gillian and Ava. "He was only protecting Ava, and you know that."

"He's my true love. I need him."

Gillian rolled her eyes. "Oh cut the lame true love garbage. You just don't want to be a part of us anymore."

"That's not true. Why would you even say that?"

"Oh come on. From the very beginning, you've complained about all this. You knew this was your life, and you knew it was dangerous to keep him around."

"I want to be with him."

"He can't be part of this."

"Wait, you want this fool to become one of us?" Thomas asked.

"Yes," Peter said. "So you'd better get used to me."

Thomas clenched his jaw. "I could easily turn you into ashes."

"What like you tried to do with Ava?"

"Enough," Ava said. Why was he egging Thomas? "I just needed you all to understand before I go to Savina and Colden."

Gillian laughed. "Like they'll ever accept him."

"You know I do," Melissa said, still watching Thomas.

Lance released Thomas. "I do."

"You're kidding me." Thomas shook his head and moved aside.

Jeremy cleared his throat. "I accept him, too."

"Jeremy," Gillian screamed. "How could you even think that?" She glared at Ava. "I can't believe what's going on. You've broken this coven, do you realize that?"

"They accepted my dad."

Thomas cocked an eyebrow. "You're dad's a Halfling," he said, obviously disbelieving her.

"It's the truth."

He shrugged. "If you want to die, then go ahead and flaunt around with him. I can't promise this won't end on good terms." His voice was cold and dark.

"I never wanted to break us. But if you would just understand."

"We've nothing more to say to you," Gillian spat. "Traitor."

"You're making a huge mistake," Peter said. His voice was fierce and he glared at Gillian. "You'll need her."

"I'll be the judge of that. If you're with her, she'll be much weaker."

Melissa let out a disgusted sigh and then guided Peter and Ava out of the cabin.

Once outside, Ava exhaled.

"Look, I'm more than willing to support you, you know that," Melissa said. "But next time could we at least have some sort of warning?"

"I'm sorry, Mel."

"It was my fault." Peter said.

Lance came outside and walked down the stairs. "Well, that went well," he said sarcastically. "What do we do now?"

"I have to speak to Savina," Ava said.

"I talked to her when she came." Melissa said. "I told her that you were with Peter and that he saw everything last night."

Ava's stomach dropped. "You what?"

"I also told her that you two love each other and that it would do you a disservice to erase his mind. Ava, you're completely miserable without him. You're stronger with him."

Ava looked at Peter and then took a deep breath. "What did she say?"

"She said she felt it, but didn't think you were ready for him to become one of us."

"She's right. I'm scared."

Peter moved in front of her and softly placed his hands on both sides of her face. "Then we'll face it together. I love you, and we can do this. I'm not afraid of this or anyone. But above all, I will keep you safe."

"It isn't me that I'm worried about."

"If Thomas really wanted to hurt me, he would've done it in there."

"He's right," Lance said. "Thomas just doesn't want to admit that you two are over and that you weren't right for each other. His ego's bruised."

Ava nodded. "I need to face her. Will you two take Peter home?"

Lance shook his head. "You're not going alone."

"It will be better if we all go, so they'll see *we* understand," Melissa said.

Peter took her hand. "And I've already told you I'm not

leaving your side."

She rolled her eyes. "Fine. Let's go."

They got in Lance's car and strapped in.

Ava felt like she was about to walk into a lion's den. But she could only hope Savina and Colden would hear them out before deciding anything. And Ava needed to prove that she was ready for Peter to join.

Melissa twisted around in her seat. "Ava, are you going to talk to Savina about your mom?"

"Yes."

"Do you know who could have killed her?" Lance asked.

"No. My dad mentioned before that they couldn't find some Enchanters from Corbin's army to imprison. But why were they after my mom?"

"Maybe the same reason Devon is after us," Lance said. "I mean, she was a Water Enchanter, right?

"Yes, but they wouldn't have killed her. Taken her powers, yes."

"Maybe they were trying to get to you," Peter said.

"I was only seven. I didn't have any powers."

"Right, but couldn't they have tried taking you and raised you in their army? Then, by the time your powers developed you would have been stronger than what you are now."

"I hadn't thought of that. What if that's what they've been trying to do all along? What if this didn't start with Devon?"

"Who else could have started it?" Lance asked.

"I don't know, but it would explain how Devon escaped," Ava said. "Someone had to have helped him. Someone strong enough to bust him out of the Cruciari."

"I don't know," Melissa said. "I mean, if someone else was behind this, where have they been for ten years? Wouldn't they have tried more than once to get us?"

"Good point," Lance said, and then shrugged. "Maybe they got killed from some of our Enchanters."

"Or maybe they were waiting to find someone who could absorb powers," Ava said.

"Yeah, but Devon was around when Corbin was alive.

They knew where he was. Why would they wait ten years to break him out?"

"If this prison is as tough as you all say, maybe it took that long to plan his escape," Peter said.

"Maybe." Melissa gave a dismissive gesture. "I don't know. Just seems far-fetched."

It did seem that way, but Ava would find out. And she would learn who her mother's killer was, track them down, and take vengeance.

The lights from Lance's car illuminated the path to Blackhart Manor. The majestic house stood strong against the howling winds. Other cars were parked in the grass on the side of the house. They got out and made their way to the door.

"How does she get the flowers to look so amazing?" Peter asked as they trailed through the autumn garden. Lush orange, red, and yellow flowers bloomed surrounded by greenery.

"Magic," Ava said.

After three knocks, the door opened and Savina greeted them with a worried expression.

"Ava, I'm so glad you're okay." She drew her into an embrace.

Ava pulled away, and took a deep breath. "I'm sorry I left today and worried everyone. We know this isn't the best time, but we need to talk."

"Of course, we can come back if that's better," Melissa quickly said.

Savina's gaze flashed back and forth between them. "No, please, come in."

Ava felt Savina's critical eyes on her as she walked inside with Peter. If he was scared, he never gave any indication.

Colden emerged from the kitchen and slowed near the library. Ava's heart accelerated. What was he doing there? Had they found Devon? Did that mean he was dead?

His eyes were worried, but relieved. "What is it, Sister?"

"They need to speak to us."

"Of course."

Savina led them into the library, where several lamps lit the enormous room. To Ava's amazement, books lined the walls from floor to ceiling with a sliding ladder in front of the shelves. Three dark round tables rested in the center of the room with chairs around them. A fire crackled in the rock-laid fireplace that was on the far end of the room. A short hallway was in between the walls of books that had even more aisles.

"Please sit." She sank into the chair next to the fireplace and Colden stood near the fire, while Melissa and Lance took seats next to each other at a table, and Ava and Peter remained standing.

"We ask that you hear us out before saying anything," Melissa said.

"I agree, but where are Thomas and Gillian?" Savina asked.

Ava squeezed Peter's hand, but then loosened her grip, afraid she'd break it.

"It's okay," he whispered.

She nodded. "I don't even know where to begin. I never meant to break my oath or betray our Aureole, but I did. I know you meant to erase Peter's mind of me, but I can't let you. Gillian and Thomas aren't here because they—they don't approve of Peter and me. I know Thomas and I are in the same coven, and that we were probably set up to be together, but I can't be with him."

Savina gave a confused look. "Whatever do you mean?"

Ava removed her jacket to reveal the darkened scars on each arm. "I mean, it's obvious that Thomas and I aren't right for each other."

She gaped, bolted from her chair, and investigated Ava's arms. "Good gracious. What happened?"

"Thomas. I don't know if he knows how to control himself, but he does not believe Peter and I should be together."

"Why did you not inform us of this sooner?" Colden

asked. His face twisted in bewilderment.

"I don't know. I didn't want to bother you."

Colden shook his head. "Ava, please, you can come to us about anything."

"You should know that," Savina said, almost offended. Slowly, her hands tickled over the scars and Ava watched in astonishment as they disappeared. Then, Savina returned to her seat. "You are bound to Thomas only by this coven, as you are to Jeremy and Lance. You are by no means supposed to stay together forever. It just so happened that your Aureole ended up like that."

Melissa was right all along.

"I am sorry for what Thomas did to you, and I will speak to him."

"I know you told me to stay away from Peter, but I love him, and I-I told him everything about us." Her fear came through her voice. She tried to sound stronger, but it was no use.

Savina observed them for what seemed like forever. "There is a lot of energy flowing between you two. It reminds me of your mother and father." She smiled wistfully for a brief moment. "Do you remember your oath?"

She wanted to look away from Savina's disappointing eyes, but held her place. "Yes."

"Perfect love and perfect trust."

Colden placed a hand on Savina's shoulder. "Savina, they are young. They are bound to make mistakes."

"I realize that. And you all are naïve. It was my fault to believe you all could be mature, but it is obvious to me that it has taken quite a lot for you to understand the grave importance of this."

Ava felt herself shrinking.

"I feel the abundance of mistrust in your Aureole, and yes, you have broken your oath and coven. We cannot have such a coven to fight with us. It is too risky because they can sense weakness. Especially now is not a good since there is a pending war."

"War?" Melissa asked.

Colden frowned. "We did not find Devon. It was a false trail."

Ava could see the guilt in his eyes. As if it was his fault they failed. She wanted to console him.

"Trudy and Xavier have left and retreated to Devon. We will need to prepare for a battle soon. We fear that Devon is gathering as many troops as he can."

Ava's heartbeat picked up. "They're coming after us?"

"Yes. You were right in that he wants the Elemental powers. We must practice as much as we can."

This changed everything. The thought of having Peter join and then go straight to war sickened her.

"I instructed you that now was not a good time to be consorting with an Ephemeral," Savina said. "And you disobeyed me. There is no time to train him for this war."

Melissa stood, almost knocking her chair backwards. "But he protects her. And she can't be without him."

"Sister, please reconsider," Colden said.

"I have made my decision."

Ava's heart sank, and her throat tightened. She'd brought him here to have him become one of them, but instead, Savina rejected her request.

Peter cleared his throat politely. "Ava explained everything to me. I do not wish to cause rifts with your coven, but could I have the opportunity to decide for myself?"

Savina scrutinized him. "Do you know what you're asking? You would become an Enchanter forever. There is no going back."

"I know," Peter said. "I want this."

"This war is a serious matter. You could very easily die without the proper and extensive training. It takes days for your strength and powers to develop fully. We cannot afford such delays."

"But you said he might be a Paramortal," Ava blurted. "He could already have some strength."

"It's true that I have been unable to read your mind, but I

believe that is because your guard is up. Xavier was able to use his powers against him."

"She feels no pain when she's with him," Melissa said.

"Xavier wasn't able to use his ability on me last night because Peter was there. I think he acts as a shield."

"He cannot be a part of this right now. It is not a good time."

"I'm sorry, but I think I became a part of this when Xavier kidnapped me," Peter said. "Even if you were to erase my mind, Xavier would try again, knowing what I'm capable of doing."

"They're right, Sister. If Xavier showed interest in Peter, he will come after him again."

Savina stood and gave Peter a curious look. Her lips pursed, and she was deep in thought. "How exactly can you protect Ava?"

He shrugged. "I have no idea."

"He did it tonight," Lance uttered. "Thomas was about to attack Ava, and Peter pushed him to the ground."

The words obviously upset Savina as the anger in her eyes set. Ava couldn't figure out which part angered her, though.

"We can show you," Melissa said. "I could try to poison Ava and Peter could protect her.

"We haven't exactly practiced this," Ava said.

"I would like to see," Savina said.

"I haven't ever produced poison, but there's a first time for everything. Hold your breath, Peter." She pulled an orange camellia out of the vase that sat on the small table in between two chairs by the door. She held it for a moment, and then handed it to Ava.

Ava took the flower, and then took a deep breath.

CHAPTER THIRTY-SEVEN
PROTECTION

As Ava deeply inhaled, she quickly grimaced from the strong chemical-like scent. She waited for the poison to take over and make her weak, but nothing happened. "Nothing."

Melissa threw the flower into the fire. "See?" She looked at Savina. "He keeps her safe."

Savina moved closer and crossed her arms. "This is impossible. How are you doing it?"

"I don't know exactly." He shrugged. "I just—something just overcomes me and I can't let anything happen to Ava."

Colden stared in amazement with his lips slightly parted. "This is extraordinary. How is this even possible?"

"I've never seen anything like this," Savina said. "Can you protect anyone else?"

"I-I don't know."

"Ava, drown Lance. Peter, I want you to protect him."

"I don't know if I can."

"It's okay, I won't completely drown him," Ava said, and then she imagined Lance in the ocean. Her body warmed as energy pulsated to the ends of her extremities. Rough waves tossed him about like a doll, and the water pulled him under as he flailed his arms.

Lance bent over, coughed, and gasped for air, but then immediately stopped. He stood upright and breathed deeply. Ava kept the image in her head alive, but nothing happened.

Melissa shook her head. "Amazing."

"What were you thinking, Peter?" Savina asked.

"Just protecting him from harm."

"Truly fascinating," she said.

Lance smiled. "Yeah, just don't piss off Ava."

Savina paced, and pointed her finger at nothing in particular. "We could use you in this war."

Those weren't exactly the words Ava wanted to hear. She didn't want Peter used only in the war. Was that the only reason Savina agreed?

Melissa gave an uneasy look. "We just have one slight problem."

"What?" Colden asked.

"Thomas and Gillian will never agree."

Savina stopped pacing. "They will have to after speaking with me. He can be a vital aspect to this Aureole."

"And he cannot be separated from Ava," Colden said.

"I see he is very protective of you, and even you two, Melissa and Lance."

"What about Thomas?" Lance asked. "Can Peter protect him?"

"I do foresee an issue, but Thomas is in pain. He will heal, though. Peter, we invite you to join. I would prefer you spend time thinking about it, however, there isn't much. We'll need to know by tomorrow."

"We will need all of you here tomorrow for training," Colden said.

"I'd be more than glad to join," Peter said.

"Do not be too hasty." Her green eyes locked onto his. "Please think about it tonight. This includes a lifetime of the unknown."

"However, if we end this war once and for all, we can live peacefully." Colden gave a warm smile.

Savina moved to the door and opened it. "I will see you all

here tomorrow. I can see that you need rest."

Ava wanted answers about her mother. "Can we talk? Just you and me?"

"Of course," Savina said. "The rest of you, please make yourselves welcome in the parlor. Peter, it was lovely seeing you once again."

"You as well. And thank you for hearing us out." He released Ava's hand, and followed Lance, Melissa, and Colden outside.

Savina turned to her. "Are you okay, dear?"

She wanted to choose her words carefully, and didn't want to stumble over them or place blame. "When Trudy made me see my mother die again, it wasn't from my memory. It was someone else's." She kept her voice calm, but stared down at the Persian rug and its elaborate design. "It was like I was in their skin. Pulling the lightning from the sky and directing it at my mom. She was murdered, wasn't she?" Her eyes watered.

Savina frowned. "Yes."

"Why didn't you tell me?" she yelled.

"I would have, but you were not ready to know."

"Who are you to decide that?"

"No child is ready for that knowledge."

"I'm not a child anymore. I could have handled it." A tear dropped and she swatted at her face to erase the trail. "Does my dad know?"

"No, but I'm sure he suspects."

"Who killed her?"

"We do not know. There are many things we are investigating—."

"You've been saying that this whole time," she snapped. She was tired of all the vague answers. "What's taking so long? Why aren't we out there killing Devon and his army? There are too many unanswered questions floating around."

Savina cupped Ava's chin and peered into her eyes. "Do not be blinded by hate, my child. We are not vengeful. We are better than that. They will pay for their crimes in due time."

She released Ava.

Ava took a deep breath. "I'm sorry."

"Don't be. You are not the only one seeking answers. I promise we will end this. Now, get some rest and come back tomorrow."

"Okay." She nodded and Savina left.

But if something didn't happen soon, Ava was going to find her mother's killer by herself no matter what. How could she not be vengeful?

"Is everything okay?" Gabriel's voice came from the doorway.

Ava looked up and then felt her cheeks redden. "Fine and dandy."

"I know that look," he said.

She met his crystal blue eyes. "What?"

"The 'I'm going to do this myself' look."

"Leave me alone." She crossed her arms and brushed past him to leave, but he caught her arm.

"Hey, she's right you know. If we're angry, they'll take advantage of that."

"Did she tell you that as well?"

He let go of her. "No. I learned that myself."

"How can I not be angry? How could she keep something like that from me?"

"If you'd known, you would have stopped at nothing trying to find the killer. Which is a suicide mission, especially for such a young Enchanter."

"I take it you're still seeking answers?"

He gave a lopsided grin. "Not exactly. Corbin killed my parents."

Now she felt like an idiot. "I'm so sorry. I didn't mean…"

"It's okay. I've had a few years to cope."

"How long did you sit and wait to find out?"

"I didn't. I was that naïve Enchanter set on finding the truth. Needless to say, it didn't go well. Just don't let that rage take over. You'll only end up regretting it."

"Noted." She wanted to know what had happened, but

she kept her questions to herself. She felt her shoulders relax.

"I'm sorry about what happened to you. We were all worried."

"Thanks. Guess I'll see you tomorrow."

He nodded and gave a slight smile. "Looking forward to it. Sleep well."

CHAPTER THIRTY-NINE
FIRE

Lance dropped Ava and Peter off at her house. She was sure her father wouldn't like the idea of Peter staying over, but she was too tired to care now. Her body ached for rest. Maybe the stamina came with practice. Then again, she'd been up three days straight.

Her eyes felt heavy as she yawned. Exhaustion clung to her like wet clothes.

She quietly walked inside, careful not to wake her father, who was passed out in his chair. She didn't want to wake him, and have him yell or be worried. She'd talk to him tomorrow.

They crept upstairs into her moonlit room.

Peter unzipped his jacket and tossed it into her desk chair, and then sank onto the edge of her bed.

Ava stood in front of him. "All this time I've felt like it was me who had to keep you safe. But it's the opposite."

"And I'll always be here," he whispered. "I can't lose you."

She felt his arms around her waist and he pulled her close. She ran her hands through his soft hair and then kissed his head.

Ava couldn't believe her secret wish for Peter to join them had come true. Just last night she wept thinking that he wouldn't even know her and all the memories they had shared. But here he was, in her arms. They were together. However, she still feared going into battle with Devon and his army. What would happen to them? Had they prepared enough? Would any of them die?

He pulled away slightly and looked up at her. "What are you thinking?"

"I'm just scared. Have you really, and I mean really, thought about this? I've wanted nothing more than to be with you and to have you by my side, but this isn't a game at all. We really are about to go to war."

He grabbed her hands, and held them close to his chest. "I know it's all happening so fast, but I don't need to think about it anymore. Xavier kidnapped me and I was tortured. I want to fight them just as much as you do. I can do this and I'm ready."

"You could easily be killed, Peter." A tear escaped down her cheek.

"I would rather die, than live one day of life without you."

She crushed her lips to his, and his arms tightened around her. He pulled her onto the bed next to him as they continued kissing.

His lips grazed the hollow of her neck and she let out a low moan. Ava slid her hands under his shirt and she touched his smooth chest. He kissed her neck, cheek, and lips. Her fingers ran across his stomach and up his back and she felt him quiver. Her heart pounded, and then her necklace grew warm with Thomas's anger. She clutched the pendant.

"What is it?" he asked, breathless.

She picked it up and stared at the single glowing red point at the bottom. "He's furious. I guess even with a broken Aureole they can still tell what we're feeling."

"He won't hurt you anymore."

Ava let go of the necklace and looked at Peter. The moon reflected in his eyes in little white dots. "I know."

"Am I going to know what you feel?"

"Yes."

"What's it like?"

"You feel like you're angry or whatever emotion, but you know who's producing it. It can be intense sometimes."

"Like now?"

She nodded. "Yeah."

Ava didn't want to hurt Thomas, but maybe this would teach him to control his anger. She was envious of her mom for not having to go through this. She wished she could have talked to her mom about Peter, or that she could have met him.

He leaned over and kissed her forehead. She cuddled closer to him and felt his soft hands slowly rub her back. Then, she gave into the flood of tears. He held her so tight it was as if he squeezed the tears out even more. She wept until she couldn't breathe.

"I'm so sorry," he said.

Vengeful or not, Ava would find her mother's killer.

The warmth of her necklace spread throughout her body, making her sweat. She kicked off the blankets, and untangled herself from Peter's arms, but it was still hot. She took a deep breath, but coughed as a thick air entered. She immediately opened her eyes.

Ava sat up, and gasped. Orange flames licked the side of the house, reaching her window. Black smoke swelled inside her room faster than she could operate.

"Peter!" She choked. The entire room glowed orange.

With a jerk, he quickly rose and cursed. He grasped her hand, and they shot out of bed.

"Dad," she yelled as they fled the room.

The smoke cut the inside of her throat like a razor. Her eyes stung and she couldn't breathe. They kept their heads below the filling air. Both of them constantly coughed.

"Dad," Ava called. She was on her hands and knees in the hallway and pushed open his bedroom door. Through the incredibly thick smoke, she felt around for his bed. She hit the sheets to find him but found it empty. He was still downstairs.

She turned to follow Peter down the hall. A creak sounded as if something were to give way. The ceiling to the bedroom collapsed and pieces of debris fell on her. The cool night's air kissed her, and smoke escaped through the wide hole in the roof.

"Ava," Peter yelled, and then scrambled to help her.

He seized her hand and then they stumbled down the stairs, skipping two at a time. She scurried into the living room on her hands and knees, blindly feeling. She touched his hand and shook him.

"Dad! Dad!"

"The front door is too hot," Peter shouted. "We have to go out the back."

She pulled her dad from the chair, and Peter hoisted him over his shoulder. She fumbled with the latch on the sliding glass door, and finally opened it. They staggered out the door, and then collapsed on the cold dead lawn.

Her lungs were grateful for the fresh air.

"Dad." Her voice was hoarse as she tried to yell, hoping to wake him. She rolled him on his back, and checked his pulse in the now well-lit night, feeling the heat from the fire that engulfed her home. She hovered over his limp body.

His eyes were wide and still. Blood gushed out of the top his head and trickled out of his mouth. His clothes were shredded and his body singed.

This wasn't right. This was what her mother had looked like when she was killed.

Ava clenched her teeth and forced the image from her head. She closed and opened her eyes. Her father looked normal.

Trudy was there. She looked back at the woods and all around them.

"Stay with him," she told Peter, and got to her feet, still searching for any movement in the woods.

"What are you doing?"

"Trudy's here."

Then, she saw straight ahead some branches rustling and bolted for the forest.

"Ava," Peter cried. "Don't go."

Now was her chance to get answers from Trudy. Her mind was clear and she was ready to attack as water dripped from her fingertips. She hoped her coven would realize she was in danger and come to help.

CHAPTER THIRTY-NINE
BLIND HOPE

Ava raced through the forest to find Trudy. Her throat was scratchy from the smoke, and her eyes watered from the cold. She saw a movement to her left, and picked up the pace. She collided with something and fell to the ground.

She looked down and realized she had fallen on a woman. Black hair sprawled all around her face. She opened her eyes and they were a piercing green.

"Who are you?" Ava asked, and pushed off her.

The woman grabbed Ava's arms and flung her in the air. Ava landed hard on her back, but shot to her feet. Water built around her hands, and she discharged it at the woman, but missed.

Then, a bright flash ignited. It was so bright, Ava had to cover her eyes, and she lost her balance. She felt the woman slam her to the ground and hold her.

Ava couldn't see anything but white flashes behind her lids. Her eyes refused to adjust in the dark night.

She heard several footsteps coming closer and she struggled to get to her feet, but the woman's grasp was tight.

"There's no use struggling," the woman said. "You're surrounded."

When her eyes finally adjusted, she looked around. Xavier and his Halflings stood in a circle. The woman grabbed Ava by the shoulders and jerked her to her feet.

"You're all doing this against your will," she said, meeting the eyes of the Halflings. "Don't you see what's happening?"

Xavier had a sly smile and sauntered closer. "Some of us are under our own will." He touched her cheek, and she flinched.

Water trickled down her arms. "So you gladly support this? Without anyone compelling you?"

He laughed. "I was the one who helped Devon escape. You all thought it was over, but it's only just begun."

Xavier was an Enchanter. Not a Halfling. How long had he been around?

She glared at him. "You know who killed my mom."

"Aww, did you just find out that she was murdered? She wouldn't cooperate. Which is what will happen to you if you don't."

Ava clenched her fists, and envisioned him drowning. His eyes bulged, and his face turned red, then purple. He clawed at his neck and gasped for air. Xavier collapsed to his knees.

Then, a flash of bright light blinded Ava and she lost her concentration.

She felt something slam her body to the ground. Ava knew she had threatened Xavier's ego.

"You can't kill me," Xavier said, and then he punched her in the face.

Her jaw throbbed and a liquid leaked out of her mouth.

"Enough," someone shouted.

Ava blinked several times before her eyes came into focus. She couldn't wait to get rid of the black-headed woman to stop the blinding. A tall man emerged from behind Xavier. His hair was white-blond, and his eyes were a vibrant green. He looked way too young to be a leader of a revolt, but ages were deceiving. His lips were set in a wicked grin, as he walked closer to Ava. She assumed he was Devon.

The black-haired woman jerked her to her feet once more.

Ava was tired of the woman pushing her around. Where was everyone? Didn't they know she was in danger? She just needed to hold on a little bit longer.

If she could punch the woman holding her, shoot water in Devon's face, and somehow conjure enough water to disable everyone, she could escape.

"Hello, Ava," Devon said. "I really hate to do this, because I can tell you will be a very valuable Enchanter. But after Havok has all of your powers, he won't need you."

There was that name again. Did he think of himself in the third person?

"You'll never succeed."

He smirked. "We'll see." He raised his hand as if to touch her, and then she could feel a strange pull that left her cold and dizzy.

Ava focused her strength. She could do this.

She fought against the pulling sensation, and quickly elbowed the woman in the throat, knocking her backwards. Then, she shot water at Devon. It was powerful enough to bring him to his knees. And then all the men froze, seemingly in a trance.

Natalia appeared through the forest with a fierce look, and Ava never thought she'd be so glad to see her. The wind blew, and picked up. Fireballs shot near Xavier and Devon. The ground shook as rocks collected near a tree and Ava assumed Melissa stood there.

Jeremy, Thomas, Lance, and Gillian came into view. The black-headed woman grabbed Ava, and then punched her. She grappled with the woman, and tried imagining her underwater, but then the woman's hands wrapped around Ava's throat. She squeezed tightly, cutting off her air. Ava punched and fought but she was slowly losing strength.

"You can't kill me," Ava tried to say.

"Try me."

Flashes of fire and lightning surrounded her. Screams and explosions were muffled, and thunderous sounds shook the ground. All while Ava was slowly dying.

CHAPTER FORTY
DOWNFALL

Ava gasped for air. The black-headed Enchanter had her hands wrapped around Ava's neck, squeezing. She hit the woman but she never loosened her grip. She pictured the woman once more underwater. It was a weak image, but it was all she had. The woman coughed, and then the pressure around her throat was gone. She scrambled away from the woman. Her throat ached and it felt as if she couldn't get the air in fast enough.

She looked up and saw Joss, the petite Enchanter, electrocuting Devon. He twitched and fell to his knees. He continued to twitch, and then he was still.

Ava drew a shaky breath. Devon was dead. She looked to her left and saw the black-headed woman lying in an unnatural position.

Gabriel held out his hand for Ava. "Are you okay?"

"Yeah." She nodded, took his hand, and he helped her to her feet.

Her coven held Kristen and the rest of the Halflings captive. Xavier was on his knees with Aaron's hand on his shoulder. Eric, Maggie, and Kira stood next to Natalia, and Savina and Colden stood nearby.

Ava walked toward Xavier. She wanted to kill him for kidnapping all the innocent Ephemerals, for taking Peter, her friends, and her, for bombing the school, and for setting fire to her house.

"He won't hurt you now," Aaron said. "I've weakened his powers."

Melissa stepped forward. "How did you do that?"

"That's what I do. I can weaken or enhance."

"He should die," Ava said.

"Ava, don't," Savina said. "We will take him to the Cruciari."

"We can't take him there. He helped Devon escape, so he knows how to get out."

"She has a point," Colden said. "Perhaps we could keep him hostage."

"Devon escaped on his own," Xavier said. "You just can't believe someone could actually leave that place like he did."

"You said you helped him," Ava said.

He laughed. "Maybe I did. Maybe I didn't. But you think putting me there will stop us? Others believe Corbin's vision. This isn't over by a long shot."

Ava drew her hand back, curled it into a fist, and drove it into his face. He fell back, unconscious. She'd wanted to do that for some time.

Melissa let out a hard laugh. "Nice hook."

"Not exactly ladylike," Savina said.

"Let us go," Kristen screamed, and squirmed against Lance.

"What do we do with them?" Ava asked.

"I will heal them of their mind control," Savina said. She moved to Kristen, and gently touched her. Within seconds, Kristen relaxed, but then her eyes widened as she looked around. It reminded Ava of the boys in the hall who almost kissed her.

"W-what are you all doing?" she asked. "Why am I here? What are you doing to me?"

"They don't know anything," Ava said. "They didn't have

321

a choice."

"There are ways to help them transition," Gabriel said. "And if they choose not to continue as an Enchanter, Aaron can weaken their ability, and we can have their mind erased."

"That's terrible."

Colden lifted Xavier over his shoulder. "They will be fine. Thomas, burn the dead."

"You got it," Thomas said.

Savina finished lifting the mind control off the Halflings. "Let's go back to the Manor. We have much to discuss."

"I have to go back to my dad," Ava cried. "They burned my house." She took off through the woods once more rushing to get back. She couldn't believe she had left Peter and her dad unprotected. What if other Cimmerians took Peter and her dad?

Ava broke through the woods and found the house still ablaze. Smoke rose into the indigo sky. There was no sign of Peter or her dad. She called their names but received no answer. Where were they? Had they been taken?

"Peter," she screamed. Her heart pounded as she frantically searched. "Dad."

"Ava," someone called.

She turned around and was face-to-face with Gabriel. Her body shook and tears fell in an endless stream. "I can't find them. They're not here."

"What happened before the fight in the woods?"

"We woke up to the house burning. We got out and my dad was unconscious. And then I saw a vision like what Trudy did the other night. So I ran after her."

"Do you think Peter could have called 911?"

Ava froze. She didn't even think of that. "I don't know. Could they be at the hospital?"

"They might. I can take you there."

He pulled Ava close to his body. He was warm and oddly comforting, though it was a little awkward. She closed her eyes and a second later, they were at the hospital. They jogged inside and walked up to the check-in desk.

"Connor Hannigan," Ava said, breathless. "Do you have a patient by that name?" She sped through her words, but the old woman seemed to be moving at a snail's pace.

She clicked on her computer and Ava saw the reflection of the screen in the woman's glasses. Ava wanted to tell the nurse to hurry up as she kept clicking, but she held her tongue.

"He's in the ER," the nurse finally said. "Room 404."

For a moment, Ava was relieved, but then she darted down the hallway with Gabriel behind her. He grabbed her hand and headed for the stairs. Then suddenly they were on the fourth floor. Ava pushed open the stairwell door and found Peter halfway down the hall. He was sitting on the floor with his knees up and his head in his hands.

A lump rushed to the base of her throat and then she ran, dodging people. The hallway seemed to get longer and longer as she made her way to him.

"Peter," she cried.

He raised his head and locked eyes with her. He was covered in soot, but she was thankful to see him.

Peter got to his feet and rushed up to her. "Ava," he said, with relief.

Ava collided with him, wrapping her arms around him, and squeezing him so tight. She felt his arms fit perfectly around her.

He kissed the top of her head and forehead and then lips. He cupped his hands on her face, his brown eyes gazing into hers. "Are you okay? Your neck is bruised."

She nodded. "Yes. I'm fine. I thought they took you. I thought—."

"I'm okay." He hugged her and she buried her face in his neck. "Your dad's okay. They said he inhaled quite a bit of smoke, but we got him out in time."

"Thank you for saving him." She turned around and met Gabriel's eyes. "Thank you for your help."

"You're welcome," he said.

Ava squeezed Peter's hand, and then opened the door to

his room. Seeing her father hooked up to an oxygen mask and an IV angered her, but also brought up memories of when she was in the hospital for pneumonia. He was sleeping and there was a constant beep.

"Dad," she said and moved beside his bed. "I'm here, Dad."

The door opened and Ava twisted her head and saw Savina quietly enter.

"How is he?" she asked.

"The doctors told Peter he had inhaled a lot of smoke."

It was odd seeing Savina in such a normal atmosphere. She seemed so otherworldly. Ava watched her glide to the other side of the bed and slowly moved her hands over him.

Ava bit her lip and twirled her ring.

Her father's eyes gradually opened, and tears overflowed and raced down her face.

"Dad," she cried, and then kissed his forehead. The door closed, and she realized they were alone. "I'm so sorry," she whispered.

"For what?" His voice was a little scratchy, but his color had returned. He sat up and moved his feet to hang over the side.

"I should've been more alert. This is my fault."

"Ava, what are you talking about?"

"They came after us. They could've killed us. I almost died and Devon almost took my powers and—."

"Slow down," he cut her off. "What happened?"

Ava took a deep breath and explained everything.

"So Devon is dead."

"Yes. But I ran after Trudy and left you and Peter. I'm so sorry. I thought they took you and Peter."

"Stop. It wasn't your fault. What you should be apologizing for is how you left without saying a word for an entire day. But, thank you for saving me."

"Peter did. He got you here. I'm so glad you're okay."

He squeezed her hand. "Speaking of Peter. I take it you talked to him."

Ava sat next to him on the bed. "Yes."

"And," he urged.

"He didn't freak out once. He just accepted it. What happened when Mom told you?"

He took a deep breath. "Well, at first, I didn't know what to think or say. I was scared, but the more I learned about them the more I felt comfortable. Savina and Aaron welcomed me as if I were meant to be, or as if I were family."

She nodded. "Savina didn't want him at first. She said no. And she said she could tell we were in love, but she didn't think we'd have time with everything going on."

"What changed?"

"We showed her that he can protect us. She says he could be a Paramortal."

"Wow. What are the odds?"

"I never expected this."

"Of course not. You can't expect anything in life."

"What will happen to him? I mean, is this right of me? I feel selfish bringing him into all this and then with all these expectations."

"You may have fought for him, but he ultimately made his decision. I've seen the way he looks at you and cares for you. I think he's loved you for some time now, and this is what he wants. He chose you, Ava. Just like I chose your mother."

She nodded, and felt his arm around her, pulling her close. She rested her head on his shoulder. "I just worry about him."

"I know. Your mom was worried, too, but she knew she couldn't be happy without me, and I felt the same. There isn't a day that goes by I don't wish I could've protected her that day."

Ava stiffened, and then raised her head. "You know?"

"I had suspected."

"Do you know who"

He shook his head. "No, but I'm sure they are locked up at the Cruciari."

Ava had wondered that herself, but she still wanted to

know for sure.

There was a soft knock on the door, and then Savina entered. "How are you, Connor?"

"I'm well. Thank you for healing me."

"Of course." She smiled warmly.

"How did this happen?" her father asked.

"A Halfling named Kristen was under their influence. She caused the lightning to strike your house, catching it on fire."

"Are they okay?" he asked. Even in such a time, her father thought of others.

"They are in shock, but we will get them better. They are staying at the Manor for the time being. Ava saved them."

"Hardly," she said.

"If you had not chased after them, we may not have gotten to them. Now, Devon is dead. Rest assured."

"But is it really over?" Ava asked. "Trudy is still out there. What if she starts a revolution?"

"There weren't many strong supporters of Corbin after we imprisoned them. Trudy can't do it alone. And we have Xavier. Soon, he will join the rest at the Cruciari."

Something didn't seem right. It felt like everything wrapped up in a nice, neat package. Killing Devon and his rather small army was too easy. Was Xavier right? Was there someone else out there who had actually started this?

"You worry too much, Ava," Savina said. "I promise you we will be fine. We will still practice as much as we can to make you all stronger. But the security at the Cruciari has tightened, so no one will escape."

Ava nodded. Hearing Savina's voice calmed her. They would be safe at the Manor. "Thank you," she said and hugged Savina, inhaling the strong scent of oranges. "Thank you for everything."

She felt Savina's hands softly on her back, stroking her hair. She was warm and comforting and motherly. Ava missed that.

"You do not have to thank me," Savina said. "I would do anything for you."

"Let's go home, Sweetie," her father said.

They both stood, but Ava stopped. It hadn't occurred to her that they had no home to go to anymore. Everything was gone, including all the pictures of her mom. Tears rolled down her face. The only memory Ava had of her mother was in her head, and that faded each day.

"What is it?" Her father pulled her close.

"Dad, our house was burned. There's nothing left."

He nodded and took a deep breath. "We'll find a place." He kissed her forehead.

"I have rooms for you at the Manor," Savina said.

"You're too kind, but we can just get a hotel."

"I insist."

Ava knew her father didn't do well with handouts, but he nodded. "We'll be out as soon as we find a home."

"Stay as long as you like. Come now, let us go."

They walked out of the room where Gabriel waited for them. Ava looked around but didn't see Peter.

"Where's Peter?" she asked.

"I took him to the Manor," Gabriel said. "He's with Seth."

Ava couldn't even imagine what that conversation was like, and hoped Peter would be safe there with Thomas and Gillian.

The four of them left the hospital and Gabriel made one stop on the way to the Manor at the request of Ava's father.

Frosty dew coated the brown lawn. The early sun's red tip was barely visible beyond the horizon. The last time Ava had watched the sunrise, was right after her mother died and she and her dad stayed up watching the peaceful scene. The world was silent, almost like it was in awe of such a beautiful incident.

But when she turned her head, she stared at the blackened shell that was once their home. Smoke lingered from the desolate sight. Nothing was salvageable.

Her father held her hand tightly. "I can't believe it's all gone."

"What are we going to do?" she asked. "There's nothing

left."

"We'll manage. We still have each other. Come on," he said, and Gabriel teleported them to the Blackhart Manor, leaving the burned remains of their lives behind.

CHAPTER FORTY-ONE
TOGETHER

Ava was hesitant to cross the threshold of her new home. She didn't want to stay at the Manor. It was big, and felt more like a hotel of sorts. She wasn't used to having so many people around. It had been just her and her dad for ten years. But she forced herself inside and it was warm. She inhaled deeply and her stomach rumbled at the aroma of something familiar. It smelled like the stew she had had on their first night back.

Laughter from the library flowed into the hall and the foyer and Ava realized she had missed that sound. How long had it been since she had a good laugh?

Ava looked to her dad as if asking if he wanted to join her.

"You go ahead," he said. "I'll be down in a bit."

"We will all have a meeting about Peter," Savina said.

"Tonight?" Ava asked.

"Yes, but we will discuss other things."

Ava nodded and then strode down the hall to the library. Both Aureoles sat close to one another while the Halflings and Peter were at their own table. Did no one want to be around them?

"Ava," Melissa cried and rushed up to her. She hugged her tightly. "Where did you learn how to hit like that? Did you guys see her hit Xavier?"

Ava rolled her eyes. "He deserved it."

Gillian twirled a curl around her finger. "I can't believe we didn't kill him."

"But then we couldn't torture him," Joss said. "Gotta see the positive in things."

"Only you would say that," Eric joked, and then kissed her tiny nose.

Conversations picked up again, and Ava leaned closer to Melissa. "Has Peter been okay with Thomas and Gillian here?"

"Thomas has been eyeing him, but he assumes Peter's only here for Seth's sake." She frowned and nodded toward the Halfling's table. "They're all pretty shaken. I can't imagine what they're going through."

Ava turned and saw Kristen staring off into space while Nicole had an arm around her shoulder whispering to her. Nothing Nicole said seemed to faze Kristen. Peter talked to Seth, Link, Scott, and Liza.

"Kristen and Link are in shock," Melissa continued. "They hate what they did."

"Link?"

"You can call him Mr. Timebomb."

"What?" Ava turned to her. "How does he even do that?"

"You got me."

"I'm going to go talk to them." She meandered toward their table and she saw all their eyes on her. "How are you all?"

Kristen looked up, her eyes watered and her chin quivered. "I'm so sorry, Ava."

"Don't apologize," she said. "You have to know that wasn't your fault."

"Doesn't make it any better."

"I don't blame you and I never will."

"I can't do this. I know she gave us a choice, but I can't continue…"

Nicole hugged her tightly. "No one's making you. They'll

fix you right up and you won't even remember any of this. You'll go on in a new place and start fresh."

Ava never thought she would see the day when Nicole Eckrich would be comforting Kristen Miller.

"What if they find me again?"

Ava kneeled down beside Kristen's chair. She wasn't sure what to say because there was no guarantee that she would be one hundred percent safe. She met Kristen's beady brown eyes and placed a hand on hers.

"Devon is dead. And Xavier is a prisoner. They won't find you. You'll be so far away from all of this."

Kristen nodded and wiped her tear-stained cheeks. "Thank you."

"Anytime."

Savina, Colden, Aaron, Maggie, and Kira entered the room and suddenly the blithe atmosphere changed to a serious one. Ava stood upright and then felt Peter's hand intertwine with hers.

Savina clasped her hands together in front of her torso as she and Colden stood in front of the fireplace. Aaron, Maggie, and Kira flanked them.

"There is much to discuss tonight," Savina began. Her green eyes swept over each person. "First, we have six Halflings that were unfortunately turned against their will. We have spoken to each of them and gave them a choice to stay or leave."

Colden frowned. "We know what a difficult situation you have been placed in, but we would welcome you as our own and we would also respect your wishes if you decide to go."

Seth stood and turned his attention to the front. "I want to stay," he said.

Had Peter talked him into it or did Seth really want this?

"I want to stay as well," Link said.

"Liza and I are leaving," Scott told them. A pang of sadness hit Ava for some reason as she watched Scott hold a very distraught Liza.

How often did this happen? Corbin never turned

Ephemerals against their will; he just killed them. Would Trudy try to do the same as Devon? She didn't turn Milo for whatever reason.

"I'm leaving," Kristen said, still clutching onto Nicole.

Nicole loosened Kristen's grip and rose from her chair. "I wish to stay."

"Nicole, no," Kristen cried.

"We welcome those who are staying," Savina said. "And we will care for the others."

Ava detected a hint of sadness in Savina's eyes but then they quickly changed back to the serious look.

"As some of you are aware," she continued. "We have a potential new member, Peter McNabb. He is a Paramortal with the unusual ability to protect. I have asked him to join us to be with Ava. As you all remember, Ava's mother did the same for her father. If Peter agrees, we must all accept him in order for him to join. Peter, your answer?

"I—."

"This is ridiculous," Thomas shouted. He narrowed his eyes and the muscles in his jaw twitched. "You can't seriously do this. You should banish them both." He pointed to Ava and Peter.

"Thomas, please," Savina said. "You have not seen what he can do. Peter protects her and can protect us all. Including you, but you must give him a fair reason. Now, Peter, your answer."

Peter took a deep breath. "I wish to join." He glanced at Ava and squeezed her hand.

"Great." Savina smiled warmly. "Now I need you to show the group what all you can do. Joss, try to shock Ava."

Joss moved from beside Eric. A blue electrical arc formed between her hands as the sound hummed like a power line. She pointed the current toward Ava, and it hit her, but she didn't feel anything. Joss tried once more. Again, the shock did not hurt Ava.

Kira stepped forward to inspect Ava. Her long white hair tickled Ava's arm. "Wow," she said. "It's like he formed a shield around her. That's incredible."

"Even if I'm injured, when I'm around him, I feel no pain," Ava added.

"Can you protect yourself?" Colden asked.

"I don't know," Peter replied.

Aaron crossed his arms. "Joss, try your power on Peter."

She turned to Peter and tried to shock him, but nothing happened. Everyone watched, mesmerized. Ava wondered if Peter felt a little uncomfortable to have them all watch him and test his ability, but if he was, he never showed it.

"He knows it's coming, though," Aaron said. "What if someone just attacks him without—?"

Thomas darted for him, ripping Peter's hand from Ava's grasp, as he tackled him to the ground. Peter's head snapped back from the impact. Thomas's hands burst into flames and he pressed them into Peter. Peter cried out, but only for a second. He quickly blocked the fire.

"Thomas," Ava screamed. "That's enough." She tried pulling his arm but he jerked away from her.

Lance roughly seized his arm and dragged him away. "Calm down."

Ava helped Peter up from the ground and noticed a hole in his sweatshirt from Thomas. The skin underneath was red. "Are you okay?"

"I'm fine. He just caught me off guard."

"That is good though," Colden said. "You'll need to learn to be on your guard and ready for anything. I accept."

Aaron stroked his chin. "That was quite interesting."

Ava squeezed Peter's hand. She was sure Aaron wouldn't allow him. She wasn't sure why she felt that way. Maybe it was because of how she'd let him down by not killing Trudy.

"I accept Peter to be with us," Aaron said, and Ava felt herself relax.

"I'm convinced," Eric said.

"Yes," Kira and Maggie added together.

"I agree, as long as these kids don't let their drama get in the way of anything," Natalia nonchalantly said.

Joss rolled her beautiful violet eyes, and then smiled at Peter. "Of course I accept you."

"Me, too," Gabriel said. "It makes sense."

Ava glanced at him and thought she saw a flash of sadness in his crystal blue eyes. Had he fallen in love with an Ephemeral but something happened to her? Had he tried to bring her into this?

"Now the rest of you," Savina asked the others.

Melissa smiled. "Of course."

"Yes," Lance said.

Jeremy cleared his throat. "Yes."

Gillian wouldn't look at either Ava or Peter, but she smiled at Savina. "Absolutely."

Ava wondered what changed her mind so quickly.

Then they all turned to Thomas.

"I know you're hurting and angry," Aaron said. "But you must learn to accept this change."

"Why are we not punishing her? Didn't she break her oath?"

"Peter was already a target for Devon," Aaron told him. "He already knew some things."

Thomas sighed. "Fine. Doesn't look like I really have a choice."

Aaron placed a hand on Thomas's shoulder and then whispered something in his ear. Ava felt guilty for hurting his feelings and hoped he would move on.

"We should all get some rest now," Savina said. "We are safe."

Like a domino effect, everyone stood and filed out of the room. Melissa, Lance, Jeremy, and Gillian walked up to Peter and Ava.

"Thank you all," Ava said. "For understanding."

"Don't think I really wanted this," Gillian said. "There's just no point in me fighting the Elders. But don't think for one second that I'm your friend." She glared at Ava and then left the room.

Her words cut through Ava.

"She doesn't mean that," Jeremy said, but Ava knew he was only trying to make her feel better. "Welcome, Peter."

"Thanks," Peter said, and Jeremy walked out.

Savina made her way toward them. "Ava, I will show you your new room."

Ava nodded, even though she didn't want to think of it as her room. "Sleep well," she told Melissa and Lance.

Melissa gave a teasing smile. "You, too."

Ava rolled her eyes, knowing she was ragging on Ava about being in the same room as Peter.

She and Peter followed Savina up to the second floor and Savina opened a thick wooden door.

"Your father is right across the way," she said. "I have a room for you as well, Peter, if you wish to stay the night."

"Sure," he said and then walked with her down the hall.

Ava looked around the immense, timeless room. Three small arched windows allowed the late morning sun to filter its light across the dark hardwood floors. To the left, a mahogany canopy bed rested against the wall with a dark red curtain behind the headboard. Two Queen Anne chairs occupied the corner near the windows with a small, round table between them. Double doors on the right of the bed were open to a walk-in closet that seemed to have clothes hanging. And across the bed, a door opened to the white-marbled bathroom.

This was Ava's new home. It was beautiful, but it would take some getting used to. She still didn't want to be there, but every nerve inside her pleaded her for rest.

She heard the door close behind her, and then felt arms around her waist. She twisted around and came face-to-face with Peter. They both smelled of smoke, but she didn't care. His eyes locked onto hers and she reached up and softly touched his cheek.

He kissed her, slow, yet yearning, and then he tangled his hand in her hair. She reached around his neck, and pulled him closer. He kissed her as if he never wanted to let go. He made her forget the attack, and the loss she encountered. She immersed herself in the kiss, knowing that they were together now.

PLAYLIST

Breathing Underwater -- Metric
Haunted – Evanescence
Body and Soul – Tori Amos
Stand My Ground – Within Temptation
Flume – Bon Iver
Miseria Cantare (The Beginning) – AFI
Changes – 3 Doors Down
The Red – Chevelle
Cruel – Tori Amos
Silver and Cold – AFI
Taking Over Me – Evanescence
The Bat's Mouth – Bat For Lashes
Hysteria – Muse
Bonfires – Blue Foundation
All I Need – Radiohead
Hopeless – Breaking Benjamin
Here With Me – Dido

ABOUT THE AUTHOR

Carrigan Richards graduated from Kennesaw State University with a degree in English. The year before she began KSU, she started writing what would become Under a Blood Moon, and eleven years later, published it. She lives near Atlanta with her fiancé and their two dogs.

You can visit her online at www.carriganrichards.com.

ALSO BY CARRIGAN RICHARDS

PIECES OF ME

Made in the USA
Charleston, SC
06 October 2014